HONOUR GUARD

HIS DROVER'S DISGUISE flapping about him, an Infardi gunman clambered up the mudguard of the command Salamander and raised his autopistol, a yowl of rabid triumph issuing from his scabby lips.

Gaunt's bolt-round hit him point-blank in the right cheek and disintegrated his head in a puff of liquidised tissue.

'One to honour guard units! Infardi ambush to the right! Turn and repel!'

Gaunt could hear further missile impacts and lots of small arms fire. The chelons, viced in by the road edge on one side and the Imperial armour on the other, were whinnying with agitation and banging the edges of their shells up against vehicle hulls.

'Turn us! Turn us around!' Gaunt yelled at his driver.

'No room, sir!' the Pardus replied desperately. A brace of hard-slug shots sparked and danced off the Salamander's cowling.

'Damn it!' Gaunt bellowed. He rose in the back of the tank and fired into the charging enemy, killing one Infardi and crippling a mature chelon. The beast shrieked and slumped over, crushing two more of the ambushers before rolling hard into the tank behind.

A WARHAMMER 40,000 NOVEL

Gaunt's Ghosts

HONOUR GUARD

Dan Abnett

*For Colin Fender, honorary guardsman
and Marco, patience of a saint*

A BLACK LIBRARY PUBLICATION

Games Workshop Publishing
Willow Road, Lenton,
Nottingham, NG7 2WS, UK

First US edition, August 2001

10 9 8 7 6 5 4 3 2 1

Distributed by Simon & Schuster
1230 Avenue of the Americas
New York, NY 10020

Cover illustration by Martin McKenna
Map by Ralph Horsley

ISBN 0-7434-1167-6

Set in ITC Giovanni

Printed and bound in Great Britain by
Omnia Books Ltd, Glasgow, UK

See the Black Library on the Internet at
www.blacklibrary.co.uk

Find out more about Games Workshop
and the world of Warhammer 40,000 at
www.games-workshop.com

HONOUR GUARD

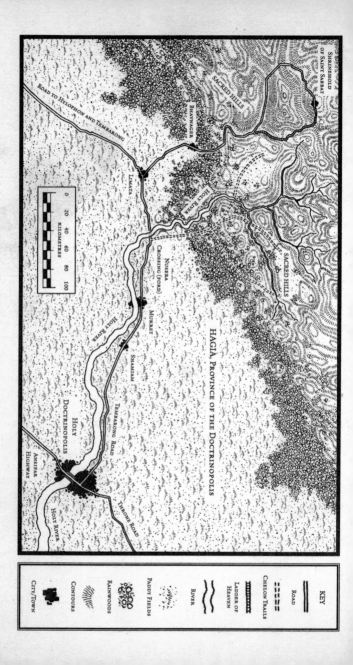

HAGIA, PROVINCE OF THE DOCTRINOPOLIS

KEY

ROAD
CHELON TRAILS
LADDER OF HEAVEN
RIVER
PADDY FIELDS
RAINWOODS
CONTOURS
CITY/TOWN

SHRINEHOLD OF SAINT SABRAT

SACRED HILLS

ROAD TO HYLOPHON AND IEMBARONG

BHAVNAGER

HOLY RIVER

SACRED HILLS

NGERA CROSSING (FORD)

MORKEL

SHANIAM

IRON RIVER

HOLY DOCTRINOPOLIS

TAMBARONG ROAD

ANSIFAR HIGHWAY

THRONE ROAD

HOLY RIVER

0 20 40 60 80 100 KILOMETRES

T HE MONUMENTAL IMPERIAL *crusade to liberate the Sabbat Worlds cluster from the grip of Chaos had been raging for over a decade and a half when* Warmaster Macaroth began his daring assaults on the strategically vital Cabal system. This phase of reconquest lasted almost two whole years, and featured a bravura, multi-point invasion scheme devised by Macaroth himself. Simultaneous Imperial assaults were launched against nineteen key planets, including three of the notorious fortress-worlds, shaking the dug-in resolve of the numerically superior but less well-orchestrated enemy.

From his war room logs, we know that Macaroth fully appreciated the scale of his gamble. If successful, this phase of assault would virtually guarantee an overall Imperial victory for the campaign. If it failed, his whole crusade force, an armed host over a billion strong, might well be entirely over-run. For two, bloody, bitter years, the fate of the Sabbat Worlds Crusade hung in the balance.

Serious analysis of this period inevitably focuses on the large-scale fortress-world theatres, most particularly on the eighteen month war to take the massive fortress-world Morlond. But several of the subsidiary crusade assaults conducted during this phase are deserving of close study, especially the liberation of the shrineworld Hagia and the remarkable events that afterwards unfolded there...

— from *A History of the Later Imperial Crusades*

ONE
A DAY FOR HEROES

*'Betwixt the wash of the river and the waft of the wind,
let my sins be transfigured to virtues.'*

— Catechism of Hagia, bk I, chp 3, vrs xxxii

THEY'D STRUNG THE king up with razor wire in a city square north
of the river.

It was called the Square of Sublime Tranquillity, an eight-
hectare court of sun-baked, pink basalt surrounded by the
elegant, mosaic walls of the Universitariate Doctrinus. Little in
the way of sublime tranquillity had happened there in the last
ten days. The Pater's Pilgrims had seen to that.

Ibram Gaunt made a sharp, bat-like shadow on the flagstones as he ran to new cover, his storm coat flying out behind
him. The sun was at its highest and a stark glare scorched the
hard ground. Gaunt knew the light must be burning his skin
too, but he felt nothing except the cool, blustering wind that
filled the wide square.

He dropped into shelter behind an overturned, burnt-out
Chimera troop carrier, and dumped the empty clip from his
bolt pistol with a flick-click of his gloved thumb. He could hear

9

a popping sound from far away, and raw metal dents appeared in the blackened armour of the dead Chimera's hull. Distant shots, their sound stolen by the wind.

Far behind, across the cooking pink stones of the open square, he could see black-uniformed Imperial Guardsmen edging out to follow him.

His men. Troopers of the Tanith First-and-Only. Gaunt noted their dispersal and glanced back at the king. The high king indeed, as he had been. What was his name again?

Rotten, swollen, humiliated, the noble corpse swung from a gibbet made of tie-beams and rusting truck-axles and couldn't answer. Most of his immediate court and family were dangling next to him.

More popping. A hard, sharp dent appeared in the resilient metal next to Gaunt's head. Crumbs of paint flecked off with the impact.

Mkoll ducked into cover beside him, lasrifle braced.

'Took your time,' Gaunt teased.

'Hah! I trained you too fething well, colonel-commissar, that's all it is.'

They grinned at each other.

More troopers joined them, running the gauntlet across the open square. One jerked and fell, halfway across. His body would remain, sprawled and unmourned in the open, for at least another hour.

Larkin, Caffran, Lillo, Vamberfeld and Derin made it across. The five scurried in beside the Ghosts' leader and Mkoll, the regiment's scout commander.

Gaunt assayed a look out past the Chimera cover.

He ducked back as distant pops threw rounds at him.

'Four shooters. In the north-west corner.'

Mkoll smiled and shook his head, scolding like a parent. 'Nine at least. Haven't you listened to anything I've told you, Gaunt?'

Larkin, Derin and Caffran laughed. They were all Tanith, original Ghosts, veterans.

Lillo and Vamberfeld watched the apparently disrespectful exchange with alarm. They were Vervunhivers, newcomers to the Ghosts regiment. The Tanith called them 'fresh blood' if they were being charitable, 'scratchers' if they weren't really thinking, or 'cannon trash' if they were feeling cruel.

The new Vervunhive recruits wore the same matt-black fatigues and body armour as the Tanith, but their colouring and demeanour stood them apart.

As did their newly stamped, metal-stocked lasguns and the special silver, axe-rake studs they wore on their collars.

'Don't worry,' said Gaunt, noting their unease and smiling. 'Mkoll regularly gets too big for his boots. I'll reprimand him when this is done.'

More pops, more dents.

Larkin fidgeted round to get a good look, resting his fine, nal-wood-finished sniper weapon in a jag of broken armour with experienced grace. He was the regiment's best marksman.

'Got a target?' Gaunt asked.

'Oh, you bet,' assured the grizzled Larkin, working his weapon into optimum position with a lover's softness.

'Blow their fething faces off then, if you please.'

'You got it.'

'How... How can he see?' gasped Lillo, craning up. Caffran tugged him into cover, saving him an abrupt death as las-shots hissed around them.

'Sharpest eyes of all the Ghosts,' smiled Caffran.

Lillo nodded back, but resented the Tanith's cocky attitude. He was Marco Lillo, career soldier, twenty-one years in the Vervun Primary, and here was a kid, no more than twenty years old all told, telling him what to do.

Lillo shuffled round, aiming his long lasgun.

'I want the king, high king whatever-his-name-is,' said Gaunt softly. Distractedly, he rubbed at a ridge of an old scar across his right palm. 'I want him down. It's not right for him to be rotting up there.'

'Okay,' said Mkoll.

Lillo thought he had a shot and fired a sustained burst at the far side of the square. Lattice windows along the side of the Universitariat exploded inwards, but the hard breeze muffled the noise of the impacts.

Gaunt grabbed Lillo's weapon and pulled him down.

'Don't waste ammo, Marco,' he said.

He knows my name! He knows my name! Lillo was almost beside himself with the fact. He stared at Gaunt, basking in every moment of the brief acknowledgement. Ibram Gaunt was like a god to him. He had led Vervunhive to victory out of the surest defeat ten months past. He carried the sword to prove it.

Lillo regarded the colonel-commissar now: the tall, powerful build, the close-cropped blond hair half-hidden by the commissar's cap, the lean cut of his intense face that so matched his name. Gaunt was dressed in the black uniform of his breed, overtopped by a long, leather storm coat and the trademark Tanith camo-cape. Maybe not a god, because he's flesh and blood, Lillo thought... but a hero, none-the-less.

Larkin was firing. Hard, scratchy rasps issued from his gun.

The rate of fire spitting over their ducked heads reduced.

'What are we waiting for?' asked Vamberfeld.

Mkoll caught his sleeve and nodded back at the buildings behind them.

Vamberfeld saw a big man... a very big man... rise from cover and fire a missile launcher.

The snaking missile, trailing smoke, struck a coronet on the west of the square.

'Try again, Bragg!' Derin, Mkoll and Larkin chorused with a laugh.

Another missile soared over them, and blew the far corner of the square apart. Stone debris scattered across the open plaza.

Gaunt was up and running now, as were Mkoll, Caffran and Derin. Larkin continued to fire his expert shots from cover.

Vamberfeld and Lillo leapt up after the Tanith.

Lillo saw Derin buckle and fall as las-fire cut through him.

He paused and tried to help. The Tanith trooper's chest was a bloody mess and he was convulsing so hard it was impossible for Lillo to get a good grip on him. Mkoll appeared beside the struggling Lillo and together they dragged Derin into cover behind the makeshift gibbet as more las-fire peppered the flagstones.

Gaunt, Caffran and Vamberfeld made it to the far corner of the square.

Gaunt disappeared in through the jagged hole that Bragg's missile had made, his power sword raised and humming. It was the ceremonial weapon of Heironymo Sondar, once-lord of Vervunhive, and Gaunt now carried it as a mark of honour for his courageous defence of that hive.

The keening, electric-blue blade flashed as it struck at shapes inside the hole.

Caffran ducked in after him, blasting from the hip. Few of the Ghosts were better than him in storm clearance. He was fast and ruthless.

He blocked Gaunt's back, gun flaring.

Niceg Vamberfeld had been a commercia cleric on Verghast before the Act of Consolation. He'd trained hard, and well, but this was all new to him. He followed the pair inside, plunging into a suddenly gloomy world of shadows, shadow-shapes and blazing energy weapons.

He shot something point blank as he came through the crumpled stone opening. Something else reared up at him, cackling, and he lanced it with his bayonet. He couldn't see the commissar-colonel or the young Tanith trooper any more. He couldn't see a gakking thing, in fact. He started to panic. Something else shot at him from close range and a las-round spat past his ear.

He fired again, blinded by the close shot, and heard a dead weight fall.

Something grabbed him from behind.

There was an impact, and a spray of dust and blood. Vamberfeld fell over clumsily, a corpse on top of him. Face down in the hot dirt, Vamberfeld found his vision returning. He was suffused in blue light.

Power sword smoking, Ibram Gaunt dragged him up by the hand.

'Good work, Vamberfeld. We've taken the breach,' he said.

Vamberfeld was dumbstruck. And also covered in blood.

'Stay sane,' Gaunt told him, 'It gets better...'

They were in a cloister, or a circumambulatory, as far as the dazed Verghastite could tell. Bright shafts of sunlight stippled down through the complex sandstone lattices, but the main window sections were screened with ornately mosaiced wood panels. The air was dry and dead, and rich with the afterscents of las-fire, fyceline and fresh blood.

Vamberfeld could see Gaunt and Caffran moving ahead, Caffran hugging the cloister walls and searching for targets as Gaunt perused the enemy dead.

The dead. The dreaded Infardi.

When they had seized Hagia, the Chaos forces had taken the name Infardi, which meant 'pilgrims' in the local language, and adopted a green silk uniform that mocked the shrineworld's religion. The name was meant to mock it too; by choosing a name in the local tongue, the enemy were defiling the very sanctity of the place. For six thousand years, this had been the shrineworld of Saint Sabbat, one of the most beloved of Imperial saints, after whom this entire star cluster – and this Imperial crusade – were named. By taking Hagia and proclaiming themselves pilgrims, the foe were committing the ultimate desecration. What unholy rites they had conducted here in Hagia's holy places did not bear thinking about.

Vamberfeld had learned all about Pater Sin and his Chaos filth from the regimental briefings on the troop ship. Seeing it was something else. He glanced at the corpse nearest him: a large, gnarled man swathed in green silk wraps. Where the wraps parted or were torn away, Vamberfeld could see a wealth of tattoos: images of Saint Sabbat in grotesque congress with lascivious daemons, images of hell, runes of Chaos overstamping and polluting blessed symbols.

He felt light-headed. Despite the months of training he had endured after joining the Ghosts, he was still out of shape: a desk-bound cleric playing at being soldier.

His panic deepened.

Caffran was suddenly firing again, splintering the dark with his muzzle-flashes. Vamberfeld couldn't see Gaunt any more. He threw himself flat on his belly and propped his gun as Colonel Corbec had taught him during Fundamental and Preparatory. His shots rattled up the colonnade past Caffran, supporting the young Tanith's salvoes.

Ahead, a flock of figures in shimmering green flickered down the cloister, firing lasguns and automatic hard-slug weapons at them. Vamberfeld could hear chanting too.

Chanting wasn't the right word, he realised. As they approached, the figures were murmuring, muttering long and complex phrases that overlapped and intertwined. He felt the sweat on his back go cold. He fired again. These troops were Infardi, the elite of Pater Sin. Emperor save him, he was in it up to his neck!

Gaunt dropped to his knee next to him, aiming and firing his bolt pistol in a two-handed brace. The trio of Imperial guns pummelled the Infardi advance in the narrow space.

There was a flash and a dull roar, and then light streamed in ahead of them, cutting into the side of the Infardi charge.

Blowing another breach in the cloister, more Ghosts poured in, slaughtering the advancing foe.

Gaunt rose. The half-seen fighting ahead was sporadic now. He keyed his microbead intercom.

There was a click of static that Vamberfeld felt in his own earpiece, then: 'One, this is three. Clearing the space.' A pause, gunfire. 'Clearance confirmed.'

'One, three. Good work, Rawne. Fan inward and secure the precinct of the Universitariat.'

'Three, acknowledged.'

Gaunt looked down at Vamberfeld. 'You can get up now,' he said.

DIZZY, HIS HEART pounding, Vamberfeld almost fell back out into the sunlight and wind of the square. He thought he might pass out, or worse, vomit. He stood with his back to the hot cloister stonework and breathed deeply, aware of how cold his skin was.

He tried to find something to focus his attention on. Above the stupa and gilt domes of the Universitariat thousands of flags, pennants and banners fluttered in the eternal wind of Hagia. He had been told the faithful raised them in the belief that by inscribing their sins onto the banners they would have them blown away and absolved. There were so many... so many colours, shapes, designs...

Vamberfeld looked away.

The Square of Sublime Tranquillity was now full of advancing Ghosts, a hundred or more, spilling out across the pink flagstones, checking doors and cloister entranceways. A large group had formed around the gibbet where Mkoll was cutting the corpses down.

Vamberfeld slid down the wall until he was sitting on the stone flags of the square. He began to shake.

He was still shaking when the medics found him.

MKOLL, LILLO AND Larkin were lowering the king's pitiful corpse when Gaunt approached. The colonel-commissar looked dourly at the tortured remains. Kings were two a penny on Hagia: a feudal world, controlled by city-states in the name of the hallowed God-Emperor, and every town had a king. But the king of Doctrinopolis, Hagia's first city, was the most exalted, the closest Hagia had to a planetary lord, and to see the highest officer of the Imperium disfigured so gravely offended Gaunt's heart.

'Infareem Infardus,' Gaunt muttered, remembering at last the high king's name from his briefing slates. He took off his cap and bowed his head. 'May the beloved Emperor rest you.'

'What do we do with them, sir?' Mkoll asked, gesturing to the miserable bodies.

'Whatever local custom decrees,' Gaunt answered. He looked about. 'Trooper! Over here!'

Trooper Brin Milo, the youngest Ghost, came running over at his commander's cry. The only civilian saved from Tanith, saved by Gaunt personally, Milo had served as Gaunt's adjutant until he had been old enough to join the ranks. All the Ghosts respected his close association with the colonel-commissar. Though an ordinary trooper, Milo was held in special regard.

Personally, Milo hated the fact that he was seen as a lucky charm.

'Sir?'

'I want you to find some of the locals, priests especially, and learn from them how they wish these bodies to be treated. I want it done according to their custom, Brin.'

Milo nodded and saluted. 'I'll see to it, sir.'

Gaunt turned away. Beyond the majestic Universitariat and the clustering roofs of the Doctrinopolis rose the Citadel, a vast white marble palace capping a high rock plateau. Pater Sin, the unholy intelligence behind the heretic army that had taken the Doctrinopolis, the commanding presence behind the entire enemy forces on this world, was up there somewhere. The Citadel was the primary objective, but getting to it was proving to be a slow, bloody effort for the Imperial forces as they claimed their way through the Doctrinopolis street by street.

Gaunt called up his vox-officer, Raglon, and ordered him to patch links with the second and third fronts. Raglon had just reached Colonel Farris, commander of the Brevian Centennials at the sharp end of the third front pushing in through the north of the city, when they heard fresh firing from the Universitariat. Rawne's unit had engaged the enemy again.

FOUR KILOMETRES EAST, in the narrow streets of the quarter known as Old Town, the Tanith second front was locked in hard. Old Town was a warren of maze-like streets that wound between high, teetering dwellings linking small commercial yards and larger market places. A large number of Infardi, driven out of the defences on the holy river by the initial push of the Imperial armour, had gone to ground here.

It was bitter stuff, house to house, dwelling to dwelling, street to street. But the Tanith Ghosts, masters of stealth, excelled at street fighting.

Colonel Colm Corbec, the Ghost's second-in-command, was a massive, genial, shaggy brute beloved of his men. His good humour and rousing passion drove them forward; his fortitude and power inspired them. He held command by dint of sheer charisma, perhaps even more than Gaunt did, certainly more than Major Rawne, the regiment's cynical, ruthlessly efficient third officer.

Right now, Corbec couldn't use any of that charismatic leadership. Pinned by sustained las-fire behind a street corner drinking trough, he was cursing freely. The microbead intercom system worn by all Guardsmen was being blocked and distorted by the high buildings all around.

'Two! This is two! Respond, any troop units!' Corbec barked, fumbling with his rubber-sheathed earpiece. 'Come on! Come on!'

A drizzle of las-blasts rocked the old sandstone water-tub, scattering chips of stone. Corbec ducked again.

'Two! This is two! Come on!'

Corbec had his head buried against the base of the water-tub. He could smell damp stone. He saw, in sharp focus, tiny spiders clinging to filmy cones of web in the tub's bas-relief carvings, inches from his eyes.

He felt the warm stone shudder against his cheek as las-rounds hit the other side.

His microbead gurgled something, but the broken transmission was drowned by the noise of a tin ladle and two earthenware jugs falling off the edge of the trough.

'Say again! Say again!'

'–chief, we–'

'Again! This is two! Say again!'

'–to the west, we–'

Corbec growled a colourful oath and tore out his earpiece. He sneaked a look around the edge of the tub and threw himself back. A single lasround whipped past, exploding against the wall behind him. It would have taken his head off if he hadn't moved.

Corbec rolled back onto his arse, his back against the tub, and checked his lasrifle. The curved magazine of the wooden-stocked weapon was two-thirds dry, so he pulled it out and snapped in a fresh one. The right-hand thigh pocket of his body armour was heavy with half-used clips. He always changed up to full-load when there was a chance. The half-spent were there at hand for dug-in resistance. He'd known more than one trooper who'd died when his cell had drained out in the middle of a firefight, when there was no time to reload.

There was a burst of firing ahead of him. Corbec spun, and noted the change in tone. The dull snap of the Infardi weapons was intermingled with the higher, piercing reports of Imperial guns.

He lifted his head above the edge of the tub. When he didn't get it shot off, he rolled up onto his feet and ran down the narrow alleyway.

There was fighting ahead. He leapt over the body of an Infardi sprawled in a doorway. The curving street was narrow and the dwellings on either side were tall. He hurried between hard shadow and patches of sunlight.

He came up behind three Ghosts, firing from cover across a market yard. One was a big man he recognised at once, even from the back.

'Kolea!'

Sergeant Gol Kolea was an ex-miner who'd fought through the Vervunhive war as a part of the 'scratch company' resistance. No one, not even the most war-weary and cynical Tanith, had anything but respect for the man and his selfless determination. The Verghastites practically worshipped him. He was a driven, quiet giant, almost the size of Corbec himself.

The colonel slid into cover beside him. 'What's new, sarge?' Corbec grinned over the roar of weaponsfire.

'Nothing,' replied Kolea. Corbec liked the man immensely, but he had to admit the ex-miner had no sense of humour. In the months since the new recruits had joined the Ghosts, Corbec hadn't managed to engage Kolea at all in small talk or personal chat, and he was pretty sure none of the others had managed it either. But then the battle for Vervunhive had taken his wife and children, so Corbec imagined Kolea didn't have much to laugh or chat about any more.

Kolea pointed out over the crates of rotting produce they were using as cover.

'We're tight in here. They hold the buildings over the market and west down that street.'

As if to prove this, a flurry of hard-round and laser fire spattered down across their position.

'Feth,' sighed Corbec. 'That place over there is crawling with them.'

'I think it's the merchant guild hall. They're up on the fourth floor in serious numbers.'

Corbec rubbed his whiskers. 'So we can't go over. What's to the sides?'

'I tried that, sir.' It was Corporal Meryn, one of the other Ghosts crouched in the cover. 'Sneaked off left to find a side alley.'

'Result?'

'Almost got my arse shot off.'

'Thanks for trying,' Corbec nodded.

Chuckling, Meryn turned back to his spot-shooting.

Corbec crawled along the cover, passing the third Ghost, Wheln, and ducked under a metal handcart used by the market's produce workers. He looked the market yard up and down. On his side of it, Kolea, Meryn and Wheln had the alley end covered, and three further squads of Ghosts had taken firing positions in the lower storeys of the commercial premises to either side. Through a blown-out window, he could see Sergeant Bray and several others.

Opposing them, a salient of Infardi troops was dug into the whole streetblock. Corbec studied the area well, and took in other details besides. He had always held that brains won wars faster than bombs. Then again, he also believed that when it really came down to it, fighting your balls off never hurt.

You're a complex man, Sergeant Varl had once told him. He'd been taking the piss of course, and they'd both been off their heads on sacra. The memory made Colm Corbec smile.

Head down, Corbec sprinted to the neighbouring building, a potter's shop. Shattered porcelain and china fragments littered the ground inside and out. He paused near a shell hole in the side wall and called.

'Hey, inside! It's Corbec! I'm coming in so don't hose me with las!'

He swung inside.

In the old shop, troopers Rilke, Yael and Leyr were dug-in, firing through the lowered window shutters. The shutters were holed in what seemed to Corbec to be a million places and just as many individual beams of light shafted in through them, catching the haze of smoke that lifted through the dark shop's air.

'Having fun, boys?' Corbec asked. They muttered various comments about the wanton proclivities of his mother and several other of his female relatives.

'Good to hear you're keeping your spirits up,' he replied. He began stamping on the pottery-covered floor.

'What the sacred feth are you doing, chief?' asked Yael. He was a youngster, no more than twenty-two, with a youngster's insubordinate cheek. Corbec liked that spirit a lot.

'Using my head, sonny,' smiled Corbec, pointing to his size eighteen field boot as he stomped it again.

Corbec raked away some china spoil and dragged up a floor-hatch by the metal yoke.

'Cellar,' he announced. The trio groaned.

He let the hatch slam down and crawled up to the window with them. 'Think about it, my brave Tanith studs. Take a look out there.'

They did, peering though the shredded shutter-slats.

'The market's raised... a raised podium. See there by that pile of drums? Gotta be a hatch. My money's on a warren of produce cellars under this whole market... and probably under that guild hall too.'

'My money's on you getting us all dead by lunchtime,' growled Leyr, a hard-edged, thirty-five year old veteran of the Tanith Magna militia.

'Have I got you dead yet?' asked Corbec.

'That's not the point–'

'Then shut up and listen. We'll be here til doomsday unless we break this deadlock. So let's fight smart. Use the fact this cess-pit of a city is a trazillion years old and full of basements, crypts and catacombs.'

He keyed his microbead intercom, adjusting the thin wire arm of the mike so it was close to his lips.

'This is two. You hearing me, six?'

'Six, two. Yes I am.'

'Bray, keep your men where they are and give the front of that hall a good seeing to in about... oh, ten minutes. Can you do that?'

'Six, got it. Firestorm in ten.'

'Good on you. Two, nine?'

'Nine, two.' Corbec heard Kolea's tight voice over the channel.

'Sarge, I'm in the pottery vendor's down from you. Leave Meryn and Wheln put and get over here.'

'Got you.'

Kolea scrambled in through the shell hole a few seconds later. He found Corbec shining his lamp-pack into the open cellar hatch.

'You know about tunnels, right?'

'Mines. I was a miner.'

'Same difference, it's all underground. Prep, we're going down.' He turned to Leyr, Rilke and Yael. 'Who's got a yen for adventure and a satchel full of tube-charges?'

Again, they groaned.

'You're safe, Rilke. I want you popping at those windows.' Rilke was a superb sniper, second only to the regimental marksmanship champion Larkin. He had a long-pattern needle-las. 'Give up any tubes you got to these plucky volunteers.'

Leyr and Yael moved back to the hatch. Each of them, like Corbec and Kolea, wore twenty kilos of matt-black composite body armour over their fatigues and under their camo-cloaks. Most of that weight came from the modular webbing pouches filled with ammo, lamp-packs, sheathed blades, waterproof microbead sets, coiled climbing rope, rolls of surgical tape, ferro-plastic binders, Founding-issue Imperial texts, door-spikes, flashbombs, and all the rest of the standard issue Imperial Guard kit.

'Gonna be tight,' mused Leyr sourly, looking down into the hole where Kolea's flashlight played.

Kolea nodded and pulled off his camo-cloak. 'Ditch anything that will get hung up.' Leyr and Yael did so, as did Corbec himself. The cloaks went onto the floor, as did other loose items. All four copies of the Imperial Infantryman's Uplifting Primer hit the cloaks at the same time.

The men looked at Corbec, almost ashamed.

'Ahh, it's all up here,' Corbec said, tapping his temple.

Sergeant Kolea tamped a spike into the tiled floor and ran the end of his climbing rope through the eye. He dropped the snake of cable down into the hole.

'Who's first?' he asked.

Corbec would have preferred to let Kolea lead, but this was his call and he wanted them to know he trusted it.

He grabbed the rope, slung his lasrifle over his shoulder, and clambered down into the hole.

Kolea followed, then Leyr. Yael brought up the rear.

The cellar shaft was eight metres deep. Almost immediately, Corbec was struggling and sweating. Even though he had ditched a lot of kit, the sheer bulk of his webbing and body armour was confining him and screwing with his centre of balance.

He landed on a floor in the darkness and switched on his lamp-pack.

The air was thick and foetid. He was in a cellar space four metres wide, dripping with ancient fluid and rot. His boots sloshed through semi-solid waste and murk.

'Oh feth!' spat Leyr as he made the ground.

There was an arched conduit snaking off towards the under-yard. It was less than a metre high and only half a metre wide. With kit and weapons, even stripped down, they had to hunch and edge in sideways, single file. The liquid ooze on the floor sucked up around their boot-tops.

Corbec attached his lamp-pack to the bayonet fitting under his lasgun's muzzle. He swung the weapon back and forth as best he could side on, bent over, and led them on into the soupy darkness.

'Probably wasn't the best idea in the galaxy to send either of us on this,' said Kolea behind him.

It was the closest Corbec had ever heard to a joke from the scratch sergeant. Apart from 'Try Again' Bragg, he and Kolea were the biggest men in the Tanith First. Neither Leyr and Yael topped out over two metres.

Corbec smiled. 'How did you manage? In the mines?'

Kolea slid round, passing Corbec in an awkward hunch. 'We crawled when the seams dipped. But there are other ways. Watch me.'

Corbec shone his light onto Kolea so that he and the two Tanith behind him could see. Kolea leaned back against the conduit wall until he was almost in a sitting position. Then he skirted along through the muck, bracing his back against the wall so that the top half of his body could remain upright. His feet ran against the foot of the far wall to prevent him slipping out.

'Very saucy,' said Corbec in admiration.

He followed suit, and so did Leyr and Yael. The quartet slid their way down the conduit.

Overhead, through the thick stone, they heard heavy fire. The ten minutes were up. Bray had begun his promised firestorm.

They were behind, too slow.

The conduit fanned and then opened out into a wide box. The stinking ooze was knee deep. Their flashlights found bas-relief markers of old saints on the walls.

At least the roof was higher here.

Straightening up, they headed forward through the tarry fluid. They were directly under the centre of the market yard now, by Corbec's estimation.

Another conduit led away towards what he presumed was the guild hall. Now Corbec led the way, double-time, back-crawling down the low conduit as Kolea had taught them.

They came on a shaft leading up.

By flashlight, they could see the sides were smooth brick, but the shaft was narrow, no more than a metre square.

By force of thighs alone, it was possible to edge up the shaft with back braced against one wall and feet against the other. Corbec led again.

Grunting and sweating, he climbed the shaft until his face was a few centimetres from a wooden hatch.

He looked down at Kolea, Yael and Leyr spidered into the flue below him.

'Here goes,' he said.

He pushed the hatch up. It didn't budge initially, then it slumped open. Light shone down. Corbec waited for gunfire but none came. He shuffled up the last of the shaft, shoul-derblade by shoulderblade, and pushed out into the open.

He was in the guild hall basement. It was boarded up and empty, and there were several corpses on the floor, drizzled with flies.

Corbec pulled himself out of the shaft into the room. The others followed.

Rising, their legs wet and stinking from the passage, they moved out, lasguns ready, lamp-packs extinguished.

The percussive throb of las-fire rolled from the floor above.

Yael checked the corpses. 'Infardi scum,' he told the colonel. 'Left to die.'

'Let's help their pals join them,' Corbec smiled.

The four took the brick stairs in the basement corner as a pack, guns ready. A battered wooden door stood between them and the first floor.

His foot braced against the door, Corbec looked back at the three Ghosts clustered behind him.

'What do you say? A day for heroes?'

All three nodded. He kicked in the door.

TWO
SERVANTS OF THE SLAIN

*'Let the sky welcome you, for therein dwells
the Emperor and his saints.'*

— Saint Sabbat, proverbs

BRIN MILO, HIS lasgun slung muzzle-down over his shoulder,
made his way against the press of traffic approaching the square
from the south. Detachments of Tanith and light mechanised
support from the Eighth Pardus Armoured were pouring into
the Universitariat district from the fighting zones to the south-
west, moving in to support the commissar's push. Milo ducked
into doorways as troop carriers and Hydra batteries grumbled
past, and slid sideways to pass platoons marching four abreast.

Friends and comrades called greetings to him as they moved
by, a few breaking step to quiz him on the front ahead. Most of
them were caked in pink dust and sweating, but morale was
generally high. Fighting had been intense during the last fort-
night, but the Imperial forces had made great gains.

'Hey, Brinny-boy! What lies in store?' Sergeant Varl called,
the squad of men with him slowing into a huddle that blocked
the street.

'Light stuff, the commissar's opened it up. The Universitariat is thick with them though, I think. Rawne's gone in.'

Varl nodded, but questions from some of his men were drowned by an air horn.

'Come on, move aside!' yelled a Pardus officer, rising up in the open cab of his Salamander command vehicle. A line of flamer tanks and tubby siege gun platforms was bottling up behind him. More horns sounded and the coughing motors raised pink dust in the air of the narrow street.

'Come on!'

'All right, feth it!' Varl responded, waving his men back against the street wall. The Pardus machines rumbled past.

'I'll try and leave some glory for you, Varl!' the armour officer called out, standing in the rear of his bucking machine and throwing a mock salute as he went by.

'We'll be along to rescue you in a minute, Horkan!' Varl returned, raising a single digit in response to the salute that all the Tanith in his squad immediately mimicked.

Brin Milo smiled. The Pardus were a good lot, and such horseplay typified the good humour with which they and the Tanith co-operated in this advance.

Behind the light armour came Trojans and other tractor units hauling heavy munitions and stowed field artillery, then Tanith pushing handcarts liberated from the weavers' barns. The carts were laden with ammunition boxes and tanks of promethium for the flamers. Varl's men were called over to help lift a cart out of a drain gutter and Milo moved on.

Hurrying against the flow of men and munitions, the young trooper reached the arch of the great red-stone bridge over the river. Shell holes decorated its ancient surface, and sappers from the Pardus regiment were hanging over the sides on ropes, shoring up its structure and sweeping for explosives. In this part of the Doctrinopolis, the river surged through a deep, man-made channel, its sides formed by the basalt river walls and the sides of the buildings. The smooth water was a deep green, deeper than the shade of the Infardi robes. A sacred river, Milo had been told.

Milo took directions from the Tanith corporal directing traffic at the junction, and left the main thoroughfare by a flight of steps that brought him down onto a riverwall path leading under the bridge itself. The water lapped at the stone three metres below and reflected ripples of white off the dark underside of the bridge.

He made his way to an archway overlooking the water further along the wall. It was the river entrance to one of the lesser shrines and tired, hungry-looking locals loitered around the entrance.

The shrine had been turned into a makeshift hospital early in the assault by local physicians and priests, and now, on Gaunt's orders, Imperial medical personnel had moved in to take charge.

Troops and civilians were being treated side by side.

'Lesp? Where's the doc?' Milo asked, striding into the lamplit gloom and finding the lean Tanith orderly at work sewing up a Pardus trooper's scalp laceration.

'In the back there,' Lesp replied, blotting the sutured wound with a swab of alcohol-soaked cloth. Stretcher parties were arriving all the time, mostly with civilian injured, and the long, arched shrine was filling up. Lesp looked harried.

'Doctor? Doctor?' Milo called. He saw Hagian priests and volunteers in cream robes working alongside the Imperial medics, and attending to the particular customs and rites of their own people. Army chaplains from the Ecclesiarchy were ministering to the needs of the off-world Imperials.

'Who's calling for a doctor?' asked a figure nearby. She rose, straightening her faded red smock.

'Me,' said Milo. 'I was looking for Dorden.'

'He's in the field. Old Town,' said Surgeon Ana Curth. 'I'm in charge here.' Curth was a Verghastite who had joined the Tanith along with the Vervunhive soldiery at the Act of Consolation. She'd taken to combat trauma well during the hive-siege and Chief Medic Dorden had been amazed and grateful at her decision to join.

'Will I do?' she asked.

'The commissar sent me,' answered Milo with a nod. 'They've found...' he dropped his voice and steered her into a private corner. 'They've found the local lord. A king, I think. He's dead. Gaunt wants his body dealt with according to local custom. Dutiful respect, that sort of thing.'

'Not really my field,' Curth said.

'No, but I figured you or the doc might have got to know some of the locals. Priests, maybe.'

She brushed her fringe out of her eyes and led him through the infirmary crowds to where a Hagian girl in the coarse cream robes of a scholar was re-dressing a throat wound.

'Sanian?' The girl looked up. She had the long-boned, strong-featured look of the local population, with dark eyes and well-defined eyebrows. Her head was shaved except for a bound pony-tail of glossy black hair hanging from the back of her skull.

'Surgeon Curth?' Her voice was thin but musical.

She's no older than me, Milo thought, but with the severe shaved head it was difficult to guess an age.

'Trooper Milo here has been sent by our commanding officer to find someone with a good knowledge of Hagian lore.'

'I'll help if I can.'

'Tell her what you need, Milo,' said Curth.

MILO AND THE Hagian girl went out of the hospital into the hard sunlight of the river wall. She put her hands together and made brief nods of respect to the river and the sky before turning to him.

'You're a doctor?' Milo asked.

'No.'

'Part of the priesthood, then?'

'No. I am a student, from the Universitariat.' She gestured to her pony-tail. 'The braids mark our station in life. We are called esholi.'

'What subject do you study?'

'All subjects, of course. Medicine, music, astrography, the sacred texts... is that not the way on your world?'

Milo shook his head. 'I have no world now. But when I did, students at advanced levels specialised in their study.'

'How... strange.'

'And when you've finished your study, what will you become?'

She looked at him quizzically.

'Become? I have become what I will become. Esholi. Study lasts a lifetime.'

'Oh.' He paused. A line of Trojans rattled by over the bridge above them. 'Look, I have some bad news. Your king is dead.'

The Hagian put her hands to her mouth and bowed her head.

'I'm sorry,' Milo said, feeling awkward. 'My commander

wants to know what should be properly done to... to care for his remains.'

'We must find the ayatani.'

'The who?'

'The priests.'

A WAILING NOISE made Rawne swing round, but it was only the wind.

He felt the movement of air against his face, gusting down the stone hallways and vaults of the Universitariat. Many windows had been blown out, and shell holes put through the walls, and now the windy air of Hagia was getting in.

He stood for a thoughtful moment, stealth cape swept back over one shoulder, lasgun slouched barrel-down across his belly staring into...

Well, he didn't rightly know what. A large room, scorched and burned out, the twisted, blackened limbs of fused sconces adhering to the sooty walls like stomped spiders. Millions of glass fragments littered the burnt floor. There were seared tufts of carpeting around the room edges.

What great purpose this room had once had was no longer important. It was empty. It was clear. That was all that mattered.

Rawne turned and went back out into the hallway. The wind, leaking through shell holes and exposed rafters, whined after him.

His clearance squad moved up. Feygor, Bragg, Mkillian, Waed, Caffran.. and the women.

Major Rawne still hadn't sorted his head out about the women. There were a fair number of them, Verghastites who had elected to join the Ghosts during the Act of Consolation. They could fight – feth! – he knew that much. They'd all been baptised in combat during the war for Vervunhive, common workers and habbers forced into fighting roles.

But still they were women. Rawne had tried to speak to Gaunt about it, but the colonel-commissar had droned on about various illustrious mixed or all female units in guard history blah blah blah and Rawne had pretty much blanked him out.

He wasn't interested in history. He was interested in the future. And in being there to enjoy it.

Women in the regiment put a strain on them all. Cracks were already showing. There had been a few minor brawls on the troop ships: Verghastite men protecting the 'honour' of their women; men falling out over women; women fighting off men...

It was a powder keg and soon there'd be more than a few split lips and broken teeth to show for it.

Bottom line was, Rawne had never really trusted women much. And he'd certainly never trusted men who put too much trust in women.

Caffran, for example. One of the youngest Ghosts: compact, strong, a fine soldier. On Verghast, he'd gotten involved with a local girl and they'd been inseparable ever since. A couple, would you believe? And Rawne knew for a fact the girl had a pair of young children who were cared for amongst the other non-combatants and camp-followers in the regimental escort ships.

Her name was Tona Criid. She was eighteen, lean and hard, with spiky bleached hair and gang tattoos that spoke of a rough life even before the Vervunhive war. Rawne watched her as she walked with Caffran down the shattered Universitariat hallway, covering each other, checking doors and alcoves. She moved with easy grace. She knew what she was doing. The black Ghost uniform fitted her well. She was... good looking.

Rawne turned away and scratched behind his ear. These women were going to be the death of someone.

The clearance squad prowled forward, picking their way down empty halls over the glass of broken windows and the kindling of shattered furniture. Rawne found himself moving level with the other female in his squad. Her name was Banda, an ex-loom worker from Vervunhive who'd fought in the famous guerilla company run by Gol Kolea. She was lively, playful, impetuous with close-cut curly brown hair and a figure that was a tad more rounded and feminine than that of the lithe ganger Criid.

Rawne signalled her on with a silent gesture and she did so, with a nod and a wink.

A wink!

You didn't wink at your commanding officer!

Rawne was about to call a halt and shout into her face when Waed signalled.

Everyone fell into shadows and cover, pressing against the hallway walls. They were reaching a turn. A wooden, red-painted door lay ahead, closed, and then further down the corridor, around the turn, there was an archway. The carpet in the halls had been rucked up and was stained and stiff with dried blood.

'Waed?'

'Movement. In the archway,' Waed whispered back.

'Feygor?'

Rawne's adjutant, the ruthless Feygor, nodded to confirm.

Rawne gestured some orders in quick succession. Feygor and Waed moved up, hunched low, hugging the right-hand wall. Bragg took the corner as cover and got his big autocannon braced. Banda and Mkillian went up the left side of the corridor until they reached the cover of a hardwood ottoman pushed against the wall.

Caffran and Criid slung their lasrifles over their shoulders, drew their blunt-nosed laspistols and went to the red door. If, as seemed likely, it opened into the same room as the archway, this could open their field of fire. And double checking it covered their arses.

Total silence. They were all Ghosts, moving with a Ghost's practiced stealth.

Caffran grasped the door handle, turned it, but didn't open it. He held it fast as Criid leaned down and put her ear to the red-painted wood. Rawne saw how she brushed her bleached hair out of the way to do it. He–

He was going to have to fething concentrate, he realised.

Criid looked round and made the open-handed sign for 'no sound'.

Rawne nodded, made sure all the squad could see him, raised three fingers and then dropped them one by one.

As the third finger dropped, Criid and Caffran went through the door low and fast. They found themselves in a large stone chamber that had once been a scriptorium before rockets had blown out the vast lancet windows opposite the door and shattered the wooden desks and writing tables. Caffran and Criid dropped for cover amid the twisted wooden wreckage. Las-shots spat their way from an archway at the far end of the room.

At the sound of gunfire from the room, Rawne's team opened up at the corridor arch. Fire was hastily returned.

'Caffran! What have you got?' Rawne snarled into his vox-link.

'The room doesn't go right along to your archway, but there's access through.'

Caffran and Criid crawled forward, popping the occasional shot off at the doorway over the broken lecterns and cracked stools. The floor was soaked with spilled ink and their palms were quickly stained black. Criid saw how the explosions had blown sprays of ink up the walls of the scriptorium: spattered patterns like reversed-out starmaps.

Caffran pulled open his hip-case and yanked out a tube-charge.

'Brace for det!' he yelled, ripping the foil strip off the chemical igniter and tossing the metal tube away through the doorway.

There was a bang that shook the floor and clouds of vapour and debris burst out of the hallway arch. Feygor tried to move forward to get a look in.

Criid and Caffran had risen and approached the inner doorway. Smoke wreathed the air and there was a pungent smell of fyceline. Just short of the doorway, Criid unslung her lasrifle and took something out of her pocket. It was the pin-mount of a brooch or a medal, the surface polished into a mirror. She hooked it over the muzzle of her weapon and pushed it into the room ahead of her. A turn of the wrist and the mirror slowly revealed the other side of the doorway.

'Clear,' she said.

They moved in. It was an annex to the scriptorium. Metal presses lined one wall. Three Infardi, killed by Caffran's charge, lay near the doorway. They were spattered and drenched by multi-coloured inks and tinctures from bottles exploded by the blast.

Rawne came in through the hallway arch.

'What's through there?' he asked, pointing to a small curtained door at the back of the annex.

'Haven't checked,' Caffran replied.

Rawne went to the door and pushed the curtain aside. A burst of las-fire pelted at him, punching through the cloth.

'Feth!' he cried, taking cover behind a mixing table. He fired through the doorway with his lasrifle and saw an Infardi crash sideways into a rack of vellum, spilling the whole lot over.

Rawne and Caffran went through the door. It was a parchment store, with no other exits. The Infardi, his green robes yanked up over his face, was dead.

But there was still shooting.

Rawne turned. It was outside in the corridor.

'We've picked up some–' MKillian's voice spat over the link.

'Feth!' That was Feygor.

Rawne, Criid and Caffran hurried to the corridor archway, but the force of crossfire outside prevented them from sticking their heads out. Las-shots smacked into the archway's jamb and ricocheted back into the annex room. One put a burn across Rawne's chin.

'Feth!' He snapped back in, smarting, and keyed his microbead. 'Feygor! How many!'

'Twenty, maybe twenty-five! Dug-in down the hall. Gods, but they're putting up a wall of fire!'

'Get the cannon onto it!'

'Bragg's trying! The belt-feed's jammed! Oh crap–!'

'What? What? Say again?'

Nothing but ferocious las-fire for a second, then Feygor's voice crackled over the link again.

'Bragg's down. Took a hit. Feth, we're pinned!'

Rawne looked around, exasperated. Criid and Caffran were over by the blasted window arches in the main scriptorium. Criid was peering out.

'What about this?' Caffran called to the major.

Rawne hurried over. Criid was already up and out on the ledge, shuffling along the stone sill.

'You've got to be kidding...' Rawne began.

Caffran wasn't. He was up on the sill too, following Criid. He reached a hand down for Rawne.

The major put his rifle strap over his shoulder and took the hand. Caffran pulled him up onto the stone ledge.

Rawne swore silently. The air was cold. They were high up. The stone flanks of the Universitariat dropped away ninety metres below the scriptorium window, straight down into the green, opaque channel of the river. Above the scriptorium's sloping, tiled roof, domes and spires rose. Rawne swayed for a second.

Criid and Caffran were edging down the ledge, stepping gingerly over leaded rainwater spouts and gutter trays. Rawne followed them. Bas-relief wall carvings, some in the form of saints or gargoyles, all weathered by age, stuck out, in some places wider than the ledge. Rawne found they had to go side-long with their backs to the drop so they could hunch and belly around such obstructions.

He felt his foot go into nothingness and put his arms round a saint's stone neck, his heart thundering, his eyes closed.

When he looked again, he could see Caffran about ten metres away, but there was no sign of the girl Criid. Feth! Had she fallen off? No. Her bleached-blonde head appeared out of a window further down, urging them on. She was back inside.

Caffran pulled Rawne in through the broken window. He ripped his kneecaps on the twisted leading and toothy stubs of glass in the frame and it took him a minute to get his breathing rate down again. He looked around.

A seriously big artillery shell had taken this chamber out. It had come through the windows, blown out the floor and the floor beneath. The room had a ring of broken floorboards jutting out around the walls and a void in the centre. They worked their way round on the remains of the floor to the hallway door. The firing was now a way behind them.

Caffran led the way out into the corridor. The shell blast had blown the room's wooden door, complete with frame, out across the hall and left it propped upright against the far wall. The three Ghosts scattered back down the hall at a run, coming in behind the enemy position that was keeping the rest of their team pinned.

The Infardi, twenty-two of them, were dug in behind a series of barricades made from broken furniture. They were blazing away, oblivious to anything behind them.

Rawne and Caffran drew their silver Tanith knives. Criid pulled out her chain-dagger, a gang-marked legacy of her low-life Vervunhive days. They went into the cultists from behind and eight were finished before the rest became aware of the counter-attack.

Then it came to hand to hand, a frantic defence. But Rawne and Criid had begun to open fire with their lasguns and Caffran had pulled out his pistol.

An Infardi with a bayonet charged Rawne, screaming, and Rawne blew his legs and belly out, but the momentum of the charge threw the body into the major and knocked him down.

He tried to scramble out from under the slippery, twitching body. Another Infardi appeared above him, swinging down with one of those wicked, twist-bladed local axes.

A headshot toppled him.

Rawne got up. The Infardi were dead and his squad was moving up.

'Feygor?'

'Nice move, boss,' Feygor replied.

Rawne said nothing. He could see no point in mentioning that the sneak attack had been Caffran's and Criid's idea.

'What's the story?' he asked.

'Waed's taken a scratch. He's okay. But Bragg's got a shoulder wound. We'll need to vox up a team to stretcher him out.'

Rawne nodded. 'Good headshot,' he added. 'That bastard had the drop on me there.'

'Wasn't me,' said Feygor, jerking a dirty thumb at Banda. The ex-loom girl grinned, patted her lasgun.

And winked.

'Well... Good shooting,' Rawne mumbled.

IN A PRAYER yard east of the Universitariat precinct, Captain Ban Daur was controlling traffic when he heard the colonel-commissar calling his name.

Colonel Corbec's second front push had woken up the Old Town, and civilians who had been hiding there in cellars and basements for the best part of three weeks were now fleeing the quarter en masse.

In the long narrow prayer yard, the tide of filthy, frightened bodies moved west in slow, choked patterns.

'Daur?'

Ban Daur turned and saluted Gaunt.

'There are thousands of them. It's jamming up the east-west routes. I've been trying to redirect them into the basilica at the end of that street. We've got medical teams and aid workers from the city authorities and the Administratum down there.'

'Good.'

'There's the problem.' Daur pointed to a row of stationary Hydra battery tractors from the Pardus unit drawn up against the far side of the yard. 'With all these people, they can't get through.'

Gaunt nodded. He sent Mkoll and a group of Tanith away into a nearby chapel and they returned with pews which they set up as saw-horses to channel the refugees away.

'Daur?'

'Sir!'

'Get down to this basilica. See if you can't open up some of the buildings around it.'

'I was taking a squad into the Old Town, sir. Colonel Corbec has asked for more infantry team support in the commercia.'

Gaunt smiled. Daur meant market district, but he used a term from Vervunhive. 'I'm sure he has, but the war will keep. You're good with people, Ban. Get this working for me and then you can go get shot at.'

Daur nodded. He respected Gaunt beyond measure, but he wasn't happy about this order. It seemed all too characteristic of the jobs he'd found himself doing since joining the Ghosts.

In truth, Daur felt empty and unfulfilled. The fight for Vervunhive had left him hollow and grim, and he'd joined the Tanith mainly because he couldn't bear to stay in the shell of the hive he had called home. As a captain, he was the senior ranking Vervun Primary officer to join the Tanith, and as a result he'd been given a place in the regimental chain of command on a par with Major Rawne, as officer in charge of the Verghast contingent, answering only to Corbec and Gaunt.

He didn't like it. Such a role should have gone to a war hero like Kolea or Agun Soric, to one of the men who had pulled himself up by his bootstraps to earn the respect of the men in the scratch companies. The majority of the Verghastite men and women who had joined the Ghosts were workers turned warriors, not ex-military. They just didn't have the sort of respect for a Vervun Primary captain they had for a hero like Gol Kolea.

But that wasn't the way it was done in the guard, apparently. So Daur was caught in the middle, with a command role he didn't like, giving orders to men who he knew should be his commanders, trying to keep the rivalry between Tanith and Verghastite under control, trying to win respect.

He wanted to fight. He wanted to badge himself with the sort of glory that would make the troops look up to him.

Instead, he found most of his days spent on squad details, deployment orders, refugee supervision. He could do that kind of thing well, and Gaunt knew it. So he was always the one

Gaunt asked for when such tasks came up. It was as if Gaunt didn't think about Ban Daur as a soldier. Just as a facilitator. An administrator. A people person.

Daur snapped out of his reverie as shots rang out and the refugees around him scattered and screamed. Some of Mkoll's makeshift saw-horses pitched over in the press. Daur looked around for a sniper, a gunman in the crowd...

One of the gun crew officers on the stationary Pardus vehicles was taking pot-shots with his pistol at the clusters of votive kites and flags that fluttered over the prayer yard. The flags and banners were secured on long tether-lines to brass rings along the temple wall. The officer was pinking at them for the entertainment of his crew.

'What the gak are you doing?' Daur shouted as he approached the Hydra mount. The men in their baggy tan fatigues and slouch caps looked down at him in puzzlement.

'You!' Daur yelled at the officer with the pistol in his hand. 'You trying to cause a panic?'

The man shrugged. 'Just passing the time. Colonel Farris ordered us up to help assault the Citadel Hill, but we're not getting anywhere, are we?'

'Get down here,' Daur ordered.

With a glance to his men, the officer holstered his service pistol and climbed down from the tractor. He was taller than Daur, with pale, freckled skin and blond hair. Even his eyelashes were blond.

'Name?'

'Sergeant Denil Greer, Pardus Eighth Mobile Flak Company.'

'You got a brain, Greer, or do you get through life with only that sneer?'

'Sir.'

Gaunt approached and Greer lost some of his bluster. His sneer subsided.

'Everything in order, Captain Daur?'

'High spirits, commissar. Everything's fine.'

Gaunt looked at Greer. 'Listen to the captain and be respectful. Better he reprimands you than I do.'

'Sir.'

Gaunt moved away. Daur looked back at Greer. 'Get your crews down and help us get these people off the road in an orderly fashion. You'll move all the quicker that way.'

Greer saluted halfheartedly and called his men down off the parked vehicles. Mkoll and Daur quickly got them to work moving civilians off the thoroughfare.

Daur moved through the filthy crowd. No one made eye contact. He'd seen that shocked, war-wrecked, fatigued look before. He'd worn it himself at Vervunhive.

An old woman, stick-thin and frail, stumbled in the crowd and went over, spilling open a shawl full of possessions. No one stopped to help. The refugees plodded on around her, stepping over her reaching hands as she tried to recover her possessions.

Daur helped her up. She was as light as a bag of twigs. Her hair was shockingly white and pinned back against her skull.

'There,' he said. He stooped and picked up her few belongings: prayer candles, a small icon, some beads, an old picture of a young man.

He found she was looking at him with eyes filmed by age. None of them had found his eyes out like that.

'Thank you,' she said, her voice richly flavoured with antique Low Gothic. 'But I don't matter. We don't matter. Only the saint.'

'What?'

'You'll protect her, won't you? I think you will.'

'Come on now, mother, let's move you along.'

She pressed something into his hand. Daur looked down. It was a small figurine, made of silver, worn almost featureless.

'I can't take this, it's–'

'Protect her. The Emperor would will it of you.'

She wouldn't take the trinket back, damn her! He almost dropped it. When he looked round again, she had disappeared into the river of moving bodies.

Daur looked about, confused, searching the moving crowd. He thrust the trinket in his pocket. Nearby, waving refugees past him, Daur saw Mkoll. He started to ask the scout leader if he'd seen the old woman.

A woman fell against him. A man just ahead dropped to his knees suddenly. Nearby in the crowd, someone burst in a puff of cooked blood.

Daur heard the shooting.

Not even twenty metres away, through the panicking crowd, he saw an Infardi gunman, shooting indiscriminately with a lasrifle. The killer had dragged back the dirty rags that had been concealing his green silk robes. He'd snuck in amid the refugee streams like a wolf coming through in the thick of a herd.

Daur drew his laspistol, but he was surrounded by jostling, screaming people. He heard the rifle firing again.

Daur fell over a body on the flagstones. He stumbled, looking through the running legs around him, catching sight of green silk.

The cultist's gunfire brought down more of the shrieking people. It made a gap.

Clutching his laspistol two-handed, Daur fired and put three shots through the gunman's torso; at almost exactly the same moment, Mkoll put a las-round through his skull from another angle.

The killer twisted and fell down onto the pink stones. Gleaming blood leaked out of him and threaded between the edges of the flags. There were bodies all around him.

'Sacred soul!' said Mkoll, moving through. Other Tanith troopers ran past, pushing through the crowd and heading for the north-east end of the yard. The vox-link buzzed and crackled.

More shooting, fierce exchanges, from the direction of the Old Town Road.

Daur and Mkoll pushed against the almost stampeding flow of refugees. At the north-east end of the prayer yard, a large sandstone pylon led through onto a long colonnade walk between temple rows. Ghosts were grouped in cover around the pylon, or were daring short runs down into the colonnade to shelter around the bases of black quartzite stelae spaced at regular intervals.

Gunfire, like a blizzard of tiny comets, churned up and down the colonnade. The long sacred walkway was littered with the bodies of native Hagians, sprawled out in twisted, undignified heaps.

More Ghosts ran up behind them, and some of the Pardus artillery men too, pistols drawn. Daur glimpsed Sergeant Greer.

'Go! Go left!' Mkoll yelled across at Daur, and immediately darted along from the arch towards the plinth of the nearest right-hand stelae. Four of his men gave him covering fire and a couple ran after him. Las-shots stitched across the walkway's flags and smacked chippings off the ancient obelisk.

Daur moved left, feeling the heat of a close round across his neck. He almost fell into the shadows of the nearest obelisk plinth. Other Ghosts tumbled in with him: Lillo, Mkvan and another Tanith whose name he didn't know. A Pardus crewman attempted to follow, but he was clipped in the knee and collapsed back into cover yelping.

Daur dared a look out, and glimpsed green movement further down the colonnade. The heaviest fire seemed to be coming from a large building on the left side of the colonnade which Daur believed was a municipal census hall.

'Left, two hundred metres,' Daur barked into his link.

'I see it!' Mkoll replied from the other side of the colonnade. Daur watched as the scout leader and his fireteam tried to advance. Withering fire drove them back into cover.

Daur ran again, reaching the next obelisk plinth on the left side. Shots were suddenly coming across him from the right and he turned to see two Infardi straddling the sloping tiles of a building, raking shots down into the shadows of the street.

Daur fired back, hastily, dragging his lasrifle off his shoulder. Lillo and Nessa reached his position around the same time and joined his fire. They didn't hit either of the Infardi but they drove them back off the roof out of sight. Broken tiles from the section of roof they had bombarded slithered off and crashed down onto the flagstones.

Mkvan reached their position too. The crossfire was intense, but they were a good twenty metres closer to the census hall than Mkoll's fireteam.

'This way,' Daur said, making sure he signed the words as he did so. Nessa was an ex-hab worker turned guerilla and like a fair number of the Verghastite volunteers, she was profoundly deaf from enemy shelling at Vervunhive. Signed orders were a scratch company basic. She nodded she understood, her fine, elfin features set in a determined frown as she slid a fresh ammunition cell into the port of her sniper-pattern lasgun.

Running stooped and low, the quartet left the main colonnade and ventured through the airy cool and shadows of a hypostyle hall. This temple, and the next which they crossed into via a small columned passage, was empty: what decoration and ornament the faithful hadn't taken and hidden prior to the invasion had been plundered by the Infardi during their occupation. Lamp braziers were overturned, and puddles of loose ash dotted the ceramic tiles of the floor. Splintered wood from broken furniture and prayer mats was scattered around. Along one east-facing wall, in a pool of sunlight cast by the hypostyle's high windows, a row of buckets and piles of rags showed where local people had attempted to scrub the Infardi's heathen blasphemies off the temple walls.

The four of them moved in pairs, providing bounding cover, two stationary and aiming while the other two swept forward to the next contact point.

The back of the second temple led into a subsidiary precinct that connected to the census hall. Here, the walls were faced in black grandiorite, but some Infardi hand had taken a sledge-hammer to the ancient wall-carvings.

The Infardi had posted lookouts at the back of the census hall. Mkvan spotted them, and brought the Ghosts into cover as laser and solid shots cut into the arched doorway of the precinct and blew dusty holes in the ashlar.

Nessa settled and aimed. She had a good angle and two single shots brought down a couple of the enemy gunmen. Daur smiled. The vaunted Tanith snipers like 'Mad' Larkin and Rilke would have to guard their reputations against some of the Verghastite girls.

Daur and Mkvan ran forward through the archway, back into the bright sunlight, and tossed tube-charges in through the rear doors of the census hall. A row of small glass windows overlooking the alley blew out simultaneously and smoke and dust rolled back out of the doors.

The four Ghosts went in, knives fixed as bayonets, firing short bursts into the smoke. They came into the Infardi position from behind. The intense firefight began to split the airy interior of the census hall.

DAUR'S STRIKE IMMEDIATELY diluted the Infardi barrage from the front of the building, allowing the pinned forces in the colonnade ample chance to push in. Three fireteams of Ghosts, including Mkoll's, circled in down the colonnade.

By then, Gaunt had moved up to the front line amongst the stelae. 'Mkoll?'

'The front's barricaded firmly, sir,' the scout leader reported over the link. 'We've got their attention turned away from us... I think that's Daur's doing.'

Gaunt crouched behind a stelae and waved a signal down the line of crouching Ghosts ranged along the side of the colonnade. Trooper Brostin ran forward, the tanks of his flamer unit clanking.

'What kept you?' Gaunt asked.

'Probably all the shooting,' Brostin replied flippantly. The colonel-commissar indicated the census hall facade.

'Wash it out, please.'

Brostin, a big man with ursine shoulders and a ragged, bushy moustache, who always reeked of promethium, hefted the flamer around and thumbed the firing toggle. The tanks made a coughing gurgle and then retched a spear of liquid fire out at the census hall. The jet of flame arced downwards with yellow tongues and noxious black smoke curling off it like a mane.

Fire drizzled and trickled across the boarded front of the hall. Painted panels suddenly scorched black and caught fire. Paint peeled and beaded in the heat. The tie-beams over the door burst into flames.

Brostin took a few steps forward and squirted flame directly in through some of the tight firing slits in the hall's defences. Gaunt liked watching Brostin work. The burly trooper had an affinity with fire, an understanding of the way it ran and danced and leapt. He could make it work for him; he knew what would combust quickly and what slowly, what would burst in fierce incandescent flames and what would smoulder; he knew how to use wind and breeze to fan flames up into target dugouts. Brostin wasn't just hosing an enemy emplacement with flames here, he was artfully building an inferno.

According to Sergeant Varl, Brostin's skill with fire came from his background as a firewatcher in Tanith Magna. Gaunt could believe this. It wasn't what Trooper Larkin said, though. Larkin said Brostin was an ex-convict with a ten-year sentence for arson.

The fire, almost white, coiled up the hall front and caught the roof. A significant section of the front wall blew out into the street as fire touched off something volatile, perhaps an Infardi's satchel of grenades. Another section guttered and fell in. Three green-clad men came out of the hall door mouth, firing las-weapons down the colonnade. The robes of one of the trio were burning. Ghost weapons opened up all around and the three toppled.

A couple of grenades flew from the burning hall and exploded in the middle of the street. Then two more Infardi tried to break out. Mkoll killed both within seconds of them appearing at the doorway.

Now, under Gaunt's orders, the Ghosts were firing into the burning facade. A Pardus Hydra platform clanked down the centre of the colonnade, trailing a bunch of prayer-kite tails that had snagged on its barrels and aerial mount, and rolled in beside Gaunt's position.

Gaunt climbed up onto the plate behind the gunner and supervised as the NCO swung the four long snouts of the anti-aircraft autocannons down to horizontal.

'Target practice,' Gaunt told him.

The gunner tipped a salute and then tore the front of the census hall into burning scraps with his unforgiving firepower.

INSIDE, AT THE rear of the hall, Daur and his comrades were moving back the way they had come in. Thick black smoke boiled out from the main body of the hall. Daur, choking, could smell promethium and knew a flamer had been put to good work. Now there was a hell of a noise out front. Heavy fire, and not something man-portable.

'Come on!' he rasped, waving Nessa, Lillo and Mkvan back. The four staggered through the smoke wash, coughing and spitting, half blind. Daur prayed they hadn't lost their sense of direction.

They were remarkably unscathed. Mkvan had a scratch across the back of his hand and Lillo was cut along the forehead, but they'd hit the Infardi hard and lived to tell of it.

More heavy firing from the colonnade side. A couple of murderously powerful shots, glowing tracers, tore through a wall behind them and passed over their heads. The shots had passed right through the bulk of the census hall.

'Gak!' cried Lillo. 'Was that a tank?'

Daur was about to reply when Nessa gave out a gasping cry and doubled over. He swung around, eyes stinging with the smoke and saw five Infardi rushing them from the main hall area. Two were firing lasrifles. Another's robes had all been burnt off his seared body.

Daur fired, and felt the kiss of a las-round past his shoulder. Daur's gunfire blew two of the Infardi over onto their backs.

Another charged Mkvan and was impaled on the Tanith's out-thrust bayonet. Thrashing, fixed, the Infardi shot Mkvan through the face point-blank with his pistol. Both bodies toppled over in the smoke.

Lillo was borne down by the other two who, weaponless, clawed at him and ripped into his clothes and skin with dirty, hooked fingernails. One got his hands on Lillo's lasrifle and was trying to pull it free, though the sling was hooked. Daur threw himself at the rebel and they went over, crashing back through the doorway and into the fire-swamped main hall.

The heat took Daur's breath away. The Infardi was hitting and biting and clawing. They rolled through fire. The enemy had his hands around Daur's throat now. Daur thought about his knife, but remembered it was still attached to the bayonet lug of his lasrifle, and that was lying out in the next room next to Mkvan's corpse.

Daur rolled, allowing the frantic Infardi to get on top of him, and then bucked and reeled, kicking up with his legs, throwing the cultist head first over the top of him. The cultist bounced off a burning table as he landed, throwing up a cloud of sparks. He got up, muttering some obscene oath, a smouldering chair leg in his hands, ready to wield as a club.

The roof came in. A five tonne beam, rippling from end to end with a thick plumage of yellow and orange flame, crushed the Infardi into the ground.

Daur scrambled up. His tunic was on fire. Little blue flames licked down the sleeve and the cuff, and around the seams of the pockets. He beat at himself, stumbling towards the door. He hadn't taken a breath in what seemed like two or three minutes. His lungs were full of searing heat.

In the annex at the back of the census hall, Lillo was trying to drag Nessa out through the back portico. Tarry black smoke was gusting out of the rafters and the air was almost unbearably toxic.

Daur stumbled towards them, over the burning bodies of the Infardi. He helped Lillo manhandle Nessa's dead weight. She'd been shot in the stomach. It looked bad, but Daur was no medic. He had no idea how bad.

A dull rumble echoed through the blazing hall as another roof section collapsed, and a gust of smoke, sparks and super-heated air bellowed out around them. As they staggered through the portico into the rear yard, Daur heard something fall from his tunic and clink on the ground behind him.

The trinket. The old woman's trinket.

They dragged Nessa clear across the yard and Lillo collapsed by her side, coughing from the bottom of his lungs and trying to vox for a med-team.

Daur crossed back to the flaming portico, tearing off his smouldering tunic. The heat and flames had scorched the fabric and burst the seams. One of the pockets was hanging off by singed threads and it was from there that the silver trinket had fallen.

Daur saw it on the flagstones, lying just inside the portico. He hunkered down under the seething mass of black smoke that filled the upper half of the archway and roiled up into the windy blue sky. He reached for it and closed his fingers around the trinket. It was painfully hot from the blaze.

Something bumped into him and knocked him to his knees. He turned to face an Infardi cultist, his flesh baked raw and bloody, who had come blindly out of the inferno.

He reached out his blistered hands, clawing at Daur, and Daur snapped his laspistol from its holster and put two rounds through his heart.

Then Daur fell over.

Lillo ran across to him, but Daur couldn't hear what the trooper was shouting.

He looked down. The engraved hilt of the ritual dagger was sticking out of his ribcage and blood as dark and rich as berry juice was pumping out around it. The Infardi hadn't just bumped into him at all.

Daur started to laugh inanely, but blood filled his throat. He stared at the Infardi weapon until his vision became like a tunnel and then faded out altogether.

THREE
PATER SIN

'Fortune deliver you by the nine holy wounds.'

— ayatani blessing

HIS FATHER TURNED from the workbench, put down a greasy spanner and smiled at him as he wiped his oily hands on a rag. The machine shop smelled of cog-oil, promethium and cold metal.

He held out the piping hot cup of caffeine, a cup so big his small hands clutched it like a chalice, and his father took it gratefully. It was dawn, and the autumn sun was gliding up over the stands of massive nalwood trees beyond the lane that led down from the river road to his father's machine shop.

The men had arrived at dusk the previous night, eight raw-palmed men from the timber reserve fifteen leagues down river. They had a big order to meet for a cabinet maker in Tanith Magna and their main woodsaw had thrown its bearings. A real emergency... could the best mechanic in Pryze County help them out?

The men from the reserve had brought the saw up on a flatbed wagon, and they helped his father roll it back into the workshop. His father had sent him to light all the lamps. It was going to be a late hour before work would be finished.

He waited in the doorway of the shop as his father made a last few adjustments to the woodsaw's big motor and then screwed the grille cover back in place. Collected sawdust had spilled out of the recesses of the cover and the room was suddenly perfumed with the pungent fragrance of nalwood.

As he waited for his father to test the saw, he felt his heart beating fast. It had been the same as long as he could remember, the excitement of watching his father perform magic, of watching his father take dead lumps of metal and put them together and make them live. It was a magic he hoped he'd inherit one day, so that he could take over when his father had done with working. So that he'd be the machinesmith.

His heart was beating so fast now, it hurt. His chest hurt. He clutched the doorframe to steady himself.

His father threw the switch on the sawblock and the machine shrilled into life. Its rasping shriek rattled around the shop.

The pain in his chest was quite real now. He gasped. It was all down one side, down the left, across his ribs. He tried to call out to his father, but his voice was too weak and the noise of the running saw too loud.

He was going to die, he realised. He was going to die there in the doorway of his father's machine shop in Pryze County with the smell of nalwood in his nose and the sound of a woodsaw in his ears and a great big spike of impossible pain driving into his heart–

COLM CORBEC OPENED his eyes and added a good thirty-five years to his life. He wasn't a boy any more. He was an old soldier with a bad wound in a grim, grim situation.

He'd been stripped to the waist, with the filthy remnants of his undershirt still looped about his shoulders. He'd lost a boot. Where the feth his equipment and vox-link had gone was anybody's guess.

Blood, scratches and bruises covered his flesh. He tried to move and pain felled him back. The left side of his ribcage was a mass of purple tissue swelling around a long laser burn.

'D-don't move, chief,' a voice said.

Corbec looked around and saw Yael beside him. The young Tanith trooper was ash-white and sat with his back against a crumbling brick wall. He too had been stripped down to his breeches and dried blood caked his shoulders.

Corbec looked around. They were sprawled together in the old, dead fireplace of a grand room that the war had brutally visited. The walls were shattered skins of plaster that showed traces of old decorations and painting, and the once-elegant windows were boarded. Light stabbed in through slits between the planks. The last thing Corbec remembered was storming into the guild hall. This, as far as he could tell, wasn't the guild hall at all.

'Where are we? What h–'

Yael shook his head gently and gripped Corbec's arm tightly.

Corbec shut up fast as he followed Yael's look and saw the Infardi. There were dozens of them, scurrying into the room through a doorway out of sight to his left. Some took up positions at the windows, weapons ready. Others moved in, carrying ammo crates and bundles of equipment. Four were manhandling a long and obviously heavy bench into the room. The feet of the bench scraped on the stone floor. The Infardi spoke to each other in dull, low voices.

Now he began to remember. He remembered the four of them taking the main chamber of the guild hall. God Emperor, but they'd punished those cultist scum! Kolea had fought like a daemon, Leyr and Yael at his side. Corbec remembered pressing ahead with Yael, calling to Kolea to cover them. And then–

And then pain. A las-shot from almost point-blank range from an Infardi playing dead in the rubble.

Corbec pulled himself up beside Yael, wincing at the pain.

'Let me look,' he whispered, and tried to see to the young man's injury. Yael was shaking slightly, and Corbec noticed that one of the boy's pupils was more dilated than the other.

He saw the back of Yael's head and froze. How was the boy still alive?

'Kolea? Leyr?'

'I think they got out. I didn't see...' Yael whispered back. He was about to say something else, but he fell suddenly dumb as a sigh wafted through the room.

Corbec felt it rather than heard it. The Infardi gunmen had gone quiet and were backing to the edges of the chamber beyond the fireplace, heads bowed.

Something came into the room, something the shape, perhaps, of a large man, if a man can be clothed in a whisper. It was something like a large, upright patch of heat haze, fogging and distorting the air, humming like the low throb of a drowsy hornet's nest.

Corbec stared at the shape. He could smell the way it blistered reality around itself, smell that cold hard scent of the warp. The shape was simultaneously translucent and solid: vapour-frail but as hard as Imperator armour. The more Corbec looked, the more he saw in the haze. Tiny shapes, twinkling, seething, moving and humming like a billion insects.

With another sigh, the refractor shield disengaged and dissolved, revealing a large figure wrapped in green silk robes. The compact generator pack for the body-shield swung from a belt harness.

It turned to face the two guard prisoners in the empty fireplace.

Well over two metres, built of corded muscle, with skin, where it showed past the rich emerald silk, decorated with the filthy tattoos of the Infardi cult.

Pater Sin smiled down at Colm Corbec.

'You know who I am?'

'I can guess.'

Sin nodded and his grin broadened. An image of the Emperor tortured and agonised was tattooed across his left cheek and forehead, with Sin's bloodshot left eye forming the screaming mouth. Sin's teeth were sharpened steel implants. He smelled of sweat and cinnamon and decay. He hunched down in front of Corbec. Corbec could feel Yael quaking with fear beside him.

'We are alike, you and I.'

'I don't think so...' said Corbec.

'Oh yes. You are a son of the Emperor, sworn to his service. I am Infardi... a pilgrim devoted to the cults of his saints. Saint Sabbat, bless her bones. I come here to do homage to her.'

'You come here to desecrate, you vile bastard.'

The steel grin remained even as Sin lashed out and kicked Corbec in the ribs.

He blacked out. When his mind swam back, he was crumpled in the centre of the room with Infardi all around him. They were chanting and beating time on their legs or the stocks of their rifles. He couldn't see Yael. The pain in his ribs was overwhelming.

Pater Sin reappeared. Behind him was the bench his minions had dragged in. It was a workbench, Corbec now saw. A stone-cutter's bench with a big rock drill clamped to it. The drill whined. The noise had been in Corbec's dream.

He had thought it was a woodsaw.

'Nine holy wounds the saint suffered,' Sin was saying. 'Let us celebrate them again, one by one.'

His men threw Yael on the bench. The drill sang.

There was nothing Corbec could do.

TO THE NORTH of its area, the Old Town rose steeply, clinging to the lower scarps of the Citadel plateau. A main thoroughfare called, confusingly enough, Infardi Mile, curved up from the Place of Wells and the livestock markets and climbed through a more salubrious commercial neighbourhood, the Stonecutters Quarter.

One glimpse of the temples, the stelae, the colonnades – any of the Doctrinopolis's triumphant architecture – told a visitor how exalted the work of the stonecutters and the masonic guilds was. The most massive work, the great sarsens and grandiorite blocks, were brought in by river or canal from the vast upland quarries, but in their workshop houses on the skirts of the Citadel mount, the stonecutters carved their intricate statuary, gargoyles, ceiling bosses, cross-facings and lintels.

At the bottom end of Infardi Mile, the Tanith chief medic Tolin Dorden had set up a field aid-post in a ceramic-tiled public washhouse. Some of the men had carried in buckets or helmets full of water from the fountain pools in the square to sluice the washrooms out. Dorden had personally taken a disinfectant rub to the worktops where the clothes had been scrubbed. There was a damp, stale scent to the place, undercut by the warm, linty aroma that drifted from the drying cupboards over the heating vents.

He was just finishing sewing up a gash on Trooper Gutes's thumb when a Verghastite Ghost wandered in from the harsh sunlight in the square. The rattling thump of Pardus mortars shelling the Citadel rolled in the distance. Out in the square, Dorden could see huddles of Tanith resting by the fountains.

He sent Gutes on his way.

'What's the trouble?' he asked the newcomer, a broad-faced, heavy jawed man in his thirties.

'It's me arm, doc,' he replied, his voice full of the Verghastite vowel-sounds.

'Let me take a look. What's your name?'

'Trooper Tyne,' the man replied, dragging up his sleeve. The upper part of his left arm was a bloody, weeping mess, with infection setting in.

Dorden reached for a swab to start cleaning.

'This is infected. You should have brought it to me before now. What is it, a shrapnel wound?'

Tyne shook his head, wincing at the touches of the alcohol-soaked swab. 'Not really.'

Dorden cleaned a little more blood away and saw the dark green lines and the knife marks. Realising what it was, he cleaned a little more.

'Didn't the commissar issue a standing order about tattoos?'

'He said we could mark 'em if we knew how to do it.'

'Which you clearly don't. There's a man in eleven platoon, one of yours, what's his name... Trooper Cuu? They say he does a good job.'

'Cuu's a gak-head. I couldn't afford him.'

'So you did it yourself?'

'Mm.'

Dorden washed the wound as best he could and gave the trooper a shot. The Tanith were, to a man, tattooed. Mostly these were ritual or family marks. It was part of the culture. Dorden had one himself. But the only Verghastite volunteers with tattoos were gangers and slum-habbers wearing their allegiances and clan-marks. Now almost all of them wanted a mark – an axe-rake, a Tanith symbol, an Imperial aquila.

If you didn't have a mark, the sentiment went, you weren't no Ghost.

This was the seventeenth infected home-made mark Dorden had treated. He'd have to speak to Gaunt.

Someone was shouting out in the square. Trooper Gutes ran back in. 'Doc! Doc!'

Outside, everyone was on their feet. A group of Tanith Ghosts had appeared from the direction of the fighting down in the merchant market, carrying Trooper Leyr on a makeshift stretcher. Gol Kolea was running beside the prostrate man.

There was shouting and confusion. Calmly, Dorden pushed his way through the mob and got the stretcher down on the ground so he could look.

'What happened?' he asked Kolea, as he started to dress the las-wound in Leyr's thigh. The man was hurt, battered, covered in minor wounds and semi-conscious, but he wouldn't die.

'We lost the colonel,' Kolea said simply.

Dorden stopped his work abruptly and looked up at the big Verghastite. The men all around went quiet.

'You what?'

'Corbec took me and Yael and Leyr in under the guild hall. We were doing pretty well but there were too many. I got out with Leyr here, but Colonel Corbec and the lad... They got them. Alive. As we shot our way out of the hall, Leyr saw the bastards dragging both of them away.'

There was murmuring all around.

'I had to get Leyr to an aid-station. That's done. I'm going back for Corbec now. Corbec and Yael. I want volunteers.'

'You'll never find them!' said Trooper Domor, stunned and miserable.

'The bastards were taking them north. Into the high part of the Old Town, towards the Capital. They're holding positions up there. My guess is they're going to interrogate them. Means they'll be alive for a while yet.'

Dorden shook his head. He didn't agree with the brave Verghastite's assessment. But then he'd seen a great deal more of the way Chaos worked.

'Volunteers! Come on!' Kolea snapped. Hands went up all around. Kolea selected eight men and turned.

'Wait!' said Dorden. He moved forward and checked the minor wounds on Kolea's face and chest. 'You'll live. Let's go.'

'You're coming?'

Corbec was pretty much beloved by all, but he and the old doctor had a special bond. Dorden nodded. He turned to Trooper Rafflan, the vox-operator. 'Signal the commissar. Tell him what we're doing and where we're going. Tell him to get a medic down here to man the aid-post and an officer to supervise.'

Dorden gathered up a makeshift kit and hurried after the troopers moving out of the square.

* * *

'YOU'RE BEHIND SCHEDULE, Gaunt,' said the clipped voice from the vox speaker. The lips of Lord General Lugo's three dimensional holographic image moved out of sync with his utterance. Lugo was speaking via vox-pictor from Imperial Base Command at Ansipar City, six hundred and forty kilometres south-west of the Doctrinopolis, and atmospherics were causing a communications lag.

'Noted, sir. But with respect, we're inside the Holy City four days ahead of your pre-assault strategy prediction.'

Gaunt and the other officers present in the gloomy command tractor waited while the lag coped with the reply. Seated in harness restraints to the rear, astropaths mumbled and muttered. The hologram flickered, jumped and then Lugo spoke again.

'Quite so. I have already applauded the work done by Colonel Furst's Pardus units in breaking you in.'

'The Pardus have done excellent work,' Gaunt agreed smoothly. 'But the colonel himself will tell you the Infardi put up little outer resistance. They didn't want to meet our armour head on. They fell back into the Doctrinopolis where the density of the buildings would work to their advantage. It's going street by street with the infantry now, and by necessity, it's slow.'

'Two days!' the vox crackled. 'That was the estimate. Once you'd entered the walls of the Holy City, you said you'd need two days to retake and consolidate. Yet you're not even near the Citadel!'

Gaunt sighed. He glanced around at his fellow officers: Major Kleopas, the squat, plump, ageing second-in-command of the Pardus armour; Captain Herodas, the Pardus's infantry liaison officer; Major Szabo of the Brevian Centennials. None of them looked comfortable.

'We're shelling the Citadel with mortars,' Szabo began, his hands in the patch-pockets of his mustard drab jacket.

Herodas cut in. 'That's true. We're getting medium firepower close to the Citadel. The heavies will pull in once the infantry have cleared the streets. Commissar Gaunt's representation of the theatre is accurate. Getting into the city proved to be four days easier than you estimated. Getting through it is proving harder.'

Gaunt shot the young Pardus captain an appreciative nod. A calm, united front was the only way to deal with tactically obsessed top brass-hole like Lugo.

The holographic figure jerked and fizzled again. A phantom of green light and mist, Lord General Lugo stared out at them. 'Let me tell you now that we are all but done here at Ansipar. The city is burning and the shrines are ours. My troops are rounding up the enemy stragglers for execution as we speak. Furthermore, Colonel Cerno reports his forces are within a day of taking Hylophan. Colonel Paquin raised the aquila above the royal palace at Hetshapsulis yesterday. Only the Doctrinopolis remains in enemy hands. I gave you the job of taking it because of your reputation, Gaunt. Was I wrong?'

'It will be taken, lord general. Your faith was not misplaced.'

A lag-pause. 'When?'

'I hope to begin full assault on the Capital by sundown. I will advise you of our progress.'

'I see. Very well. The Emperor protects.'

The four officers repeated the abjuration in a mumbled chorus as the hologram fizzled out.

'Damn him,' Gaunt murmured.

'He's there to be damned,' Major Kleopas agreed. He pulled down one of the metal frame slouch-seats from the wall of the tractor hull, sat his rotund bulk down and scratched at the scar tissue around the augmetic implant that served as his left eye. Herodas went to fetch them all caffeine from the stove rack by the rear hatch.

Gaunt took off his peaked and braided cap, set it on the edge of the chart display and tossed his leather gloves into it. He knew well what Kleopas meant. Lugo was new blood, one of the 'New Minted' generals Warmaster Macaroth had brought with him when he superseded Slaydo and took command of the Sabbat Worlds Crusade almost six sidereal years before. Some, like the great Urienz, had proved themselves just as able as the Slaydo favourites they replaced. Others had proved only that they were book-learned tacticians with years of campaign in the war-libraries of Terra and none at the front line. Lord General Lugo was desperate to prove himself, Gaunt knew. He'd botched command of his first theatre, Oscillia IX, turning a sure-thing into a twenty-month debacle, and there were rumours that an enquiry was pending following his lightning raids on the hives of Karkariad. He needed a win, and a victor's medal on his chest, and he needed them quickly before Macaroth decided he was dead weight.

The liberation of Hagia was to have been given to Lord Militant General Bulledin, which was why Gaunt had gladly approved his Ghosts for the action. But at the last minute, presumably after much petitioning behind the scenes by Lugo's faithful, Macaroth had replaced Bulledin and put Lugo in charge. Hagia was meant to be an easy win and Lugo wanted it.

'What do we do?' asked Szabo as he took a cup from Herodas.

'We do as we're told,' Gaunt replied. 'We take the Citadel. I'll pull my men back out of Old Town and the Pardus can shell it to pieces. Clear us a path. Then we'll storm the Citadel.'

'That's not how you want it to go, is it?' asked Kleopas. 'There are still civilians in that district.'

'There may be,' Gaunt conceded, 'but you heard the lord general. He wants the Doctrinopolis taken in the next few days and he'll make us scapegoats for any delay. War is war, gentlemen.'

'I'll make arrangements,' said Kleopas grimly. 'Pardus armour will be rolling through Old Town before the afternoon is old.'

There was a metallic rap at the outer hatch. A Tanith trooper on duty opened it and spoke to the figure outside as cool daylight streamed into the dim tactical chamber.

'Sir?' the trooper called to Gaunt.

Gaunt walked to the hatch and climbed down out of the massive armoured mobile command centre. The tractor, a barn-sized hull of armoured metal on four massive track sections, had been parked in a narrow street beside the basilica where the city's refugees were now being housed. Gaunt could see rivers of them still issuing from the Old Town district, pouring into the massive building under the supervision of Ghost troopers.

Milo was waiting for him, accompanied by a local girl in cream robes and a quartet of old, distinguished men in long gowns of austere blue silk.

'You asked for me?' Gaunt said to Milo.

The young Tanith nodded. 'This is ayatani Kilosh, ayatani Gugai, ayatani Hilias and ayatani Winid,' he said, indicating the men.

'Ayatani?' Gaunt asked.

'Local priests, sir. Devotees of the saint. You asked me to find out about–'

'I remember now. Thank you, Milo. Gentlemen. My trooper here has undoubtedly explained the sad news I bear. For the loss of Infareem Infardus, you have my commiserations.'

'They are accepted with thanks, warrior,' ayatani Kilosh replied. He was a tall man, bald save for a silver goatee. His eyes were immeasurably weary.

'I am Colonel-Commissar Ibram Gaunt, commander of the Tanith First and over all commander of the action here at the Doctrinopolis. It is my wish that your high king, so miserably murdered by the arch-enemy, should receive every honour that is due to him.'

'The boy has explained as much,' said Kilosh. Gaunt saw how Milo winced at the word 'boy'. 'We appreciate your efforts and your respect for our customs.'

'Hagia is a holy world, father. The honour of Saint Sabbat is one of the primary reasons for our crusade. To retake her homeworld is my chief concern. By honouring your customs, I do no more than honour the God-Emperor of Mankind himself.'

'The Emperor protects,' the four priests echoed in concert.

'So what must be done?'

'Our king must be laid to rest in sanctified soil,' said Gugai.

'And what counts as sanctified?'

'There are a number of places. The Shrinehold of the Saint is the most holy, but here in the Doctrinopolis, the Citadel is the high hallowed ground.'

Gaunt listened to Kilosh's words and turned to look out past the jagged roofs of the Old Town towards the towering plateau of the inner Citadel. It was swathed in smoke, the white after-fog of heavy mortar shelling wisping away into the windy blue air.

'We have just drawn plans to retake the Citadel, fathers. It is our imperative. As soon as the way is clear, I will allow you through to perform your rites and lay your gracious ruler to rest.'

The ayatani nodded as one.

There, thought Gaunt. It's decided for me. Hell take Lugo's wishes, we have a need to recapture the Citadel now. Kloepas, Herodas and Szabo had emerged from the command tractor now and Gaunt waved them over. He signalled to his waiting vox-officer too.

'We're go for the Citadel,' Gaunt told the officers. 'Get the armour ready. I want shelling to begin in an hour from now. Beltayn?'

The Tanith vox-officer stepped up. 'Signal the Tanith units in the Old Town area to withdraw. The word is given. Armour assault begins in an hour.'

Trooper Beltayn nodded and hitched his vox-set around to his hip, coding in the orders for transmission.

'THAT ONE'S YOUR leader?' Sanian asked Milo as they waited in the shadow of the command tractor.

'That's him.'

She studied Gaunt thoughtfully. 'It is his way,' she said.

'What?'

'His way. It is his way and it suits him. Do you not have a way, Trooper Milo?'

'I... I don't know what you mean...'

'By "way", the esholi means destined path, boy,' said ayatani Gugai, looming at Milo's left side. Sanian bowed her head in respect. Milo turned to the old priest.

Gugai was by far the most ancient of the four priests Sanian had found for him. His skin was wizened and deeply scored with innumerable lines. His eyes were clouding and dim, and his body, beneath the blue silk robes, was twisted and hunched from a lifetime that had been both long and hard.

'I'm sorry, father... with respect, I still don't understand.'

Gugai looked cross at Milo's reply. He glanced at the bowed Sanian. 'Explain it to the off-worlder, esholi.'

Sanian looked up at Milo and the old priest. Milo was struck by the peerless clarity of her eyes.

'We of Hagia believe that every man and woman born in the influence of the Emperor–' she began.

'Fate preserve him, may the nine wounds mark his fortune,' intoned Gugai.

Sanian bowed again. 'We believe that everyone has a way. A destiny preordained for them. A path to follow. Some are born to be leaders, some to be kings, some to be cattlemen, some to be paupers.'

'I... see...' Milo said.

'You don't at all!' Gugai said with contempt. 'It is our belief, given to us by the saint herself, that everyone has a destiny.

Sooner or later, God-Emperor willing, that destiny will realise itself and our way become set. My way was to become a member of the ayatani. Commander Gaunt's way, and it is clear, is to be a warrior and a leader of warriors.'

'That is why we esholi study all disciplines and schools of learning,' Sanian said. 'So that when our way becomes apparent to us, we are ready, no matter what it brings.'

Milo began to understand. 'So you have yet to find your... way?' he asked Sanian.

'Yes. I am esholi yet.'

Gugai sat his old bones down on an empty ammo box and sighed. 'Saint Sabbat was a low-born, daughter of a chelon herdsman in the high pastures of what we now call the Sacred Hills. But she rose, you see, she rose despite her background, and led the citizens of the Imperium to conquest and redemption.'

The best part of six years in the Sabbat Worlds Crusade had told Milo that much. Saint Sabbat had, six thousand years before, come from poverty on this colony world to command Imperial forces and achieve victory throughout the cluster, driving the forces of evil out.

He had seen images of her, bare-headed and tonsured, dressed in Imperator armour, decapitating the daemons of filth with her luminous sword.

Milo realised the girl and the old priest were staring at him.

'I have no idea of my way,' he said quickly. 'I'm a survivor, a musician... and a warrior, or that's what I hope to be.'

Gugai stared some more and then shook his head. It was the strangest thing. 'No, not a warrior. Not simply a warrior. Something else.'

'What do you mean?' asked Milo, disarmed.

'Your way is many years hence...' Gugai began then stopped abruptly.

'You'll find it. When the time comes.' The old priest rose stiffly and wandered away to rejoin his three brethren, talking together quietly in the stepped portico of the basilica.

'What the feth was that about?' Milo barked, turning to the girl.

'Ayatani Gugai is one of the Doctrinopolis elders, a holy man!' she exclaimed defensively.

'He's an old madman! What did he mean I wasn't a warrior? Was that some kind of prophesy?'

Sanian looked at Milo as if he'd just asked the dumbest question in the entire Imperium.

'Of course it was,' she said.

Milo was about to reply when his earpiece squawked and combat traffic crackled into his link. He listened for a moment and then his face went dark.

'Stay here,' he told the girl student. He hurried towards Gaunt, who stood with the other Imperial officers at the rear steps of the command tractor. Sunlight barred down between the high roofs of the temple district and made pools on the otherwise dark street. Rat-birds, their plumage grey and dirty, fluttered between the eaves or roosted and gurgled in the gutters.

As Milo strode towards Gaunt he could see that the Tanith commander was listening to his own headset.

'You heard that, sir?'

Gaunt nodded.

'They've got Colonel Corbec. Kolea's leading a rescue party.'

'I heard.'

'So call off the withdrawal. Call off the armour.'

'As you were, trooper.'

'What?'

'I said – As you were!'

'But–' Milo began and then shut up. He could see the dark, terrible look in Gaunt's face.

'Milo... if there was a chance of saving Corbec, I'd hold up the entire fething crusade. But if he's been taken by the Infardi, he's already dead. The lord general wants this place taken quickly. I can't suspend an attack in the slim hope of seeing Colm again. Kolea and his team must pull out with the others. We'll take the Citadel by nightfall.'

There were many things Brin Milo wanted to say. Most of them were about Colm Corbec. But the look of Colonel-Commissar Gaunt's face denied them all.

'Corbec's dead. That's the way of war. Let's win this in his name.'

'SIGNAL HIM "NO",' Kolea drawled.

'Sir?' vox-officer Rafflan queried.

'Signal him a "no", gak take you! We're not withdrawing!'

Rafflan sat down in a corner of the ruined Old Town dwelling they had secured. Trooper Domor and four others moved past to the cracked and bare windows and aimed their lasguns. The old doctor, Dorden, weighed down with his medicae kit and loose-fitting black smock, was last into the building.

'I can't, sir, with respect,' said Rafflan. 'The colonel's signalled a priority order, code Falchion, verified. We are to withdraw from the Old Town now. Shelling is to commence in forty-six minutes.'

'No!' Kolea snapped. The men looked round from their positions.

Dorden settled in beside Kolea on the slope of plaster and rubble under the window.

'Gol... I don't like this any more than you, but Gaunt's made an order.'

'You never break one?'

'An order from Gaunt? You're kidding!'

'Not even on Nacedon, when he ordered you to abandon that field hospital?'

'Feth! Who's been talking?'

Kolea paused for a moment. 'Corbec told me,' he said.

Dorden looked down and ran a hand through his thinning grey hair. 'Corbec, huh? Damn it...'

'If they start shelling, we'll be hit by our own guns,' Trooper Wheln said.

'It's Corbec,' Dorden said simply.

'Don't signal,' said Kolea, reaching forward and unplugging Rafflan's headset. 'Just don't signal, if it makes you feel better. We've got to do this. You just never got the order.'

Mkvenner and Sergeant Haller called back that the street was clean. They were on the edge of the Stonecutters' district.

'Well?' Dorden looked at Kolea.

'Come on!' he replied.

TWO HOURS AFTER the midday chimes had peeled from the dozen or more clock towers in the Universitariat district, to be echoed by the clocks of the Old Town and beyond, the Pardus armour was unleashed.

Led by Colonel Furst aboard the legendary Shadow Sword super-heavy tank *Castigatus*, a storm-shoal of fifty Leman Russ Conquerors, thirty-eight Thunderer siege tanks and ten Stygies-pattern Vanquishers slammed into the southern lip of the Old Town.

Long-range bombardment from Basilisk units and
Earthshaker platforms out in the marshes south of the city
perimeter fell for twenty minutes until the tank squadrons were
poised at the limits of the Old Town district. By then,
firestorms were boiling through the street blocks from the livestock market north to Haemod Palisade and all the way across
to Infardi Mile.

The tank groups plunged forward, their main weapons blasting as they went. Vanquishers and Conquerors followed the
street routes, churning up the Mile like determined beetles
under a rising pall of smoke and firedust that quickly shrouded
the entire city. The hefty siege tanks ploughed straight through
terraced habitation blocks and ancient dwelling towers with
their dozer blades, bricks and building stone and tiles cascading off them. The thump and roar of the tank guns quickly
became a drum beat heard by all of the citizens and soldiery in
the Doctrinopolis. The Ghosts had fallen back into the suburbs
south of the Old Town, and the Brevians had withdrawn clear
of the firefield to the Northern Quarter above the
Universitariat. Vox-officers reported to the tactical teams that
Sergeant Kolea's team had not been recorded.

The fire splash of the tank wave rippled through the Old
Town all the way up to the base of the Citadel. Twenty thousand homes and businesses burned or were flattened by
shelling. The Chapel of Kiodrus Militant was blown apart. The
public kitchens and the studios of the iconographers were
blasted through and trampled under churning tracks. The
Ayatani Scholam and the subsidiaries of the esholi were
destroyed, and their brick litter toppled into the holy river. The
ancient stones of the Indehar Sholaan Sabbat Bridge were
hurled a hundred and fifty metres into the air.

The Pardus armour ploughed on, directed by Colonel Furst
and Major Kleopas. They were one of the best armour units in
this segmentum.

Old Town, and everything and everyone in it, didn't stand a
chance.

FOUR
THE COLONEL AT BAY

*'Lay a fire within your soul and another between your hands,
and let both be your weapons.
For one is faith and the other is victory and neither
may ever be put out.'*

— Saint Sabbat, lessons

THE ROOM SHOOK. The walls and floor jarred slightly. Dust dribbled from the rafters. Onion-flasks full of water clinked against each other.

No one seemed to notice at first, except Corbec himself. He was sprawled on the floor, and he could feel the flagstones stirring under his palms and fingertips.

He looked up, but none of the Infardi had felt it. They were too busy with Yael. The boy was dead now; for that much Corbec was thankful, though it meant it would soon be his own turn on the bench. But the Infardi were still finishing their ritual butchery, adorning the corpse with shunned symbols while they muttered verses from polluted texts.

The room shook again. The bottles clinked. More dust trickled down.

Despite the gravity of his situation, perhaps even because of it, Colm Corbec smiled.

A shadow fell across him.

'Why do you smile?' Pater Sin asked.

'Death's coming,' Corbec replied, spitting a wad of bloody saliva into the floor dust.

'Do you welcome it?' Sin's voice was low, almost breathless. Corbec saw that Sin's metal teeth were so sharp they cut the inside of the bastard's own lips.

'I welcome death all right,' Corbec said. He sat up slightly. 'Takes me away from you for one thing. But I'm smiling 'cause it's not coming for me.'

The room shook again. Pater Sin felt it and looked around. His men stopped what they were doing. With curt words and gestures, Sin sent three of them hurrying from the room to investigate.

Corbec didn't need anyone to tell him what it was. He'd been close to enough mechanised assaults in his time to know the signs. The hard shocks of shells falling, the background vibration of heavy armour...

The room shook yet again, and this time there was a triple-peal of noise loud enough to be clearly identified as explosions. The Infardi were gathering up their weapons. Sin stalked over to one man who had a light vox unit and exchanged calls with other Infardi units.

By then, the shaking and the sound of the explosions was a constant background noise.

Sin looked over at Corbec.

'I expected this, sooner or later. You presume it's taken me by surprise, but in fact it's precisely what I...'

He paused, as if unwilling to give away secrets even to a half-dead old foot-slogger.

Sin made several guttural noises – Corbec decided they must be command words in the Infardi's private combat-code – and the gunmen made ready to leave en masse. Four of them grabbed Corbec and dragged him up with them. Pain flared through his torso, but he bit his lip.

His captors pulled and shoved him along dirty hallways and across an open courtyard behind the main body of the Infardi gunmen. In the yard, the sunlight was harsh and painful to Corbec, and the open air brought the sounds of the

Imperial assault to him with greater clarity: the overlapping, meaty thump of explosions, the swooping air-rush of shells, the clanking grind of tracks, the slithering collapses of masonry.

Corbec found himself almost hopping along, trying to favour the foot with the boot on it. The Infardi punched and jabbed him, cursing him. They wanted to move faster than he could go. Besides, keeping one hand on him meant they each had only one hand free to manage ammo satchels, lasrifles and their other accoutrements.

They pressed on through the interior of a stonecutter's workshop where everything was coated thumb-deep in white stone dust, before emerging through a set of wooden shutters into a steep, cobbled street.

Above, not more than two kilometres away, rose the Citadel. It was the closest Corbec had been to the building. Its bleached cliff edges, fringed in mauve mosses and feathery lichens, thrust up above the skirt of roofs and towers formed by Old Town and the eastern hill quarters of the Doctrinopolis, supporting the ashlar-dressed pillars and temples of the holy city's royal precincts. The monumental buildings were flesh-pink against the blue of the sky. Sin's men must have taken him and Yael a good way north through the Old Town.

Looking the other way, the street swept down through the jumbled old dwellings and massy stoneshops towards the river plain where the Old Town started. The sky that way was a whirling haze of black and grey smoke. Fire licked through the town's flanks. Corbec could see series after series of shell-strikes fan in ripples through the streets. Geysers of flame, smoke, earth and masonry blew up into the air.

His guards pulled at him again and forced him up the slope of the street. Most of the other Infardi had already disappeared into the surrounding buildings.

The gunmen jostled him off the street, through a cast-iron gate into a level yard where stones and tiles were stacked ready for use. To one side, under an awning, sat three flat-pan work barrows and some cutter's tools; to the other, a pair of heavy old-pattern servitors that had been deactivated.

The men pushed Corbec down on the barrows. Pater Sin reappeared with eight other men, moving from an inner door across the yard, and words were exchanged.

Corbec waited. The barrows were covered in dusty sacking. The masons' tools were nearby: four big adzes, a worn mallet, some chisels, a diamond-bladed trowel. Even the smaller items were not small enough for him to conceal.

A whistling scream shook the yard as a shell passed directly overhead. It detonated in the neighbouring building and blew brick chips and smoke back over them with a boneshaking roar. Corbec pressed his head down into the sacking.

He felt something under the sacking, reached for it.

A heavy weight, small, about the size of a child's fist or a ripe ploin, with a cord attached. A stonecutter's plumb-line; a hard lead weight on the end of four metres of plaited silk string. Trying not to let them see, he tugged it out of the sacking on the barrow and wound it into his hand.

Pater Sin barked some more orders to his men, and then engaged his body-shield, effectively vanishing from view. Corbec saw his hazy shape, crackling in the dustclouds kicked up from the near-hit, leave the yard by the far side, accompanied by all but three of the men.

They turned back to him, approaching.

A salvo of tank shells fell on the street around with numbing force and noise. Luck alone had caused them to bracket the yard or, Corbec realised, he and his captors would have been pulped. As it was, all three Infardi were knocked over on their faces. Corbec, who had a more experienced ear for shelling times and distances than the cultists, had braced himself at the first whistle of the incoming shells.

He leapt up. One of the Infardi was already rising groggily, lasrifle swinging up to cover the prisoner.

Corbec spun the looped plumb-line in his hand quickly, letting the lead soar free on the third turn. It smashed into the gunman's left cheek with a satisfying crack and sent him tumbling back to the floor.

Corbec now spun the line over his head at the full length of its cord. He had built up enough force by the time the second gunman jumped up that it wrapped four times around his throat and cinched tight.

Choking, the cultist fell, trying to get the tough, tight cord off his throat.

Corbec grabbed his lasrifle, and managed to roll with it and fire off a pair of shots as the first Infardi got up again. He was firing as he rose, the dent of the plumb-weight bruising his face. Corbec's shots went through his chest and tossed him over on to his back.

Clutching his captured weapon, Corbec stood up. More shells fell close by. He put a shot through the head of the Infardi who was still trying to get the line off his neck.

The third was face down, dead. The close blast had buried a piece of tile in his skull.

The rolling thunder of the barrage was coming closer. There was no time to search the bodies for ammo or liberate a replacement boot. Corbec figured if he headed up the Old Town hill he could get around the side of the Citadel plateau and perhaps stay alive. It was undoubtedly what the Infardi were doing.

He went through the doors on the far side of the yard, in the direction Sin had taken. He kept hopping as shards of debris dug into the sole of his unprotected foot. He passed down a tiled hallway where the force of the blasts had brought the windows and blinds in, then on into a bay area where iron scaffolding was stored near to a loading ramp.

Between the beat of explosions, close and distant, he heard voices. Corbec crouched and peered through the loading area. The outer doors, tall and old and wooden, had been levered open, and a pair of eight-wheel cargo trucks had been backed in. Infardi, about a dozen of them, were loading sheet-wrapped objects and wooden crates into the rear of the vehicles.

There was no sign of Pater Sin.

Corbec checked the power-load of his appropriated weapon. Over three-quarters yield.

Enough to make them sit up and take notice at least.

THE BURNING STREETS were alive. Humans, locals, fleeing from their devastated homes and hiding places with bundles of possessions, driving thin, scared livestock before them.

And vermin... tides of vermin... pouring out of the inferno, sweeping down the hill streets of Old Town towards the river.

Kolea's team moved against the tide.

Chasing uphill at a run, with rebreather masks buckled over their faces to shut out the searing smoke, they tried to head away from the blast front of the encroaching armour brigade while steering a path towards the masons' district.

Now and then, shells fell so close they were all thrown off their feet by the shockwaves. Torched dwellings collapsed across streets to block their route. In places, they waded through living streams of rodents, guard-issue boots crunching on squirming bodies.

The eight Ghosts sprinted across another street junction, wafer-shreds of ash billowing around them, and took shelter in a leather worker's shop. It had been gutted by shells, just an empty ruin.

Dorden pulled off his rebreather and started coughing. By his side, Trooper Mkvenner rolled onto his side and tried to pull a shard of hot glass shrapnel out of his thigh.

'Let me see to it,' Dorden coughed. He used his medicae kit tweezers to tug the sliver out and washed the deep cut with antiseptic from a spray bottle.

Dorden sat back, mopping his brow.

'Thanks, doc,' whispered Mkvenner. 'You okay?'

Dorden nodded the question away. He felt half-cooked, wilted, choked. He couldn't draw breath properly. The heat from the burning buildings all around was like an oven.

By an exploded doorway in the far wall, Kolea and Sergeant Haller looked out.

'It's clear that way,' Kolea muttered, pointing.

'For now,' Haller conceded. He waved up troopers Garond and Cuu and sent them dashing over to secure the premises next door.

Dorden noted that Haller, a Verghastite recruit himself, and a veteran of the Vervun Primary regiment, favoured the troops he knew from his homeworld: Garond and Cuu, both Verghastites.

Haller was a cautious soul. Dorden felt the sergeant sometimes had too much respect for the heroic Tanith to give them orders.

The old medic eyed the other members of the squad: Mkvenner, Wheln, Domor and Rafflan, the other Tanith men. Harjeon was the only other Vervunhiver. A small, blond man with a wispy moustache, Harjeon cowered in the shelled out corner of the premises.

Dorden noted he could see a pecking order now. Kolea's in charge, and he's a war hero, so no one argues. Haller's ex-hive military, and so's Garond. Cuu... well, he's a law unto himself, an ex-ganger from the lowest hive levels, but no one doubts his mettle or his fighting smarts.

Harjeon... An ex-civilian. Dorden wasn't sure what Harjeon's calling had been in pre-guard life. A tailor? A teacher? Whatever, he rated lowest of all.

If they ever got out of this alive, Dorden knew he'd have to talk to Gaunt about evening up the prejudices that the new influx brought with them.

Volcanically, shells splashed down across the end of the street. They were showered with debris.

'Let's move!' Haller cried and took off after Cuu and Garond. Kolea waited, waving Harjeon and the Tanith past.

Dorden reached the doorway, and looked at Kolea as he adjusted his rebreather mask.

'We really should go back...' he began.

'Into that, doctor?' Kolea asked, gesturing back at the firestorm that boiled up through Old Town after them.

'We're out of options, I'm afraid,' Kolea said. 'Just to stay alive, we've got to keep ahead of the shells. So we might as well keep on and see if we can find Corbec.'

They ran through a wall of heat into the next ruin. Dorden saw the bare skin on his wrists and forearms was blistering in the crisping air.

They darted into the next building. It was remarkably intact and the air within mercifully cool. From the window, Dorden watched as shells slammed down close by. The building across the street seemed to shunt sideways, whole and complete, before disintegrating.

'Close, huh, Tanith?'

Dorden glanced round and met the eyes of Trooper Cuu.

Trooper Cuu. Lijah Cuu. Something of a legend already in the regiment. Just under two metres, slim, corded with muscle. Lean with a face like a bad lie. That's how Corbec had described him.

Cuu had been a ganger in Vervunhive before the war. Some said he'd killed more men in gang fights than he had in battle. He was tattooed extensively, and sold his ability with ink and needle to appreciative Verghastites. A long scar split his face top to bottom.

Trooper Cuu called everyone 'Tanith', like it was a scornful insult.

'Close enough for me,' Dorden said.

Cuu flexed around and checked over his lasrifle. His movements were feline and quick, Dorden thought. A cat, that's just what he is. A scarred and ragged tomcat. Even down to his chilly green eyes. Dorden had spent the last odd years in the company of exceptionally dangerous men. Rawne, that ruthless snake... Feygor, a soulless killer... but Cuu...

A casebook sociopath, if ever he'd seen one. The man had made a life of gang-fights and blade-wars long before the crusade had come along to legitimise his talents. Just being close to Cuu with his vivid tattoo gang marks and cold, lifeless eyes made Dorden uneasy.

'What's the matter, doc? Got no stomach for it?' Cuu chuckled, sensing Dorden's unease. 'Better you stayed at your nice safe aid station, huh?'

'Absolutely,' Dorden said and moved across to a place between Rafflan and Domor.

Trooper Domor had lost his eyes on Menazoid Epsilon, and augmetic surgeons had rebuilt his face around a pair of military gauge optic sensors. The Tanith men called him 'Shoggy', after the bug-eyed amphibian they decided he now resembled.

Dorden knew Domor well, and counted him a friend. He knew that Domor's implants could read heat and movement through stone walls and brick facades.

'You see much?'

'It's all empty ahead,' Domor replied, the milled focus rings of his implants whirring as they moved around on automatic. 'Kolea should put me up front. Me and Mkvenner.'

Dorden nodded. Mkvenner was one of the Tanith's elite scout troopers, trained by the infamous Mkoll himself. Between his senses and Domor's augmetic sight, they could be moving ahead with a great deal more confidence.

Dorden decided to speak to Kolea and Haller about it. He moved forward towards the bulky shape of the big miner and the lean figure of Haller, who still wore his spiked Vervun Primary helmet as part of his battledress.

A shockwave threw him off his feet into the far wall. Plaster smashed and slid away as he hit it.

For a fleeting, peaceful second, he saw his wife, and his daughter, long gone with Tanith itself and his son Mikal, dead these last few months on Verghast far away...

Mikal smiled, and detached himself from the embrace of his sister and his mother. He stepped towards his father.

'Sabbat Martyr,' he said.

'What?' Dorden replied. His mouth and nose were full of blood and he couldn't talk clearly. The joy and pain of seeing his son was making him cry. 'What did you say?'

'Sabbat Martyr. Don't die, dad. It's not your time.'

'Mikal, I...'

'Doc! Doc!'

Dorden opened his eyes. Pain shuddered through his waking body. He couldn't see.

'Oh feth,' he gurgled, blood filling his mouth.

Rough hands yanked his mask off and he heard liquid pattering on the rubble. He blinked.

Wheln and Haller were bent over him, anxious looks on their faces. 'W-what?' Dorden mumbled.

'Thought you were fething dead!' Wheln cried.

They helped him sit up. Dorden wiped his face and saw his hand came away bloody. He checked his face and realised his nose was streaming blood. The nosebleed had filled his mask and blinded his eye-slits.

'Feth!' he snarled, getting up. His head swam and he sat back.

'Who did we lose?' he asked.

'No one,' Haller said.

Dorden looked around. The shell had taken out the west wall of the building, but all his comrades were intact: Kolea, Cuu, Garond, Rafflan, Mkvenner, Harjeon.

'Charmed lives,' said Cuu with a chuckle.

With the help of Wheln and Haller, Dorden got to his feet. He felt like the spirit had been blasted out of him.

'You all right?' Kolea asked.

Dorden spat clotted blood and wiped his face. 'Just dandy,' he said. 'If we're going, let's just go, right?'

Kolea nodded, and signalled the party to their feet.

Firestorms were ripping down both sides of the street by them, and further shells were adding to the inferno. Behind the dwelling, they found that the shell had blown open a watercourse gurgling below street level in a brick defile.

Kolea and Mkvenner leapt down into it. The brackish water, perhaps an ancient tributary of the holy river, surged around their boots.

Dorden followed them down. It was cooler here, and the moving water seemed to wash away the thick smoke.

'Let's move along it,' Kolea suggested. No one argued.

In a tight line, the seven Ghosts tracked up the watercourse through the fires.

They'd gone no more than a hundred metres when Trooper Cuu suddenly held up his hand. The crude tats of a skull and crossbones marked his knuckles.

'Hear that?' he asked. 'Las fire!'

CORBEC'S SHOTS TORE through the loading bay. Two Infardi were slammed back off the side of one of the trucks. Another toppled, dropping the crate he had been carrying.

They started firing back almost immediately, pulling handguns from their sashes or grabbing the lasrifles leaning up against the wall. Glittering laser fire and whining hard rounds hammered into the stacked scaffolding around Corbec.

He didn't flinch. Kicking over a stack of scaffolding, he ran down the length of the bay's side wall, firing from the hip. Another Infardi clutched his throat, fell on his back and slithered off the bed of one of the trucks.

A bullet creased his tricep. A las-round tore through the thigh pocket of his combat pants.

He threw himself into cover behind an archway pillar.

It went unpleasantly quiet. Gunsmoke and the coppery stink of las discharge filled the air.

Corbec lay still, trying to slow his breathing. He could hear them moving around.

An Infardi came around the pillar and Corbec shot him through the face. A torrent of shots poured in his direction and the Tanith colonel started to crawl on his hands and knees down the stone passage. The wood-panelled walls above began to splinter and shred into the air as solid and energy rounds rained into them.

There was a doorway to his left. He rolled across into it, and got up. His hands were shaking. His chest hurt so much he could barely think any longer.

The room was an office of some sort. There were book cases and a large clerical desk lined with pigeon holes. Sheets of paper coated the floor, some fluttering in the breeze from the small, broken window high in the end wall.

There was no way out. The window was about large enough for him to stick his arm out of and that was it.

'Feth me..' Corbec murmured to himself, wiping a hand through his matted beard. He hunched down behind the heavy desk and laid the barrel of his weapon over the desktop, pointing at the doorway.

The gun's power cell was all but a quarter spent now. It was an old, battered Imperial issue job, with an L-shaped piece of metal brace welded on in place of the original stock. The makeshift brace jutted into his collarbone, but he aimed up as best he could, remembering all the things Larkin had taught him about spot shooting.

A figure in green silk darted across the door mouth, too fast for Corbec to hit. His wasted shot smacked into the far wall. Another swung round into the doorway, firing on auto with a small calibre machine pistol. The spray of bullets went high over Corbec's head and destroyed a bookshelf. Corbec put a single round into the Infardi's chest and threw him back out of sight.

'You messed with the wrong man, you bastards!' he yelled. 'You should have finished me when you had the chance! I'm gonna take the head off anyone who comes through that door!'

I just hope they don't have grenades, he thought.

Another Infardi ducked in, fired twice with his lasgun and jumped back out. Not fast enough. Corbec's shot didn't kill him but it went through his arm. He could hear whimpering outside.

Now a lasgun came around the doorframe, held out blind and firing. Two shots hit the desk hard enough to jerk it back against him. He shot back and the gun disappeared.

Now he could smell something. An intense chemical stink.

Liquid promethium.

They had a flamer out there.

GOL KOLEA SNAPPED his fingers and made three quick gestures.

Mkvenner, Harjeon and Haller sprinted forward to the left, down the side of the stonemason's shop. Domor, Rafflan and Garond ran right, around to the gaping entrance of the loading bay that opened onto the narrow back street. Cuu headed forward, jumped up onto a rainwater tank and from there swung up onto the sloping roof.

With Dorden at his heels, Kolea moved after them. The chatter of las and solid firing from inside the buildings was audible over the roar of the advancing tank assault down the hill behind them.

Domor, Rafflan and Garond rushed the bay doors, firing tight bursts. They came in on half a dozen Infardi who turned in abject surprise to meet their deaths.

Mkvenner, Harjeon and Haller kicked in big leaded windows and fired into the bay, cutting down a trio of Infardi who were running back through, alerted by the sudden firing.

Cuu shot in a skylight and began picking off targets below.

Kolea went in through a side door, firing twice to drop an Infardi trying to flee that way.

Dorden watched the Ghosts at work with awe. It was a stunning display of precision tactics, exactly the sort of work that the Tanith First-and-Only was famous for.

Caught from several angles at once, the enemy panicked and started to die.

One of the trucks spluttered into life and spun its heavy wheels as it started to speed out of the bay. Domor and Rafflan were in its way, and stood their ground, firing their lasguns from the shoulder, peppering the cab. Garond, to the side, raked the vehicle as it ran past.

Sharp-edged punctures stung the cab's metalwork. The windows shattered. It veered drunkenly, smashing a crate waiting to be stacked and rolling over the sprawled corpses of two Infardi with nauseating crunches.

At the last moment, Rafflan and Domor dived aside. The truck sped right across the back alley and battered nose-first into the opposite wall, which caved in around it.

Rafflan and Domor advanced into the bay, joining up with Garond and then with Kolea and Dorden. The soldiers formed a straggled knot, firing safety shots into corners where the collecting weapon-smoke blocked vision.

Dorden felt his pulse racing. He felt exposed, and more, he felt elated. To be part of this. Killing was misery and war was a bestial waste, but glory and valour... they were something else. Pleasures so intense and so fundamentally contiguous with the horrors he abominated, they made him feel guilty to cherish them. At times like this, he understood why mankind made war, and why it celebrated its warriors above all others. At times like this he could understand Gaunt himself. To see well-trained men like Kolea's squad take down a significantly larger force with discipline, skill and daring....

'Check the other vehicle,' Kolea snapped, and Rafflan turned aside to do so. Domor went ahead and covered the corner into a short passageway.

'Flamer!' he cried, leaping back, and a moment later fire gouted out of the passageway mouth.

Kolea pushed Dorden into cover and keyed his microbead. 'Haller?'

'Inside, sir! We're coming at you from the east. A little light opposition.' From the bay they could all hear the las exchanges.

'Go slow: we've got a flamer.'

'Understood.'

'I can get him, sure as sure,' Cuu's voice crackled.

'Do it,' Kolea instructed.

Trooper Cuu moved across the shop roof and swung his lithe body down through a gap between broken shutters. He could see the Infardi with the flamer now, cowering in a passageway outside some kind of office with two other gunmen.

Cuu could smell the sweet promethium reek.

From thirty metres, he put a las round through the flamer operator's skull, then picked off the other two as they stumbled up in alarm.

'Clear!' he reported, gleefully. He crept forward.

'Who's out there?' a hoarse voice called from the office.

'That you, colonel?'

'Who's that? Lillo?'

'Nah, it's Cuu.'

'Is it clear?'

'Clear as clear.'

Corbec limped cautiously out of the doorway, gun raised, glancing around.

'Gak, ain't you a mess, Tanith,' smiled Cuu. He flicked open his bead.

'I found Colonel Corbec. Do I win a prize?'

'THAT'LL DO UNTIL we reach a proper aid post,' Dorden said, taping the last dressing tightly across Corbec's chest. 'You can forget about the war, colonel. This'll see you bed-ridden for a good two weeks.'

Weary and broken by pain, Corbec simply nodded. They were seated on crates in the bay while the other Ghosts regrouped. Cuu and Wheln were checking bodies.

'You find Sin?' Corbec asked.

Kolea shook his head. 'We count twenty-two dead. No sign of Sin, leastways not anybody who matches your description.'

Outside, the tremulous rumble of the armour wave was closer.

'What's Gaunt doing sending the infantry ahead of the tanks?' Corbec asked.

Kolea didn't reply. Rafflan looked away, embarrassed.

'Sergeant?'

'This is unofficial,' Dorden replied for Kolea. 'We came hunting for you.'

Corbec shook his head. 'Against orders?'

'The Pardus armour is putting Old Town to the torch. The assault on the Citadel has begun. The commissar ordered all infantry groups out.'

'But you came looking for me? Feth, was this your idea, Kolea?'

'We all kind of went along,' said Dorden.

'I thought you had more sense, doc,' Corbec growled. 'Help me up.'

Dorden supported Corbec as he shuffled over to the bay doors.

The colonel took a long look down the hill at the nightmare of fire and destruction moving up towards them.

'We're dead if we stay here,' Corbec said glumly.

'Right enough,' Mkvenner said. 'I reckon we should use that truck. Drive on over the hill, away from the assault.'

'That's Infardi territory!' Garond exclaimed.

'True, but I rate our chances that way higher. Besides, I'd guess they were falling back by now.'

'What's the matter, colonel?' Dorden asked, seeing a look on Corbec's face.

'Pater Sin,' he said. 'I can't figure it. We thought he was up in the Capital. I don't understand why he was down here in Old Town.'

'Driving his men? Hands on, like Gaunt?'

Corbec shook his head. 'There was something else. He almost told me.'

Haller got up into the cab of the truck and turned the engine over. On the flatbed, Harjeon had opened one of the crates.

'What's this?' he called.

The crate was full of icons and holy statuettes, prayer texts, reliquaries. The men opened the other crates and found them all to be full of similar artefacts.

'Where is this all from?' asked Rafflan.

Kolea shrugged.

'The shrines of the Citadel. They must have plundered them all.' Corbec gazed down into one of the open crates.

'But why? Why take all this stuff? Why not just smash it? It's not sacred to them, is it?'

'Let's work it out later.'

The Ghosts climbed up into the rear of the truck. Haller took the wheel with Wheln riding shotgun beside him.

They rolled out of the battle-torn bay onto the backstreet, edged around the wreck of the other truck, and sped away up the hill.

JUST AFTER SIX O'CLOCK, local time, a brigade-strength force of Brevian Centennials led by Major Szabo scaled the Holy Causeway and entered the Citadel. They met no resistance. The storm assault of the Pardus tanks had broken the back of the Infardi grip on the Doctrinopolis. Sixteen square kilometres of the city, the areas of Old Town flanking the noble plateau, were on fire and dead. Scout recons estimated what little numbers the Infardi could still muster had fled north, out of the city and into the rainwoods of the hinterland.

A victory, Gaunt realised, as Szabo's initial reports were relayed to him by the vox-operator. They had taken the Doctrinopolis and driven the foe out. Pockets of resistance remained – there was a hell of a street fight raging in the western suburbs – and it would take months to hunt out the Infardi who had gone to ground outside the city. But it was a victory. Lord General Lugo would be pleased. Or at least satisfied. In short order, Szabo's men would raise the Imperial standard above the Citadel, and under the fluttering aquila, the place would be theirs again. Hagia was theirs. A world liberated.

Gaunt climbed down from the command tractor and wandered alone down the street. He felt oddly out of sorts. There had been precious little glory in this theatre. His men had acquitted themselves well, of course, and he was happy to see the Tanith working confidently and efficiently alongside the Verghastite newcomers.

But it hadn't gone the way he would have liked. It might have cost him more in time and casualties, but he resented the fact that Lugo hadn't allowed him to clear Old Town and make a clean job of it. The Pardus were exemplary soldiers, and they'd cracked this nut. But the city had suffered unnecessarily.

He stood alone for a while in a prayer yard, watching the votive flags and kites dancing in the wind. The yard was littered with chips of stained glass thrown out when tank shells had gutted a nearby shrine.

This was the sacred beati's world, Saint Sabbat's world. He would have taken it whole, out of respect for her, not ruined it to crush the foe.

The darkening evening sky was thick with sooty smoke. Thanks to Lugo and his hunger for victory, they had razed a third of one of the most holy sites in the Imperium. He would resent this all his life, he realised. If Lugo had left him alone, he could have liberated the Doctrinopolis and left it standing.

Macaroth would hear of this.

Gaunt stepped into the cold silence of the ruined shrine and removed his brocaded cap before advancing down the temple aisle. Glass shards cracked under his jack boots with every pace. He reached the altar and knelt down.

Sabbat Martyr!

Gaunt started and looked round. The whisper had come from right behind him, in his ear.

There was no one in sight.

His imagination...

He settled back onto one knee. He wanted to make his peace with the saint in this holy place, to see if he could make amends for the excessive way they had driven out the infidel. And there was Corbec too, a loss that he would really feel.

But his mouth was dry. The words of the Imperial catechism would not form. He tried to relax, and his mind sought out the words of the Throne Grace he'd been taught as a child at the Scholam Progenium on Ignatius Cardinal.

Even that simple, elementary prayer would not come.

Gaunt cleared his throat. The wind moaned through the broken window lights.

He bowed his head and–

Sabbat Martyr!

The hiss again, right beside him. He leapt up, drawing his boltgun and holding it out at arm's length.

'Who's there? Come out! Show yourself!'

Nothing stirred. Gaunt snapped his aim around, left, right, left again.

Slowly, he slid the heavy hand gun back into his leather button-down holster. He turned back to the altar and knelt again.

He let out a long breath and tried to pray again.

'Sir! Commissar sir!'

Vox-trooper Beltayn was running frantically in through the temple doors, his vox-set falling off his shoulder and swinging round on its strap to bump against the end of the pews.

'Sir!'

'What is it, Beltayn?'

'You've got to hear this, sir! Something's awry!'

Awry. Beltayn's favourite word, always used as a masterpiece of understatement. 'The invading orks have killed everyone, sir! Something's awry!'... 'Everything's been awry since the genestealers turned up, sir!'...

'What?'

Beltayn thrust out the headset to his commander.

'Listen!'

MAJOR SZABO'S BREVIANS moved into the Citadel, fanning out, weapons ready. The towering shrines were silent and empty, pinkish stone gleaming in the light of the setting sun.

As they moved out of the sunlight into the slanted shadows of the temple pylons, Szabo felt a chill, as cold as anything he'd suffered in the winter-wars on Aex Eleven.

The men had been chatting freely and confidently as they advanced up the Citadel hill. Now their voices were gone, as if stolen by the silence of these ancient tombs and empty temples.

There was nothing, Szabo realised. No priests, no Infardi, no bodies, not even a speck of litter or a sign of damage.

He fanned the Brevians out with a few brisk hand signals. In their mustard-drab fatigues and body armour, the fire-teams clattered forward down parallel avenues of stelae.

Szabo selected a vox-channel.

'Brevia one. Zero resistance in the Citadel. It's damn quiet.'

He looked around, and sent Sergeant Vulle ahead into the lofty Chapel of the Avenging Heart with twenty men. Szabo himself advanced into a smaller chapter house where the Ecclesiarchy choir had lived.

Inside the portico, he saw the row of empty alcoves where the household shrine should have been.

Vulle voxed in from Avenging Heart. Every holy item, every icon, every text, every worship statuette, had been removed from the famous chapel. Other fire-teams voxing in from around the temple precinct reported the same. Altars were empty, votive alcoves were bare, relic houses were empty.

Szabo didn't like it. His men were edgy. They'd expected some fighting, at least. This was meant to be Pater Sin's bolt hole, the place where he'd make his last stand.

The Brevians spread out through the vast colonnades and temple walks. Nothing stirred except the wind across this high plateau.

With a lag-team of eight men, Szabo entered the main shrine, the Tempelum Infarfarid Sabbat, a towering confection of pink ashlar and cyclopean pillars, rising three hundred metres above the heart of the Citadel precinct. Here too the altar was bare. The size of a troop carrier, the colossal, gilt-swathed altar bore no branches of candelabras, no censers, no triptych screen, no aquila.

There was an odd scent in the air, a tangy smell like thick oil being fried, or pickled fish.

Szabo's lips were suddenly moist. He licked them and tasted copper.

'Sir, your nose...' his scout said, pointing.

Szabo wiped his nose and realised blood was weeping out of it. He looked around and saw that every man in his squad was leaking blood from their nose or their eyes. Someone started whimpering. Trooper Emith suddenly pitched over onto his face, stone dead.

'Great God-Emperor!' Szabo cried. Another of his men fell in a faint as blood poured out his tear ducts.

'Vox-officer!' shouted Szabo. He reached out. The smell was getting stronger, a thousand times more intense. Time seemed to be slowing down. He watched his own hand as he reached it out in front of him. How slow! Time and the very air around

them seemed to have become treacle-thick and heavy. He saw
his men, slowed down in time like insects in sap. Some half-
fallen, limbs outstretched, some convulsing, some on their
knees. Perfect, glinting droplets of blood hung in the air.

Someone had done this. Someone had been ready. They'd
stripped the shrines of their holy, warding charms. And left
something else in their place.

Something lethal.

'A trap! A trap!' Szabo yelled into the vox. His mouth was full
of blood. 'We've set something off by coming in here! We–'

The choking overwhelmed him. Szabo let go of the vox
handset and retched blood onto the polished floor of the
Tempelum Infarfarid Sabbat.

'Oh Holy Emperor...' Szabo mumbled. There were maggots
in the blood.

Time stopped dead. Over the Doctrinopolis, night fell pre-
maturely.

In a flare of blue light, like the petals of a translucent orchid
a kilometre across, the Citadel exploded.

FIVE
THE BECKONING

'From this high rock, from this peak, let the light of worship shine so that the Emperor himself might see it from his Golden Throne.'

— dedication on the high altar of the
Tempelum Infarfarid Sabbat

THE CITADEL BURNED for many days. It burned without flames, or at least without any flames known to mankind. Mist-blue and frost-green tongues of incandescent energy leapt kilometres into the air like some flailing part of an aurora display anchored to the plateau. They fluttered helplessly in the wind. Their glare cast long shadows in daylight, and illuminated the night. At their base, the blues and greens became white hot, a blistering inferno that utterly consumed the temples and buildings of the Citadel, and the heat could be felt half a kilometre away down the hillslopes.

No one could approach closer than that. The few scout squads that ventured nearer were driven back by nausea, spontaneous bleeding or paroxysms of insane fear. Observations

made from a safe distance by scopes or magnoculars revealed
that the stone cliffs of the plateau were melting and twisting.
Rock bubbled and deformed. One observer went mad, raving
that he'd seen screaming faces form and loom out of the ooz-
ing stone.

At the end of the first day, a delegation of local ayatani and
ecclesiarchs from the Imperial Guard retinues set up temporary
shrines around the slopes of the Citadel and began a vigil of
supplication, appeasement and banishment.

A dismal mood of defeat settled on the Doctrinopolis. This
was an unparalleled disaster, worse even than the Infardi's
annexation of the holy city. This was desecration. This was the
darkest possible omen.

Gaunt was withdrawn. His mood was black and few dared to
disturb him, even his most trusted Ghosts. He lurked in private
chambers in the Universitariat, brooding and reviewing
reports. He slept wretchedly.

Even the news that Corbec had been recovered, injured but
alive, failed to lift his spirits much. Many believed that Gaunt's
mood was so dark he would now mete severe punishment on
Kolea's unit for disobeying the withdrawal orders, despite the
fact they had saved the colonel.

The ayatani conducted a service of thanksgiving for the holy
icons and relics Kolea's unit had brought back in the captured
truck. It was a small, redemptive consolation in the face of the
Citadel's destruction. The items were solemnly rededicated and
placed in the Basilica of Macharius Hagio at the edge of the Old
Town.

The surviving Brevians, two brigades who had not deployed
into the Citadel with Szabo, entered into a ritual of remorseful
fasting and mourning. A mass funeral oration was made on the
second day, during which the roll of the fallen was read out,
name by name. Gaunt attended, in full dress uniform, but
spoke to no one. The guns of the Pardus Armour thundered the
salute.

On the morning of the fourth day, Brin Milo crossed the
Square of Sublime Tranquillity and hurried up the steps of the
Universitariat's south gate with a feeling of dread inside him.
Tanith sentries at the gatehouse let him past, and he walked
through echoing halls and drafty chambers where teams of
esholi worked in silence to salvage what they could of the

books, papers and manuscripts the Infardi had left torn and scattered in the ransacked rooms.

He saw Sanian, industriously picking paper scraps from a litter of glass chips under a shattered window, but she didn't acknowledge him. Afterwards, he wondered if it had actually been her. With their white robes and shaved heads, the female esholi affected an alarming uniformity.

He turned at a cloister corner, trotted up a set of stone stairs under the watchful, oil-painted stares of several ex-Universitariat principals, and crossed a landing to a pair of wooden doors.

Milo took a deep breath, tossed the folds of his camo-cape over his shoulder and knocked.

The door opened. Trooper Caffran let him through.

'Hey, Caff.'

'Brin.'

'How is he?'

'Fethed if I know.'

Milo looked around. Caffran had let him into a small anteroom. A pair of shabby couches had been pulled up under the window to serve as makeshift daybeds for the door guards. On a side table were a few dirty mess trays, some ration packs, and some bottles of water and local wine. Sergeant Soric, Caffran's partner on watch duty, sat nearby, playing Devils and Dames Solo with a pack of buckled cards. He was using an upturned ammo box as a table.

He looked up and grinned his one eyed, lop-sided grin at Milo.

'He hasn't stirred,' he said simply.

Milo didn't have the measure of Soric yet. A squat, slabby barrel of a man, Agun Soric had been an ore smeltery boss on Verghast, then a guerrilla leader. Though overweight, he had massive physical power, the legacy, like his hunched posture, of hard years at the ore face as a youth. And he was old, older than Corbec, older even than Doc Dorden, who was the oldest of the Tanith. He had the same avuncular manner as Corbec, but was wilder somehow, more unpredictable, more given to anger. He'd lost an eye at Vervunhive, and had refused both augmetic implant or patch. He wore the puckered wink of scar tissue proudly. Milo knew the Verghastite Ghosts adored him, maybe even more than they did the noble, taciturn Gol Kolea, but he

sensed Soric was still a Verghast man in his heart. He'd do anything for his own men, but was less forthcoming with the
Tanith. To Milo, he typified the few amongst both Tanith and
Verghastite who perpetuated the divide rather than seeking to
close it.

'I have to see him,' Milo said. He wanted to say that Major
fething Rawne had told him to come and see Gaunt because
Major fething Rawne didn't fancy doing it himself, but there
was no point getting into it.

'Be my guest,' Soric grinned disparagingly, gesturing to the
inner doors.

Milo looked at Caffran, who shrugged. 'He won't let us in
except to bring him meals, and he doesn't eat half of those.
Gets through a feth of a lot of these, though.' Caffran pointed
to the empty wine bottles.

Milo's unease grew. He'd been worried about disturbing
Gaunt when his mood was bad. No one wanted to confront an
ill-disposed Imperial commissar. But now he was worried
about Gaunt himself. He'd never been a drinker. He'd always
had such great composure and confidence. Like all commissars,
he had been created to inspire and uplift.

Milo knew things here on Hagia had turned bad, but now he
was afraid they might have taken Gaunt with them.

'Do you knock, or should I just–' Milo began, pointing at the
inner doors. Caffran backed off with a shrug and Soric point-
edly refused to look up from his dog-eared cards.

'Thanks a lot,' Milo said, and walked to the doors with a sigh.

The inner chambers were dark and quiet. The drapes were
drawn and there was an unpleasantly musty smell. Milo edged
inside.

'Colonel-commissar?'

There was no answer. He walked further in, blind in the
gloom as his night vision tried to adjust.

Groping his way, he slammed into a book stand and sent it
crashing over.

'Who's there? Who the feth is there?'

The anger in the voice made Milo start. Gaunt loomed in
front of him, unshaven and half-dressed, his eyes fierce and
bloodshot.

He was pointing his bolt pistol at Milo.

'Feth! It's me, sir! Milo!'

Gaunt stared at Milo for a moment, as if he didn't recognise him, and then turned away, tossing his gun onto a couch. He was wearing only his jackboots and uniform breeches, and his braces dangled slackly around his hips. Milo glimpsed the massive scar across Gaunt's trim belly, the old wound he had taken at Dercius's hands on Khed 1173.

'You woke me,' Gaunt growled.

'I'm sorry.'

Gaunt lit an oil lamp with clumsy fingers and sat down on a tub chair. He began leafing urgently through an old, hide-bound tome. Gazing at the book, he reached out without looking to snatch up a glass tumbler from a side table. He took a deep swig of wine and set it down again.

Milo moved closer. He saw the stacks of unread military communiqués piled by the chair. The top few had been torn into long shreds, and many of these paper tassels now marked places in the book Gaunt was studying.

'Sir–'

'What?'

'Major Rawne sent me, sir. The lord general is on his way. You should make ready.'

'I am ready.' Gaunt took another swig, his eyes never leaving the book.

'No you're not. You need a wash. You really need a wash. And you look like shit.'

There was a very long silence. Gaunt's hands stopped flipping the pages. Milo tensed, regretting his boldness, waiting for the other shoe to drop.

'This doesn't answer anything, you know.'

'What, sir?' Milo asked, and realised Gaunt was referring to the old book.

'This. The Gospel of Saint Sabbat. I felt sure there would be an answer in here. I've been through it line by line. But nothing.'

'An answer to what, sir?'

'To this,' Gaunt said, gesturing about himself. 'To this... monstrous disaster.' He reached for his glass again without looking and succeeded in knocking it onto the floor.

'Feth. Get me another.'

'Another?'

'Over there, over there!' Gaunt snapped impatiently, pointing to a sideboard where numerous bottles and old glasses stood.

'I don't think you need another drink. The lord general's coming.'

'That's precisely why I need another drink. I don't intend to spend a moment of my time in the company of that turd-brained insect if I'm sober.'

'I still don't–'

'Feth you, you Tanith peasant!' Gaunt snapped venomously and got up, tossing the book to Milo as he strode over to the sideboard.

Milo caught the book neatly.

'See if you can do better,' Gaunt hissed as he went through the bottles one by one until he found one that wasn't empty.

Milo looked at the book, thumbing through, seeing the passages Gaunt had feverishly underlined and scribbled over.

'Defeat is but a step towards victory. Take the step with confidence or you will not ascend.'

Gaunt swung round sharply, sloshing the overfilled glass he had just poured.

'Where does it say that?'

'It doesn't. I'm paraphrasing one of your speeches to the men.'

Gaunt hurled the glass at Milo. The boy ducked.

'Feth you! You always were a clever little bastard!'

Milo dropped the book onto the seat of the tub chair. 'The lord general's coming. He'll be here at noon. Major Rawne wanted you to know. If that's all, I request permission to leave.'

'Permission granted. Get the feth out.'

'WHAT DID HE say? How was he?' Caffran asked as Milo stepped out of the inner rooms and closed the doors behind him.

Milo just shook his head and walked on, out through the ruined hallways of the Universitariat, into the windy sunlight.

TEN MINUTES BEFORE noon, the sound of distant rotors thumped across the Doctrinopolis. Five dots appeared in the sky to the south-west, but in the glare of the Citadel fire it was hard to resolve them.

'He's here,' Feygor called.

Major Rawne nodded and smoothed the front of his clean battledress, made sure the campaign medals were spotless, and carefully put on his cap. He took one last look at himself in the full-length mirror. Despite the crazed cracks in it, he could tell he still looked every fething centimetre the acting first officer of the Tanith First Regiment.

He turned, and strode out of the derelict dressmaker's shop that had served as his ready room.

Feygor, Rawne's adjutant, whistled and fell in step beside him. 'Look out ladies, here comes the major.'

'Shut up.'

Feygor smiled. 'You're looking very sharp, I must say.'

'Shut up.'

They marched down a debris-strewn side street and out onto the massive concourse of the high king's royal summer palace on the holy river. The area had been cleared to allow the lord general's aircraft to land. Round the edges of the concourse, four platoons of Ghosts, two platoons of Brevians and three platoons of Pardus stood as an honour guard, along with delegations of local officials and citizens. There was a military band too, their brass instruments winking as they caught the sunlight.

The uniforms of the honour guard were clean and spotless. Colonel Furst, Major Kleopas and Captain Herodas had all put on dress kit. Medals were on show.

Rawne and Feygor approached them across the concourse.

'When you put on your cap, it was just the way Gaunt does it. Brim first.'

'Shut up.'

Feygor smiled and shrugged.

'And fall in,' added Rawne. Feygor, his own matt-black Ghost battle dress immaculate, doubled-timed and took his place at the end of the Ghost file. Rawne joined the officers. Furst nodded to him and Herodas stepped back to make room.

The band started to play. The old hymn 'Splendid Men of the Imperium, Stand Up and Fight'. Rawne winced every time they missed the repeated harmonic minor in the refrain.

'I didn't know you were a music lover, Major Rawne,' Captain Herodas said quietly.

'I know what I like,' Rawne said through gritted teeth, 'and what I'd like right now is for someone to jam that bass horn up the arse of the bastard who's molesting it.'

All four officers coughed as they stifled their laughter.

The lord general's transport approached.

The four ornithopter gunships flying escort thundered overhead, tearing the air with the beating chop of their massive rotors. They were painted ash-grey with a leopard pattern of khaki blotches. Rawne admired their power, and the bulbous gun turrets on their chins and the ends of their elongated tails.

Lord General Lugo's aircraft was a massive delta wing with a spherical glass cockpit at the prow. It was matt silver with beige jag-stripes and yellow chevrons on the wingtips alongside the Imperial aquila.

Its shadow fell across the honour guard as it paused in mid-air and the giant jet turbines slowly cranked around in their gimbal mounts from a horizontal position. With jets now flaring downwards, the huge transport descended, whirling up dust and extending delicate landing struts from cavities in the underwing.

It bounced slightly once, settled, and the screaming jets slowly powered down. A ramp set flush into the sky-blue painted belly gently unfolded and seven figures emerged.

Lord General Lugo strolled down the ramp, a tall, bony man in a white dress uniform, his chest burdened by the weight of medals on it. At his heels, two battle-armoured troopers in red and black from the Imperial Crusade staff marched in escort, hellguns raised. Behind them came a towering, stick-thin woman of advancing years dressed in the black leather and red braid of the Imperial tacticians, two colonels from the Ardelean Colonials with glittering breastplates and bright sashes of orange satin, and a thickset man in the uniform of an Imperial commissar.

The group advanced across the concourse and saluted the visitors.

Lugo eyed them all suspiciously, particularly Rawne.

'Where's Gaunt?'

'He... Sir... He...'

'I'm here.'

Dressed in full ceremonial uniform, Ibram Gaunt strode out across the concourse flagstones. From the attentive ranks of the honour guard, Milo sighed. He was relieved to see that Gaunt was clean and shaved. Gaunt's silver-trimmed black leather uniform was immaculate. Perhaps the unpleasant incident in the Universitariat had been just an aberration...

Gaunt saluted the lord general and introduced his fellow officers. The band played on.

'This is Imperial Tactician Blamire,' said Lugo, indicating the tall, elderly woman. She nodded. Her face was lean and pinched and her greying hair was cropped.

'I am here because of that...' Lugo said flatly, turning to look across the concourse and the holy city beyond to the flaring aurora flames flickering over the Citadel.

'That, lord, is an abomination we all regret,' Gaunt said.

'You will bring me up to speed, Gaunt. I want a full report.'

'And you'll have it,' said Gaunt, guiding the lord general across the concourse to the waiting land cars and their Chimera escort.

Lugo sniffed suddenly.

'Have you been drinking, Gaunt?'

'Yes, sir. A cup of altar wine during the morning obeisance conducted by the ayatani. It was symbolic and expected of me.'

'I see. No matter then. Now show me and tell me what I need to know.'

'Starting where, sir?'

'Starting with how this simple liberation turned into a pile of crap,' said Lugo.

'YOU REALISE IT'S a signal,' said Tactician Blamire, lowering her magnoculars.

'A signal?' echoed Colonel Furst.

'Oh yes. The adepts of the Astropathicus have confirmed it as such... it's generating a significant psychic pulse with an interstellar range.'

'For what purpose?' asked Major Kleopas.

Blamire fixed him with a craggy gaze, a patient smile on her lips. 'Our imminent destruction, of course.'

The party of officers stood on the flat roof of the treasury, escorted by over fifty guardsmen. Prayer kites and votive flags cracked and shimmied in the air above them.

'I don't follow,' said Kleopas, 'I thought that it was just a spiteful parting gift from the enemy. A booby trap to sour our victory.'

Blamire shook her head. 'Well, it's not, I'm afraid. That phenomenon—' she gestured to the flickering blaze on top of the Citadel plateau. 'That phenomenon is an operating instrument of the warp. An astropathic beacon. Don't think of it as fire. What happened up there four days ago wasn't an explosion in any conventional sense. Its purpose wasn't to destroy the Citadel, or to kill those unfortunate Brevian troops. Its purpose is to beckon.'

'Beckon who?' asked Furst.

'Don't be dense,' said Gaunt quietly. He fixed Blamire with a direct gaze. 'The site was significant, of course. Sacred ground.'

'Of course. The warp-magic of their ritual required the dese-cration of one of our shrines.'

'That was why they removed all the relics and icons?'

'Yes. And then withdrew to wait for the Brevian Centennials to move in and act as the blood sacrifice to set it off. This Pater Sin clearly planned this contingency well in advance when it looked like his forces would be ousted.'

'And is it working?' Gaunt asked.

'I'm sorry to say it is.'

There was a long silence broken only by the whip and buffet of the flags and kites above them.

'We have detected an enemy fleet massing and moving through the immaterium towards us,' said Lord General Lugo.

'Already?' queried Gaunt.

'This summons is clearly something they don't intend to ignore or be slow about responding to.'

'The fleet... How big?' There was an anxious tone on Kleopas's voice. 'What is the scale of the enemy response?'

Blamire shrugged, rubbing her gloved hands together uncomfortably. 'If it is even a quarter the size we estimate, the combined liberation force here will be obliterated. Without question.'

'Then we need to reinforce at once! Warmaster Macaroth must retask crusade regiments to assist. We–' Lugo cut Gaunt off.

'That is not an option. I have communicated the situation to the Warmaster, and he has confirmed my fears. The reconquest of the Cabal system is now fully underway. The Warmaster has committed all the crusade legions to the assault. Many are already en route to the fortress-worlds. There are categorically no reinforcements available.'

'I refuse to accept that!' Gaunt cried. 'Macaroth is fully aware of this world's sacred significance! The saint's home world! It's a vital part of Imperial belief and faith! He wouldn't just let it burn!'

'The point is moot, colonel-commissar,' said Lugo. 'Even if the Warmaster was able to assist us here – and I assure you, he is not – the nearest Imperial contingents of any useful size are six weeks distant. The arch-enemy's fleet is twenty-one days away.'

Gaunt felt helpless rage boil up inside him. It reminded him in the worst way of Tanith and the decisions he had been forced to make there. For the greater good of the Sabbat World's Crusade, another whole damned planet was going to be sacrificed.

'I have received orders from the Warmaster,' said Lugo. 'They are unequivocal. We are to commence immediate withdrawal from this planet. All Imperial servants, as well as the planetary nobility and priesthood, are to be evacuated with us, and we are to remove the sacred treasures of this world: relics, antiquities, holy objects, works of learning. In time, the crusade will return and liberate Hagia once more and, at such a time, the shrines will be restored and rededicated. Until then, the priests must safeguard Hagia's holy heritage in exile.'

'They won't do it,' said Captain Herodas. 'I've spoken to the local people. Their relics are precious, but only in conjunction with the location. As the birthplace of Saint Sabbat, it is the world that really matters.'

'They will be given no choice,' snapped Lugo. 'This is no time for flimsy sentiment. An intensive program of evacuation begins tonight. The last ship leaves here no later than eighteen days from now. You and your officers will all be given duties overseeing the smooth and efficient running of said program. Failure will result in the swiftest censure. Any obstruction of our work will be punishable by death. Am I safe to assume you all understand what is required?'

Quietly, the assembled officers made it clear they did.

'I'm hungry,' Lugo announced suddenly. 'I wish to dine now. Come with me, Gaunt. I wish to explain your particular duties to you.'

'LET'S BE FRANK about this, Gaunt,' said Lugo, deftly shucking the shell of a steamed bivalve harvested from celebrated beds a few kilometres down river. 'Your career is effectively over.'

'And how do you figure that, sir?' Gaunt replied stiffly, taking a sip of wine. His own dish of gleaming black shellfish lay largely untouched before him.

Lugo looked up from his meal at Gaunt and finished chewing the nugget of succulent white meat in his mouth before replying. He dabbed his lips with the corner of his napkin. 'I assume you're joking?'

'Funny,' said Gaunt, 'I assumed you were, sir.' He reached for his glass, but realised it was empty, so instead picked up the bottle for a refill.

Lugo chased a morsel of food out of his cheek with his tongue and swallowed. 'This,' he said, with an idle gesture that was intended to take in the entire city rather than just the drafty, empty dining chamber where they sat, 'this is entirely your fault. You never were in particular favour with the Warmaster, despite your few colourful successes in the last couple of years. But there's certainly no coming back from a disgrace like this.' He took up another bivalve and expertly popped the hinged shell open.

Gaunt sat back and looked around, knowing if he spoke now it would be the beginning of a swingeing rant that would quite certainly end with him at the wrong end of a firing squad. Lugo was a worm, but he was also a lord general. Shouting at him would achieve nothing productive. Gaunt waited for his anger to subside a little.

The dining chamber was a high ceilinged room in the summer palace where the high king had once held state banquets. The furniture had been cleared except for their single table with its white linen cloth. Six Ardelean Colonial infantrymen stood watch at the doors, letting through the serving staff when they knocked.

With Lugo and Gaunt at the table was the heavily-built commissar who had arrived with the lord general's party. His name was Viktor Hark, and he had said nothing since the start of the meal. Nothing, in fact, since he had stepped off the aircraft. Hark was a few years younger than Gaunt, with a short, squat stature that suggested a brute muscular strength generously upholstered in the bulk of good living. His hair was thick and black and his heavy cheeks and chin were cleanly shaven. His silence and refusal to make any kind of eye contact was annoying Gaunt. Hark had already finished his shellfish and was mopping up the cooking juices from the dish with chunks of soda bread torn from a loaf in the basket on the table.

'You're blaming me for the loss of the Citadel?' Gaunt asked gently.

Lugo widened his eyes in mock query and replied through his mouthful. 'You were the commanding officer in this theatre, weren't you?'

'Yes, sir.'

'Then who else would I blame? You were charged with the liberation of the Doctrinopolis, and the recapture, intact, of the holy Citadel. You failed. The Citadel is lost, and furthermore, your failure has led directly to the impending loss of the entire shrineworld. You'll lose your command, naturally. I think you'll be lucky to remain in the Emperor's service.'

'The Citadel was lost because of the speed with which it was retaken,' Gaunt said, choosing every word carefully. 'My strategy here was slow and methodical. I intended to take the holy city in such a way as to leave it as intact as possible. I didn't want to send the tanks into the Old Town.'

'Are you,' Lugo paused, washing his oily fingers in a bowl of petal-scented water and drying them carefully on his napkin, 'are you possibly trying to suggest that I am in some way to blame for this?'

'You made demands, lord general. Though I had achieved my objectives ahead of the planned schedule, you insisted I was running behind. You also insisted I ditch my prepared strategy and accelerate the assault. I would have had the Citadel scouted and checked in advance, and such care may have resulted in the safe discovery and avoidance of the enemy trap. We'll never know now. You made demands of me, sir. And now we are where we are.'

'I should have you shot for that suggestion, Gaunt,' said Lugo briskly. 'What do you think, Hark? Should I have him shot?'

Hark shrugged wordlessly.

'This is your failure, Gaunt,' said Lugo. 'History will see it as such, I will make sure of that. The Warmaster is already demanding severe reprimand for the officer or officers responsible for this disaster. And, as I pointed out just now, you're hardly a favourite of Macaroth's. Too much of old Slaydo about you.'

Gaunt said nothing.

'You should have been stripped of your rank already, but I'm a fair man. And Hark here suggested you might perform with renewed dedication if given a task that offered something in the way of redemption.'

'How kind of him.'

'I thought so. You're a capable enough soldier. Your time as a commanding officer is over, but I'm offering you a chance to temper your disgrace with a mission that would add a decent footnote to your career. It would send a good message to the troops, too, I think. To show that even in the light of calamitous error, a true soldier of the Imperium can make a worthy contribution to the crusade.'

'What do you want me to do?'

'I want you to lead an honour guard. As I have explained, the evacuation is taking with it all of the priesthood, the what do you call them...?'

'Ayatani,' said Hark, his first spoken word.

'Quite so. All of the ayatani, and all the precious relics of this world. Most precious of all are the remains of the saint herself, interred at the Shrinehold in the mountains. You will form a detail, travel to the Shrinehold, and return here with the saint's bones, conducted with all honour and respect, in time for the evacuation transports.'

Gaunt nodded slowly. He realised he had no choice anyway. 'The Shrinehold is remote. The hinterlands and rainwoods outside the city are riddled with Infardi soldiers who've fled this place.'

'Then you may have trouble on the way. In which case, you'll be moving in force. Your Tanith regiment, in full strength. I've arranged for a Pardus tank company to travel with you as escort. And Hark here will accompany you, of course.'

Gaunt turned to look at the hefty commissar. 'Why?'

Hark looked back, meeting Gaunt's eyes for the first time. 'For the purposes of discipline, naturally. You're broken, Gaunt. Your command judgment is suspect. This mission must not be allowed to fail and the lord general needs assurance that the Tanith First is kept in line.'

'I am capable of discharging those duties.'

'Good. I'll be there to see you do.'

'This is not–'

Hark raised his glass. 'Your command status has always been thought of as strange, Gaunt. A colonel is a colonel and a commissar is a commissar. Many have wondered how you could perform both those duties effectively when the primary rationale of a commissar is to keep a check on the unit's commander. For a while, Crusade command has been considering appointing a commissar to the Tanith First to operate in conjunction with you. Events here have made it a necessity.'

Gaunt pushed back his chair with a loud scrape and rose.

'Won't you stay, Gaunt?' Lugo asked with a wry smile. 'The main course is about to be served. Braised chelon haunch in amasec and ghee.'

Gaunt nodded a curt salute, knowing that there was no point saying he had no appetite for the damned meal or the company. 'My apologies, lord general. I have an honour guard to arrange.'

SIX
ADVANCE GUARD

*'What raised me will rest me. What brought
me forth will take me back. In the high country of Hagia,
I will come home to sleep.'*

— Saint Sabbat, epistles

THE HONOUR GUARD left the Doctrinopolis the next morning at daybreak, crossing the holy river and travelling west out of the Pilgrim Gate onto the wide track of the Tembarong Road.

The convoy was almost three kilometres long from nose to tail: the entire Ghost regiment, carried in a line of fifty-eight long-body trucks: twenty Pardus mainline battle tanks, fifteen munition Chimeras and four Hydra tractors, two Trojans, eight scout Salamanders and three Salamander command variants. Their dust plume could be seen for miles and the throaty rumble of their collective turbines rolled around the shallow hills of the rainwoods. A handful of motorcycle outriders buzzed around their skirts, and in their midst travelled eight supply trucks laden with provisions and spares and two heavy fuel tankers. The tankers would get them to Bhavnager, two or three days away, where local fuel supplies would replenish them.

Gaunt rode in one of the command Salamanders near the head of the column. He had specifically chosen a vehicle away from Hark, who travelled with the Pardus commander, Kleopas, in his command vehicle, one of the Pardus regiment's Conqueror-pattern battle tanks.

Gaunt stood up in the light tank's open body and steadied himself on the armour cowling against the lurching it made. The air was warm and sweet, though tinged with exhaust fumes. He had twenty-five hundred infantry in his retinue, and the force of a mid-strength armour brigade. If this was his last chance to experience command, it was at least a good one.

His head ached. The previous night he'd retired alone to his chambers in the Universitariat and drunk himself to sleep over a stack of route maps.

Gaunt looked up into the blue as invisible shapes shrieked over, leaving contrails behind them that slowly dissipated. For the first hour or two, they'd have air cover from the navy's Lightnings.

He looked back, down the length of the massive vehicle column. Through the dust wake, he could see the Doctrinopolis falling away behind them, a dimple of buildings rising up beyond the woodlands, hazed by the distance. The flickering light storm of the Citadel was still visible.

He'd left many valuable men back there. The Ghosts wounded in the city fight, Corbec among them. The wounded were due to be evacuated out in the next few days as part of the abandonment program. He was going to miss Corbec. He was sadly struck by the notion that his last mission with the Ghosts would be conducted without the aid of the bearded giant.

And he wondered what would happen to the Ghosts after his removal. He couldn't imagine them operating under a commander brought in from outside, and there was no way Corbec or Rawne would be promoted. The likelihood was the Tanith First would simply cease to be once he had gone. There was no prospect for renewal. The troopers would be transferred away into other regiments, perhaps as recon specialists, and that would be that.

His looming demise meant the demise of his beloved Tanith regiment too.

* * *

IN ONE OF the troop trucks, Tona Criid craned her head back to look at the distant city.

'They'll be fine,' said Caffran softly. Tona sat back next to him in the bucking truckbed.

'You think?'

'I know. The servants of the Munitorium have cared for them so far, haven't they?'

Tona Criid said nothing. At Vervunhive, thanks to circumstance, she had become the de facto mother of two orphaned children. They now accompanied the Tanith First war machine as part of the sizeable and extended throng of camp followers. Many of that group, the cooks and mechanics and munition crew, were travelling with them, but many had been left behind for the evacuation. Children, wives, whores, musicians, entertainers, tailors, peddlers, panders. There was no place for them on this stripped-down mission. They would leave Hagia on the transports and, God-Emperor willing, would be reunited with their friends, and comrades and clients in the First later.

Tona took out the double-faced pendant she wore around her neck and looked wistfully at the faces of her children, preserved in holoportraits and set in plastic. Yoncy and Dalin. The babe in arms and the fretful young boy.

'We'll be with them again soon,' Caffran said. He thought of them as his too now. By extension, by the nature of the relationship he had with Tona, Dalin called him Papa Caff. They were as close to an actual family unit as it was possible to get in the Imperial Guard.

'Will we, though?' Tona asked.

'Old Gaunt would never lead us into harm, not if he thought he could get out of it,' Caffran said.

'The word is he's finished,' said Larkin from nearby, overhearing. 'Word is, we're finished too. He's a broken man. Dead on the wire, so to speak. He's going to be stripped of command and we're going to be kicked around the Imperial Guard in search of a home.'

'Are we now?' said Sergeant Kolea, moving down the truck bay, catching Larkin's words.

'S'what I heard,' said Larkin defensively.

'Then shut up until you know. We're the fighting Tanith First, and we'll be together until the end of time, right?'

Kolea's words got a muted chorus of cheers from the troops in the truck.

'Oh, you can do better than that! Remember Tanith! Remember Vervunhive!'

That got a far more resounding cheer.

'What's that you've got, Criid?' Kolea asked as he shambled back down the truck.

She showed him the pendant. 'My kids, sir.'

Kolea looked into the pendant's portraits for a curiously long time.

'Your kids?'

'Adopted them on Verghast, sir. Their parents were killed.'

'Good... good work, Criid. What are their names?'

'Yoncy and Dalin, sir.'

Kolea nodded and let go of the pendant. He walked to the end of the lurching truck and looked out into the rainwoods and irrigated field systems as they passed.

'Something the matter, sarge?' asked Trooper Fenix, seeing the look on Kolea's face.

'Nothing, nothing...' Kolea murmured.

They were his. The children in the pendant portrait were his children. Children he thought long gone and dead on Verghast.

Some god-mocking irony had let them survive and be here. Here, with the Ghosts.

He felt sick and overjoyed all at the same time.

What could he say? What could he begin to say to Criid or Caffran or the kids?

Tears welled in his eyes. He looked out at the rainwoods sliding by and said nothing because there was nothing he could say.

THE TEMBARONG ROAD ran flat, wide and straight through the arable lowlands and rainwoods west of the Doctrinopolis. The lowlands were formed by the broad basin of the holy river, which irrigated the fields and ditch systems of the local farmers every year with its seasonal floods. There was a fresh, damp smell in the air and for a lot of the way, the road followed the curving river bank.

Sergeant Mkoll ran ahead of the main convoy in one of the scout Salamanders with troopers Mkvenner and Bonin and the driver. Mkoll had used Salamanders a couple of times before, but he was always impressed with the little open-topped track-machines' turn of speed. This one wore Pardus Armour insignia on its coat of blue-green mottle, carried additional tarp-wrapped equipment slouched like papooses to the side sponsons, and had its pair of huge UHF vox-antennas bent back over its body and tied off on the rear bars. The driver was a tall, adenoidal youth from the Pardus Armour Aux who wore mirrored glare-goggles and drove like he wanted to impress the Tanith.

They dashed down the tree-lined road at close to sixty kph, waking out a fan tail of pink dust behind them off the dry earth surface.

Mkvenner and Bonin clung on, grinning like fools and enjoying the ride. Mkoll checked his map book and made notes against the edges of the glass-paper charts with a wax pencil.

Gaunt wanted to make the most of the Tembarong Road. He wanted a quick motorised dash for the first few days as far as the sound highway lasted. Their speed was bound to drop once the trail entered the rainwoods, and after that, as they wound their way up into the highlands things might get very slow altogether. There was no way of telling what state the hill roads were in after the winter rains, and they were hoping to pass a great many tonnes of steel along them.

As scout commander, Mkoll had special responsibilities for route-tasking and performance. He'd spent a while talking to Captain Herodas the night before, assessing the mean road and off-road speeds the Pardus could manage. He'd also spoken to Intendant Elthan, who ran the Munitorium's freight motor-pool. He and his drivers were crewing the troops trucks and tankers. Mkoll had taken their conservative estimates of speed and mileage and revised them down. Both Herodas and Elthan were imagining a trip of five or six days to travel the three hundred or so kilometres to the Shrinehold, roads permitting. Mkoll was looking at seven at least, maybe eight. And if it was eight, they'd have barely a day to collect up what they'd come for and turn around for the home run, or they'd miss Lord General Lugo's eighteen-day evacuation deadline.

For now, the going was clear. The sky was still violet blue, and a combination of low altitude and the trees kept the breezes down. It was hot.

At first they passed few people on the road except the occasional farmer, or a family group, and once or twice a drover
with a small train of livestock. The farmfolk had tried to maintain cultivation during the Infardi occupation, but they had
suffered, and Mkoll saw that great areas of the field-stocks and
water beds were neglected and overgrown. The few locals they
saw turned to watch them pass and raised a hand of greeting or
gratitude.

There was no sign of Infardi, many of whom had apparently
fled out this way. The road and its environs showed some sign
of shelling and air damage, but it was old. The war had passed
over this area briefly months ago, but most of the conflict on
Hagia had been focused on the cities.

Every once in a while, their passing engines scared flocks of
gaudy-feathered fliers up out of trees and roosts. The trees were
lush green and roped with epiphytes, their trunks tall, curved
and ridged. To Mkoll, raised in the towering, temperate nalwood forests of Tanith, they seemed slight and decorative, like
ornamental shrubs, despite the fact that some of them were in
excess of twenty metres tall.

At regular intervals through the trees, they caught racing
glimpses of the sunlight on the river. Along one half kilometre
stretch where the highway ran right beside the water's edge,
they motored past a line of fishermen wading out into the river
stream, casting hand nets. The fishers all wore sunhats woven
from the local vineleaves.

The river dictated the way of life in the floodplains. The few
roadside dwellings and small settlements they went through
were built up on wood-post stilts against the seasonal water
rise. They also passed ornately carved and brightly painted
boxes raised three metres high on intricately carved single
posts. These were occasional things, appearing singly by the
roadside or in small groups in glades set from the highway.

In the hour before noon, they ran through an abandoned village of overgrown, unkept stilt houses and came around one of
the road's sharper bends, almost head first into a herd of chelons and their drovers.

The Pardus driver gave out a little gasp, and hauled on the
steering yoke, pulling the Salamander half up onto the bushy
verge, into the foliage and to an undignified halt.
Unconcerned, the chelons, more than forty of them, lowed and

grunted as they shambled past. They were the biggest Mkoll had yet seen on Hagia, the great bell-domed shells of the largest and most mature towering above their vehicle. The smallest and youngest had blue-black skins that gleamed like oil and a fibrous dark patina to their shells, while the elders' hides were paler and less lustrous, lined with cracks and wrinkles, their massive shells limed almost white. A haze of dry, earthy animal smells wafted from them: dung, fodder, saliva in huge quantities.

The three drovers ran over to the Salamander the moment it came to rest, waving their jiddi-sticks and exclaiming in alarm. All three were tired, hungry men in the earth-tone robes of the agricultural caste.

Mkoll jumped down from the back step and raised his arms to calm their jabberings while Mkvenner directed the Pardus driver as he reversed the light tank back out of the thorn breaks.

'It's fine, no harm done,' Mkoll said. The drovers continued to look unhappy, and were busy making numerous salutes to the Imperials.

'Please... If you feel like helping, tell us what's ahead. On the road.' Mkoll pulled out his mapbook and showed the route to the men, who passed it between themselves, contradicting each other's remarks.

'It's very good,' said one. 'The road is very clear. We come down now this month from the high pastures. They say the war is over. We come down in the hope that the markets will be open again.'

'Let's hope so,' said Mkoll.

'People have been hiding in the woods, whole families, you know,' another said. His ancient weather-beaten skin was as lined and gnarled as that of the chelons he drove. 'They were afraid of the war. The war in the cities. But we have heard the war is over and many people will come out of the woods now it is safe.'

Mkoll made a mental note. He had already suspected that a good proportion of the rural population might have fled into the wilderness at the start of the occupation. As the honour guard pressed on, they might encounter many of these people emerging back into the lowlands. With the threat of Infardi guerrillas all around, that made their job harder. Hostiles and ambushes would be harder to pick out.

'What about the Infardi?' Mkoll asked.

'Oh, certainly,' said the first drover, cutting across the gabble of his companions. 'Many, many Infardi now, on the road and in the forest paths.'

'You've seen them?' Mkoll asked with sharp curiosity.

'Very often, or heard them, or seen the signs of their camps.'

'Many, you say?'

'Hundreds!'

'No, no... Thousands! More every day!'

Feth! Mkoll thought. A couple of pitched fights will slow us right down. The chelon-men might be exaggerating for effect, but Mkoll doubted it. 'My thanks to you all,' he said. 'You might want to get your animals off the road for a while. There's a lot more of this stuff coming along,' he pointed to the Salamander, 'and it's a fair size bigger.'

The men all nodded and said they would. Mkoll was a little reassured. He wasn't sure who would win a head-on collision between a Conqueror and a mature bull chelon, but he was sure neither party would walk away smiling. He thanked the drovers, assured them once more they had done him and his men no harm, and got back aboard the Salamander.

'Sorry,' the driver grinned.

'Maybe a tad slower,' Mkoll replied. He pulled out the handset for the tank's powerful vox set and sent a pulse hail to the main convoy. Mkvenner was still standing in the road, gently and politely trying to refuse the honking chelon calf that one of the drovers was offering him to make amends.

'Alpha-AR to main advance, over.'

The speaker crackled. 'Go ahead Alpha-AR.' Mkoll immediately recognised Gaunt's voice.

'Picking up reports of Infardi activity up the road. Nothing solid yet, but you should be advised.'

'Understood, Alpha-AR. Where are you?'

'Just outside a village called Shamiam. I'm going ahead as far as Mukret. Best you send at least a couple more advance recon units forward to me.'

'Copy that. I'll send Beta-AR and Gamma-AR ahead. What's your ETA at Mukret?'

'Another two to three hours, over.' Mukret was a medium-sized settlement on the river where they had planned to make their first over night stop.

'God-Emperor willing, we'll see you there. Keep in contact.'

'Will do, sir. You should be aware that there are non-coms on the road. Families heading back out of hiding. Caution advised.'

'Understood.'

'And about an hour ahead of you, there's a big herd of live-stock moving contra your flow. Lots of livestock and three harmless herdsmen. They may be off road by the time you reach them, but be warned.'

'Understood.'

'Alpha-AR out.' Mkoll hung up the vox-mic and nodded at the waiting Pardus driver. 'Okay,' he said.

The driver throttled the Salamander's turbine and pointed her nose up the brown mud-cake of the highway.

A GOOD FIFTEEN kilometres back down the Tembarong Road, the honour guard convoy slowed and came to a halt. The big khaki troop trucks bunched up, nose to nose, and shuddered their exhaust stacks impatiently as they revved. A few sounded their horns. The sun was high overhead and gleamed blindingly off the metalwork. To the left of the convoy, the blue waters of the holy river crept by on the other side of a low levee.

Rawne got up in the back of his transport and climbed up on the guardrail so he could look out along the length of the motorcade over the truck's cab. All he could see was stationary armour and laden trucks right down to the bend in the road three hundred metres away.

He keyed his microbead as he glanced back down at Feygor.

'Get them up,' Rawne told his adjutant.

Feygor nodded and relayed the glib order to the fifty or so men in the transport cargo area. The Ghosts, many of them sweating and without headgear, roused and readied their weapons, scanning the tree-line and field ditches to the right of the road.

'One, three,' said Rawne into his link. There was a lot of vox traffic. Questioning calls were running up and down the convoy.

'Three, one,' replied Gaunt from up ahead.

'One, what's the story?'

'One of the munition Chimeras has thrown a track section. I'm going to wait fifteen minutes and see how the techs do. Longer than that, I'll leave them behind.'

Rawne had seen the battered age of the worn Chimeras they'd been issued by the Munitorium motorpool. It would take more than fething fifteen minutes to get one running in his opinion.

'Permission to recreationally disperse my men along the river edge.'

'Granted, but watch the tree-line.'

Setting two men on point to cover the right-hand side of the road, Rawne ordered the rest of his troops off the truck. Joking, pulling off jackets and boots, they jogged down to the river edge and started bathing their feet and throwing handscoops of water on their faces. Other troop trucks pulled off the hardpan onto the levee shoulder and disembarked their men. A Trojan tank tractor grumbled past, edging up along the length of the stationary column from the rear echelon to assist with the spot repairs.

Rawne wandered down the line of vehicles to where Sergeants Varl, Soric, Baffels and Haller stood on the levee. Soric was handing out stubby cigars from a waxed card box and Rawne took one. They all smoked for a while in silence, watching the Ghosts, both Verghastite and Tanith, engage in impromptu water fights and games of kickball.

'Is it always like this, major?' Soric asked, jerking a thumb at the unmoving convoy. Rawne didn't warm to people much, but he liked the old man. He was a capable fighter and a good leader, but he wasn't afraid to ask questions that revealed his inexperience, which in Rawne's book made him a good student and a promising officer.

'Always the same with motorised transportation. Breakdowns, bottlenecks, bad terrain. I always prefer to shift the men by foot.'

'The Pardus equipment looks alright,' said Haller. 'Well maintained and all.'

Rawne nodded. 'It's just the junk transports the Munitorium found for us. These trucks are as old as feth, and the Chimeras...'

'I'm surprised they've made it this far,' said Varl. The sergeant gently windmilled his arm, nursing the cybernetic shoulder joint the augmeticists had given him on Fortis Binary several years before. It still hurt him in humid conditions. 'And we'll be fethed without them. Without the munitions they're carrying anyway.'

'We're fethed anyway,' said Rawne. 'We're the Imperial fething Guard and it's our lot in life to be fethed.'

Haller, Soric and Varl laughed darkly, but Baffels was silent. A stocky, bearded man with a blue claw tattoo under one eye, Baffels had been promoted to sergeant after old Fols was killed at the battle for Veyveyr Gate. He still wasn't comfortable with command, and took his duties too seriously in Rawne's opinion. Some common troopers – Varl was a good example – were sergeants waiting to happen. Baffels was an honest footslogger who'd had responsibility dumped on him because of his age, his dependability and his good favour with the men. Rawne knew he was finding it hard. Gaunt had had a choice when it came to Fols's replacement: Baffels or Milo, and he'd opted for Baffels because to give the lead job to the youngest and greenest Ghost would have smacked of favouritism. Gaunt had been wrong there, Rawne thought. He had no love for Milo, but he knew how capable he'd proved to be and how dearly the men regarded him as a lucky totem. Gaunt should have gone with his gut – ability over experience.

'Good smoke,' Varl told Soric, glancing appreciatively at the smouldering brown tube between his fingers. 'Corbec would have enjoyed them.'

'Finest Verghast leaf,' smiled Soric. 'I have a private stock.'

'He should be here,' Baffels said, meaning the colonel. Then he glanced quickly at Rawne. 'No offence, major!'

'None taken,' Rawne replied. Privately, Rawne was enjoying his new-found seniority. With both Corbec and that upstart Captain Daur out of the picture, he was now the acting second of the regiment, with only the Pardus Major Kleopas and the outsider Commissar Hark near to him in the taskforce pecking order. Mkoll was the Ghosts' number three officer for the duration, and Kolea had been given Daur's Verghastite liaison tasks.

It still irked Rawne that he was forced to maintain the callsign 'three' to Gaunt's 'one'. Gaunt had explained it was to preserve continuity of vox recognition, but Rawne felt he should be using Corbec's 'two' now.

What irked him more was the notion that Baffels was right. Corbec *should* be here. It went against Rawne's impulse, because he'd never liked Corbec that much either, but it was true. He felt it in his blood. What everyone knew and none wanted to talk about was that this seemed likely to be the last mission of the Tanith First. The lord general had broken Gaunt, and Rawne would lead the applause when they came to march Gaunt away in disgrace, but still...

This was the Ghosts' final show.

And, feth him, Corbec should be here.

MAD LARKIN SAT, hot and edgy, in the rear of a vacated truck, his long-pattern las resting on the bodywork. Kolea had left him and Cuu on point while the others ran to the river to cool down and blow off steam.

Larkin searched the far side of the road with his usual obsessive methods, sectioning the tree-line and the expanse of water-field by eye and then scanning each section in turn sequentially. Thorough, careful, faultless.

Each movement made him tense, but each movement turned out to be flapping forkbills or scampering spider-rats or even just the breeze-sway of the fronded leaves.

He passed the time with target practice, searching out a target and then following it through his scope's crosshairs. The red-crested forkbills were fine enough, but they were an easy target because of their white plumage and size. The spider-rats were better: creepy eight-limbed mammals the size of Larkin's hand that jinked up and down the tree trunks in skittering stop-start trajectories so fast they made a sport out of it.

'What you up to?'

Larkin looked round and up into Trooper Cuu's arrogant eyes.

'Just... spotting,' Larkin said. He didn't like Cuu at all. Cuu made him nervous. People called Larkin mad, but he wasn't mad like Cuu. Cuu was a cold killer. A psycho. He was covered in gang tatts and had a long scar that bisected his narrow face.

Cuu folded his lean limbs down next to Larkin. Larkin thought of himself as thin and small amongst the Ghosts but Cuu was smaller. There was, however, a suggestion of the most formidable energy in his wiry frame.

'You could hit them?' he asked.

'What?'

'The white birds with the stupid beaks?'

'Yeah, easy. I was hunting the rats.'

'What rats?'

Larkin pointed. 'Those things. Creepy fething bugs.'

'Oh yeah. Didn't see them before. Sharp eyes you got. Sharp as sharp.'

'Goes with the territory,' Larkin said, patting his sniper weapon.

'Sure it does. Sure as sure.' Cuu reached into his pocket and produced a couple of hand-rolled white smokes which he offered in a vee to Larkin.

'No thanks.'

Cuu put one away and lit the other, drawing deep. Larkin could smell the scent of obscura. He'd used it occasionally back on Tanith, but it was one of Gaunt's banned substances. Feth, but it smelled strong.

'Colonel-commissar'll have you for that stuff,' he said.

Cuu grinned and exhaled ostentatiously. 'Gaunt don't frighten me,' he said. 'You sure you won't..?'

'No thanks.'

'Those gakking white birds,' Cuu said after a long interval. 'You reckon you could hit them easy?'

'Yeah.'

'I'm betting they could be good in the pot. Bulk up standard rations, a few of them.'

It was a decent enough idea. Larkin keyed his link. 'Three, this is Larks. Cuu and I are going off the track to nab a few waterbirds for eating. Okay with you?'

'Good idea. I'll advise the convoy you're going to be shooting. Bag one for me.'

Larkin and Cuu dropped off the side of the truck and wandered across the road. They slithered down the field embankment into an irrigation ditch where the watery mud sloshed up around their calves. Forkbills warbled and clacked in the cycad grove ahead. Larkin could already see the telltale dots of white amongst the dark green foliage.

Skeeter flies buzzed around them, and sap-wasps droned over their heads. Larkin slid his sound suppressor out of his uniform's thigh pouch and carefully screwed it onto the muzzle of his long-las.

They came up around a clump of fallen palms and Larkin nestled down in the exposed root system to take aim. He scope-chased a spider-rat up and down a tree bole for a moment to get his eye in and then settled on a plump forkbill.

The trick wasn't to hit it. The trick was to knock its head off.

A las-round would explode a forkbill into feathers and mush if it hit the body, like taking a man out by jamming a tube-charge down his waistband. Shoot the inedible head off and you'd have a ready-to-pluck carcass.

Larkin squared up, shook his head and shoulders out, and fired. There was a slight flash and virtually no noise. The fork-bill, now with nothing but a scorched ring of flesh and feathers where its head should have joined on, dropped off into the shallow water.

In short order, Larkin pinked off five more. He and Cuu sloshed out to gather them up, hooking them by the webbed feet into their belts.

'You're gakking good,' Cuu said.

'Thanks.'

'That's a hell of a gun.'

'Sniper variant long-las. My very best friend.'

Cuu nodded. 'I believe that. You mind if I take a try?'

Cuu held his hand out and Larkin reluctantly handed the long-las to him, taking Cuu's standard lasrifle in return. Cuu grinned at the new toy, and eased the nalwood stock against his shoulder.

'Nice,' he sighed. 'Nice as nice.'

He fired suddenly and a forkbill exploded in a mass of white feathers and blood.

'Not bad, but–'

Cuu ignored Larkin and fired again. And again. And again. Three more forkbills detonated off their perches.

'We can't cook them if you hit them square,' Larkin said.

'I know. We've got enough for eating now. This is just fun.'

Larkin wanted to complain, but Cuu swung the long-las round quick fire and destroyed two more birds. The water under the trees was thick with blood stains and floating white feathers.

'That's enough,' said Larkin.

Cuu shook his head, and aimed again. He'd switched the long-las to rapid fire and when he pulled the trigger, pulse after pulse whined into the canopy.

Larkin was alarmed. Alarmed at the misuse of his beloved weapon, alarmed at Cuu's psychopathic glee...

...and most of all, alarmed at the way Cuu's wildfire blasted and crisped a half dozen spider-rats off the surrounding tree trunks. Not a shot was wasted or went wide. Skittering targets even he'd have to think twice about hitting were reduced to seared, blood-leaking impacts on the trees.

Cuu handed the weapon back to Larkin.

'Nice gun,' said Cuu, and turned back to rejoin the road.

Larkin hurried after him. He shivered despite the sun's heat that baked down over the highway. Cold killer. Larkin knew he'd be watching his back from now on.

AT THE FRONT end of the immobile convoy, Gaunt, Kleopas and Herodas stood watching the tech-priests and engineers of the Pardus regiment as they struggled to retrack the defective Chimera. A workteam of Pardus and Tanith personnel had already unloaded the armoured transport by hand to reduce its payload weight. The Trojan throbbed and idled nearby like a watchful parent.

Gaunt glanced at his chronometer. 'Another ten minutes and we'll move on regardless.'

'I might object, sir,' Kleopas ventured. 'This unit was carrying shells for the Conquerors.' He gestured to the massive stack of munitions the workteam had removed from the Chimera to get it upright. 'We can't just leave this stuff.'

'We can if we have to,' said Gaunt.

'If this was a payload of lasgun powercells, you'd say different.'

'You're right,' Gaunt nodded to Kleopas. 'But we're on the tightest of clocks, major. I'll give them twenty minutes. But only twenty.'

Captain Herodas moved away to shout encouraging orders at the engineer teams.

Gaunt pulled out a silver hip flask. It was engraved with the name 'Delane Oktar'. He offered it to Kleopas.

'Thank you, colonel-commissar, no. A little early in the day for me.'

Gaunt shrugged and took a swig. He was screwing up the cap when a voice from behind them said, 'I hear shooting.'

Gaunt and Kleopas looked around at Commissar Hark as he approached them.

'Just a little authorised foraging,' Gaunt told him.

'Do the squad leaders know? It might trigger a panic.'

'They know. I told them. Regulation 11-0-119 gamma.'

Hark made an open-handed shrug. 'You don't need to cite it to me, colonel. I believe you.'

'Good. Major Kleopas... perhaps you'd explain to the commissar here what is happening. In intricate detail.'

Kleopas glared at Gaunt and then turned to smile at Hark. 'We're retracking the Chimera, sir, and that involves a heavy lifter as you can see...'

Gaunt slipped away, removing himself from the commissar's presence. He walked back down the line of vehicles, taking another swig from the flask.

Hark watched him go. 'What are your thoughts on the legendary colonel-commissar?' he asked Kleopas, interrupting a lecture on mechanised track repair.

'He's as sound a commander as ever I knew. Lives for his men. Don't ask me again, sir. I won't have my words added to any official report of censure.'

'Don't worry, Kleopas,' said Hark. 'Gaunt's damned any way you look at it. Lord General Lugo has him in his sights. I was just making conversation.'

Gaunt walked back a hundred metres and found Medic Curth and her orderlies sitting in the shade cast by their transport.

Curth got up. 'Sir?'

'Everything fine here?' Gaunt asked. He was unhappy with the fact that Dorden had stayed behind in the Doctrinopolis to see to the wounded. Curth was a fine medic, but he wasn't used to her being in charge of the taskforce's surgical team. Dorden had always been his chief medic, since the foundation of the Ghosts. Curth would take a little getting used to.

'Everything's fine,' she said, her smile as appealing as her heart-shaped face.

'Good,' said Gaunt. 'Good.' He took another swig.

'Any of that going spare?' Curth asked.

Surprised, he turned and handed her the flask. She took a hefty slug.

'I didn't think you'd approve.'

'This waiting makes me nervous,' she said, wiping her mouth and handing the hip flask back to Gaunt.

'Me too,' Gaunt said.

'Anyway,' said Curth. 'Trust me. It's medicinal.'

* * *

ALPHA-AR PULLED INTO Mukret in the late afternoon. The Salamander rolled down to a crawl and Mkoll, Mkvenner and Bonin leapt out, lasguns raised, trailing the light tank down the main highway as it passed through the jumble of stilt houses and raised halls. A slight breeze had picked up with the approach of evening, and it lifted dust and leaf-litter across the bright sunlit road and the dark spaces of shadow between and under the dwellings.

The sun itself, big and yellowing, shone sideways through a stiff break of palms and cypresses towards the river.

The township was deserted. Doors flapped open and epiphytic creepers roiled around window frames and stack posts. There was broken crockery on the house-walks, and litters of ragged clothing in the gutters. At the far end of the town sat long, brick and tile smokehouses. Mukret's main industry was the smoke-drying of fish and meats. The Tanith could still pick out the tangy background scent of woodsmoke in the air.

Behind the rolling tank, the three scouts prowled forward, lasguns held in loose, fluid grips. Bonin swung and aimed abruptly as forkbills mobbed out of a tree.

The Salamander rumbled.

Mkoll moved ahead and switched Bonin left down a jetty walk to the river itself with a coded gesture.

Ahead, something stirred. It was a chelon, an immature calf, wandering out into the main road, dragging its reins in the dust. A short-form clutch saddle was lashed to its back.

It wandered past Mkoll and Mkvenner, trailing its bridle. Mkoll could hear sporadic knocking now. Mkoll signalled for Mkvenner to hold back as cover and walked forward towards the noise.

An old man, skinny and gnarled, was hammering panels into place on an old and ransacked stilt-chapel. It looked like he was trying to board up broken windows using only a length of tree-limb as a hammer.

He was dressed in blue silk robes. Ayatani, Mkoll realised. The local priesthood.

'Father!'

The old man turned and lowered his tree-limb. He was bald, but had a triumphantly long, tapering white beard. It was so long, in fact, that he'd tucked it over his shoulder to keep it out of the way.

'Not now,' he said in a crotchety tone, 'I'm busy. This holy shrine won't just repair itself.'

'Maybe I can help you?'

The old man clambered back down to the roadway and faced Mkoll. 'I don't know. You're a man with a gun... and a tank, it appears. You may be intending to kill me and steal my chelon which, personally speaking, I would not find helpful. Are you a murderer?'

'I'm a member of the Imperial liberation force,' Mkoll replied, looking the old man up and down.

'Really? Well now...' the old man mused, using the tip of his long beard to mop his face.

'What's your name?'

'Ayatani Zweil,' said the old man. 'And yours?'

'Scout Sergeant Mkoll.'

'Scout Sergeant Mkoll, eh? Very impressive. Well, Scout Sergeant Mkoll, the Ershul have fouled this shrine, this sacred house of our thrice beloved saint, and I intend to rebuild it stick by stick. If you assist me, I will be grateful. And I'm sure the saint will be too. In her way.'

'Father, we're heading west. I need to know if you've seen any Infardi on the road.'

'Of course I have. Hundreds of them.'

Mkoll reached for his vox link but the old man stopped him.

'Infardi I've seen plenty of. Pilgrims. Flocking back to the Doctrinopolis. Yes, yes... plenty of Infardi. But no Ershul.'

'I'm confused.'

The ayatani gestured up and down the sunlit road through Mukret. 'Do you know what you're standing on?'

'The Tembarong Road,' said Mkoll.

'Also known in the old texts of Irimrita as the Ayolta Amad Infardiri, which literally means the "approved route of Infardi procession" or more colloquially the Pilgrim's Way. The road may go to Tembarong. That way. Eventually. Who wants to go there? A dull little city where the women have fat legs. But that way–' He pointed the direction Mkoll had appeared from.

'In that direction, pilgrims travel. To the shrines of the Doctrinopolis Citadel. To the Tempelum Infarfarid Sabbat. To a hundred places of devotion. They have done for many hundreds of years. It is a pilgrim's way. And our name for pilgrims is "Infardi". That is its proper sense and I use it as such.'

Mkoll coughed politely. 'So when you say Infardi you mean real pilgrims?'

'Yes.'

'Coming this way?'

'Positively flocking, Scout Sergeant Mkoll. The Doctrinopolis is open again, so they come to give thanks. And they come to prostrate themselves before the desecrated Citadel.'

'You're not referring to soldiers of the enemy then?'

'They stole the name Infardi. I won't let them have it! I won't! If they want a name, let them be Ershul!'

'Ershul?'

'It is a word from the Ylath, the herdsman dialect. It refers to a chelon that consumes its own dung or the dung of others.'

'And have you seen... uhm... Ershul? On your travels?'

'No.'

'I see.'

'But I've heard them.' Zweil suddenly took Mkoll by the arm and pointed him west, over the roofscape of Mukret, towards the distant edges of the rainwoods, which were becoming hazed and misty in the late afternoon. A dark stain of storm-clouds was gathering over the neighbouring hills.

'Up there, Scout Sergeant Mkoll. Beyond Bhavnager, in the Sacred Hills. They lurk, they prowl, they wait.'

Mkoll involuntarily wanted to pull away from the old man's tight grip but it was strangely reassuring. It reminded him of the way Archdeacon Mkere used to steer him to the lectern to read the lesson at church school back on Tanith, years ago.

'Are you a devout man, Scout Sergeant Mkoll?'

'I hope I am, father. I believe the Emperor is god in flesh, and I live to serve him in peace and war.'

'That's good, that's good. Contact your fellows. Tell them to expect trouble on their pilgrimage.'

TWENTY KILOMETRES EAST, the main convoy was moving again. The munitions Chimera had been repaired well enough for the time being, though Intendant Elthan had warned Gaunt it would need a proper overhaul during the night rest.

They were making good time again. Gaunt sat in the open cab of his command Salamander, reviewing the charts and hoping they'd make it to Mukret before nightfall. Mkoll had just checked in. Alpha-AR had reached Mukret and found it deserted, though the dour scout had repeated his warning about Infardi sightings.

Gaunt put the maps aside and turned to his battered, annotated copy of Saint Sabbat's gospel, as he had done many times that day. Trying to read the text in the jolting Salamander made his head hurt, but he persisted. He flicked through to the most recent of the paper place-markers he'd left. The mid-section, the Psalms of Sabbat. Virtually impenetrable, their language both antique and mysteriously coded with symbols. He could read everything and nothing into them as meaning, but nothing was all he took away.

Except that it was the most beautiful religious verse he'd ever read. Warmaster Slaydo had thought so too. It was from him, Gaunt had got his love of the Sabbat psalms. His hands lowered the book to his knees as he looked up and remembered Slaydo for a moment.

He felt a lurch as the tank slowed suddenly, and stood up to look. His mount was third from the front of the convoy, and the two scout Salamanders ahead had dropped speed sharply. Red brake lights came on behind their metal grilles, stark and bright in the twilight.

A large herd of massive chelons was coming towards them, driven by several beige-robed peasants. It was half blocking the road. The convoy leaders were being forced to pull into tight single file against the riverwards edge of the highway.

Mkoll had warned him about this. Lots of livestock and three harmless herdsmen, he'd said, though he'd seemed certain they'd be off the road before the convoy met them.

'One to convoy elements,' Gaunt said into his vox on the all-channel band. 'Drop your speed and pull over to the extreme left. We've got livestock on the road. Show courtesy and pass well clear of them.'

The drivers and crews snapped back responses over the link. The convoy slowed to a crawl and began to creep along past the straggled line of lowing, shambling beasts. Gaunt cursed this fresh delay. It would be a good ten minutes until they were clear of the obstruction.

He looked out at the big shell-backs as they went by close enough to lean out and touch. Their animal odour was strong and earthy, and Gaunt could hear the creak of their leathery armour skin and the gurgle of their multi-chambered stomachs.

They broke noxious wind, or groaned and snuffled. Blunt muzzles chewed regurgitated cuds. He saw the drovers too. Large
labourers in the coarse off-white robes of the agrarian caste, urging the beasts on with taps of their jiddi-sticks, their hoods and
face-veils pulled up against the dust. A few nodded apologeti-
cally to him as they passed. Most didn't spare the Imperials a
look. Religious war and sacred desecration ravages their world
and for them, it's business as usual, thought Gaunt. Some lives
in this lethal galaxy were enviably simple...

Lots of livestock and three harmless herdsmen. He remembered
Mkoll's report with abrupt clarity. Three harmless herdsmen.

Now he was level with them, he counted at least nine.

'One! This is one! Be advised, this could be–'

His words were cut off by the bang-shriek of a shoulder-
launched missile. Two vehicles back, a command Salamander
slewed wildly and vomited a fierce cone of flame and debris
out of its crew-space. Metal fragments rained down out of the
air, tinking off his own vehicle's bodywork.

The vox-link went mad. Gaunt could hear sustained bursts of
las fire and auto weapons. Herdsmen, suddenly several dozen
in number, were surging out from the cover of their agitated
animals. They had weapons. As their robes fell away, he saw
body art and green silk.

He grabbed his bolt pistol.

The Infardi were all over them.

SEVEN
DEATH ON THE ROAD

'Let me rest, now the battle's done.'

— Imperial Guard song

HIS DROVER'S DISGUISE flapping about him, an Infardi gunman clambered up the mudguard of the command Salamander and raised his autopistol, a yowl of rabid triumph issuing from his scabby lips. He stank of fermented fruit liquor and his eyes were wild-white with intoxicated frenzy.

Gaunt's bolt round hit him point-blank in the right cheek and disintegrated his head in a puff of liquidised tissue.

'One to honour guard units! Infardi ambush to the right! Turn and repel!'

Gaunt could hear further missile impacts and lots of small arms fire. The chelons, viced in by the road edge on one side and the Imperial armour on the other, were whinnying with agitation and banging the edges of their shells up against vehicle hulls. 'Turn us! Turn us around!' Gaunt yelled at his driver.

'No room, sir!' the Pardus replied desperately. A brace of hard-slug shots sparked and danced off the Salamander's cowling.

'Damn it!' Gaunt bellowed. He rose in the back of the tank and fired into the charging enemy, killing one Infardi and crippling a mature chelon. The beast shrieked and slumped over, crushing two more of the ambushers before rolling hard into the Chimera behind. It began to writhe, baying, shoving the tank into the verge.

Gaunt swore and grabbed the firing grips of the pintle-mounted storm bolter. Infardi were appearing in the road ahead and he raked the hardpan, dropping several. Some had swarmed over the leading scout tank ahead and were murdering the crew. The vehicle slewed to a drunken, sidelong halt.

A tank round roared off close behind him. He heard the hot detonation of superheating gas, the grinding clank of the recoiling weapon, the whoosh of the shell. It fell in the ditch-field to the right of the road and kicked up a huge spout of liquid muck. More tanks now fired their main guns, and turret-mounted bolters chattered and sprayed. Another big chelon, hit dead centre by a tank shell, exploded wholesale and a big, stinking cloud of blood mist and intestinal gas billowed down the convoy.

Gaunt knew they had the upper hand in terms of strength, but the ambushers had been canny. They'd slowed the convoy down with the livestock and pinned it against the road wall so it couldn't manoeuvre.

He fired the weapon mount again, chopping through an Infardi running up to position a missile launcher. Dead fingers convulsed anyway and the missile fired and immediately dropped, blowing a deep crater in the road.

Something grabbed Gaunt from behind and pulled him off the storm bolter. He fell back into the tank's crewbay, kicking and fighting for his life.

THE FIRST THIRD of the honour guard convoy was under hard assault, jammed and slowed to such an extent by the herd that the trailing portion of the convoy, straggled back to a more than four kilometre spread now, couldn't move up to successfully support.

Larkin found himself next to Cuu, firing down from their troop truck body into the weeds as Infardi swarmed up out of the waterline, shooting as they came. Cuu was giggling gleefully as he killed. An anti-tank rocket wailed over their heads, and las-fire exploded around them, killing a trooper nearby and blowing out the windows of the truck cab.

'Disperse! Engage!' Sergeant Kolea yelled, and the Tanith leapt from the trucks en masse, charging the attackers with fixed bayonets and blazing las-fire.

Criid and Caffran charged together, hitting the first of the Infardi hand to hand, clubbing and gutting them. Caffran dropped for a wide shot that sent another ambusher tumbling back down the ditch into the field. Criid fell, got up, and laced las-blasts into the shins of the Infardi stampeding towards them. A Pardus tank roared nearby, blindly shelling the herd.

Rawne's truck, further down the line, was mobbed by Infardi. The cargo bed rocked as bodies piled onto it. Rawne fired his lasgun into the thick press, and saw Feygor rip an enemy's throat out with his silver Tanith knife. The darkening evening air was crisscrossed by painfully bright las-fire. A second later, gusting flames surged down the roadside gulley. From Varl's truck, Trooper Brostin was washing the roadline with bursts from his flamer.

Major Kleopas tried to turn his Conqueror, but a massive chelon, bucking and hooting, slammed into his bull-bars and shunted the entire tank around. For a full five seconds, the tank's racing tracks dragged at thin air as the weight of the bull chelon drove its nose into the road.

Then the tracks grabbed purchase again. Kleopas's tank lurched forward.

'Ram it!' Kleopas ordered.

'Sir?'

'Screw you! Full power! Ram it!' Kleopas barked down at his driver.

The Conqueror battle tank, named *Heart of Destruction* according to the hand-painted hull logo, scrambled sideways in a vast spray of dust and then drove its bulldozer blade into the legs of the big bull chelon. Kleopas's tank maimed the animal and rammed it off the highway, though the Conqueror dented its hull plating against the chelon's shell in the process.

Squealing, the chelon fell down into the waterfield ditch and rolled over on its back, squashing eight Infardi troopers in the irrigation gulley.

The *Heart of Destruction* dipped off the roadside and down into the waterbed, tracks churning. As his main gunner and gun layer pumped shells into the breaks of trees beyond the road, Kleopas manned the bolter hardpoint and blasted tracer shots across the irrigation ditches.

His manoeuvre began to break the deadlock. Three tanks followed him through the gap he'd cut and rattled round into the tree-line off the road, wasting the dug-in Infardi with turret bolters and flamers.

In the closed truck carrying the medical supplies, Ana Curth flinched as stray shots punched through the hardskin and her racks of bottled pharmaceuticals. Glass debris spat in all directions. Lesp stumbled to his knees, a dark line of blood welling across his cheek from a sliver of flying glass.

Two Infardi clambered up the rear gate of the truck. Curth kicked one away with a boot in the face, and then dragged out a laspistol Soric had given her and fired twice. The second Infardi attacker fell off the truck.

Curth turned to see if Lesp was all right. She saw the alarm in his face, half-heard the warning shout coming from his mouth, and then felt herself grabbed and pulled bodily out of the truck.

Her world spun. Terror viced her. She was jerked upside down, held carelessly by the legs, her face in the dirt. The Infardi were all over her, clawing and tearing. She could smell their wretched sweat-stink. All she could see was a jumble of green silk and tattooed flesh.

There was a sudden glare of hard blue light and a sizzling sound. Hot liquid sprayed over her, and she realised, with professional detachment, that it was blood. She swung as the grip on her half-released.

The blur of blue light carved the air again and something yelped. She collapsed onto the road, flat on her belly, and rolled up in time to see Ibram Gaunt raking his glowing power sword around in an expert figure-six swing that felled an Infardi like a tree. Gaunt had lost his cap and his clothes were torn. There was an unnerving look of unquenchable fury in his eyes. He wielded the sacred blade of her home-hive two-handed now, like a champion of antique myth. Dismembered bodies piled around him and the gritty sand of the road was soaked with gore for metres in every direction.

A hero, she thought abruptly, realising it truly in her mind for the first time. Damn Lugo and his disdain! This man is an Imperial hero!

Lesp, his face running with blood, appeared suddenly behind the commissar in the back gatehatch of the medical truck and began laying down support fire with his lasgun. Gaunt staked his power sword tip-down in the road and knelt next to it, scooping up a fallen Infardi lasrifle. His short, clipped bursts of fire joined Lesp's, stinging across the road and into the mob of Infardi. Green-clad bodies tumbled onto the road or slithered back down the trench into the field.

Curth scrambled over to Gaunt on her hands and knees. Once she was safely beside him, she too knelt and began firing with a purloined Infardi weapon. She had none of the Commissar's trained skill with an assault las, nor as much as Trooper Lesp, but she made a good account of herself with the unfamiliar weapon nevertheless. Gaunt, grim and driven, handled his firing pattern with an assured expertise that would have shamed even a well-drilled infantryman.

'You didn't scream,' Gaunt said to her suddenly, firing steadily.

'What?'

'You didn't scream when they grabbed you.'

'And that's good – why?'

'Waste of energy, of dignity. If they'd killed you, they'd have taken no satisfaction in it.'

'Oh,' she said, nonplussed, not sure if she should be flattered.

'Never give the enemy anything, Ana. They take what they take and that's more than enough as it is.'

'Live by that, do you?' she asked sourly, twitching off another burst of unsteady but enthusiastic shots.

'Yes,' he replied, as if he was surprised she should ask. Sensing that, she felt surprised too. At herself, for her own stupidity. It was obvious and she'd known it all along if she'd but recognised it. That was Gaunt's way. Gaunt the Imperial hero. Give nothing. Never. Ever. Never let your guard down, never allow the enemy the slightest edge. Stay firm and die hard. Nothing else would do.

It wasn't just the commissar in him. It was the warrior, Curth realised. It was Gaunt's fundamental philosophy. It had brought him here and would carry him on to whatever death, kind or cruel, the fates had in store for him. It made him what he was: the relentless soldier, the celebrated leader, the terrifying slayer.

She felt unbearably sad for him and in awe of him all in the same moment.

Ana Curth had heard about the disgrace awaiting Gaunt at the end of this mission. That made her saddest of all. She realised he was going to be absolutely true to his duty and his calling right to the end, no matter the shadow of dishonour hanging over him. He would not falter.

Gaunt would be Gaunt until death claimed him.

FIFTY METRES AWAY, Captain Herodas fell out of a burning Salamander a few moments before a second anti-tank rocket whooshed out of the roadside trees and blew it apart.

Almost immediately, a hard-slug tore through his left knee and threw him into the dust. He blacked out in pain for a second and then fought back, trying to crawl. The Pardus trooper next to him was face down in a pool of blood.

'Lezink! Lezink!'

Herodas tried to turn the man over, but the limbs were loose and the body was hollow and empty. Herodas looked down and saw the horror of blown-out meat and bone shards that was all that remained of his own leg joint. Las-shots zinged over his head. He reached for his pistol but his holster was flapping open.

There were tears in his eyes. The dull pain was rising to overwhelm him. From all around came the sounds of screaming, shooting, killing.

The ground shook. Herodas looked up in disbelief at the cow chelon that was stampeding towards him from the trapped, terrified herd. It was a third the size of the big bulls, but still weighed in at over two tonnes.

He closed his eyes tight and braced for the bone-splintering impact that was about to come.

A thin beam of hot red energy stabbed across the road and hit the hurtling brute with such force it was blown sideways off its feet. The shot disintegrated a huge hole in the chelon and left it a smouldering husk, dripping fatty mush.

Plasma fire! thought Herodas. Thrice-damned gods! That was plasma fire!

He saw the stocky shape of Commissar Hark striding down the roadway, dark in the rising dust and evening light, his long coat rippling around him. Hark was calling out commands and pointing as he directed the units of sprinting Tanith infantry down the road and into the enemy flank. He held an ancient plasma pistol in his right hand.

Hark halted and sent three more troop units on past him as they ran up, forking them wide to disperse them into the roadside gutter. He turned and waved two Pardus Conquerors forward off the road with quick, confident gestures.

Then he spun round abruptly, brought up his weapon, and cremated an Infardi who had risen from the roadside weeds with a rifle.

Hark crossed to Herodas.

'Stay still, help's on the way.'

'Get me up, and I'll fight!' Herodas complained.

Hark smiled. 'Your courage does you credit, captain, but believe me, you're not going anywhere but to a medic cot. Your leg's a mess. Stay still.'

He turned and fired his plasma gun into the trees again at a target Herodas couldn't even see.

'They're all over us,' Herodas said.

'No, they're breaking. We've got them running,' Hark told him, holstering his plasma gun and kneeling down to apply a tourniquet to Herodas's thigh.

'The fight's out of them,' he reassured the captain, but Herodas had blacked out again.

THE FIGHT WAS indeed out of them. Overmatched and repulsed, leaving two-thirds of their number dead, the Infardi ambushers fled away into the off-road woodland, hunted by the Pardus shelling and the staccato thrash of the Hydra batteries.

The front section of the convoy was a mess: two scout Salamanders and a command Salamander ruined and burning, a supply Chimera overturned and blown out, two trucks ablaze. Twenty-two Pardus dead, fifteen Ghosts, six Munitorium crewmen. Six Ghosts and three Pardus severely injured and over eighty light wounds sustained by various personnel.

Listening to the roll call of deaths and injuries on his microbead, Gaunt strode back to his vehicle, retrieving his cap, and exchanging his torn storm coat for a short leather bomber jacket.

He sat on the rear fender of his Salamander as sweating troopers carried out the bodies of his driver and navigator.

Smoke and blood-fumes lingered over the scene. Infardi bodies were strewn everywhere, as well as the stricken chelon, some dead, some mortally hurt. The rest of the herd had broken into the waterfield and were disappearing as they moved away in the diminishing light. Gaunt could hear the snap of las-fire and the grumble of tanks as they cleared the low lying woods.

During the course of the fight, the sun had gone down, and the sky was now a smooth, luminous violet. Night breezes came up from the river and shivered the trees. They were badly behind schedule, a long way short of the planned night stop. It would be well after full dark before they reached Mukret now.

Gaunt heard someone approach and looked up. It was Intendant Elthan, wearing the stiff grey robes of the Munitorium, and a look of disdain.

'This is unacceptable, colonel-commissar,' he said briefly.

'What is?'

'The losses, the attack.'

'I'm afraid I don't follow you, intendant. War isn't "unacceptable". It's dirty and tragic and terrifying and often senseless, but it's also a fact of life.'

'This attack!' Elthan hissed, his lips tight around his yellowed teeth. 'You were warned! Your scout detail warned you of the enemy presence. I heard it myself on the vox-link. This should never have happened!'

'What are you suggesting, intendant? That I'm somehow culpable for these deaths?'

'That is exactly what I'm suggesting! You ignored your recon advice. You pressed on–'

'That's enough,' said Gaunt, getting to his feet. 'I'm prepared to put your comments down to shock and inexperience. We should just forget this exchange happened.'

'I will not!' Elthan replied. 'We all know the mess you made of the Doctrinopolis liberation. That shoddy leadership has cost you your career! And now you–'

'Menazoid Epsilon. Fortis Binary. Vervunhive. Monthax. Sapiencia. Nacedon.'

They both looked around. Hark stood watching them.

'Other examples of shoddy leadership, in your opinion, intendant?'

Elthan went a little red around the edges and then blustered on. 'I expect your support on this, commissar! Are you not here for the express purpose of disciplining and supervising this... this broken man?'

'I am here to discharge the duties of an Imperial commissar,' said Hark simply.

'You heard the recon reports!'

'I did,' said Hark. 'We were warned of enemy activity. We moved judiciously and took precautions. Despite that, they surprised us. It's called an ambush. It happens in war. It's part of the risk you take in a military action.'

'Are you siding with him?' asked Elthan.

'I'm remaining neutral and objective. I'm pointing out that even the best commander must expect attacks and losses. I'm suggesting you return to your vehicle and supervise the resumption of this convoy.'

'I don't—'

'No, you don't understand. Because you are not a soldier, intendant. We have a saying on my home world: sometimes you get the carniv and sometimes the carniv gets you.'

Elthan turned disdainfully and stalked away. Down the road, a trio of Pardus tanks had lowered their dozer blades and were ploughing the chelon carcasses off the thoroughfare. Headlamps gleamed like little full moons in the dusk.

'What's the matter?' Hark asked Gaunt. 'You look... I don't know... startled, I suppose.'

Gaunt shook his head and didn't reply. In truth, he was startled at the way Hark had come to his defence. Elthan had been talking a lot of crap, but he'd been spot on about Hark's purpose here. It was common knowledge. Hark himself had been brutally matter of fact about it from the outset. He was Lugo's punisher, here to oversee the end of Gaunt's command. Gaunt knew little of Hark's background or past career, but the same was clearly not true in reverse. Hark had casually reeled off the most notable actions of the Ghosts under Gaunt from memory. And he'd spoken with what seemed genuine admiration.

'Have you made a particular study of my career, Hark?'

'Of course. I have been appointed to serve the Tanith First as commissar. I'd be failing in that duty if I did not thoroughly acquaint myself with its history and operations. Wouldn't I?'

'And what did you learn from that study?'

'That, despite a history of clashes with the upper echelons of command, you have a notable service record. Hagia is your first true failure, but it is a failure of such magnitude that it threatens to eclipse all you have done before.'

'Really? Do you really believe I deserve sole blame for the disaster in the Doctrinopolis?'

'Lord General Lugo is a lord general, Gaunt. That is the most complete answer I can give you.'

Gaunt nodded with an unfriendly smile. 'There is justice beyond rank, Hark. Slaydo believed that.'

'Rest his good soul, the Emperor protects. But Macaroth is Warmaster now.'

The candid honesty of the response struck Gaunt. For the first time, he felt something other than venom towards Commissar Viktor Hark. To be part of the Imperial Guard was to be part of a complex system of obedience, loyalty and service. More often than not, that system forced men into obligations and decisions they'd otherwise not choose to make. Gaunt had butted up against the system all his career. Was he now seeing that mirrored in another? Or was Hark just dangerously persuasive?

The latter notion seemed likely. Charisma was one of the chief tools of a good commissar, and Hark seemed to have it in spades. To say the right thing at the right time for the right effect. Was he just playing with Gaunt?

'I've detailed some platoons to bury the dead here,' Hark said. 'We can't afford to carry them with us. A small service should do it, consecrated by the Pardus chaplain. The wounded are a bigger problem. We have nine serious, including Captain Herodas. Medic Curth tells me at least two of them won't live if they don't reach a hospital by tomorrow. The others will perish if we keep them with us.'

'Your suggestion?'

'We're less than a day out from the Doctrinopolis. I suggest we sacrifice a truck, and send them back to the city with a driver and maybe a few guards.'

'That would be my choice too. Arrange it, please, Hark. Select a Munitorium driver and one Ghost trooper, one single good man, as armed escort.'

Hark nodded. There was a long pause and Gaunt thought Hark was about to speak again.

Instead he walked away into the gathering gloom.

* * *

IT WAS APPROACHING midnight when the last elements of the honour guard convoy rolled in to the deserted village of Mukret. Both moons were up, one small and full, the other a large, perfect geometric semicircle, and dazzling ribbons of stars decorated the dark blue sky.

Gaunt looked up at them as he jumped down from his command vehicle. The Sabbat Worlds. The battleground he had come to with Slaydo all those years before. The starscape of the crusade. For a moment he felt as if it all depended on this little world, on this little night, on this little continent. On him.

They were the Sabbat Worlds because this was Sabbat's world. The saint's place. If ever a soldier had to face his final mission, none could be more worthy. Slaydo would have approved, Gaunt considered. Slaydo would have wanted to be here. They weren't storming some fortress-world or decimating the legions of the arch-enemy. Such worthy glories and battle honours seemed slight and meaningless compared to this.

They were here for the saint.

Alpha-AR had secured the empty town. The tanks and carriers rolled in, choking the cold night air with their thunderous exhausts and dazzling lamps.

The main town road was full of vehicles and disembarking troops. Braziers were lit, and pickets arranged.

Mkoll saluted Gaunt as he approached. 'You had some trouble, sir.'

'Sometimes the carniv gets you, sergeant,' Gaunt replied.

'Sir?'

'From tomorrow, we run a spearhead under your command. Hard armour, fast moving.'

'Not my way, sir, but if you insist.'

'I do. We were caught napping. And paid for it. My mistake.'

'No one's mistake, sir.'

'Perhaps. But it can only get worse from here. Spearhead, from Mukret, at dawn. Can you manage that?'

Mkoll nodded.

'Do you want to choose the formation or do you trust me to do it?'

The scout sergeant smiled. 'You call the shots, sir. I've always preferred it that way.'

'I'll consult Kleopas and let you know.'

They walked through the bustle of dismounting personnel.

'I've met a man here,' Mkoll said. 'A sort of vagrant priest. You should talk to him.'

'To confess my sins?'

'No sir. He's... Well, I don't know what he is, but I think you'll like him.'

'Right,' said Gaunt. He and Mkoll sidestepped as Tanith troopers backed across their path carrying ammo boxes and folded mortars for the perimeter defence.

'Sorry, sir,' said Larkin, struggling with a heavy shell crate.

'As you were, Larks,' Gaunt smiled.

'Tough luck about Milo,' said Larkin.

Gaunt felt his blood chill. For one dreadful moment, he wondered if he'd missed Brin's name on the casualty roll.

'Tough luck?'

'Him going back to the city like that. He'll miss the show.'

Gaunt nodded warily, and called over Sergeant Baffels, Milo's platoon commander. 'Where's Trooper Milo?'

'Heading back to the Doctrinopolis with the wounded. I thought you knew, sir.' Baffels, chunky and bearded, looked awkwardly up at the colonel-commissar.

'Hark selected him?'

Baffels nodded. 'He said you wanted a good man to ride shotgun for the wounded.'

'Carry on, sergeant.'

Gaunt walked through the busy activity of the convoy, away, down to the river's edge, where the rippling water reflected back the moons and the chirrup of night insects filled every angle of the darkness.

Milo. Gaunt had always joked about the way the men saw Brin Milo as his lucky charm. He'd teased them for their superstitious foolishness. But in his heart, silently, he'd always felt that it was actually true. Milo had a charmed life. He had the pure flavour of lost Tanith about him. He was their last and only link to the Ghosts' past.

Gaunt had always kept him close for that reason, though he'd never, ever admitted it.

Hark had chosen Milo to be the one to return to the holy city. Accident? Coincidence? Design?

Hark had already stated he had studied the Tanith records. He had to know how psychologically important Brin was to the Ghosts. To Gaunt.

Gaunt had a nasty feeling he'd been deliberately under-mined.

Worse still, he had a feeling of doom. For the first time, they were going out without Milo. He already knew this mission was going to be his last.

Now, with a sense of terrifying premonition, he felt it was going to turn bad. Very bad indeed.

FAR AWAY NOW, chasing back down the Tembarong Road towards the Doctrinopolis, the lone troop truck thundered through the night.

Milo had ridden in the cab for the first part of the overnight journey, but the obese Munitorium driver had proved to be surly and taciturn, and then had begun to exhibit a chronic flatulence problem that would have been offensive even in an open-topped car.

Milo had climbed back to spend the rest of the trip with the wounded men.

Commissar Hark had singled him out for this duty. Milo wondered why. There were any number of troopers who could have done the job.

Milo wondered if Hark had chosen him because he hadn't been a proper trooper long. Despite his uniform, some of the Ghosts still regarded him as the token civilian. He resented that. He was a fething Imperial Guardsman and he'd take physical issue with anyone who doubted that. Even more, he resented missing out on what he knew would be the last action of the Tanith Ghosts under Ibram Gaunt. He doubted there would be much glory in the mission, but still he yearned to be there.

He felt cheated.

Then, as he watched the moons' light flickering on the river dashing by, he wondered if Gaunt had told Hark to select him. His encounter with Gaunt in the Universitariat still stung. Had Gaunt really wished him away?

Most of the wounded were unconscious or asleep. Milo sat beside Captain Herodas in the back of the rocking truck. The captain was pale from blood loss and trauma and his face was pinched. Milo was afraid Herodas wasn't going to make it back to the Doctrinopolis, despite Medic Curth's ministrations. He'd lost so much blood.

'Don't you go dying on me, sir,' he growled at the supine officer.

'I won't, I swear it,' Herodas murmured.

'Just a bad wound. They'll fix you up. Feth, you'll get an augmetic knee, soon as look at you!'

Herodas laughed but no sound came out of him.

'Sergeant Varl in my mob, he's got an augmetic shoulder. The latest fething bionics!'

'Yeah?' whispered Herodas. Milo wanted to keep him talking. About anything, any old nonsense. He was worried what might happen if Herodas fell asleep.

'Oh yes, sir. The latest thing! Claims he can crack nalnuts in his armpit now, he does.'

Herodas chuckled. 'You're gonna miss all the fun coming back with us,' he said.

Milo grimaced. 'Not so much fun. The colonel-commissar's swansong. No great glory in being there for that.'

'He's a good man,' mumbled Herodas, moving his body as much as the pain allowed to resettle more comfortably. 'A fine commander. I didn't know him well, but from what I saw, I'd have been proud to be numbered as one of his.'

'He does his job,' said Milo.

'And more. Vervunhive! I read the dispatches about that. What an action! What a command! Were you there for that?'

'Hab by fething hab, sir.'

Herodas coughed and smiled. 'Something of note. Something to be proud of.'

'It was just the usual,' Milo lied, his eyes now hot with angry tears.

'Glory like that, you take it with you to the end of your days, trooper.' Herodas fell silent and seemed to be sleeping.

'Captain? Captain?'

'What?' asked Herodas, blinking up.

'I– nothing. I see the lights. I see the Doctrinopolis. We're almost there.'

'That's good, trooper.'

'Milo. It's Milo, sir.'

'That's good, Milo. Tell me what you see.'

Milo rose up in the flatbed of the bouncing truck and looked out through the windy dark at the lambent flames burning distantly on the Citadel. They made a beacon in the night.

'I see the holy city, sir.'

'Do you?'

'Yes, I see it. I see the lights.'

'How I want to be there,' Herodas whispered.

'Sir? What did you say? Sir?' Milo looked down out of the wind, holding on tight to the truck's stanchions.

'My name is Lucan Herodas. I don't feel like being a "sir" any more. Call me by my name.'

'I will, Lucan.'

Herodas nodded slowly. 'Tell me what you see now, Milo.'

'I see the city gates. I see the roofs and towers. I see the temples glowing like starflies in the dark.'

Lucan Herodas didn't reply. The truck rolled in under the Pilgrim Gate. Dawn was just a suggestion at the horizon.

Ten minutes later, the truck drew up in the yard of the western city infirmary.

By then, Herodas was dead.

EIGHT
THE WOUNDED

'As I have been called to the holy work,
so I will call others to me.'

— Saint Sabbat, epistles

'A FINE, FAIR, BRIGHT morning, Colm, you old dog,' Dorden announced as he walked into the little side room that had been reserved for the Tanith second-in-command. Early daylight poured in like milk through the west facing casement. The air was cool with the promise of a hot day ahead. A smell of antiseptic wafted in from the hospital halls.

There came no immediate reply, but then Corbec was a notoriously heavy sleeper.

'Did you sleep well?' Dorden asked conversationally, moving towards the cabinet beside the gauze-veiled bed.

He hoped the sound of his voice would slowly, gently rouse the colonel so he could check him over. More than one orderly had received a slap in the mouth for waking Corbec too abruptly.

Dorden picked up a small pottery flask of painkillers. 'Colm? How did you sleep? With all the noise, I mean?'

The sounds of the relentless evacuation had gone on all night, and even now, he could hear the thump of equipment and bustle of bodies in the street outside. Every half hour, the ascending wail of transporter jets roared over the Doctrinopolis as bulk transports lifted away into the sky.

The considerable, gothic manse of the Scholam Medicae Hagias lay on the west bank of the holy river facing the Universitariat, and thus occupied the heart of one of the most populated and active city quarters. A municipal infirmary and teaching hospital attached to the Universitariat, the Scholam Medicae was one of the many city institutions sequestered by the Imperial liberation force to treat wounded men.

'Funny, I don't seem to be sleeping at all well myself,' Dorden said absently, weighing the pill-bottle in his hand. 'Too many dreams. I'm dreaming about my son a lot these days. Mikal, you know. He comes to me in my dreams all the time. I haven't worked out what he's trying to tell me, but he's trying to tell me something.'

Below the little room's window, an argument broke out. Heated voices rose in the still, clear air.

He went to the window, unlatched the casement and leaned out. 'Keep it down!' he yelled into the street below. 'This is meant to be a hospital! Have you no compassion?'

The voices dropped away and he turned back to face the veiled bed.

'This feels light to me,' he said softly, gesturing with the flask. 'Have you been taking too many? It's no joke, Corbec. These are powerful drugs. If you're abusing the dose...'

His voice trailed off. He stepped towards the bed and pulled back the gauzy drapes.

The bed was empty. Rucked, slept in, but empty.

'What the feth–?' Dorden murmured.

THE BASILICA OF Macharius Hagia was a towering edifice on the east side of the Holyditch chelon markets. It had four steeples clad in grey-green ashlar, a stone imported from off-world and which contrasted starkly with the pinks and russets and creams of the local masonry. A massive statue of the Lord Solar in full armour, raising his lightning claws to the sky in a gesture of defiance or vengeance, stood upon a great brick plinth in the entrance arch.

Inside, out of the day's rising heat, it was cold and expansive. Doves and rat-birds fluttered in the open roof spaces and flickered across the staggeringly broad beams of sunlight that stabbed down into the nave.

The place was busy, even at this early hour. Blue-robed ayatani bustled about, preparing for one of the morning rites. Esholi fetched and carried for them, or attended the needs of the many hundreds of worshippers gathering in the grand nave. From the east side, the breeze carried the smells of cooking fish and bread, the smells of the public kitchens adjoining the temple, whose charitable work was to produce alms and free sustenance twice a day for the visiting pilgrims.

The smells made Ban Daur hungry. As he limped in down the main colonnade amidst the other faithful, his stomach gurgled painfully. He stopped for a moment and leaned hard on his walking stick until the dizzying discomfort passed. He hadn't eaten much since taking his wound, hadn't done much of anything, in fact. The medics had banned him from even getting out of bed, but he knew best how he felt. Strong, surprisingly strong. And lucky. The ritual blade had missed his heart by the most remarkably slim margin. The doctors worried the wound might have left a glancing score across the heart muscle, a weakness that might rupture if he exerted himself too soon.

But he could not just lie in bed. This world, Hagia... It was coming to an end. The streets were full of military personnel and civilians trying to pack up and ship out the contents of their lives. There was fear in the air, and a strange sense of unreality.

He started to walk again, but had to stop quickly. He was still light-headed, and sometimes the wound ache in his chest came in bitter waves.

'Are you all right, sir?' asked a passing esholi, a teenage boy in cream silk robes. There was concern in the eyes of the shaven-headed youth.

'Can I help you to a seat?'

'Mmmh... Perhaps, yes. I may have overdone things.'

The student took his arm and guided him across to a nearby bench. Daur lowered himself gratefully onto it.

'You're very pale, sir. Should you even be on your feet?'

'Probably not. Thank you. I'll be fine now I'm sitting.'

The student nodded and moved on, though Daur saw him again some minutes later, talking to several ayatani and pointing anxiously Daur's way.

Daur ignored them and sat back to gaze up at the high altar. The shortness of breath was the worst thing. Exertion got him out of breath so quickly and then he couldn't catch it back because taking deep breaths was agony on his wound.

No, that wasn't the worst thing. A knife in the chest wasn't the worst thing. Being injured in battle and missing the last mission of his regiment.... even that wasn't the worst thing.

The worst thing was the thing in his head, and that wouldn't leave him alone.

He heard voices exchanging hard words nearby and looked round. So did all the worshippers in earshot. Two ayatani were arguing with a group of officers from the Ardelean Colonials. One of the Colonials was repeatedly gesturing to the reliquary. Daur heard one of the priests say '...but this is our heritage! You will not ransack this holy place!'

Daur had heard the same sentiments expressed several times in the last day or so. Despite the abominable evil that moved towards them with the clear intent to engulf the entire world, few native Hagians wanted the evacuation. Many of the ayatani, in fact, saw the removal of icons and relics for safekeeping tantamount to desecration. But Lord General Lugo's decrees had been strict and inflexible. Daur wondered how long it would be before a Hagian was arrested for obstruction or shot for disobedience.

He felt an immeasurable sympathy for the faithful. It was almost as if his wounding had been an epiphany. He'd always been a dutiful man, dutiful to the Imperial creed, a servant of the God-Emperor. But he'd never thought of himself as especially... devout.

Until now. Until here on Hagia. Until, it seemed to Ban Daur, the very moment an Infardi dagger had punched between his ribs. It was like it had changed him, as if he'd been transformed by sharp steel and his own spilt blood. He heard about men undergoing religious transformations. It scared him. It was in his head and it wouldn't leave him alone.

He felt he needed to do something about it, desperately. Limping his way from the infirmary to the nearest temple was a start, but it didn't seem to achieve much. Daur didn't know what he expected to happen. A sign, perhaps. A message.

Such a thing didn't seem very likely.

He sighed, and sat back with his eyes closed for a moment. He was scheduled to join a troop ship with the other walking wounded at six that evening. He wasn't looking forward to it. It felt like running away.

When he opened his eyes, he saw a familiar figure amongst the faithful at the foot of the main altar. It was such a surprise, Daur blinked in confusion.

But he was not mistaken. There was Colm Corbec, his left arm webbed in a sling tight against his bandaged chest, the sleeve of his black fatigue jacket hanging empty, kneeling in prayer.

Daur waited. After a few minutes, Corbec stood up, turned, and saw Daur sitting in the pews. A look of puzzlement crossed the grizzled giant's face. He came over at once.

'Didn't expect to see you here, Daur.'

'I didn't expect to see you either, colonel.'

Corbec sat down next to him.

'Shouldn't you be resting in bed?' Corbec asked. 'What? What's so funny?'

'I was about to ask you that.'

'Yeah, well...' Corbec murmured. 'You know me. Can't abide to be lying around idle.'

'Has there been any word from the honour guard?'

Corbec shook his head. 'Not a thing. Feth, but I...'

'You what?'

'Nothing.'

'Come on, you started to say something.'

'Something I don't think you'd understand, Daur.'

'Okay.'

They sat in silence for a while.

'What?' Daur looked round sharply at Corbec.

'What what?' growled Corbec.

'You spoke.'

'I didn't.'

'Just then, colonel. You said–'

'I didn't say anything, Daur.'

'You said "Sabbat Martyr". I heard you.'

'Wasn't me. I didn't speak.'

Daur scratched his cheek. 'Never mind.'

'What... what were those words?'

'Sabbat Martyr. Or something like that.'

'Oh.'

The silence between them returned. The basilica choir began to sing, the massed voices shimmering the air.

'You hungry, Ban?'

'Starving, sir.'

'Let's go to the public kitchens and get some breakfast together.'

'I thought the temple kitchens were meant to serve the faithful.'

'They are,' said Corbec, getting to his feet, an enigmatic half-smile on his lips. 'Come on.'

THEY GOT BOWLS of fish broth and hunks of crusty, huskseed bread from the long-canopied counters of the kitchens, and went to sit amongst the breakfasting faithful at the communal trestle tables under a wide, flapping awning of pink canvas.

Daur watched as Corbec pulled what looked like a couple of pills from his coat pocket and gulped them down with the first sip of broth. He didn't comment.

'There's something not right in my head, Ban,' Corbec began suddenly through a mouthful of bread. 'In my head... or my gut or my soul or wherever... somewhere. It's been there, off and on, since I was a held captive by Pater Sin, rot his bones.'

'What sort of thing?'

'The sort of thing a man like me... a man like you too, would be my guess... has no idea what to do with. It's lurked in my dreams mostly. I've been dreaming about my father, back home on lost Tanith.'

'We all have dreams of our old worlds,' said Daur cautiously. 'It's the guard curse.'

'Sure enough, Ban. I know that. I've been guard long enough. But not dreams like this. It's like... there's a meaning to be had. Like... Oh, I dunno...' Corbec frowned as he struggled to find adequate words.

'Like someone's trying to tell you something?' Daur whispered softly. 'Something important? Something that has to be done?'

'Sacred feth!' growled Corbec in amazement. 'That's it exactly! How did you know?'

Daur shrugged, and put his bowl down. 'I can't explain. I feel it too. I didn't realise... Well, I didn't until you started describing it there. It's not dreams I'm having. Gak, I don't think I'm dreaming much at all. But a feeling... like I should be doing something.'

'Feth,' murmured Corbec again.

'Are we mad, do you think? Maybe what we both need is a priest who's a good listener. A confessor. Maybe a head-doctor.'

Corbec dabbed his bread into the broth distractedly. 'I don't think so. I've nothing to confess. Nothing I haven't told you.'

'So what do we do?'

'I don't know. But I know there's no way in feth I'm getting on that troop ship tonight.'

HE'D STOLEN A few hours' sleep in a corner of the western city infirmary's entrance hall. But as the sun rose and the noise of people coming and going became too much to sleep through, Brin Milo shouldered his pack and rifle and began the long walk up the Amad Road into the centre of the Doctrinopolis.

Hark had told him to report to Guard command once he'd escorted the wounded party to safety. He was to present himself and arrange his place on an evacuation ship.

The city seemed like a place of madness around him. With the fighting over, the streets had filled up with hurrying crowds, honking motor vehicles, cargo trains hauled by servitors, processions of worshippers, pilgrims, protesters, refugees. The city was seething again, like a nalmite nest preparing to swarm.

Milo remembered the last, final hours in Tanith Magna, the same atmosphere of panic and activity. The memories were not pleasant. He decided he wanted to be out of here now, on a troop ship and away.

There was nothing here now he wanted to stay for, or needed to stay for.

A flustered Brevian Centennial on crowd control duties told him that Evacuation command had been established in the royal treasury, but the roads approaching that edifice were jammed with foot traffic and vehicles. The commotion was unbearable.

Transport shuttles shivered the sky as they lifted up over the holy city. A pair of navy fighters screamed overhead, low and fast.

Milo turned and headed for the Scholam Medicae where the Tanith wounded were being cared for. He'd find his own men, maybe Colonel Corbec, he decided. He'd leave with them.

'BRINNY BOY!' a delighted voice boomed behind him, and Milo was snatched up off his feet in a one-armed bear hug of crushing force.

'Bragg!' he smiled, turning as he was released.

'What are you doing here, Brin?' beamed Trooper Bragg.

'Long story,' said Milo. 'How's the arm there?'

Bragg glanced contemptuously at his heavily bandaged right shoulder.

'Fixing up. Fething medics refused to let me join the honour guard. Said it was a safe ticket out for me, feth 'em! It's not bad. I could've still fought.'

Milo gestured to the busy hallway of the Scholam Medicae Hagias they stood in. 'Anyone else around?'

'A few. Most of 'em in a bad way. Colonel's here somewhere, but I haven't seen him. I was in a bed next to Derin. He's on the mend and cussing his luck too.'

'I'm going to try and find the colonel. What ward are you in?'

'South six.'

'I'll come and find you in a bit.'

'You better!'

Milo pushed on through the hectic hallway, through the smells of blood and disinfectant, the hurrying figures, the rattling carts. He passed several doors that opened onto long, red-painted wards lined with critically injured guardsmen in rows of cots. Some were Ghosts, men he recognised. All were too far gone from pain and damage to register him. After asking questions of several orderlies and servitors, he found his way to Dorden's suite of offices on the third floor. As he approached, he could hear the shouting coming from inside down the length of the corridor.

'...don't just get up and walk off when you feel like it! For the Emperor's sake! You're hurt! That won't heal if you put a strain on it!'

An answering mumble.

'I will not calm down! The health of the regimental wounded is my business! Mine! You wouldn't disobey Gaunt's orders, why the feth do you think you can disobey mine?'

Milo walked into the office. Corbec was sitting on an examination couch facing the door, and his eyes opened wide when he saw Milo. Dorden, shaking with rage, stood facing Corbec and turned sharply when he read Corbec's expression.

'Milo?'

Corbec leapt up. 'What's happened? The honour guard? What the feth's happened?'

'There was an ambush on the road last night. We took a few injured, some bad enough Surgeon Curth wanted them brought back here. Commissar Hark volunteered me to ride shotgun. We got back here at dawn.'

'Are you meant to return?'

Milo shook his head. 'I'd never catch up with them now, colonel. My orders are to join the evacuation now I'm here.'

'How were they doing? Apart from the ambush, I mean?'

'Not so bad. They should've made it to the overnight stop at Mukret.'

'Did we lose many in the attack?' Dorden asked softly. His anger seemed to have dulled.

'Forty-three dead, fifteen of them Ghosts. Six Ghosts amongst the injured I brought back.'

'Sounds bad, Milo.'

'It was quick and nasty.'

'You can show me on the map where it happened,' Corbec told him.

'Why?' snapped Dorden. 'I've told you already, you're not going anywhere. Except to the landing fields this evening. Forget the rest, Colm. I mean it. I have seniority in this, and Lugo would have my fething head. Forget it.'

There was a loaded pause.

'Forget... what?' Milo dared to ask.

'Don't get him started!' Dorden roared.

'The boy's just asking, doc...' Corbec countered.

'You want to know, Milo? Do you?' Dorden was livid. 'Our beloved colonel here has this idea... No, let me start at the beginning. Our beloved colonel here decides he knows doctoring better than me, and so gets himself out of bed against my orders this morning! Goes wandering around the fething city!

We didn't even know where he was! Then he shows up again without so much as a by your leave, and tells me he's thinking of heading up into the mountains!'

'Into the mountains?'

'That's right! He's got it into his thick head that there's something important he's got to do! Something Gaunt, an armour unit and nigh on three thousand troopers can't manage without his help!'

'Be fair, I didn't quite say that, Doc...'

Dorden was too busy ranting at the rather stunned Milo. 'He wants to break orders. My orders. The lord general's orders. In a way, Gaunt's own orders. He's going to ignore the instructions to evacuate tonight. And go chasing up into the Sacred Hills after Gaunt. On his own! Because he has a hunch!'

'Not on my own,' Corbec growled in a whisper.

'Oh, don't tell me! You've persuaded some other fools to go along with you? Who? Who, colonel? I'll have them chained to their fething beds.'

'Then I won't tell you who, will I?' Corbec yelled.

'A... hunch...?' Milo asked quietly.

'Yeah,' said Corbec. 'Like one of me hunches...'

'Spare us! One of Colonel Corbec's famous battle-itches–'

Corbec wheeled round at Dorden and for a moment, Milo was afraid he was going to throw a punch. And even more afraid that the medic was going to throw one back. 'Since when have my tactical itches proved wrong, eh? Fething when?'

Dorden looked away.

'But, no... It's not like that. Not an itch. Not really. Or it's like the grandaddy of all battle-itches. It's more like a feeling–'

'That's all right then! A feth-damned feeling!' said Dorden sarcastically.

'More like a calling, then!' bellowed Corbec. 'Like the biggest, strongest calling I've ever had in me life! Pulling at me, demanding of me! Like... like if I've got the wit to respond, the balls to respond, I'll be doing the most important thing I could ever do.'

Dorden snorted. There was a long, painfully heavy pause.

'Colm... it's my job to look after the men. More than that, it's my pleasure to look after them. I don't need orders.' Dorden sat down behind his desk and fiddled with a sheaf of scripts, not making eye contact with either of the others. 'I came into Old

Town with Kolea– broke orders to do it– because I thought we might get you out alive.'

'And you did, doc, and feth knows, I owe you and the boys that one.'

Dorden nodded. 'But I can't sanction this. You– and anyone else you may have talked to– you all need to be at the muster point for evacuation at six tonight. No exceptions. It's an order from the office of the lord general himself. Any dissenters. Any absentees... will be considered as having deserted. And will suffer the full consequences.'

He looked up at Corbec. 'Don't do this to me, Colm.'

'I won't. They ask you, you don't know a thing. I'd have liked you to join me, doc, really I would, but I won't ask that of you. I understand the impossible position that'd put you in. But what I feel isn't wrong...'

'Corbec, please-'

'The last few nights, me dad's been in my dreams. Not just a memory, I mean. Really him. Bringing me a message.'

'What sort of message?' asked Milo.

'All he says is the same thing, over and over. He's in his machine shop, back in Pryze County, working the lathe there. I come in and he looks up and he says "sabbat martyr". Just that.'

'I know what's going on,' said Dorden. 'I feel it myself, it's perfectly natural. We both know this is Gaunt's last show. That Lugo's got his balls in a vice. And that means, let's face it, the end for the Ghosts. We all want to be there with Gaunt this last time. The honour guard, the last duty. It doesn't feel right to be missing it. We'd do anything... we'd think of any excuse... to get out there after him. Even subconsciously, our minds are trying to magic up ways to make it happen.'

'It's not that, doc.'

'I think it is.'

'Well then, maybe it is. Maybe it is me subconscious trying to jinx up an excuse. And maybe that's good enough for me. Gaunt's last show, doc. You said it yourself. They can court martial me, but I won't miss that. Not for anything.'

Corbec glanced at the silent Milo, patted him on the arm, and limped out of the office.

'Can you talk some sense into him, do you think?' Dorden asked Milo.

'From what I've just heard, I doubt it. In all candour, sir, I doubt I want to.'

Dorden nodded. 'Try, for my sake. If Corbec's not at the muster point tonight, I won't sell him out. But I can't protect him.'

CORBEC WAS IN his little room, sorting his pack on the unmade bed. Milo knocked at the half open door.

'You coming with me? I shouldn't ask. I won't be offended if you say no.'

'What's your plan?'

Corbec half-shrugged. 'Fethed if I know. Daur's with me. He feels the same. Really, he feels the same, you know?'

Milo said nothing. He didn't know.

'Daur's seeing if he can find any others crazy enough to come. We'll need able men. It won't be an easy ride.'

'It'll be hell. A small unit, moving west. The Infardi are everywhere. They didn't think twice about hitting a target the size of the taskforce.'

'We could so do with a scout. Local knowledge, maybe. I don't know.'

'Assuming we make it through, all the way to the Shrinehold. What then?'

'Feth me! I hope by then me dad will have told me more! Or maybe Daur will have figured it out. Or it'll be obvious...'

'It sure isn't obvious now, sir. Whatever it is, if Gaunt and the taskforce can't do it, how could we hope to?'

'Maybe they don't know. Maybe... they need to do something else.'

Corbec turned and smiled at Milo. 'You realise you've been saying "we", don't you?'

'I guess I have.'

'Good lad. It wouldn't be the same without you.'

'WELL, FETH BLESS my good soul!' said Colm Corbec. He was so touched by the sight before him, he felt he might cry. 'Did you all... I mean, are you all...?'

Bragg got up from the base of the pillar he was sitting against and stuck out his hand. 'We're all as crazy as you, chief,' he smiled.

Corbec gripped his meaty paw hard.

'Daur and Milo asked around. We're the only takers. I hope we'll do.'

'You'll do me fine.'

They stood in the shadows of the Munitorium warehouse on Pavane Street, off the main thoroughfare, out of sight. The contents of the warehouse had been evacuated that morning. It had been arranged as the rendezvous point. It was now close to six o'clock.

Somewhere, a troop ship was waiting for them. Somewhere, their names were being flagged on the commissariat discipline lists.

Corbec moved down the line as the assembled troopers got up to greet him. 'Derin! How's the chest?'

'Don't expect me to run anywhere,' smiled Trooper Derin. There was no sign of injury about him, but his arms moved stiffly. Corbec knew a whole lot of suturing and bandages lay under his black Tanith field jacket.

'Nessa... my girl.'

She threw him a salute, her long-las resting against her hip. *Ready to move out, colonel sir*, she signed.

'Trooper Vamberfeld, sir,' said the next in line. Corbec grinned at the pale, slightly out of condition Verghastite.

'I know who you are, Vamberfeld. Good to see you.'

'You said you needed local knowledge,' Milo said as Corbec reached him. 'This is Sanian. She's esholi, one of the student body.'

'Miss,' Corbec saluted her.

Sanian looked up at Corbec and appraised him frankly. 'Trooper Milo described your mission as almost spiritual, colonel. I will probably lose my privileges and status for absconding with you.'

'We're absconding now, are we?' The troopers around them laughed.

'The saint herself is in your mind, colonel. I can see that much. I have made my choice. If I can help by coming with you, I am happy to do it.'

'It won't be easy, Miss Sanian. I hope Milo's told you that much.'

'Sanian. I am just Sanian. Or esholi Sanian if you prefer to be formal. And yes, Milo has explained the danger. I feel it will be an education.'

'Safer ways of getting an education...' Derin began.

'Life itself is the education for the esholi,' said Milo smartly.

Sanian smiled. 'I think Milo has been paying too much attention to me.'

'Well, I can see why,' said Corbec, putting on the charm. 'You're welcome here with us. Do you know much about the land west of here?'

'I was raised in Bhavnager. And the western territories of the Sacred Hills and the Pilgrim's Way are fundamental knowledge for any esholi.'

'Well, didn't we just win the top prize?' grinned Corbec. 'So,' he said, turning to face the six of them. 'I guess we wait for Daur. He's in charge of transport.'

The group broke up into idle chatter for a minute or two. Suddenly, they all heard the clatter of tracks in the street outside. All of them froze, snatching up weapons, expecting the worst.

'What do you see?' Vamberfeld hissed to Bragg.

'It's the commissariat, isn't it?' said Derin. 'They're fething on to us!'

An ancient, battered Chimera rumbled into the warehouse. Its turbines coughed and rasped as they shut down. It was the oldest and worst kept piece of Munitorium armour Milo had ever seen, and that included the junk piles that had been given to the honour guard convoy.

The back hatch opened, and Daur edged out as gracefully as his aching wound allowed.

'Best I could do,' he said. 'It was one from the motorpool they're going to abandon in the evacuation.'

'Feth!' said Corbec, walking around the dirty green hulk. 'But it goes, right?'

'It goes for now,' replied Daur. 'What do you want, Corbec, miracles?'

A second man climbed out of the Chimera. He was a tall, blond, freckled individual in Pardus uniform. His head was bandaged.

'This is Sergeant Greer, Pardus Eighth Mobile Flak Company. I knew none of us could handle this beast, so I coopted a driver. Greer here... kind of owes me.'

'That's what he says,' Greer said sulkily. 'I'm just along for the ride.'

'Where'd you get the hurt?' Corbec asked him.

Greer touched his bandage. 'Glancing shot. During the action to take the census hall a few days back.'

Corbec nodded. The same action Daur had been hurt in. He shook Greer's hand.

'Welcome to the Wounded,' he said.

AT AROUND HALF past six, the names of troopers Derin, Vamberfeld, Nessa and Bragg, and of Captain Daur and Colonel Corbec, were noted in the log of the evacuation office as overdue. The lift shuttle left without them.

At a muster point further east across the Doctrinopolis, the Pardus chief surgeon noted the absence of Driver-Sergeant Greer.

Both reports were sent to Evacuation command and entered into the night log. The officer of the watch wasn't unduly taxed by this. He had over three hundred names on his list of absentees by then, and it was growing with each passing shuttle call. There were many reasons for missed muster: badly relayed orders; confusion as to the correct muster point; delays because of traffic in the holy city; un-logged deaths from the guard infirmaries. Indeed, some names on the evacuation lists were of troopers who had died in the liberation fight and as yet lay undiscovered and unidentified in the rubble.

Some, a very few, were deserters. Such names were passed to the discipline offices and the lord general's staff.

The officer of the watch passed these latest names on. It was unusual for senior officers like a colonel to fail to report.

By eight o'clock, the list had dropped onto the desk of Commissar Hychas, who was away at dinner. His aide passed it to the punishment detail, who by nine thirty had sent a four-man team led by a commissar-cadet down to the Scholam Medicae Hagias to investigate. A report was copied to Lord General Lugo's staff, where it was read by a senior adjutant shortly before midnight. He immediately voxed the punishment detail, and was told by the commissar-cadet that no trace of the missing personnel could be found at the Scholam Medicae.

At one in the morning, a warrant was issued for the arrest of Colonel Colm Corbec of the Tanith First-and-Only, along with six of his men. No one thought or knew to tally this with the warrant out for Sergeant-Driver Denic Greer of the Pardus Eighth. Or the theft report of a class gamma transport Chimera from the Munitorium motorpool.

By then, Corbec's Chimera was long gone, heading west down the Tembarong Road, five hours out from the city perimeter, thundering into the night.

It had made one stop, in the half-empty, wartorn suburb streets just short of the Pilgrim Gate. That had been around seven at night, with deep, starless dusk falling.

At the helm, Greer had seen a figure in the road ahead, waving at them. Corbec had popped the turret hatch and looked out, almost immediately calling down at Greer to pull over.

Corbec had dropped down from the waiting Chimera, his boots kissing the road dust, and had walked to meet the figure face to face.

'Sabbat martyr,' Dorden had said, tears in his eyes. 'My boy told me to. Don't think for a minute you're going without me.'

NINE
APPROACHING BHAVNAGER

'If the road is easy, the destination is worthless.'

— Saint Sabbat, proverbs

FROM MUKRET, THE highway ran due west to the Nusera Crossing where the holy river twisted across it. North of the crossing, the river's course snaked up to the headwaters in the hills, one hundred and fifty kilometres away.

The second day of the mission dawned soft and bright, with the lowland plains of the river valley dressed in thick white fogs. The scout spearhead under Mkoll left Mukret through the early fogs, travelling at a moderate rate because of the reduced visibility.

Gaunt and Kleopas had assembled three scout Salamanders carrying a dozen Ghost troopers between them, two Conqueror tanks and one of the two Destroyer tank hunters in the Pardus complement. The main taskforce set out from Mukret an hour behind them.

Gaunt's intention was to reach the farming community of Bhavnager by the second night. This meant a run of nearly ninety-five kilometres, on decent roads. But already the mists

153

were slowing their progress. At Bhavnager, so intelligence reported, they could refuel for the later stages of the journey. Bhavnager was the last settlement of appreciable size on the north-west spur of the highway. It marked the end of the arable lowlands and the start of the rainwood districts that dressed the climbing edges of the Sacred Hills. From Bhavnager, the going would become a lot tougher.

Ayatani Zweil had agreed to accompany the main taskforce, and rode with Gaunt in his command Salamander at the colonel-commissar's personal invitation. He seemed intrigued by the Imperial mission: no one had told him of the intended destination, but he clearly had ideas of his own, and once they took the north-west fork at Limata, there would be no disguising where they were heading.

'How long do these fogs last, father?' Gaunt asked him as the convoy ran through the pale, smoke-like mists. It was bright, and the fogs glowed with the sunlight beyond, but they could see only a few dozen metres ahead of themselves. The sounds of the convoy engines, amplified, were thrown back on them by the heavy vapour.

Zweil toyed with his long, white beard.

'In this part of the season, sometimes until noon. These, I think, are lighter. They will lift. And when they lift, they go suddenly.'

'You're not much like the other ayatani I've met here, if you'll forgive me saying so. They all seemed tied to a particular shrine and places of worship.'

Zweil chuckled. 'They are tempelum ayatani, devoted to their shrine places. I am imhava ayatani, which means "roving priest". Our order celebrates the saint by worshipping the routes of her journeys.'

'Her journeys here?'

'Yes, and beyond. Some of my kind are up there.' He pointed a gnarled finger at the sky, and Gaunt realised he meant space itself, space beyond Hagia.

'They travel the stars?'

'Indeed. They pace out the route of her Great Crusade, her war pilgrimage to Harkalon, her wide circuit of return. It can take a lifetime, longer than a lifetime. Few make the entire circuit and return to Hagia.'

'Especially in these times, I imagine.'

Zweil nodded thoughtfully. 'The return of the arch-enemy to the Sabbat Worlds has made such roving a more lethal undertaking.'

'But you are content to make your holy journeys here?'

Zweil smiled his broad, gap-toothed smile. 'These days, yes. But in my youth, I walked her path in the stars. To Frenghold, before Hagia called me back.'

Gaunt was a little surprised. 'You've travelled off this world?'

'We're not all parochial little peasants, Colonel-Commissar Gaunt. I've seen my share of the stars and other worlds. A few wonders on the way. Nothing I'd care to stay for. Space is over-rated.'

'I tend to find that too,' Gaunt grinned.

'The main purpose of the imhava ayatani is to retread the routes of the saint and offer assistance to the believers and pilgrims we find making their way. Guardians of the route. It is, I think, small-minded for a priest to stay at a shrine or temple to offer aid to the pilgrims who arrive. The journey is the hardest part. It is on the journey that most would have need of a priest.'

'That's why you agreed to come with us, isn't it?'

'I came because you asked. Politely, I might add. But you're right. You are pilgrims after all.'

'I wouldn't call us pilgrims quite–'

'I would. With devotion and resolve, you are following one of the saint's paths. You are going to the Shrinehold, after all.'

'I never said–'

'No, you didn't. But pilgrims usually travel east.' He gestured behind them in the vague direction of the Doctrinopolis. 'There's only one reason for heading this way.'

The vox squawked and Gaunt slid down into the driving well to answer it. Mkoll was checking in. The spearhead had just forded the holy river at Nusera and was making good speed to Limata. The fogs, Mkoll reported, were beginning to lift.

When Gaunt resumed his seat, he found Zweil looking through his ragged copy of Sabbat's gospel.

'A well-thumbed book,' said Zweil, making no attempt to set it aside. 'Always a good sign. I never trust a pilgrim with a clean and pristine copy. The texts you've marked are interesting. You can tell much of a man's character by what he chooses to read.'

'What can you tell about me?'

'You are burdened... hence the numerous annotations in the Devotional Creeds... and burdened by responsibility and the demands of office in particular... these three selections in the Epistles of Duty show that you seek answers, or perhaps ways of fighting internal daemons... that is plain from the number of paper strips you've used to mark the pages of the Doctrines and Revelations. You appreciate battle and courage... the Annals of War, here... and you are sentimental when it comes to fine devotional poetry...'

He held the book out open to show the Psalms of Sabbat.

'Very good,' said Gaunt.

'You smile, Colonel-Commissar Gaunt.'

'I am an Imperial commander leading a taskforce of war on a mission. You could have surmised all that about me without even looking at the bookmarks.'

'I did,' laughed Zweil. He carefully closed the gospel and handed it back to Gaunt.

'If I might say, colonel-commissar... the gospel of our saint does contain answers. But the answers are often not literal ones. Simply reading the book from cover to cover will not reveal them. One has to... feel. To look around the bare meanings of the words.'

'I studied textual interpretation at Scholam Progenium...'

'Oh, but I'm sure you did. And from that I'm sure you can tell me that when the saint talks of the "flower incarnadine" she means battle, and when she refers to "the fast-flowing river of pure water" she means true human faith. What I mean to say is the lessons of Saint Sabbat are oblique mysteries, to be unlocked by experience and innate belief. I'm not sure you have those. The answers you seek would have come to you by now if you had.'

'I see.'

'I meant no disrespect. There are high ayatani in the holy city who do no more than read and reread this work and fancy themselves enlightened.'

Gaunt didn't reply. He looked out of the rocking tank and saw how the fog was beginning to burn off with remarkable haste. Already the tree-lines at the river were becoming visible.

'Then how do I begin?' Gaunt asked darkly. 'For, truth be told, father, I have need of answers. Now more than ever before.'

'I can't help you there. Except to say, start with yourself. It is a journey you must make, standing still. I told you you were a pilgrim.'

Half an hour later, they reached the crossing at Nusera. The highway came down to a wide, shallow pan of shingle that broke the fast flowing water in a broad fording place. Groves of ghylum trees clustered at either bank, and hundreds of fork-bills broke upwards into the sky in an explosive fan at the sound of the motors, their wings beating the air with the sound of ornithopter gunships.

A lone peasant with an ancient cow chelon on a pull-rein waved them past. One by one, the vehicles of the honour guard ploughed over the ford, spraying up water so hard and high that rainbows marked their wake.

LIMATA WAS ANOTHER dead town. Mkoll's spearhead reached it just before eleven thirty. The fogs had vanished. The sun was climbing and the air was still. This day was going to be even hotter than the last.

The baking roofs of Limata lay ahead, dusty and forlorn, their tiles bright pink in the sunlight. No breeze, no sounds, no telltale fingers of cookfire smoke rising above the village. Here, the Tembarong Road divided, one spur heading southwest towards Hylophon and Tembarong itself. The other broke north-west into the highlands and the steaming tracts of the rainwoods. Forty-plus kilometres in that direction lay Bhavnager.

'Slow to steady,' Mkoll snapped into his vox. 'Troopers arm. Load main weapons. Let's crawl in.'

Captain Sirus, commanding the Pardus elements, voxed in immediately from his Conqueror. 'Allow us, Tanith. We'll drive 'em down.'

'Negative. Full stop.'

The vehicles came to a halt six hundred metres short of the town perimeter. The Ghosts dismounted from the Salamanders. Idling engines rumbled in the hot, dry air.

'What's the delay?' Sirus snapped over the vox.

'Stand by,' replied Mkoll. He glanced around at Trooper Domor, one of the disembarked troopers. 'You sure?'

'Sure as they call me Shoggy,' Domor nodded, carefully using a felt cloth to wipe dust grit from the lenses of his augmetic eyes. 'You can see the way the road surface there is broken and repacked.'

Most eyes couldn't but Mkoll's were sharper than any in the regiment. And Domor's field specialisation was in landmines.

'Want me to sweep?'

'Might be an idea. Unship your kit, but don't advance until I say.'

Domor went over to his Salamander with troopers Caober and Uril to unpack the sweeper sets.

Mkoll fanned fire-teams out into the acestus groves on either side of the roadway, Mkvenner to the left and Bonin to the right, each with three men.

Within seconds of entering the dappled shadows of the fruit trees, the men were invisible, their stealth cloaks absorbing the patterns around them.

'What's the delay?' asked Captain Sirus from behind. Mkoll turned. Sirus had dismounted from his waiting Conqueror, the *Wrath of Pardua*, and had come forward to see for himself. He was a robust man in his early fifties, with the characteristic olive skin and beak nose of the Pardus. He seemed a little gung-ho to Mkoll, and the scout sergeant had been disappointed when Kleopas had appointed him to Mkoll's spearhead company.

'We've got road mines in a tight field there. And maybe beyond.' Mkoll gestured. 'And the place is too quiet for my liking.'

'Tactics?' Sirus asked briefly.

'Send my sweepers forward to clear the road for you and infiltrate the village from the sides with my troops.'

Sirus nodded sagely. 'I can tell you're infantry, sergeant. Bloody good at it too, so I hear, but you haven't the armour experience. You want that place taken, my *Wrath* can take it.'

Mkoll's heart sank. 'How?'

'That's what the Adeptus Mechanicus made dozer blades for. Give the word and I'll show you how the Pardus work.'

Mkoll turned away and walked back to his Salamander. This wasn't his approach to recon patrols. He certainly didn't want the Pardus heavies lighting up the hill for all to see with their heavy guns. He could take Limata his way, by stealth, he was sure. But Gaunt had urged him to co-operate with the armour allies.

He reached into the Salamander and pulled out the long-gain vox mic.

'Recon Spear to one.'

'One, go ahead.'

'We've got possible obstruction here at Limata. Certainly a minefield. Request permission for Captain Sirus to go in armoured and loud.'

'Is it necessary?'

'You said to play nice.'

'So I did. Permission granted.'

Mkoll hung up the mic and called to Domor's group. 'Pack it away. It's the Pardus's turn.'

Griping, they began to disassemble the sweeper brooms.

'Captain?' Mkoll looked over to Sirus. 'It's all yours.'

Sirus looked immensely pleased. He ran back to his revving tank.

At his urging, riding high in the open hatch of his turret, the two Conquerors clanked past the waiting Salamanders and headed down the highway. The grim Destroyer waited behind them, turbines barely murmuring.

The two battle tanks lowered their hefty dozer blades as they came up on the mined area and dug in, driving forward.

Captain Sirus's mine clearance methods were as brutal as they were deafening. The massive dozer blades ploughed the hardpan of the road and kicked up the buried munitions which triggered and detonated before them. Clouds of flame and debris swirled up around the advancing tanks. If the mines had been triggered under a passing vehicle, they would have crippled or destroyed it, but churned out like the seeds of a waterapple or flints turned up by a farrier's plough, they exploded harmlessly, barely scorching the thrusting dozer blades.

It was an impressive display, Mkoll had to admit.

Smoke and dust drifted back down the road over Mkoll and the waiting Salamanders. Mkoll shielded his eyes and purposely kept his off-road fire-teams in position.

In less than six minutes, the *Wrath of Pardua* and its sister tank *Lion of Pardua* were rolling into Limata, the road buckled and burning behind them.

Mkoll got up on the fender of his Salamander and ordered all three light tanks to move forward after them.

He looked round. The Destroyer had disappeared.

'What the feth?' How did something that big and heavy and ugly disappear?

'Recon Spear command to Destroyer! Where the feth are you?'

'Destroyer to command. Sorry to startle you. Standard regimental deployment. I pulled off-road to lie low. Frontal assaults are the Conquerors' job, and Sirus knows what he's doing.'

'Read that, Destroyer.' Mkoll, who was generally inexperienced when it came to tank warfare, had already noted the clear differences between the Conqueror battle tanks and the low-bodied Destroyers. Where the Conquerors were high and proud, stately almost, with their massive gun turrets, the Destroyers were long-hulled and sleek, their one primary weapon not turret-mounted but fixed out forward from their humped backs. The Destroyers were predators, tank hunters, armed with a single, colossal laser cannon. They were, it seemed to Mkoll, the tank equivalent of an infantry sniper. Accurate, cunning, hard-hitting, stealthy.

The Destroyer appointed to the Recon Spear was called the *Grey Venger*. Its commander was a Captain LeGuin. Mkoll had never seen LeGuin face to face. He just knew him by his tank.

Through the rising pall of smoke, Mkoll saw the Conquerors were in the village now. They were kicking up dust. Abrupt small arms fire rained against their armoured bodies from the left.

The *Wrath of Pardua* traversed its turret and blew a house apart with a single shell. Its partner began shelling the right flank of the town's main drag. Stilt houses disintegrated or combusted. The sponson-mounted flamers on both Conquerors rippled through the close-packed buildings and turned them into torched ruins.

Captain Sirus's whoops of triumph came over the vox. Mkoll could see him in his turret, supporting his main weapon's blasts with rakes from the pintle mount.

'That's just showing off,' Domor said beside him.

'Tank boys,' murmured Caober. 'Always wanting to show who's boss.'

Advancing, they found the bloody, burnt remnants of maybe three dozen Infardi in the ruins Sirus had flattened. Limata was taken. Mkoll signalled the news to Gaunt and advanced the spearhead, bringing his fire-teams in and reforming the force with the Salamanders at the front. The Destroyer trundled out of hiding and joined the back of the column.

'Next stop Bhavnager!' Sirus warbled enthusiastically from his Conqueror.

'Move out,' ordered Mkoll.

WELL OVER A day behind them, Corbec's thrown-together team rolled past the site of the ambush, skirting around the wrecks of the Salamanders and the Chimera that the taskforce's Trojans had pushed to the roadside verges.

Corbec called a halt. The Chimera's turbine was overheating anyway, and the troopers dismounted for a rest.

Corbec, Derin and Bragg wandered over to the roadside where a plot of dark earth and rows of fresh-cut stakes marked the graves of the fallen.

'One we missed,' said Derin.

Corbec nodded. This site marked the first Ghosts action that he hadn't been a part of. Not properly. All the way from Tanith he'd come, to be with his men. Here, they'd fought and died while he had been lying in his bed miles away.

His chest hurt. He swallowed a couple more pain-pills with a swig of tepid water from his flask.

Greer had dismounted from the Chimera on the road and had yanked back its side cowlings to vent greasy black smoke. He reached in with a wrench, trying to soothe its ailing systems.

Milo thought he'd talk to Sanian, but the esholi had wandered down to the water's edge with Nessa. It looked like the Verghastite girl was teaching the student the rudiments of sign language.

'She likes to learn, doesn't she?'

Milo looked round and met Captain Daur's smile. 'Yes, sir.'

'I'm glad you found her, Brin. I don't think we'd last long without a decent guide.'

Milo sat himself down on a roadside stump and Daur sat next to him, cautiously nursing his wounded body down.

'What do you know, sir?' Milo asked.

'About what?'

'About this mission. Corbec said you knew as much as him. That you – uh – felt the same way.'

'I can't offer you an explanation, if that's what you're asking for. I just have this urge in my head...'

'I see.'

'No, you don't. And I know you don't. And I love you like a brother for daring to come this far in such ignorance.'

'I trust the colonel.'

'So do I. Have you not had dreams? Visions?'

'No, sir. All I have is my loyalty to Corbec. To you. To Gaunt. To the God-Emperor of mankind...'

'The Emperor protects,' Daur put in dutifully.

'That's all. Loyalty. To the Ghosts. That's all I know. For now, that's all I need.'

'But you delivered to us our guide,' a calm, frail voice said suddenly.

'I did what?'

Daur paused and blinked.

'What?' he asked Milo, who was looking at him mistrustfully.

'You said "but you delivered to us our guide"... just then. Your voice was strange.'

'Did I? Was it?'

'Yes, sir.'

'I meant Sanian...'

'I know you did, but that was a pretty odd way of saying it.'

'I don't remember... Gak, I don't remember saying that at all.'

Milo looked at Daur dubiously. 'With all respect, captain, you're weirding me out here.'

'Milo, I think I'm weirding myself out,' he said.

'Doc.'

'Corbec.'

They stood in the groves overlooking the burial place. It was the first chance they'd got to talk alone since leaving the Doctrinopolis.

'Your son, you say? Mikal?'

'My son.'

'In your dreams?'

'For days now. I think it started when I was looking for you in Old Town, you old bastard.'

'You haven't dreamt of Mikal before?'

Mikal Dorden had died on Verghast. He had been the only Tanith to escape the destruction of that world with a blood relative alive. Trooper Mikal Dorden. Chief Medic Tolin Dorden. Ghosts together, father and son, until... Vervunhive and Veyveyr Gate.

'Of course. Every night. But not like that. This was like Mikal wanted me to know something, to be somewhere. All he said was "sabbat martyr". When you said the words too, I realised.'

'It's going to be hard,' said Corbec softly, 'getting up there.' He pointed up towards the Sacred Hills, which lingered distantly, partly obscured by the smudge of a rainstorm over the woods.

'I'm ready, Colm,' Dorden smiled. 'I think the others are too. But keep your eye on Trooper Vamberfeld. His first taste of combat hasn't gone down well. Shock trauma. He may get past it naturally, but some don't. I don't think he should be here.'

'In truth, none of us should. I took what I could get. But point taken. I'll be watching him.'

'I RESPECT YOU.'

'I'm sure you do, buddy,' said Greer, nursing the old Chimera's engines back to health.

'But I do, I respect you,' repeated Trooper Vamberfeld.

'And why's that?' asked Greer off-hand as he unclamped a fuel pipe.

'To join this pilgrimage. It's so holy. So, so holy.'

'Oh, it's so holy sure enough,' growled Greer.

'Did the spirit of the saint speak to you?' Vamberfeld asked.

Greer looked round at him with a cynical eyebrow cocked. 'Did she speak to you?'

'Of course she did! She was triumphant and sublime!'

'That's great. Right now, I've got an engine to fix.'

'The saint will guide your work...'

'Will she crap! The moment Saint Sabbat manifests here and helps me flush out the intercooler, then I'll believe.'

Vamberfeld looked a little crestfallen. 'Then why do you come?'

'The gold, naturally,' Greer said, over-stressing each word as one would to a child.

'What gold?'

'The gold. In the mountains. Daur must've told you about it?'

'N-no...'

'Only reason I'm here! The gold ingots. My kind of come-on.'

'But there is no treasure. Nothing physical. Just faith and love.'

'Whatever you reckon.'

'The captain wouldn't lie.'

'Of course he wouldn't.'

'He loves us all.'

'Of course he does. Now if you'll excuse me...'

Vamberfeld nodded and walked away obediently. Greer shook his head to himself and returned to work. He didn't get these Tanith, too intense for his liking. And ever since he'd arrived on Hagia he'd heard men rambling on and on about faith and miracles. So, it was a shrineworld. So what? Greer didn't hold with that sort of stuff much. You lived, you died, end of story. Sometimes you got lucky and lived well. Sometimes you got unlucky and died badly. God and saints and fricking angels and stuff was the sort of nonsense men filled their with heads with when bad luck came calling.

He wiped his hands on a rag, and cinched the hose clamp tighter. This mob of losers was a crazy lot. The colonel and the doctor and that complete sad-case Vamberfeld were mooning on about visions and saints, clearly all out of their heads. The deaf girl he didn't get. The big guy was an idiot. The boy Milo was way too up himself, and only here because he had the hots for that local girl, who was incidentally a nutjob in Greer's humble opinion. Derin was the only one who seemed remotely okay. Greer was sure that was because Derin was along for the gold too. Daur must have persuaded the rest of the lunatics to sign on by buying into their saint fixations.

Daur was a hard case. He looked all clean-cut and stalwart, the very model of a young, well-bred officer. But under the surface ticked the heart of a conniving bastard. Greer knew his type. Greer hadn't liked Daur since the moment they'd met in the prayer yard. Dressing him down in front of his men like that. Greer had only ended up wounded because he'd been going balls-out in the fight to prove his mettle and win back his rep. But Daur had needed a driver, and he'd cut Greer in on the loot. Temple gold, stacks of ingots, taken secretly from the Doctrinopolis treasury to a place of hiding when the Infardi invaded. That's what Daur had told him. He'd got the inside track from a dying ayatani. Worth deserting for in Greer's book.

He wouldn't be surprised if Daur intended to waste the others once they were home and dry. Greer would be watching his back when the time came. He'd get in first if he had to. For now though, he knew he was safe. Daur needed him more than any of the others.

Vamberfeld was the one he worried about most. Daur had recruited everyone except Sanian and Milo from the hospital, from amongst the injured, and they all had bandaged wounds to prove it. Except Vamberfeld. He was a psych case, Greer knew. The timid behaviour, the thousand-metre stare. He'd seen that before in men who were on the way to snapping. War fever.

Greer didn't want to be around when the snap came.

HE CLOSED THE engine cowling. 'She's running! Let's go if we're going!'

The company moved back to rejoin the Chimera. For the umpteenth time that day, Corbec wondered what he had got himself into. Sometimes it felt so decisively right, but the rest of the time the doubts plagued him. He'd broken orders, and persuaded eight other guardsmen to do the same. And now he was heading into enemy country. He wondered what would happen if they got into a situation. Milo was sound and able bodied, but the doc and Sanian were non-combatants. Nessa was strapped up with a healing las-wound in her belly, Bragg's shoulder was useless, Daur and Derin had chest wounds that slowed them down badly, Greer had a head-wound, and Vamberfeld was teetering on the edge of nervous collapse. Not to mention his own, aching wounds.

Hardly the most able and fit fire-team in the history of guard actions. Nor the best equipped. Each trooper had a lasrifle – in Nessa's case a long-las sniper model – and Bragg had his big autocannon. They had a box of tube-charges but were otherwise short on ammo. As far as he knew they had only half a dozen drums for the cannon. The Chimera had a storm bolter on its pintle, but given its performance so far, Corbec wasn't sure how much longer it would be before they were all walking.

He wondered what Gaunt would do in this situation. He was pretty sure he knew.

Have them all shot.

* * *

THROUGH THE TREES, thick roadside glades of acestus and slim-trunked vipirium, they began to see the outlines of Bhavnager.

It was late afternoon, the sun was infernally bright and hot, and the heat haze was distorting every distance. The Recon Spear had made excellent time, and word on the vox was that the main convoy was only seventy minutes behind them.

Mkoll pulled them to a halt and headed out into the groves with Mkvenner to do a little scouting. They crouched in the slanting shadows of the wild fruit trees and panned their mag-noculars around. The air was still and breathless, as dry and hot as baked sand. Insects ticked like chronometers in the gorse thickets.

Mkoll compared what he saw with the town plan on his map. Bhavnager was a large place, dominated by a large white-washed temple with a golden stupa to the east and a massive row of brick-built produce barns to the south-west. Prayer kites and flags dangled limply from the golden dome in the breeze-less air. The road they were following entered in the south-eastern corner, ran in south of the temple to what looked like a triangular market place which roughly denoted the town centre, and then appeared again north of large buildings on the far outskirts that Mkoll took to be machine shops. A streetplan of smaller roads radiated out from the market, lined with shops and dwellings.

'Looks quiet,' said Mkvenner.

'But alive this time. Figures there, in the market.'

'I see them.'

'And two up there, on the lower balcony of the temple.'

'Lookouts.'

'Yeah.'

The pair moved forward and down a little, parallel to the highway. Once the road came out of the fruit groves it was open and unprotected for over fifteen hundred metres right down to the edge of the town. Trees had been felled and brush cleared.

'They don't want anyone sneaking up on them, do they?'

Mkoll held up his hand, the signal for quiet. They both now detected movement in the trees twenty metres to their right, right on the road itself.

With Mkvenner a few paces behind him in cover, las raised, Mkoll slid forward silently through the dry undergrowth. He slipped his silver blade from its sheath.

The man was watching the road from a small culvert under the trees, His back was to Mkoll. The vehicles of the Recon Spear were out of sight beyond the road turn, but he must have heard their engines. Had he sent a signal already or was he waiting to see what came around the bend?

Mkoll took him out with a fast, sudden lunge. The man didn't have time to realise he was dead.

He was dressed in green silk, his filthy skin livid with tattoos. Infardi.

Mkoll checked the corpse and found an old autorifle but no vox set. Tucked into a hand-dug hole in the side of the culvert was a round mirror. Simple but effective signalling, perhaps to another invisible spotter down the road. How many others? Had they already rolled in past some?

He looked back at the town in time to see sunlight glint and flash off something on the temple balcony. A minute or so later, it repeated.

An answer? A question? A routine check? Mkoll wondered whether to use the mirror or not. He'd tip them off if he got the signal wrong, but would a lack of response be as bad?

The flash from the temple came again.

'Chief?' Mkvenner hissed over the headset vox.

'Go.'

'I see flash-signals.'

'On the temple?'

'No. Far side of the road from you, about thirty metres, right where the tree-line ends.'

Mkvenner had a better angle. Mkoll moved back out of the culvert softly and edged down a little way, his stealth cloak pulled around him. He could see the man now, on the far side of the road under a swathe of camo-netting. The man was looking up the highway and seemed not to have made out Mkoll yet.

Mkoll sheathed his blade and took up his lasrifle. The sound suppressor was screwed in place. He seldom took it off in country.

He waited for the man to shift around and raise his mirror again and then put a single shot through his ear. The Infardi spotter tumbled back out of sight.

The scouts headed back to the Recon Spear. Sirus was waiting, with the commander of the other Conqueror.

'No idea of numbers but the place is held by the enemy,' explained Mkoll. 'We picked off a couple of lookouts on the road. They're watching the approach carefully and they've made the south edge of the town clear. I'd prefer to take the time to disperse my troops into the woods here to clear for other spotters and maybe make a crawl approach after dark, but I think the clock's against us. They'll notice their spotters are quiet before long, if they haven't already.'

'We'll have the whole bloody convoy bunching up behind us in less than an hour,' said Sirus.

'Maybe that's how to play it,' said the other commander, a short man called Farant or Faranter, Mkoll hadn't quite caught it. 'Wait until the main elements arrive and then just go in, full strength.'

It made sense to Mkoll. They could waste a lot of time here trying to be clever. Maybe this was an occasion where sheer brute force and might were the best course. Simple, direct, emphatic. No messing about.

'I'll get on the vox and run it past the boss,' he said, and walked over to his Salamander.

There was a faint, distant bang, muffled by the dead air of the hot afternoon. A second later, a whooping shriek came down out of the sky.

'Incoming!' Sirus yelled. All the men broke for cover.

With a roar, the shell hit the roadline twenty-five metres short of them and blew a screen of trees out onto the track. After a moment, two more exploded in the trees to their left, hurling earth and flames into the cloudless blue.

Soil drizzled down over them. Both Conquerors came around the Salamanders, the *Wrath of Pardua* leading the way. More shells now, detonating all around them. The enemy had either done an excellent job of range-finding or had just got very lucky.

'Hold! Sirus, hold back!' Mkoll yelled into the vox as his Salamander lurched forward. He had to duck as debris from a perilously close shell rattled across the hull.

This was shelling from more than one gun. Multiple points, field guns maybe, large calibre ordnance by the size of the shell strikes. Where the hell were they hiding a battery of artillery?

Farant's Conqueror suddenly came apart in a huge fireball. The explosion was so fierce the shockwave punched Mkoll off his feet. Splintered armour shards rained down. Caober cried out as one ripped his forehead.

The blazing remains of the Pardus tank filled the centre of the road, turret disintegrated, bodywork fused and twisted, tread segments disengaged and scattered. The *Wrath* was beyond it, moving down the roadway.

'Enemy armour! Enemy armour!' Sirus bawled over the vox-link.

Mkoll saw them. Two main battle tanks, painted bright lime green, main guns roaring as they tore their way out through the fruit tree stands and onto the road ahead.

That was why he'd seen no artillery positions. It wasn't artillery.

The Infardi had armoured vehicles. Lots of them.

TEN
THE BATTLE OF BHAVNAGER

'Do not shirk! Do not falter!
Give them death in the name of Sabbat!'

— Saint Sabbat, at the gates of Harkalon

HEEDLESS OF THE 105mm shells tearing into the highway and trees around him, Sirus confronted the Infardi armour head-on. The *Wrath of Pardua* sped forward with a clank of treads and fired its main gun. The hypervelocity round hit the nearest of the two enemy vehicles, exploding into the rear mantlet of its turret with such force the entire turret mount spun round through two hundred and ten degrees. The tank clearly retained motive power, because it continued to churn along the road, but its traverse system was crippled and the turret and weapon swung around slackly with the motion. The *Wrath* fired again, mere seconds before a shell from the second tank glanced lengthways along its starboard flank. The hit buckled and tore its track guards and then fragmented off into the trees.

The *Wrath's* second shot had missed. The disarmed Infardi machine was closing to less than forty metres now, and its hull-mounted lascannon began to spit bolts of blue light at Sirus's

171

Conqueror. The other enemy tank was trying to pull around its wounded colleague for a clearer shot, knocking down a row of saplings and small acestus trees as it hauled half its bulk off the highway and through the verge underbrush. Heavy shelling from as yet unseen Infardi units continued to lacerate the position.

With furious las-fire from the injured tank now splashing off the *Wrath of Pardua's* front casing, Sirus ordered his layer to address the other tank coming around the first. Re-laying the gun took a vital second. In that time, the second tank fired again and hit the *Wrath* squarely. The impact was enough to lurch all sixty-two tonnes of armoured machine several metres sideways. But it didn't penetrate the twenty centimetre-thick armour skin. Inside, the crew was dazed, and they'd lost most of the forward scopes. Sirus bellowed to retask, but the tank was now right on them and looming for the kill.

A devastating lance of laser fire raked past the *Wrath* and cut through the assaulting vehicle below the turret. Internally stored munitions went off and the tank exploded with such force that the main body and track assemblies cartwheeled over in a blistering fireball. The blast wake and shrapnel cleared a semicircle of woodland twenty metres in radius.

The Destroyer *Grey Venger* had struck.

From the open cab of his rapidly reversing Salamander, Mkoll saw the long, low Destroyer prowl past, palls of heat discharge spuming from the vent louvres around its massive fixed laser cannon. It nudged aside the burning wreck of Farant's dead Conqueror and came up alongside the *Wrath*.

But the crew of the *Wrath of Pardua* had recovered their wits and swiftly nailed the remaining aggressor hard at short range, blowing out its port track sections and shunting it away lame with the shell impact. It began to burn.

By then, the trio of scout Salamanders had reversed far enough to be able to turn.

'Break off and retreat!' Mkoll shouted into the vox. 'Fall back to waymark 00.58!'

LeGuin immediately acknowledged, but Mkoll got nothing from Sirus.

Fething idiot wants to stay in the fight, Mkoll thought. From his machine's tactical auspex, he counted at least ten good-size targets moving up towards their position from Bhavnager.

But Sirus suddenly appeared out of the *Wrath's* top hatch, looking back through the gusting smoke to Mkoll. The last hit had taken out his vox system and intercom. Mkoll made damn sure Sirus understood his hand signals.

The *Grey Venger* stood its ground and walloped two more incandescent blasts down the road at targets Mkoll couldn't see. Probably just discouragement tactics, he thought. Who wants to ride an MBT into woodland cover when you know an Imperial Destroyer is waiting for you?

The *Wrath of Pardua* reversed hard and swung around to follow the Salamanders, traversing its turret to the rear to cover their backs. Then, as it too began bravura discouragement shelling, the *Venger* came about and trundled after them all so fast its hull rocked and rose nose up on its well-sprung torsion bar traction.

Deafened and a little bloodied, the Recon Spear made off down the highway away from the bombardment, which continued for some fifteen minutes after they had withdrawn. There was no sign of pursuit.

Mkoll voxed the bad news to Gaunt.

KEEPING A WEATHER eye on the northern approaches for signs of the enemy, the Recon Spear waited to rendezvous with the main honour guard strength at waymark 00.58, a west-facing escarpment of grass pasture fifteen kilometres south of Bhavnager.

The sun was beginning to sink and the intense heat of the day was dissipating. A southerly was blowing cooler air down from the misty shapes of the Sacred Hills, which now could be seen rising above the wide green blanket of the rainwoods on the northern horizon.

Mkoll got out of his Salamander, passing Bonin who was field stitching the gash in Caober's face, and walked towards the *Wrath of Pardua*. He took the time to gaze at the Sacred Hills: dark uplands seventy kilometres away, then behind them, higher peaks fading to an insubstantial grey in the distance. Behind them still, about a hundred kilometres beyond, the majestic jagged summits of the Sacred Hills proper: transparent, icy titans with their heads lost in ribbons of cloud, nine thousand metres above sea level.

It was quite a prospect.

The fact that getting there involved struggling past at least one enemy tank unit dug into their only guaranteed fuel depot, then rainwood jungle, then increasingly high mountains, made it all the more chilling.

Thunder, the reveille call of a too hot day in summer, crackled around the neighbouring hills. The taste of rain was a promise on the rising breeze. Swells of grey cloud, as mottled as Imperial air-camo schemes, rolled in from the north, staining a sky that had otherwise been cloudless and blue since the fogs lifted that morning.

Small chelons and goat-like herbivores grazed and ruminated in the lush meadows beyond the raised pasture of the waymark point. Their throat bells clanged dully as they moved.

Sirus and his men were running emergency repairs to the great, wounded *Wrath of Pardua*. They were joking and laughing with their captain, revelling in the details of the recent combat and the fact they had come away alive. No one spoke of the dead crew. There would be due time for recognition later. Mkoll felt sure that once the obstacle of Bhavnager was done with, there would be more than one Conqueror to mourn.

A figure approached him across the wind-shivered grass. Mkoll knew at once it was the so far unseen LeGuin. He was a short, well-made man in his thirties, dressed in tan Pardus fatigues and a fleece-lined leather coat. He unbuttoned his leather skull-guard as he approached, unplugging the wire of his headset.

His skin was darker than most of the Pardus men, his eyes glittering blue.

'Cool head, sergeant,' he said, offering Mkoll his hand.

'Looked mighty tight there for a minute,' Mkoll replied.

'It was, but so are the best fights.'

'I thought Sirus might blow it,' Mkoll ventured.

LeGuin smiled. 'Anselm Sirus is a bravo and a glory hound. He's also the best Conqueror boss in the Pardus. Except maybe for Woll. They have a rivalry. Both multi-aces. But permit Sirus his heroics. He's the very best.'

Mkoll nodded. 'I know similar infantrymen. I thought they'd got him there, though. But for you.'

'My greatest pleasure in life is using my girl's main mount to effect. I was just doing my job.'

The *Grey Venger* lay nearby, hull down in a grassy lea, its massive muzzle pointing north up the road. Mkoll reflected that if he'd ever been schooled into armour, a Destroyer would have been his machine of choice. As far as fifty-plus tonnes of rattling armoured power could be said to be stealthy, it was a silent predator. A hunter. Mkoll had a kinship with hunters. He'd been one all his adult life before the guard and, in truth, he'd been one ever since too.

Some of the grazers in the meadow below suddenly looked up and began to move away west.

A minute later, they heard the gathering thunder from the south.

'Here they come,' said LeGuin.

THE HONOUR GUARD assembled at the waymark, spreading its strength out in a firm defensive line facing the north. As the tanks took up station, the Hydra batteries behind them, the infantry dismounted and dug in.

'Now we'll see fun, sure as sure,' Trooper Cuu informed Larkin as they took position in the grasses.

'Not too much fun, I hope,' Larkin mumbled back, test-sighting up his long-las.

As the force secured the position, Gaunt called his operational and section chiefs for a briefing. They assembled around the back of his Salamander: Kleopas, Rawne, Kolea, Hark, Surgeon Curth, tank commanders, squad leaders, platoon sergeants. Some brought dataslates, some charts. Most clutched tin cups of fresh brewed caffeine or smokes.

'Opinions?' he asked, drawing the briefing to order.

'We've got no more than four hours of light left. Half of that will go getting into position,' Kleopas said. 'I take it we're looking at dawn instead.'

'That means we're looking at noon at least to refuel and turn around, provided we can break Bhavnager,' replied Rawne. 'That's half a day chopped off our timetable just like that.'

'So what?' Kleopas asked cynically. 'Are you saying we rush ahead and hit them up tonight, major?'

Some of the Pardus laughed.

'Yes,' Rawne answered coldly, as if it was so obvious Kleopas must be a fool to miss it. 'Why lose the daylight we have left? Is there another way?'

'Airstrike,' said Commissar Hark. To a man, the tank soldiers moaned.

'Oh, please! This is a prime opportunity to engage with armour,' said Sirus. 'Leave this to us.'

'I'll tell you what it is, captain,' said Gaunt darkly. 'This is a prime opportunity to discharge a mission for the God-Emperor as expediently and efficiently as we can. What it's not is an opportunity to let you heap up glory by forcing a tank fight.'

'I don't think that's what Sirus meant, sir,' said Kleopas as Sirus scowled.

'I think it's exactly what he meant,' said Hark lightly.

'Whatever he meant, I've been talking to navy strike command at Ansipar. The air wing is tied up with the evacuation. They wouldn't tell me more than that. We might get an airstrike if we wait two days. As Major Rawne pointed out, time is not for wasting. We're going to take Bhavnager ourselves, the hard way.'

Sirus smiled. There was murmuring.

Gaunt consulted the assessment reports on-slate. 'We know they have at least ten armour units. Non-Imperial MBTs.'

'At least ten,' repeated Sirus. 'I doubt they would have fielded their entire complement to chase off a raid.'

'Type and capability?' Gaunt asked, looking up.

'Urdeshi-made tanks, type AT70s,' said LeGuin. 'Indifferent performance and slow on the fire rate. 105 mil guns as standard. They're common here in this subsector and favoured by the arch-enemy.'

'They've been cranking them out of the manufactories on Urdesh ever since the foe took that world,' said LeTaw, another tank officer.

'The Reaver model by the look of the ones I saw,' LeGuin went on. 'Promethium guzzlers with cheap armour, and loose in the rear on a turn. Our Conquerors outclass them. Unless they have the numbers, of course.'

'From the hammering we got on the road, I'd say they had a minimum of five self-propelled guns too,' said Sirus.

'At the very least,' said LeGuin. 'But there's another thing. They continued to shell the roadway for quite a time after we pulled back. I bet that's because they didn't know we'd gone. They had an efficient string of spotters and lookouts, but my guess is their onboard scanners are very much lower spec than ours. No auspex. No landscape readers. Until they or their spotters actually see us, they're blind. We, on the other hand...'

'Noted,' said Gaunt. 'Okay, here's how we're going to play it. Head-on assault following the roadline. Tonight. If we think it's dicey leaving it so close to nightfall, you can bet they won't expect it. Armour comes out of the woods and spreads. Infantry behind, supporting with anti-tank weapons. I want two full strength troop assaults pushing ahead into the south of the town here. Kolea? Baffels? That's you. Around the warehouse barns.'

He pointed to his chart.

'Here's the winner. A side thrust. Maybe four or five tanks, in from the east, with infantry support and the Salamanders. Objective is the temple and then pushing through to the fuel stores. Hydra batteries will slug down from the roadline here.'

'What about civilians?' asked Hark.

'I haven't brought any, have you?'

The men laughed.

'Bhavnager is a clear and open target. I'll say it now so there's no mistake about it. We prosecute this town with maximum prejudice. Even if there are civilians, there are no civilians. Understood?'

The officers assented quickly. Gaunt ignored Curth's dark look.

'Kleopas, you have command of the main charge. I'll bring the Ghosts in behind you. Rawne? Sirus? You have the side thrust. Varl? I want you to play watchdog with a platoon on the road. Stay behind the Hydras and cover the transport and supply train. Bring them in only when we signal the town as secure. Go word is "Slaydo". Support advance is "Oktar". Retreat command is "Dercius". Vox channel is beta-kappa-alpha. Secondary is kappa-beta-beta. Any questions?'

THERE WERE NONE. With under two hours of daylight left, sunset burning off the mountains and rain on the wind, the honour guard fell upon Bhavnager.

LeGuin's *Grey Venger*, and the company's other Destroyer, the name *Death Jester* painted in crimson on its plating skirts, went in first along the highway, cleaning off the outer perimeter. Between them, they made eight kills, all Infardi MBTs covering the fruit groves on the road.

MKoll led a scout platoon in with them. They rode on the Destroyers' hulls until they reached the treecover and then scattered into the spinneys. The Ghosts rolled forward in a wave alongside the hunting tank killers, locating and cutting the observation posts of the enemy signal line by stealth.

Venger and *Jester* bellied down at the edge of the trees overlooking Bhavnager as the main assault force swooped in past them, the *Heart of Destruction* leading the way. The ground shook, and mechanical thunder rolled through the still air. Troops dismounted in full strength from the trucks behind them, and then the transporters retreated to waymark 00.60, where Varl and his unit guarded the Chimeras, Trojans and tankers.

The word was given and the word was 'Slaydo'. Under Kleopas, twelve battle machines charged towards Bhavnager from the south, eleven Conquerors and the company's single Executioner, an ancient plasma tank nicknamed *Strife*.

By then, the enemy had seen the smoke and flash of the Destroyer kills in the woods and had launched out in force. Thirty-two AT70 Reavers, all painted gloss lime, plus seven model N20 halftracks mounting 70 mil anti-tank cannons. Major Kleopas considered ruefully that this was considerably more than Captain Sirus's estimate of 'at least' ten Reavers and five self-propelled guns. This was going to be a major engagement. A chance to snatch glory from the din of battle. A chance to find death. The sort of choice the Pardus were bred to make.

Despite the appalling odds, Kleopas grinned to himself.

The Imperial Hydras, dug-in and locked out, sprayed their drizzle of rapid fire over the town from the tree-line. Two thousand Ghosts fanned out over the open approach in the wake of Kleopas's charging armoured cavalry. Already, small arms fire was cracking at them from the town edge.

The tank fight began in earnest. Kleopas's squadron was formed in a trailing V with the *Heart of Destruction* at the tip. They had the slight advantage of incline in the cleared ground between the fruit groves and the town edge and were making better than thirty kph. The enemy mass, in no ordered formation, churned up the slope to meet them, kicking rock chips and dry soil out behind them as their tracks dug in. They played out in a long, uneven line.

In the command seat of the *Heart*, Kleopas checked the readings of his auspex, glowing pale yellow in the half-light of the locked down turret, against the eyeball view through his prismatic up-scope. He used his good right eye for this, not his augmetic implant, an affectation his crew often joked about. Kleopas then adjusted his padded leather headset and flicked down the wire stalk of the voice mic.

'Lay on and fire at will.'

The Conqueror phalanx began to fire. A dozen main weapons blasting and then blasting again. Bright balls of gasflame flashed from their muzzles and discharge smoke streamed back from their muzzle brakes, fuming in long white trails of slipstream over their hulls. Three AT70s sustained direct hits and vanished in flurries of metal and fire. Two more were crippled and foundered, beginning to burn. A halftrack lurched lengthways as a round from the Conqueror *Man of Steel* punched through its crew bay and shredded it like a mess tin hit by a las-shot.

The elderly Pardus Executioner tank *Strife*, commanded by Lieutenant Pauk, was slower on its treads than the dashing Conquerors, and trailed at the end of the left-hand file. Its stubby, outsized plasma cannon razed a gleaming red spear of destruction down the slope and explosively sheared the turret off an AT70 in a splash of shrapnel and spraying oil.

The enemy mass began firing back uphill with resolved fury. The main weapons of the AT70s were longer and slimmer than the hefty muzzles of the Imperial Conquerors. Their blasts made higher, shrieking roars and sparked star-shaped gasburns from the flash-retarders at the ends of their barrels. Shells rained down across the Imperial charge.

LeGuin had been right. Examples of old, sub-Imperial standard technology, the Reavers lacked any auspex guidance of laser rangefinding. It was also clear they had no gyro stabilisers. Once the Conqueror guns were aimed, they damn well stayed aim-locked thanks to inertial dampers, no matter how much bouncing and lurching the tank was experiencing. That meant the Conquerors could shoot and move simultaneously without any appreciable loss of target lock. The AT70s fired by eye and any movement or jarring required immediate aim revision.

In the *Heart of Destruction*, Kleopas smiled contentedly. The enemy was chucking hundreds of kilos of munitions up the slope at them, but most of it was going wide or overshooting. They were not designed for efficient mobile shooting. If their supremo had only had the good sense to stop his armour dead and fire on the Imperial charge from stationary locks, he would have been ahead on points by now.

Even so, more by luck than judgement, the enemy scored hits. The Conqueror known as *Mighty Smiter* was hit simultaneously by two rounds from different adversaries, exploded and slewed to an ugly halt, greasy black smoke pouring out of the hatches. *Drum Roll*, another Conqueror, under the command of Captain Hancot, was hit in the starboard tread section and lost its tracks in a shower of sparks and steel fragments. It lurched and came to a stop, but continued to fire.

Captain Endre Woll made his second kill of the day and his crew let out a cheer. Woll was a tank ace, adored by the Pardus regiment, and Sirus's chief rival. Under the stencil reading *Old Strontium* on the side of his steed was a line of sixty-one kill marks. Sirus and the *Wrath of Pardua* claimed sixty-nine. Electric servos swung *Old Strontium's* turret basket around and Woll executed a perfect kill on a veering AT70. The noise in the Conqueror turret was immense, despite the sound-lagging and the crew's ear-protectors. When it fired, the breech of the main gun hurtled back into the turret space with one hundred and ninety tonnes of recoil force. The novice loaders and gun layers at Pardus boot camp quickly trained themselves to be alert and nimble. As the breech slammed back, a battered metal slide funnelled the red-hot spent shell case into the cartridge hopper and the loader swung round with a fresh shell from the water-jacketted magazine, thumping it into place with the ball of his palm. The layer consulted the rangefinder and the crosswind sensor, and obeyed Woll's auspex-guided instructions. Woll always kept one eye on the target reticule displayed on his up-scope. Like all good soldiers, he only trusted tech data so far.

'Target at 11:34!' Woll instructed.

'11:34 aye!' the layer repeated, jerking the recoil brake. The gun roared.

Another Reaver was reduced to a rapidly expanding ball of fire and scrap.

The Pardus armour men were trained for mobile cut and thrust. The Conquerors' time-honoured torsion-bar suspension systems and high power to weight ratio meant they were more nimble than most of the adversaries they encountered, whether super-heavy monsters or lacklustre mediums like the ones the Infardi were fielding. That meant the Conquerors were perfect cavalry tanks, built to fight on the move, to charge, to out-manoeuvre and overwhelm the foe.

But there came a crucial moment in any armour-cav charge where the decision had to be made to halt, break or break through. Kleopas knew that moment was at hand. The dream intention of any armour charge was to utterly crush the target formation. But the Infardi outnumbered them three to one, and more tanks were massing at the edge of the town. Kleopas cursed... the Infardi had mustered in division strength at Bhavnager. The major had to keep revising Sirus's original esti-mate up and up. Forget about major engagement, this was becoming historic.

The Conquerors were about to meet the enemy head-on. Kleopas had three choices: stop dead and fight it out standing, break through the enemy line and turn to finish the job, or sep-arate and pincer.

A stand-up fight was a worst case option. It would allow the Reavers to play to their strengths. Breakthrough was psycholog-ically strong, but it meant reversing the playing field, and the Pardus would then be fighting back up hill, risking their own infantry coming in behind.

'Pincer three-four! Pincer now!' Kleopas instructed his squadron. The left-hand edge of the V formation carried on with Kleopas at the head, crashing past and between the Infardi machines. The right edge, under Woll, spread wide in a lateral line and slowed right down.

Gearboxes and differentials grinding, the tanks of Kleopas's wing rotated almost on a point, spraying up loose earth, and presented at the hindquarters of the enemy line. All Leman Russ pattern tanks, like the Conquerors, delivered deliciously low ground pressure through their track arrangement, and pos-sessed fine regenerative steering. These almost balletic turns were a trademark move. Six more AT70s blew out as they were struck from the rear, and two more and a halftrack fell to Woll's straggler line.

The sloping field south of Bhavnager became a tank grave-yard. Flames and debris covered the ground, and burning wrecks littered the incline. Huddles of Infardi crew, ejected from escape hatches, ran blindly for cover. Some of the Reavers, lurching on their old-style volute spring suspension, tried to come about to engage Kleopas's line, and were blown apart from both sides. The front formation of the Infardi armour was overrun and slaughtered.

But the day was nothing like won yet.

The *Man of Steel* shuddered and lost its front end in a spurting fireball. From the edge of the town, an N20 halftrack, sensibly bedded down and unmoving, had hit it squarely with its anti-tank cannon.

Kleopas blanched as he heard Captain Ridas screaming over the vox-net as fire swamped his turret basket. Moments later, the conqueror *Pride of Memfis* was destroyed by a traversing AT70. Plasma spitting out with searing brilliance, Lieutenant Pauk's *Strife* evened the score.

As Kleopas's tanks hauled around on their regenerative steering again, Woll's line came through the kill-field, crunching and rolling over enemy wrecks. Eighteen more AT70s were spread around the town's southern limits and were bombarding steadily from standing. The shell deluge was apocalyptic. Woll counted nine Usurper-pattern self-propelled guns firing from positions behind the AT70 front. The boxy Usurpers carried howitzers, crude but efficient copies of Imperial Earthshakers, slanting forward out of their gun pulpits. Behind them came twelve more N20s, moving in a file down the marketplace road.

It was going to get worse before it got better.

'LINE UP, LINE up!' Gaunt cried, and his call was repeated down the infantry file from platoon leader to platoon leader. The Ghosts had formed in position at the edge of the tree-line, behind the four rattling Hydra batteries, and had been watching in awe and admiration for the last ten minutes as the tank fight boiled across the approach field below.

'Men of Tanith, warriors of Verghast, now we do the Emperor's duty! Advance! By file! Advance!'

Starting to jog, and then to run, the massed force of Ghosts came down the field, through the blasted landscape, bayonets fixed.

A few shells dropped amongst them. Glaring tracers spat overhead. The air was filthy with smoke. Kolea led the left-hand point of the advance, Sergeant Baffels the right, with Gaunt somewhere between them.

Gaunt allowed his designated assault leaders to move ahead, confident in their abilities, while he took time to pause and turn to yell encouragement and inspiration to the hundreds of troopers streaming down the slope. He brandished his power sword high so they could see it.

Right then, he missed Brin Milo. Milo should be here, he thought, piping the Ghosts into battle. He yelled again, his voice almost hoarse.

Commissar Hark was advancing with Baffels's mob. His shouts and urgings lacked the rousing fire of Gaunt's. He was new to them, he hadn't shared what Gaunt had shared with them. Still he urged them on.

'Destroyers signal their advance in our support,' Vox-officer Beltayn reported to Gaunt as they ran forward. Gaunt looked back to see the *Grey Venger* and the *Death Jester* rise up on their torsion springs and begin to prowl in at the heels of the infantry. It made a change to advance under armour, Gaunt thought. This was the Imperial Guard at its most efficient. This was inter-speciality co-operation. This was victorious assault.

ANA CURTH AND the medical party pushed down in the wake of the charging Ghosts. The ground they were covering was ruined by the furious tank fight and stank of fuel and fyceline. Shells had torn it up, so that the chalky bed rock was ploughed up over the black topsoil in white curds and lumps. It looked to Curth as if the very entrails of the earth had been blown out and exposed. This was a dead landscape, and they would undoubtedly extend and enlarge it before they were finished with Bhavnager.

Lesp darted to the left as a Ghost went down. Another two fell to an overshot tank round immediately ahead and Chayker and Foskin ran forward.

'Medic! Medic!' the scream rose from the massed confusion of manpower before her.

'I have it!' Mtane called to her, scrambling over the broken ground to a Ghost who was hunched over a squealing, disembowelled friend.

This is hell, Curth thought. It was her first taste of open war, of full-scale battle. She'd been through the urban horrors of

Vervunhive, but had only ever read about the experience of
pitched war in exposed territory. Battlefields. Now she understood what the term meant. It took a lot to shock Ana Curth,
and death and injury wasn't enough.

What shocked her here was the raging, callous fury of the
battle. The scale, the size, the gak-awful noise, the mass charge.

The mass wounding. The randomness of pain and hurt.

'Medic!'

She pulled open her field kit, running forward between the
plumes of fire kicked up by falling shells and heavy las-fire.

Every time she thought she knew the horrors of war, it gleefully exposed new ones. She wondered how men like Gaunt
could be even remotely sane after a life of this.

'Medic!'

'I'm here! Stay down, I'm here!'

FROM WAYMARK 07.07, the side thrust began their assault. They
congregated a kilometre to the east of Bhavnager at an outlying
farm. Even from this distance, the thunder of the main assault
four kilometres away was shaking the ground.

Rawne spat in the dust and picked up the lasrifle he had lent
against the farmyard's drybrick perimeter wall.

'Time to go,' he said.

Captain Sirus nodded and ran back towards his waiting tank,
one of six Conquerors idling behind the abandoned farmstead.

Feygor, Rawne's adjutant, armed his lasgun and roused up
the troops, close on three hundred Ghosts.

The wind was up, and the sun setting. Gold light radiated
from the bulbous stupa of the temple a kilometre away.

Rawne adjusted his vox. 'Three to Sirus. You see what I see?'

'I see the eastern flank of Bhavnager. I see the temple.'

'Good. If you're ready... go!'

The six Conquerors roared out of their holding position and
charged across the open fields and meadows towards the eastern edge of the town. Behind them came the convoy's eight
remaining Salamanders. Rawne hopped up onto the running
boards of one of the command Salamanders and rode it in,
turning back to supervise the infantry group advancing behind
him.

The five Conquerors chasing Sirus's *Wrath of Pardua* were
named *Say Your Prayers, Fancy Klara, Steel Storm, Lucky Bastard*

and *Lion of Pardua*, the latter the *Wrath's* sister tank. Rocking over terrain humps and irrigation gullies, the Pardus machines began firing, their shots hammering at the looming temple and its precincts. Puffs of white smoke plumed from the distant hits silently.

Almost immediately, four AT70 tanks appeared around the northern side of the temple. Two spurred forward into the edges of the wet, arable land, the others stopped dead and commenced shelling.

The *Fancy Klara*, commanded by Lieutenant LeTaw, crippled one of the moving tanks with a beautiful long range shot that would have made Woll himself proud. But then, as it bounced up over a tilled field, a tungsten-cored tank round hit the *Klara* squarely, penetrating the turret mantle and puncturing down through the basket. LeTaw lost his right arm and his gunlayer was instantly liquidised. The incandescent shell pierced the water jackets of the *Klara's* magazine and didn't explode.

The Conqueror swerved to a halt. LeTaw was numb with shock. He could barely pull aside his seat harness to look round. The interior of the turret was painted with a slick film of gore, the only remaining physical trace of his layer.

The loader had fallen from his metal stool, and was curled foetally on the floor of the basket, drenched in blood.

'Holy Emperor,' LeTaw murmured, looking down through the crisp-edged hole in the side of the magazine. Filthy water from the jackets dribbled out, diluting the blood on the floor. He could see sizzling fire inside the hole, the heat-shock residue of the impact.

'Get out!' he cried.

The loader looked blank, shocked out of his mind.

'Get out!' LeTaw repeated, reaching for the escape hatch pull with an arm that was no longer there.

Laughing at the macabre oddness of it, he swung around and reached up with his remaining hand. He heard the driver scrambling out through the forward hatch.

With a pop, heat-exchanger conduits in the side of the turret, weakened by the shell impact, burst. Scalding water spurted out, hitting LeTaw in the face before cascading down to broil his loader.

LeTaw tried to scream. The loader's shrieks echoed around the tank interior.

The shell had severed electrical cables in the footwell of the turret. The swirling water met the fizzling ends. LeTaw and his loader were electrocuted even as they writhed and screamed and blistered.

TARGETING A STATIONARY AT70, the *Steel Storm* exchanged shot after shot with it. Lieutenant Hellier, commanding the *Steel Storm*, realised his inertial dampers were damaged and that his auspex must consequently be out.

He shut the electronic systems down and began to aim through the reticule of the up-scope. He called out lay numbers to his aimer and was about to make a confident kill when the tank exploded, flipped over and broke apart.

The *Steel Storm* had hit the edge of the so-far undetected mine-field east of Bhavnager. The *Wrath of Pardua* crossed into the field immediately behind it, losing track pins and part of its side plating to an exploding mine.

Gunning its drive into full reverse, it was able to limp backwards a few metres while Sirus called an urgent dead stop.

The three remaining Conquerors slewed up behind him.

Bouncing up to their rear, the Salamander formations drew out in a line abreast, the infantry herding in around them. Shells from the three AT70s on the far side of the mine-field splashed all around them, chewing up the muddy irrigation system of the farmland which had already been scored with deep furrows by the hurtling armour.

'Sweepers! Sweepers forward!' Rawne ordered into his vox. Two specialist squads of three, one led by 'Shoggy' Domor, the other by a Verghastite trooper named Burone, immediately went ahead under fire.

'Infantry units! Support!' Rawne yelled.

The Ghosts began firing at the edge of the town with lasrifles, and with the heavier infantry support weapons they had brought up: four heavy stubbers and three missile launchers, plus the heavy bolters and the autocannons hull-mounted on the Salamanders.

The sweeper squads were miserably exposed, working their delicate magic as tank rounds and small arms fire whooshed around them. They had the expertise to clear a corridor through the field... if they lived long enough.

The second front advance was now dangerously delayed.

More AT70s appeared in support of the existing trio, as well as a quartet of heavy Usurper self-propelleds. Sirus wondered just how much bloody armour the enemy had to draw on at Bhavnager.

Deadlocked by the mines, the four Conquerors began free-firing at the enemy position with main guns and coaxial mounts. In the space of a few seconds, the *Lion of Pardua* comprehensively destroyed a self-propelled gun thoroughly enough to ignite its munition pile, and the *Lucky Bastard* knocked out an AT70. The detonation of the self-propelled gun was severe enough to spray shrapnel out over the minefield and trigger a few of the buried munitions off.

The *Say Your Prayers* and Sirus's *Wrath of Pardua* slung over some tank rounds that blew out the north retaining wall of the temple. The *Wrath's* driver and a Pardus tech-priest from the Salamanders took the opportunity to rig running repairs on the Conqueror's damaged track section.

In a shell-dug foxhole near to Rawne's Salamander, Criid, Caffran and Mkillian prepped one of the foot support missile launchers, known as 'tread-fethers' in the regimental slang. It was a shoulder tube of khaki-painted metal with a fore-scope, a trigger brace and fluted venturi at the back end to vent the recoil exhaust.

Heavy support weapons like this weren't commonly deployed by the stealth-specialist Ghosts; in fact Bragg was often the only trooper carrying one. But they were in the middle of a tank fight now. Caffran shouldered the tube and aimed via the crude wire crosshairs at the AT70 that had duelled with the late, lamented *Steel Storm*. Like many Ghosts, Caffran had become familiar with tread-fethers during the street-to-street war at Vervunhive, where he'd used one to knock out five Zoican siege tanks.

In fact he'd been fielding one in the burning habs when Criid had turned up to save his life from Zoican storm troops. They'd been together ever since.

Over the roar of the fighting, he heard her say 'For Verghast' as she kissed the armed rocket-grenade Mkillian handed to her. She slammed it into the launcher pipe.

'Loaded!' she yelled.

Caffran had his target. 'Ease!' he ordered.

Everyone nearby echoed the word, so that their mouths would be open when the tube fired. Anyone with closed mouths risked burst eardrums from the sudden firing pressure.

With a hollow, whistling cough, the tread-fether shot the rocket grenade at the enemy, leaving a slowly dissolving contrail of smoke behind it. The hit was clean, but the rocket exploded impotently off the heavy front armour of the Reaver. As if goaded, the AT70 came around.

'Load me!'

'Loaded!' Criid yelled.

'Ease!'

Now that was better. The AT70 shuddered and began to burn. Its cannon muzzle drooped, as if the tank itself was feigning death.

'Load me! Just to be sure!'

'Loaded!'

'Ease!'

The burning AT70 now shivered and exploded in a blizzard of machine parts, armour plating, track segments and fire.

A cheer rippled down the infantry lines.

Then, above the ceaseless warring, the sound of another, louder cheer.

Rawne leapt out of his Salamander to investigate, running hunched as tracer fire crackled over his position.

Larkin had scored magnificently with his first shot of the engagement.

'I saw it for definite,' Trooper Cuu told Rawne excitedly, tapping his lasgun's scope. 'Larks got the officer, dead as dead.'

At a distance of over three hundred metres, Larkin had put a hot-shot las round through the sighting grille of the pulpit armour on one of the Usurpers and killed the artillery officer in charge. It was one hell of a shot.

'You go, Larks!' Trooper Neskon yelled. One of the unit's flamer troopers, Neskon was reduced to firing his laspistol, his flame-gun pretty much redundant in these mid- to long-range conditions.

'Could you do better closer?' Rawne asked Larkin.

'I'd feel better further away, major... like on another planet, maybe,' Larkin said sourly.

'I'm sure, but...'

'Yes, of course, sir!' Larkin said.

'Follow Domor's team out into the field. Feygor? Form up a five-man intruder team around Larkin. Get another sniper in there if you can. Move out down the swept corridor and give the sweeper boys cover. Use the reduced range to do some real damage. I want officers and commanders picked out and killed.'

'Don't we all, major,' replied Feygor as he leapt up to obey. The voice of Rawne's adjutant had always been deep and gravelly, but ever since the final fight for Veyveyr Gate, he'd spoken through a voicebox deformed and twisted with las-burn scar tissue. He was permanently monotone and deadpan.

Feygor scrambled around and selected Cuu, Banda and the Verghast sniper Twenish to accompany himself and Larkin.

Under the storm of fire, the quintet moved out into the killing field. Domor's party, working alongside Burone's, had cleared a ten metre wide channel that ran thirty metres into the field, its edges carefully denoted by staked tapes laid by Trooper Memmo. One of Burone's squad was already dead and Mkor in Domor's had taken shrapnel in his left thigh and shoulder.

Domor's team was slightly ahead of Burone's, and this competition was a matter of pride between Tanith and Verghastite minesweepers. Domor, of course, had the advantage of his heat-reading augmetic eyes to back up the sweeper brooms.

Feygor's intruder team joined them, Larkin and Twenish immediately digging in and sighting up as Cuu and Banda gave them cover fire. The vulnerable sweepers were glad of the additional support.

'Couldn't have brought a fat stub or a tread-fether with you, I suppose?' Domor asked.

'Just keep sweeping, Shoggy,' Feygor growled.

Twenish was a damn good shot, Larkin noted. He was one of the very few Verghastite newcomers to have specialised in sniper school before the Act of Consolation. A long-limbed, humourless fellow, Twenish was ex-Vervun Primary, a career soldier. His long-las was newer than Larkin's nalwood-furnished beauty; a supremely functional weapon with grostequely enlarged night-scope array, a bipod stand and a ceramite stock individually tailored to fit its user.

The two snipers, products of entirely diverging regimental schools and training, began firing at the enemy armour. From three shots, Larkin dropped a Usurper gunlayer, an infantry leader, and the commander of an AT70 who had made the mistake of spotting from his turret hatch.

Twenish fired in quick double-shots. If the first didn't kill, it at least found range and drew his aim to his target for the second. From three of these paired shots, he made two excellent kills, including an Infardi priest rousing his men to combat. But to Larkin, it seemed like wasted effort. He knew about the double-shot method, and also was aware that many guard regiments taught the approach as standard. In his opinion, it gave the enemy too much warning, no matter how quickly you adjusted for the second squeeze.

As he lined up again, Larkin began to find the crack-pause-crack of Twenish's routine off-putting. Twenish was obsessive in his care, laying out a sheet of vizzy-cloth beside his firing position that he used to polish clean the scope lenses between each double-shot. Like a fething machine... crack-pause-crack.... polish-polish... crack-pause-crack. Enough with the precious rituals! Larkin felt like yelling, though he had more than enough of his own.

Larkin snuggled in again and with one shot killed the driver of a halftrack that was moving into the opposition line.

Banda, Cuu and Feygor knelt in the folds of soil, blazing suppressing fire freely at the enemy.

Banda was an excellent shot, and like many of her kind – female Verghastite conscripts, that was – she had wanted to specialise in marksmanship on joining the Ghosts. As it was, there was a strict limit on numbers for that specialisation and she'd been denied, although, to Banda's delight, her friend Nessa had made it. Most of the marksman places went to Vervun Primary snipers like Twenish who were carrying their specialisation over into the Ghosts with them. But Banda could shoot damn well, even with a standard, bulk-stamped lasrifle... a fact she'd proved to the gak-ass Major Rawne in the Universitariat clearance.

A swathe of autogun fire rippled across the position of the sweepers and the intruder team and every one threw themselves down. The remaining member of Burone's team was shredded, and Burone himself was hit in the hip. As they all got up again, Banda was first to realise that Twenish was dead; hammered into the soil in his prone position by the stitching fire that had raked over them.

Without hesitating, she leapt forward and prised the Verghastite long-las from Twenish's stiff grip.

'Do you know what you're doing?' Larkin called to her.

'Yes, gak you very much, Mr Tanith sniper.'

She took aim. The stock, molded for Twenish's longer reach, was awkward for her, but she persisted. This was a long-las, gak it!

No double-shots for her. An Infardi artillery officer running from one Usurper to the other crossed her sighting reticule and she blew his head off.

'Nice,' approved Larkin.

Banda smiled. And took an Infardi gunman off the balustrade of the temple at four hundred metres.

'Beat 'cha at yer own game, Larks,' Cuu simpered at Larkin. 'Sure as sure.'

'Feth off,' said Larkin. He knew how brilliantly – if psychotically – Cuu could shoot. If Cuu wanted a piece of it, let him get his belly dirty and use the damn long-las. At least Banda was eager. And damn good. He'd always suspected that about her. Since the day he'd first met her at street junction 281/kl in the suburbs of Vervunhive. The cheeky fething bitch.

As Domor's squad continued forward with their unenviably deadly task, and a fresh sweeper team ran forward to replace Burone's unit, the two Ghost snipers plied their precise and murderous trade across the enemy positions.

'Three, one. We're deadlocked!' Rawne told Gaunt via his Salamander's powerful voxcaster set.

'How long, three?'

'At this rate, an hour before we're even at the temple, one!'

'Continue as you are and await orders.'

South of Bhavnager, the infantry forces were swarming into the town itself on the smoking heels of the Pardus main armour. Tanks were engaging the enemy at short range now, in the limiting spaces of the narrow market area streets. Woll's *Old Strontium* knocked out three N20 anti-tankers during this phase of close armour, and hit a Usurper before it could train its huge tank-killing weapon down to fire.

Kloepas's *Heart of Destruction* was caught in a firefight with two Reavers, and the Conquerors *Xenophobe* and *Tread Softly* smashed down low corral walls and single-storey brick-built houses as they moved to support it.

The Executioner tank *Strife*, flanked by the Conquerors *Beat the Retreat* and P48J, crushed a squadron of halftracks and broke into the compound of the south-western produce barns. Kolea's troop spearhead swiftly moved up to support them, enduring a series of fierce, close range fights through the echoing interiors of the barns. Mkoll's scout force pushed through towards the town centre marketplace after an ambiguous but deadly confrontation in the yards of the warehouses, where bales of dried vines were stacked. A platoon under Corporal Meryn fought their way in after them, meeting a counter-assault massed by fifty Infardi gunmen.

The flame-troopers, typified by Brostin and Dremmond and the Verghastite Lubba, excelled themselves during this part of the fight, sweeping clean the hard-locked barns of any Infardi resistance.

Accompanied by Vox-officer Beltayn, Gaunt advanced through the promethium smoke and the fyceline discharge. He took the handset from Beltayn as it was offered.

'One to seven!'

'Seven, one!' Sergeant Baffel's replied, his voice eerily distorted by electromagnetics.

'Three's counter-punch is deadlocked. We need to secure the fuel depot stat. I want you to push ahead and cut us a way through. How do you feel about that?'

'Do our best, one.'

'One, seven. Acknowledged.'

SERGEANT BAFFELS TURNED to his prong of the advance, as heavy shelling whipped over them.

'Orders just got interesting, people,' he said.

They groaned.

'What the gak are we expected to do now, Baffels?' asked Soric.

'Simple,' said Baffels. 'Live or die. The fuel depot. Let's look like we mean business.'

AT WAYMARK 00.60, standing amid the parked tankers, Chimeras, Trojans and troop trucks, they could hear the rumble of battle from away through the trees at Bhavnager.

Varl's defence section stood about aimlessly, talking with the waiting Munitorium drivers, smoking, cleaning kit.

Varl paced up and down. He so fething wanted to get down there and into it. This was a good duty and all, but still...

'Sir?' Varl looked round. Trooper Unkin was approaching.

'Trooper?'

'He says he wants to advance.'

'Who does?'

'Him, sir.' Unkin pointed at the ragged old ayatani, Zweil.

'I'll deal,' Varl told his point man.

He wandered down to the old priest. 'You have to stay here, father,' he said.

'I have to do no such thing,' Zweil replied. 'In fact, it's my duty to get down there, on the path of the Ayolta Amad Infardiri.'

'The what, father?'

'The Pilgrim's Way. There are pilgrims in need of my ministry.'

'There's no such–'

A distant, powerful explosion shook the air.

'I'm going, Sergeant Varl. Right now. To do less would be desecration.'

Varl groaned as the elderly priest strode away from him and began heading down the highway through the fruit groves towards Bhavnager. Gaunt would have Varl's stripes if anything happened to the ayatani.

'Take over,' Varl told Unkin and began running after the retreating figure of the priest.

'Father! Father Zweil! Wait up!'

CAUSTIC SMOKE WAS rolling down the length of the side street, obscuring Kolea's view. Somewhere down there, somewhere close to the point where the street met the main through road just off the market square, an enemy halftrack was sitting and chopping fire from its pintle-mount at anything that moved. Every now and then, it fired its anti-tank gun too.

The wretched smoke was pouring out of a threshing mill close by. Las-fire whimpered down the thoroughfare. The tightly packed buildings in the side street degraded vox-quality. It reminded Kolea rather too much of the fighting in the outhabs of Vervunhive.

Corporal Meryn's platoon, fresh from their firefight in the barns, moved up behind Kolea's bunch. Kolea signalled Meryn by hand to force a way through the buildings to the left and out onto the street running parallel to the one that currently stymied the advance. Meryn acknowledged.

Bonin, one of the scouts, had peeled to the right and found a walk-through breezeway that opened onto a small area of open wasteland behind the street buildings. Hearing this over the vox, Kolea immediately sent Venar, Wheln, Fenix and Jajjo through to link up with Bonin. Fenix carried a 'tread-fether' in addition to his lasrifle.

From cover, Kolea continued to scrutinize the billowing smoke for signs of the gakking N20. After a while, he began to fire off rounds into the section of smoke his instinct said concealed it. He was sure he could hear his shots impacting off hull metal. A heavy burst of stub fire raked back in response, chewing into the rubble and debris on the street. Almost immediately, it was followed by a whistling bang as the anti-tank weapon fired. The shell, travelling, it seemed to Kolea, at head height, impacted explosively in a burnt-out hut behind Kolea's position. As it sped through the smoke, the projectile left behind a bizarre corkscrew wake pattern.

'Come forward, come forward, you bastard...' Kolea urged the 'track, under his breath.

'Confirmed foot targets!' the vox hiss came in his ear. Marksman Rilke, dug into cover close by Kolea, had seen movement down by the burning mill. He'd challenged by vox, using the day's code word, in case it was some of their own out of position and crossing the line of battle. No identifiers came back. Rilke lined up his long-las and began firing.

Others in Kolea's formation joined in: Ezlan and Mkoyn over a broken wall near Rilke; Livara, Vivvo and Loglas from the windows of a livery; the loom-girls Seena and Arilla from a fox hole to Kolea's right. Las and auto fire began to ripple down the street at them. Platoon-strength opposition at least.

Seena and Arilla formed, respectively, the gunner and loader of a heavy stubber team. They'd learned the skills in the Vervun war, as part of one of the many 'scratch' companies of the resistance. Seena was a plump, twenty-five year old girl who wore a black slouch cap to keep her luxuriant bangs out of her eyes; Arilla was skinny, barely eighteen.

Somehow it looked wrong for the frailer, shorter girl to always be the one lugging the hollow plasteel yoke laden with ammo hoppers. But they were an excellent team. Their matt-black stubber was packed into the lip of the foxhole tightly to prevent the tripod skating out during sustained fire. Those old-pattern stubbers could buck like a riled auroch. Seena was squirting out tight bursts, interspersing them with longer salvoes that she sluiced from side to side on the gunstand's oiled gimbal.

Ezlan and Mkoyn tossed out a few tube-charges that detonated with satisfying thumps and collapsed the street facade of a farrier's shop.

Kolea got a few shots off himself, moving along the defence line. Another anti-tank round screamed low overhead. Kolea hoped the infantry clash would bring the halftrack up in support of its troops. He got Loglas and Vivvo to prep their missile tube.

'Nine, seventeen?'

'Seventeen,' Meryn answered over the link.

'What have you got?'

'Access to the next street. Looks quiet. Advancing.'

'Steady does it. Keep in vox-touch.'

A particularly heavy spray of las-fire stippled the wall behind him, and Kolea ducked flat. He heard the stubber barking out in response.

'Nine, thirty-two?'

'Reading you, nine.'

'Any luck with that halftrack yet, Bonin?'

'We're crossing the wasteground. Can't find a route back onto the street to come in behind them. We... Hold on.'

Kolea tensed as he heard fierce shooting distorted by the vox.

'Thirty-two? Thirty-two?'

'...vy fire! Heavy fire in this area! Feth! We've got m–' Bonin's response came back, chopped by the vox-bounce off the buildings.

'Nine, thirty-two. Say again! Nine, thirty-two!'

The channel just bled white noise. Kolea could hear staccato crossfire from behind the structures to his right. Bonin's fire-team needed help. More particularly, if they were overrun, Kolea needed to make sure the gap to his flank was plugged.

'Nine, I require file support here! Map-mark 51.33!'

Within two minutes, a platoon had moved up from the warehouses along the route his team had already cleared. Kolea's old friend Sergeant Haller was at the head of it. Kolea quickly outlined the situation and the suspected position of the N20 to Haller and then grouped up a fire-team of Livara, Ezlan, Mkoyn and, from Haller's detail, Trooper Surch and the flamer-man Lubba.

'Take over here,' Kolea told Haller, and immediately led his ready-team right, down through the breezeway and onto the open ground beyond.

As if it had been waiting for the Verghastite hero to go, the halftrack suddenly clanked forward through the pungent brown smoke and fired its main mount at the Ghost line. Two of Haller's new arrivals were killed and Loglas was wounded by flying debris. Haller ran head-down through the rain of burning ash, and scooped up the missile tube as Vivvo got the dazed Loglas into cover.

'Loaded?' Haller yelled at Vivvo.

'Hell, yes sir!' Vivvo confirmed.

Haller sighted up. He put the crosshairs on the box-armoured view-slits of the N20's cab.

'Ease!'

The rocket tore open the halftrack's cab armour like a can-opener, and exploded out with enough force to spin the entire anti-tank mount around. Seena and Arilla hosed the stricken machine with stub-fire.

There was a ragged ripple of cheers from the Ghosts.

'Load me up again,' Haller told Vivvo. 'I want to make certain and kill it twice.'

BONIN'S ADVANCE TEAM had run into ferocious and extraordinary opposition centring on a shell-damaged building at the edge of the wasteground. More than twenty Infardi weapons had fired on them and then, incredibly, dozens of green-clad warriors had charged out, brandishing cleavers, pikes and rifle bayonets.

The five Ghosts reacted with extreme levels of improvisation. Fenix had been winged in the initial fire, but he was still fit to fight, and dropped to his knees, presenting a smaller target as he fired at the mob rushing them. Wheln and Venar had already fixed bayonets and countered directly, uttering blood-chilling yells as they drove forward, slashing and impaling.

Bonin sprayed his lasgun on full auto, draining out the power-cell swiftly but harvesting the opposition. Jajjo was carrying the loaded tread-fether and decided not to waste the stopping power. Yelling 'Ease!' he shouldered the tube and fired the anti-tank round into the face of the building the Infardi had charged out of. The back-blast took out several of the skirmishers and collapsed a section of the wall. Then Jajjo tossed his tube aside and leapt into the close fighting, his silver blade in his hand.

His powercell depleted, Bonin joined in the hand to hand too, clubbing with his gunstock. The Imperials, trained by the likes of Feygor and Mkoll at this sort of fighting, outclassed the cultists, despite the latter's superior numbers and bigger, slashing blades. But the Infardi had frenzy in them, and that made them lethal opponents.

Bonin broke a jaw with a swing of his lasgun, and then smacked the muzzle of his weapon into the solar plexus of another attacker. What the feth had made them charge out like this, he wondered? It was bizarre, even by the unpredictable standards of the Chaos-polluted foe. They had cover and they clearly had guns. They could have taken Bonin's intruder unit in the open.

The brutal melee lasted for four minutes and only ended when the last of the Infardi were dead or unconscious. Bonin's team were all splashed with the enemy's gore and the waste-ground was soaked. Corpses sprawled all around. The Ghosts had all sustained cuts and contusions: Bonin had a particularly deep laceration across his left upper arm and Jajjo had a broken wrist.

'What the hell was that about?' Venar groaned, stooping over, out of breath.

Bonin could feel the adrenalin surging through his body, the rushing beat of his own heart. He knew his team must be feeling the same way too, and wanted to use it before they ebbed out of that intense combat edge. He slammed a fresh powercell into his weapon.

'Don't know but I want to know,' he told Venar. 'Let's get in there and secure the damn place fast. Jajjo, use your pistol. Wheln, carry the tread-fether.'

Fenix suddenly switched round at movement behind them, but it was Kolea's support section.

'Gak me!' said Kolea, looking at the bloody evidence of the fight. 'They charge you?'

'Like fething maniacs, sir,' Bonin said, pausing to put a las-round through the head of a stirring Infardi.

'From there?'

Bonin nodded.

'Protecting something?' Ezlan suggested.

'Let's find out,' said Kolea.

'Fenix, get yourself and Jajjo back to the rear and find medics. Bonin, Lubba, you've got point.'

The nine men advanced into the ruin through the hole Jajjo's rocket had made. Lubba's flamer stuttered and then surged cones of fire into the dark spaces.

They found the Infardi troop leader sprawled unconscious amid the blast damage. His personal force shield had been overwhelmed by the rocket blast, and the portable generator pack lay shattered nearby. He'd sent his men out in a suicidal charge to cover his own escape.

Kolea looked down at the unconscious man. Tall, wiry, with a shaved head and a pot belly, his unhealthy skin was covered with unholy symbols. Bonin was about to finish him with his silver blade but Kolea stopped him.

'Vox the chief. Ask him if he wants a prisoner.'

IN THE NEXT street over, Meryn's unit had caught up with Mkoll's scout section and they moved forward together. The sounds of close fighting rolled in from the neighbouring street, but Haller had informed Meryn that the N20 had been killed and advised him to press on.

Night was now falling fast, and the darkening sky was lit all around by firelight, the flashes of explosions and the glimmer of tracers. By Mkoll's guess, the fight was not yet even half done. The Tanith were still a long way from taking Bhavnager or securing their primary objective, the fuel depot.

Strangely, the street they advanced down, a narrow lane lined with empty dwellings and plundered trading posts, was untouched by the fighting, intact, almost peaceful.

Mkoll wished urgently for full darkness. This phase of the day when light turned into night was murder on the eyes. Night vision refused to settle in. The bright moons were up, shrouded by palls of rising smoke that turned them blood red.

Meryn suddenly made a movement and fired. Swiftly, all the Ghosts opened up, moving into secure cover. Odd bursts of gunfire came back at them, chipping the bricks and stucco walls of the commonplace buildings.

Then something made a whooping bang and a building to Meryn's left dissolved in a fireball that took two Ghosts with it.

'Armour! Armour!'

Squat and ominous like a brooding toad, the AT70 crumpled a fence as it rolled out onto the road, traversing its turret to fire down on them again. The blast destroyed another house.

'Missile tube to order!' Meryn yelled as brick chips drizzled down over him.

'Firing jam! Firing jam!'

'Feth!' Meryn growled. The one tool they had that might make a dent in the tank was down. They were caught cold.

Infardi troops streamed in behind the Reaver, blasting away. A serious small arms firefight developed, lighting up the dim street with its strobing brilliance.

The tank rolled on, crushing heedlessly over the dead or wounded forms of its own foot troops. Meryn shuddered. It would soon be doing the same to his boys.

From his position, he could hear Mkoll urgently talking over the vox. He waited until Mkoll broke off before patching in.

'Seventeen, four. Do we fall back?'

'Four, seventeen. See if we can hold out a few minutes more. We can't let these infantry numbers in at our flank.'

'Understood. What about the tank?'

'Let me worry about that.'

Easy for Mkoll to say, Meryn thought. The tank was barely seventy metres away now, its 105 mil barrel lowered to maximum declension. It fired again, putting a crater in the road, and its coaxial weapon began chattering. Meryn heard two Ghosts cry out as they were hit by the spray of bolter rounds. The Infardi troops were moving up all around. This was turning into a full-on counter thrust.

Meryn wondered what the feth Mkoll intended to do about the tank. He hoped it wasn't some insane, suicidal run with a satchel of tube-charges. Even Mkoll wouldn't be that crazy, would he? Then again, he hoped Mkoll had something up his guard-issue sleeve. The AT70 was going to be all over them in a moment.

His vox crackled. 'Infantry units, brace and cover for support.'
What the feth...?

A horizontal column of light, as thick as Meryn's own thigh,
raked down the narrow street from the rear. It was so bright its
afterimage seared Meryn's retinas for minutes afterwards. There
was a stink of ozone.

The AT70 blew up.

Its turret and main gun, spinning like a child's discarded rattle, separated from the hull in the fireball and demolished the
upper storey of a house. The hull itself split open like a roast-
ing nalnut shell in a campfire and showered flames and metal
fragments everywhere.

'Feth me!' Meryn stammered.

'Moving up, stand aside,' the vox said.

LeGuin's *Grey Venger* rolled up the street, a dark predatory
shape, unlit.

'Drinks are on me,' Meryn heard Mkoll vox to the tank.

'Hold you to that. Form up and follow me in. Let's get this
finished.'

The Ghosts moved out of cover and ran up behind the
advancing tank destroyer, firing suppression bursts into the surrounding houses. The *Venger* crunched over the remains of the
Reaver. The Infardi were in flight.

Meryn smiled. In a second, the flow of battle had completely
reversed. Now they were the ones advancing with a tank.

HALF A KILOMETRE away, the *Heart of Destruction* and the P48J
finally broke through into the market place. Their steady
advance had been delayed for a while by a trio of N20s, and the
Heart's hull carried the blackened scars of that clash.

Kleopas looked away from the prismatic up-scope for the
first time in what seemed like hours.

'Load?' he asked.

'Down to the last twenty,' his gun layer said after checking the
shells left in the water-jacketted magazine.

Small arms fire began to rattle off the mantlet. Kleopas
scoped around and identified at least three fire-teams of Infardi
troops on the northern side of the market place. The two
Conquerors smashed forward through the empty wooden market stalls, shattering them and tearing off the canvas awnings.
P48J dragged one like a pennant.

The *Heart's* gun-team loaded and layed at one of the enemy fire-teams.

'Don't waste a shell on soft targets, we're low on ammo,' Kleopas growled. He pulled open a fire-control lever and aimed up the coaxial bolter. The heavy cannon destroyed one Infardi position in a blizzard of dust. The P48J followed suit – she must be running low on shells too, Kleopas decided darkly – and between them, the armoured pair pulverised the out-classed foot troops.

Kleopas's auspex suddenly showed two fast moving blips. A pair of Urdeshi-made light tanks, SteG 4s, each bouncing along on three pairs of massive tyres, sped into the square, headlamps blazing. Their tiny turrets mounted only stick-like 40 mil cannons, but if they had tungsten-cored ammo, or dis-carding sabots, they might still hurt the hefty Imperial machines.

'Lay up on that one,' said Kleopas, indicating his backlit tar-get screen as he checked the up-scope. 'Now we use our muscle.'

SERGEANT BAFFELS FELT he was under intense pressure to perform. He was sweating profusely and he felt sick. The ferocious com-bat was bad enough, but he'd seen plenty of that before. It was the command responsibility that troubled him.

His eastern prong of the infantry assault had pushed up through Bhavnager far enough to cross the main highway. Now, with the temple on their right, they fought through the streets north of the market towards the fuel depot. Gaunt him-self had charged Baffels with clearing the route to the depot. He would not fail, Baffels told himself.

The colonel-commissar had given him squad command on Verghast. He didn't want it much, but he appreciated the hon-our of it every waking moment. Now Gaunt had tasked him with the battle's crucial phase. It was an almost impossibly heavy burden to carry.

Almost a thousand Ghosts were pouring into the town behind him, platoon supporting platoon. The original plan had been that they, and a similar number under Kolea, would drive open, parallel wounds into Bhavnager's defences and crack the place wide, while Rawne took the northern depot. Now with both Kolea and Rawne basically bogged down, it was down to him.

Baffels thought about Kolea a lot, usually with envy tingeing his mood. Kolea, the great war hero, took to command so effortlessly. The troops loved him. They would do anything for him. To be fair, Baffels had never seen a trooper disobey one of his own orders, but he felt unworthy. Until Vervunhive, he'd been a common dog-soldier too. Why the feth should they do as he told them?

He thought about Milo too. Milo, his friend, his squad buddy. Milo should have had this command, he often thought.

Baffels's brigade had struggled up through the streets east of the market, winning every metre hard. Baffels had Commissar Hark with him, but he wasn't sure Hark helped much. The men were afraid of him, and suspected him of all sorts of dreadful motives. It was good to have a healthy fear of commissars, Baffels knew that much. That's what commissars were there for. And the regiment's new commissar, give him his due, was doing his job and doing it well. As he had proved the day before during the ambush, Hark was almost unflappable and he had a confident and agile grasp of field tactics. Not only was he urging the rear portions of Baffel's group on, he was directing and focussing their efforts in a way that entirely complemented the sergeant's lead.

But Baffels could tell that the men despised Hark. Despised what he stood for. Baffels knew this because it was how he felt himself. Hark was Lugo's agent. He was here to orchestrate Gaunt's demise.

The leading edge of Baffels's assault had run into especially fierce fighting at an intersection between the abandoned halls of an esholi school and the market's livestock pens. Despite monumental efforts by Soric's platoon, they had lodged tight, coming under heavy fire from N20 half tracks and several curious, six-wheeled light tanks.

Hark, picking out a squad of Nehn, Mkendrick, Raess, Vulli, Muril, Tokar, Cown and Garond, had attempted to leap-frog Soric's unit and break the deadlock. They found themselves pinned down almost immediately.

Then, more by luck than plan, Pardus armour tore up through the eastern roadway to support them – the Executioner *Strife*, the Conquerors *Tread Softly* and *Old Strontium*, the Destroyer *Death Jester*. Between them, they made a terrific mess of the north-eastern streets and left burning tank and light tank carcasses in their wake. Baffels moved his forces in behind them as they made the last push to the depot, just a few streets away. It had been bloody and slow, but Baffels had done what Gaunt had asked of him.

The delay had given Gaunt himself the opportunity to move up with the front. Baffels was almost overjoyed to see him and Hark immediately deferred to the colonel-commissar.

Gaunt approached Baffels's position as enemy las-fire criss-crossed the night air.

'You've done a fine job,' Gaunt told the sergeant.

'It's taken fething ages I'm afraid, sir,' Baffels countered.

'It was going to. The Ershul aren't giving up without a fight.'

'Ershul, sir?'

'A word ayatani Zweil taught me this afternoon. Smell that?'

'I do, sir,' said Baffels, scenting the stink of promethium fuel on the wind.

'Let's go finish it,' Gaunt said.

Supported by the blistering firepower of the Pardus, the Ghosts moved forward towards the depot. Leading one line, Gaunt found himself suddenly face to face with Infardi who had laid low and dug in, now springing out in ambush to the file. His power sword sang and his bolter spat. Around him, Uril, Harjeon, Soric and Lillo, some of the best of the Verghastite new blood, proved themselves worthy Ghosts. It was the first of seventeen separate hand-to-hand engagements the prong would encounter on the way up.

At the fifth, a messy firefight to clear a cul de sac, chance brought Gaunt and Hark up side by side in the mayhem. Hark's plasma pistol seared into the shadows.

'I'll say this, Gaunt... you fight a good fight.'

'Whatever. The Emperor protects,' Gaunt murmured, decapitating a charging Infardi with the power sword of House Sondar.

'You still don't trust me, do you?' Hark said, destroying an enemy stub-nest with a single, volatile beam.

'Are you really very surprised?' Gaunt replied tartly and, without waiting for a response, rallied his Ghosts for the next assault.

SERGEANT BRAY WAS the first platoon leader in Baffels's group to break his men through to the fuel depot proper. He found a row of massive sheds and chubby fuel tanks, guarded by over a hundred dug-in Infardi, supported by three AT70s and a pair of Usurpers.

Bray's rocket teams got busy. This was the heaviest resistance they'd yet encountered, and the attack had hardly been a picnic up until then. Bray called up for armour support.

Gaunt, Baffels, Soric and Hark clawed in, each driving a solid formation of Ghosts up to the rear of Bray's position. Gaunt could taste victory, and defeat too, intertwined. Experience told him that this was the moment, the make or break. If they endured and pushed on, they would win the town and destroy the foe. If not...

Shell, las and hard-round fire whipped into his formation. He saw the Pardus go forward, smashing through chain-link fences and across ditches as they breached the depot compound. *Strife* killed a Usurper, and *Death Jester* crippled a Reaver. The night sky was underlit by a storm of explosions and tracers.

'Regroup! Regroup!' Baffels was yelling as the shells scourged the air. Soric's section made gains, charging in through the southern fence, before being driven back by heavy fire from Infardi troops. Hark's section was backed into a corner.

Gaunt saw the Baneblade before anyone else.

His blood ran cold.

Three hundred tonnes of super-heavy tank, a captured, corrupted Imperial machine. It trundled casually out from behind the depot, its massive turret weapon rising.

A monster. A steel-shod monster from the mouth of hell.

'Baneblade! Enemy Baneblade at 61.78!' Gaunt yelled into his vox.

Captain Woll, commanding the *Old Strontium*, couldn't believe his ears.

His auspex picked up the behemoth a second before it fired and obliterated the Conqueror *Tread Softly*.

Woll layed in and fired, but his tank round barely made a dent on the massive machine's hull.

The Baneblade's secondary and sponson turrets began to fire on the Imperial positions. The immediate death toll was hideous. Staunch, loyal Ghosts broke in terror and ran as the Baneblade rolled forward.

'Stand true! Stand true, you worthless dogs!' Hark yelled at the fleeing Tanith around him. 'This is the Emperor's work! Stand true or face his wrath at my hand!'

Hark was suddenly jerked backwards as Gaunt seized his wrist tightly and spoiled the threatened aim of his plasma pistol.

'I punish the Ghosts. Me. Not you. Besides, it's a fething Baneblade, you moron. I'd be running too. Now, help me.'

Soric's and Bray's sections hurled anti-tank missiles at the looming giant, to no great avail. *Death Jester* hit it with two blinding shots and still it rolled on. The Infardi armour and infantry advanced behind it.

Gaunt realised he had been right. This had been the moment. The make or break.

And they had broken.

Weapons thumping and spitting, the Infardi Baneblade drove the Tanith First into abject retreat.

Baffels would not let go. He was still determined to prove Gaunt right in selecting him for command. He was going to win this, he was going to take the target. He was–

As men fled around him, he grabbed a fallen tread-fether, loaded up a rocket and took aim on the monster tank. It was less than twenty metres away now, a giant, fire-spitting dragon that blotted out the stars.

Baffels locked the crosshairs on a slit window near what he assumed was the driver's position. He held the tube steady and fired.

There was a bright blast of flame and for one jubilant moment, Baffels thought he'd been successful. That he'd become a hero like fething Gol Kolea.

But the Baneblade was barely bruised. One of its secondary coaxial cannons killed Baffels with a brief spurt of shots.

RAWNE'S COUNTER PUNCH finally reached the Bhavnager temple at nine thirty-five. It was dark by then, and the town was alive with firestorms and shooting.

Their slow progression through the minefield had sped up when Larkin and Domor had hit upon an improvised plan. Domor's augmetic eyes could pick out many mines just under the soil surface. He talked Larkin onto them and Larkin and Banda then set them off with pinpoint shots.

The sweepers had advanced another thirty metres and by that time, with the sun gone, Sirus's tank mob had dealt with the opposition armour. Then the tanks rolled in down the channel Domor had cleared, and lowered their combat dozer blades to clear the last few metres now they were no longer under fire.

The temple was a mess. Golden fish-scale tiles trickled off the burst dome of the once glorious stupa. Incendiary shells burned in the main nave. Prayer flags smouldered and twitched in the breeze.

The counter punch drove in at last towards the fuel depot from the east.

Captain Sirus, his tracks now repaired, thundered forward in the *Wrath of Pardua*. He had heard the strangled, unbelievable transmission from the southern front that they'd met a Baneblade.

If it was true, he wanted a piece of that. Something Woll could never beat.

The *Wrath of Pardua* came at the enemy Baneblade in the open space of the depot field. Sensing the *Wrath* by auspex, the Baneblade had begun to turn.

Sirus loaded augur shells, armour busters, into his breech, and punched two penetrating holes in the massive enemy tank's mantlet. Few Pardus tank commanders carried augur shells as a matter of course, because few ever expected to meet something genuinely tougher than themselves. Sirus was a philosophically tactical man. He was happy to sacrifice a few valuable places in his magazine for augur shells, just in case.

Now the trick was to target the holes made by the augurs and blow the enemy out from the inside with a hi-ex tank round.

The wounded Baneblade traversed its turret, locked on to the *Wrath of Pardua*, and destroyed it with a single shot from its main weapon.

Sirus was laughing in victory as he was incinerated. An instant. An instant of success all tank masters dream of. He had wounded the beast. He could die now.

The *Wrath of Pardua* exploded, skipping armour chips out around itself in the blast wake.

Old Strontium purred out from behind the shattered build-ings south of the depot. Woll had never carried augur rounds as standard, like Sirus. But he was damn well going to use the advantage.

Ignoring his auspex and sighting only by eye, referring to his rangefinder and crosswind indicator, Woll punched a hi-ex shell through one of the profound holes Sirus had made in the Baneblade's armour.

There was a brief pause.

Then the super-heavy tank blew itself to pieces in a titanic eruption of heat and noise and light.

GAUNT AND SORIC, with the help of Hark and the squad leaders, managed to slow the Ghosts' panic and bring them around towards the fuel depot. Soric himself led the charge back down the yard towards the depot, past the flaming remains of the Baneblade.

By then, Rawne's counter punch had chased in after the valiant *Wrath of Pardua*, and was cleaning out the last Infardi in the depot. It was a running gun-battle, and Rawne knew he had time to make up.

He vox-signalled seizure of the depot just before eleven.

Surviving Infardi elements fled north into the rainwoods beyond Bhavnager. The town was now in Imperial hands.

AS THE MEDICS moved around him in the smoke-stained night, Gaunt found ayatani Zweil kneeling over the ruptured corpse of Sergeant Baffels. Sergeant Varl stood attentively nearby, watching.

'Sorry, chief. He insisted. He wanted to be here,' Varl told Gaunt.

Gaunt nodded. 'Thanks for looking after him, Varl.'

Gaunt walked over to Zweil.

'This man is a special loss,' Zweil said, turning to rise and face Gaunt. 'His efforts were crucial here.'

'Did someone tell you that or do you just feel that, father?'

'The latter... Am I wrong?'

'No, not at all. Baffels led the way to the depot. He did his duty, beyond his duty. I could not have asked for more.'

Zweil closed Baffels's clouded eyes.

'I felt as much. Well, it's over now,' he said. 'Sleep well, pilgrim. Your journey's done.'

ELEVEN
THE RAINWOODS

'Though my tears be as many as the spots of rain
Falling in the Hagian woods,
One for every fallen soul, loyal to the Throne
There would not be enough.'

— Gospel of Saint Sabbat, Psalms II vii.

UNDER COVER OF darkness, the sky lit up, over a hundred and fifty kilometres away. Flashes, sudden flares, spits of light, accompanied by the very distant judder of thunder.

Once it had been going on for an hour, they all agreed it wasn't a storm.

'Full-scale action,' Corbec murmured.

'That's one feth of a fight,' Bragg agreed.

They stood in the dark, at the edge of the holy river, insects chorusing around them, as Greer and Daur worked on the engine.

'What I wouldn't give...' Derin began, and then shut up.

'I know what you mean, son,' said Corbec.

'Bhavnager,' said Milo, joining them with a flashlight and an open chart-slate.

209

'Where, boy?'

'Bhavnager. Farming town, in the approach to the foothills.'
Milo showed Corbec the area on the chart.

'It was meant to be our second night stop,' he said. 'There's a
fuel depot there.'

An especially big flash underlit the clouds.

'Feth!' said Bragg.

'Bad news for some poor bastard,' said Derin.

'Let's hope it was one of theirs,' said Corbec.

DORDEN HAD WALKED away down to the river, and stood casting
stones aimlessly into the inky water.

He started as someone came up beside him in the close dark.
It was the esholi, Sanian.

'You are no fighter, I know that,' she said.

'What?'

'I worked with the lady Curth. I saw you. A medic.'

'That's me, girl,' Dorden smiled.

'You are old.'

'Oh, thanks a bunch!'

'No, you are old. On Hagia, that is a mark of respect.'

'It is?'

'It shows you have wisdom. That, if you haven't wasted your
life, you have used it to collect up learning.'

'I'm pretty sure I haven't wasted my life, Sanian.'

'I feel like I have.'

He looked round at her. She was a shadow, a silhouette staring down into the river.

'What?'

'What am I? A learner? A student? All my life I have studied
books and gospels... and now my world ends in ruin and war.
The saint doesn't watch over us. I see men like Corbec, Daur,
even a young man like Brin. They scold themselves because all
they have learned is the art of war. But war is what matters. Here.
On Hagia, now. But for the art of war-making, there is nothing.'

'There's more to life than–'

'There is not, doctor. The Imperium is great, its wonders are
manifold, but what of it would remain but for war? Its people?
Its learning? Its culture? Its language? Nothing. War encom-
passes all. In this time, there is only war.'

Dorden sighed. She was right. After a fashion.

'War has found Bhavnager,' she remarked, looking briefly at the flashes underlighting the distant clouds.

'You know the place?'

'I was born there and raised there. I left there to become esholi and find my way. Now, even if my way in life is revealed to me, there will be nothing for me to return home to, when this is done. Because it will never be done. War is eternal. It is only mankind that is finite.'

'NOTHING ON THE vox,' Vamberfeld said.

Corbec nodded. 'You've tried all channels?'

'Yes sir. It's dead. I don't know if it's dead because we're out of range or because the Chimera's vox-caster is a pile of junk.'

'We'll never know,' said Derin.

Vamberfeld sat down on a tree stump at the edge of the road. Rain was in the air, and a true storm was gathering in defiance of the man-made one to the west. The wind stirred their hair and the first few spats of rain dropped around them.

Under the raised cowling of the Chimera, Daur and Greer worked at the engines.

Vamberfeld could hear Corbec talking to Milo just a few steps away from where he sat. It would be, he supposed, the easiest thing in the world just to stand up, get the colonel's attention, and talk to him, man to man.

The easiest thing...

He couldn't do it.

Even now, he could feel the terror crawling back into him, in through his pores, in through his veins, squirming and slithering down along his gut and up into the recesses of his mind. He began to shake.

It was so unfair. On Verghast, in the towering hive, he'd enjoyed a quiet life, working as Guilder Naslquey's personal clerk in the commercia, signing dockets, arranging manifests, chasing promissory notes. He'd been good at that. He'd lived in a decent little hab on Spine Low-231, with a promise of status promotion. He'd been very much in love with his fiancée, an apprentice seamstress with Bocider's.

Then the Zoican War had taken it all away. His job, his little hab, to an artillery shell; his fiancée to...

Well, he didn't know what. He'd never been able to find out what had happened to his dear, sweet little seamstress.

And that was all terrible. He'd lived through days and nights of fear, of hiding in ruins, of running scared, of starving. But he'd lived through them, and come out sane.

Because of that, he'd decided he was man enough to turn his back on the ruins of his life and join the Imperial Guard when the Act of Consolation made that possible. It had felt like the right thing to do.

He'd known fear during the war, and renewed the acquaintance again. The fear of leaving Verghast, never to return. The anxiety of warp travel in a stinking, confined troop ship. The trepidation of failing during the bone-wearying first week of Fundamental and Preparatory.

The true terror, the unexpected terror had come later. The first time, wriggling and chuckling at the back of his scalp, during the Hagia mass landings. He'd shaken it off. He'd been through hell on Verghast, he told himself. This was just the same kind of hell.

Then it had come again, in the first phase of the assault on the Doctrinopolis. In real fighting, for the first time, as a real soldier. Men died alongside him or, worse still as it seemed to Vamberfeld, were dismembered or hideously mutilated by war. Those first few days had left him shaking inside. The terror would not now leave him alone. It simply subsided a little between engagements.

Vamberfeld had decided that he needed to kill. To make a kill, as a soldier, to exorcise his terror. The chance had finally come when he'd been with Gaunt as they breached the Universitariat from across the Square of Sublime Tranquillity. To be baptised in war, to be badged in blood. He had been willing, and eager. He had wanted combat. He had wanted relief from the terror-daemon that was by then riding his back all the time.

But it had only made things worse.

He'd come out of that encounter shaking like an idiot, unable to focus or talk. He'd come out a total slave to that daemon.

It was so bloody unfair.

Bragg and Derin had recruited him from the hospital wards for this mission. He could hardly have refused them... he was able-bodied and that made him useful. No one seemed to see the cackling, oil-black terror clinging to him. Bragg and Derin had said Corbec had an important mission, and that was alright. Vamberfeld liked the colonel. It seemed vital. The colonel had talked about holy missions and visions. That was fine too. It had been easy for Vamberfeld to play along with that. Easy to pass off his nervousness and pretend the saint had spoken to him as well, and ear-marked him for the task.

It was all a sham. He was just saying what he thought they wanted to hear. The only thing that really spoke to him was the cackling daemon.

The words of the driver, Greer, had alarmed him. His talk of gold, of complicity with Captain Daur. Vamberfeld wondered if they were all mocking him. He was now pretty sure they were all bastard-mercenaries, breaking orders not because of some lofty, holy ideal but because of a base lust for wealth. And so he felt a fool for acting the part of the dutiful visionary.

His hands shook. He tucked them into his pockets in the hope that no one would see. His body shook. His mind shook. The terror consumed him. He cursed the daemon for fooling him into throwing in with a band of deserters and thieves. He cursed the daemon for making him shake. He cursed the daemon for being there at all.

He wanted to get up and tell Corbec about his terror, but he was shaking so much he couldn't.

And even if he could, he knew they'd most likely laugh in his face and shoot him in the bushes.

'Drink?'

'What?' Vamberfeld snapped around.

'Fancy a drink?' Bragg ask, offering him an open flask of the Tanith's powerful sacra.

'No.'

'You look like you could use some, Vambs,' Bragg said genially.

'No.'

'Okay,' said Bragg, taking a sip himself and smacking his lips in relish.

Vamberfeld realised the rain was falling hard now, bouncing off his face and shoulders.

'You should get in,' Bragg observed. 'It's coming down in buckets.'

'I will. In a minute. I'm okay.'

'Okay,' said the big Tanith, moving away.

Warm rainwater began to leak down Vamberfeld's neckline and over his wrists. He turned his face up to look into the downpour, wishing that it would wash the terror away.

'SOMETHING'S UP WITH the hive-boy, chief,' Bragg said to Corbec, passing him the flask.

Corbec took a deep swig of the biting liquor and used it to swallow a handful more painkillers. He was sucking in way too many of them, he knew. He hurt so, he needed them. Corbec followed Bragg's gesture and looked across the rain-pelted road at the figure seated with its back to them. 'I know, Bragg,' he said. 'Do me a favour. Keep an eye on him for me, would you?'

'So... HOW MUCH?' whispered Greer, tightening a piston nut.

'How much what?' replied Daur. He was soaked by the rain now.

'Don't make me say it, Verghast... The gold!'

'Oh, that. Keep your voice down. We don't want the others hearing.'

'But it's a lot, right? You promised a lot.'

'You can't imagine the amount.'

Greer smiled, and wiped the rain off his face with a cuff that stained the streaks of water running down his brow with machine oil.

'You haven't told the rest, then?'

'Ah... Just enough to get them interested.'

'You gonna cut them out when the time comes?'

'Well, I'm considering it.'

'You can count on me, Verghast, time comes... If I can count on you, that is.'

'Oh, yeah. Of course. But look for my signal before you do anything.'

'Got it.'

'Greer, you will wait for my signal, won't you?'

Greer grinned. 'Absolutely, cap. This is your monkey-show. You call the play.'

'SLOW DOWN, GIRL, slow down!' Corbec smiled, sheltering from the rain under the open hatch of the Chimera. Her hand signs were too quick for him as usual.

Is the saint really calling to you? Nessa signed, more slowly this time.

'Feth, I don't know! Something is...' Corbec had still not truly mastered the sign codes used by the Verghastites, though he'd tried hard. He knew his clumsy gestures only conveyed the pigeon-essence of his words.

Captain Daur says he has heard her, she signed expressively. *He says you and the doctor have too.*

'Maybe, Nessa.'

Are we wrong?

'I'm sorry, what? Are we wrong?'

Yes. She looked up at him, her face running with rainwater, her eyes bright.

'Wrong in what way?'

To be here. To be doing this.

'No, we're not. Believe that much at least.'

ONLY HIS HAND shook now. His left hand. By force of will, Vamberfeld had focused all the terror and the shakes down into that one extremity. He could breathe again. He was controlling it.

Down the track, through the heavy rain, he saw something stir in the darkness. He knew he should reach for his weapon or cry out, but he didn't dare in case it let the shaking spill out through him again.

The movement resolved and became visible for a second. Two yearling chelon calves, no higher than a man's knee, waddling down the muddy track towards them.

And then a girl, aged twelve or thirteen, dressed in the dingy robes of the peasant caste, rounding the calves in with her crook.

She pulled them back before they came too close to the parked Imperial transport. Just a smudge in the rainy night. A peasant girl, bringing in her herd, trying not to risk contact with the soldiers driving through her pastures.

Vamberfeld stared at her in fascination. Her eyes came up and found his.

So young. So very grimy and spattered with mud. Her eyes piercing and...

The Chimera roared into life, engines turning and racing and spitting exhaust. Vapour streamed up into the rainfall in thick geysers of steam. The main lamps and headlights burst into life.

'Mount up! Mount up!' Corbec yelled, calling them all back to the repaired transport.

Vamberfeld woke up suddenly, finding himself lying on his side in the rain-pounded mud. He'd passed out and fallen from the tree stump. He got to his feet, weak and shivering, fumbled for his gun and ran back towards the brightly lit transport.

He cast a final look back into the dark trees. The girl and her chelons had vanished.

But the daemon was still there.

Pulling his shaking hand into his jacket to hide it, he climbed into the Chimera.

DAYBREAK, STREAMING RAIN in lament over the smoking battle-ground, came up on Bhavnager.

Waking early in his tent, Gaunt leapt up suddenly and then remembered the battle was done. He sat back on the tan canvas seat of his folding stool and sighed. A half-empty bottle of amasec sat on the map table nearby. He began to reach for it and then decided not to.

Beyond his tent, he heard the grumble of tank engines being overhauled by the tech-priests. He heard the clank of the fuel bowsers as they replenished the transports. He heard the whine of hoists as tank magazines were reloaded from the Chimeras. He heard the moan of the wounded in Curth's makeshift infirmary.

Vox-officer Beltayn stuck his head in through the tent flap cautiously. 'Oh five hundred, sir,' he said.

Gaunt nodded distractedly. He got up, pulling off his blood-, soot- and oil- streaked vest, replacing it with a fresh one from his kit. The braces of his uniform pants dangling loose around his hips, he washed his face with handfuls of water from the jug and then slipped the braces up, putting on a shirt and his black dolman jacket with its rows of gold buttons and frogging.

Bhavnager. What a victory. What a loss.

He was still shaking from the combat, from the ebbing adrenalin and the weariness.

He had slept for about three hours, and that fitfully. Mad dreams, confused dreams, dreams spawned by extreme fatigue and the memories of what he had been through.

He had seen himself on a narrow shelf of ice, with the world far below, clinging on, about to fall, hurricanes of fire falling around him.

Sergeant Baffels had appeared, alive and whole. He'd been on the lip of ice, and had reached over to grab Gaunt's hands. He'd pulled Gaunt up, onto solid ground.

'Baffels...' he'd managed to gasp out, frozen to the marrow.

Baffels had smiled, just before he'd vanished.

'Sabbat Martyr,' he'd said.

Gaunt grabbed the bottle and poured a deep measure into his dirty shot glass.

He swigged it down.

'Now the ghosts of Ghosts are haunting me,' he murmured to himself.

UNDER KOLEA'S INSTRUCTION, the honour guard buried their dead – almost two hundred of them – in a mass grave beside the temple at Bhavnager. The Trojans could have dug the pit, but the Pardus Conquerors *Old Strontium, Beat the Retreat, P48J* and *Heart of Destruction* did the honours with their dozer blades, even though their crews were half dead with fatigue. Ayatani Zweil was prevailed upon to make the service of the dead. The Ghosts dutifully staked small crosses cut from ghylum wood in rows across the turned earth, one for each of the dead who slept beneath.

THE DAY CAME up, warm, muggy and blighted with heavy rain. Gaunt knew it would take weeks for a unit to recover from the shock of an action as fundamentally brutal as Bhavnager, but he didn't have weeks.

He barely had days.

At nine in the morning, he called the honour guard to order for an hour's prep and sent the Recon Spear out in advance into the rainwoods above the town. Though tired, the men in his command seemed generally to be in good spirits. A solid victory, and against such odds, would do that, despite the losses. The Pardus were more sombre than the Ghosts: they seemed more to be mourning the beloved machines they'd lost rather than the men.

Gaunt crossed the town square and stopped by a small timber store where Troopers Cocoer, Waed and Garond were guarding the Infardi officer Bonin's squad had taken the night before. No other Infardi troops had been taken alive. Gaunt presumed that was because the Infardi took their wounded with them or killed them.

The vile, tattooed thing was chained up like a canid at the back of the shed. 'Anything from him?'

'No sir,' said Waed.

Rawne and Feygor had made a preliminary attempt at interrogation the previous night, after the fight, but the prisoner hadn't responded.

'Get him ready for shipping. We'll take him with us.'

Gaunt walked up towards the depot. Major Kleopas, Captain Woll and Lieutenant Pauk stood on the sooty apron of the machine sheds as the unit's Trojans towed in the *Drum Roll* and the *Fancy Klara*. Both tanks could be repaired, Gaunt had been told. The *Drum Roll's* damaged starboard track section was a buckled, dragging mess, and the crew, led by Captain Hancot, rode on the turret of their wounded steed. Though immobilised early in the fight, they had continued to fire and make kills effectively.

But for an oddly neat hole punched into the plating of its turret, the *Klara* seemed intact. Only her driver had survived. Shutting off the electrics, tech-priests and sappers had disarmed the unexploded enemy shell that had, both directly and indirectly, killed LeTaw and his gun crew. Once it had been extracted safely from the ruptured magazine, and the magazine picked over for damaged munitions, the *Klara* was towed into Bhavnager for turret repairs. A replacement crew was assembled from survivors of slain tanks.

Gaunt crossed to the watching tank officers and properly congratulated the Pardus commander for his part in the victory. Kleopas looked tired and pale, but he gladly shook Gaunt's hand.

'One for the casebooks in the Armour Academy on Pardua,' Gaunt said.

'I imagine so.'

'I have a... a question, I suppose, colonel-commissar,' said Kleopas.

'Voice it, sir,' said Gaunt.

'You and I... all of us were briefed that while Infardi forces were still at large in the hinterlands, their numbers were minimal. The opposition they raised here at Bhavnager was huge in scale, well organised and well supplied. Not the sort of show you'd expect from a broken, running enemy.'

'I agree completely.'

'Damn it, Gaunt, we moved in on this target expecting a hard fight, but not an all-out battle. My machines faced numerical odds greater than they've ever known. Don't get me wrong, there was great glory here and I live to serve, the Emperor protects.'

'The Emperor protects,' echoed Gaunt, Woll and Pauk.

'But this isn't what they told us was out here. Can you... comment at least?'

Gaunt looked at his boots thoughtfully for a moment. 'When I was with Slaydo, just before the start of the crusade, we fell upon Khulen in winter time. I served with the Hyrkans then. Brave soldiers all. The enemy had vast numbers dug into the three main cities. It was snow-season and hellish cold. Two months it took, and we drove them out. Victory was ours. Slaydo told us to maintain vigil, and none of the command echelon knew why. Slaydo was a wily old goat, of course. He'd seen enough in his long career to have insight. His instincts proved correct. Within a month, three times as many enemy units fell upon our positions. Three times as many as we had driven out in the first place. They'd given up, you see? They'd abandoned the cities and fallen back before we'd had time to rob them of their full strength, regrouped in the wilderness, and come back in vast numbers.'

'What happened?' asked Pauk, fascinated.

'Slaydo happened, lieutenant,' smiled Gaunt and they all laughed.

'We took Khulen. A liberation effort turned into an all-out war. It lasted six months. We destroyed them. Now, consider this, a year later at the start of this crusade, liberating Ashek II. Formidable enemy strengths in the hives and the trade-towns of the archipelago. Three months' hard fighting and we were masters of the world, but the Imperial tacticians warned that the lava hills might provide excellent natural defences in which the enemy could regroup. We battened down, ready for the counter sweep. It never came. After a lot of recon we discovered that the enemy hadn't fallen back at all. They'd fought to the last man in the hives and we'd vanquished them entirely on the first phase. They hadn't even thought to use the landscape that so favoured them.'

'I'm beginning to feel like a child in tactica class,' smiled Woll.

'I'm sorry,' said Gaunt. 'I was simply illustrating a number of points.'

'That any enemy twisted by Chaos is always unpredictable?' suggested Kleopas.

'That, for one thing.'

'That because the enemy is so unpredictable, we might as well hang all the Imperial tacticians now?' chuckled Woll.

'Exactly, Woll, for two.'

'That this is what's occurring here?' asked Kleopas.

Gaunt nodded. 'You all know I have no love of Lugo. I have personal reason to object to the man.'

'Make no apologies for him,' Kleopas said. 'He's a new minted upstart with no experience.'

'Well, you said it, not me,' grinned Gaunt. 'The point is... whatever our lord general's failings... the spawn of Chaos is never predictable, never logical. You can't out-think them. To try would be madness. You can only prepare for any event. My clumsy examples were meant to illustrate that. If I failed at all at the Doctrinopolis, it was that I didn't cover every possibility.'

'I was with you, Gaunt. You were given orders that prevented you from using your experience.'

'Gracious. Thank you. That's what I feel we have here. A misguided expectation on the part of Lugo that the enemy will behave like an Imperial army. He thinks it will hold the cities until it is beaten. It will not. He thinks that only defeated remnants will flee after the battle. Not true again. I believe that the Infardi gave up the cities when they realised we had the upper hand, and purposefully backed up their main strengths into the outlying territories. Hence the weight of numbers at Bhavnager.'

'Lugo be damned,' said Woll.

'Lugo ought to listen to his officers, that's all,' said Gaunt. 'That's what made Slaydo Slaydo... or Solon Solon... the ability to listen. I fear that's lacking from the crusade's senior ranks now, even lacking in Macaroth.'

The Pardus officers shuffled uneasily.

'I'll blaspheme no more, gentlemen,' Gaunt said and drew smiles from them all. 'My advice is simply this. Prepare. Expect the unexpected. The arch-enemy is not a logical or predictable foe, but he has his own agenda. We can't imagine it, but we can suffer all too well when it takes effect.'

He stepped back as Rawne, Kolea, Varl, Hark and Surgeon Curth approached across the rockcrete apron to join them, and an impromptu operations meeting came to order. Curth handed a personnel review to the colonel-commissar.

They had two hundred and twenty-four wounded, of whom seventy-three were serious. Curth told Gaunt frankly that although they could move all the wounded with them, at least eighteen would not survive the transit more than a day. Nine would not survive the transit, period.

'Your recommendations, surgeon?'

'Simple, sir. None of them travel.'

Rawne shook his head with a dry laugh. 'What do we do? Leave them here?'

Kolea suggested they establish a stronghold at Bhavnager, where the injured might be tended in a field hospital. Though it meant leaving a reduced force at the town, vulnerable to the roaming Infardi, it might be the only hope of survival for the casualties. Besides, the honour guard would need Bhavnager's fuel resources for the return trip.

Gaunt conceded the merit of this idea. He would leave one hundred Ghosts and a supporting armoured force at Bhavnager to guard the fuel dump and the wounded while he pushed on into the Sacred Hills. Curth immediately insisted on staying, and Gaunt allowed that, selecting Lesp as the ongoing mission's chief medic. Captain Woll volunteered to command the armour guard of the Bhavnager fastness. Gaunt and Kleopas arranged to leave the *Death Jester*, *Xenophobe* and the mid-repairs *Drum Roll* and *Fancy Klara* under his command. Gaunt chose Kolea to command the position, with Sergeant Varl as his second.

Kolea accepted the task obediently, and went off to gather up the platoons under his immediate command. Varl was rather more against the choice, and as the meeting broke up, took Gaunt quietly to one side and begged to be allowed to join him on this final mission.

'It's not my final mission, sergeant,' Gaunt said.

'But sir–'

'Have you ever disobeyed an order, Varl?'

'No, sir.'

'Don't do it now. This is important. I trust you. Do this for me.'

'Yes sir.'

'For Tanith, like I know you remember her, Varl.'

'Yes, sir.'

'For Tanith.'

Then Gaunt roused up the main force and pushed on into the rainwoods, leaving the lowlands and Bhavnager behind in their dust.

Knots of Ghost and Pardus personnel watched the convoy depart. Varl stood watching for a long time after the last vehicle had vanished from sight and only dust clouds showed their progress.

'Sergeant?'

He swung around out of his reverie. Kolea and Woll had grouped squad leaders and tank chiefs around a chart table on the steps of the battered town hall.

'If you'd care to join us?' Kolea smiled. 'Let's figure out how best to get this place defended.'

FROM BHAVNAGER, THE wide road made a sharp incline for five or six kilometres as it ran north. Gaunt noticed that already the land to either side of the road was becoming less open. Field systems and cultivated areas began to disappear, except for a few well-watered paddocks and meadows, where lush stands of woodland began to flourish. Cycads and a larger variant of acestus predominated, often lush with sphagnum moss or skeins of a dark epiphyte known locally as priest's beard. Luminously coloured flowers dotted the thickets, some unusually large.

The air became increasingly humid. The woods to either side grew thicker and taller. Within the first hour after departure, sunlight began to flicker down on the travelling convoy, slanting through the ladder of the trees.

After three hours, the track levelled out and became damp sand and mud rather than dust. The air was heated and still, and clothing began to stick and cling with the airborne moisture. Every now and then, without warning or overture, heavy, warm rain began to fall, straight down, sometimes so hard visibility dropped to a few metres and headlamps went on. Then, just as abruptly, the rain would stop, as if it had never been there. Ground mist would well up almost immediately. Thunder rumbled in the heat-swollen air.

Past noon, they stopped, circulating rations and rotating driving teams. The rainwoods to either side of the trail were mysterious realms of green shadow, and a sweetly pungent vegetable smell permeated everything. Between the showers, the place was alive with wildlife: whirring beetles with wings like rubies, rivers of colonial mites, arachnids and grotesquely large shelled gastropods that left trails of glistening glue on the barks of the trees. There were many birds too: not the riverine forkbills, but shoals of tiny, coloured fliers that buzzed as they hovered and darted. Their tiny forms were small enough to be clenched in a man's fist, except their long, thin down-curved beaks which were almost thirty centimetres long.

Standing by his Salamander as he drank water and ate a ration bar, Gaunt saw eight-limbed lizards, their scaled flesh as golden as the stupa of Bhavnager's temple, flickering through the undergrowth. The whoops, whistles and cries of larger, unseen animals echoed intermittently from the woods.

'It surprises me you left Kolea at the town,' Hark said, appearing beside Gaunt. Hark had slipped off his heavy coat and jacket and stood, in shirt sleeves and a silver-frogged waistcoat, mopping sweat from his brow with a white kerchief. Gaunt hadn't heard him approach, and Hark's conversations tended to start like that, in the middle, without any hail or hello.

'Why is that, commissar?'

'He's one of the regiment's best officers. Ferociously loyal and obedient.'

'I know.' Gaunt took a swig of water. 'Who better to leave in charge of an independent operation?'

'I'd have kept him close by. Rawne is the one I'd leave behind.'

'Really?'

'He's a good enough soldier, but he fights from the head, not the heart. And there's no missing the fact he has issues with you.'

'Major Rawne and I have an understanding. He – and many other Ghosts – blame me for the death of their world. Time was, I think, Rawne would have killed me to avenge Tanith. But he's grown into command. Now, I think, he accepts that we just simply don't like each other and gets on with it.'

'I've studied his files and, over the last few days, I've studied the man. He's a cynic and a malcontent. I don't think his issues with you have subsided at all. His knife still itches for your back. The time will come. He's just become very good at waiting.'

'There was a saying Slaydo used to like: "Keep your friends close..."'

'"...and your enemies closer". I am familiar with that notion, Gaunt. Sometimes it does not work well at all.'

The cry went down the convoy to remount. 'Why don't you travel the next part in my carrier?' Gaunt asked Hark. He hoped none of the remark's irony would be lost.

FORTY MINUTES NORTH of the main convoy, the Recon Spearhead was slowing to a crawl. Rawne had chosen to accompany Mkoll's forward unit. For this, the third day, the spear comprised two scout Salamanders, a Hydra flak tractor, the Destroyer *Grey Venger* and the Conqueror *Say Your Prayers*.

The track was narrowing right down, so tight that the tree cover was beginning to meet overhead and the hulls of the big tanks brushed the foliage.

Mkoll kept checking the chart-slates to make sure they weren't off course.

'There was no other track or road,' said Rawne.

'I know, and the locator co-ordinates are right. I just didn't expect things to close down so tightly so fast. I keep feeling like we must have missed the main way and come off onto a herding trail.'

They both had to duck as a sheath of low-hanging rubbery green leaves brushed over the crewbay.

'Looks like fast-growing stuff,' said Rawne. 'You know what tropical flora can be like. This stuff may have come up in the last month's wet season.'

Mkoll looked over the side of the Salamander at the condition of the track itself. The rainwoods were packed into the spur gorges of the foothills, and that meant there was a slight gradient against them. The centre of the trackway was eroded into a channel down which a stream ran, and heavier floodaways had brought down mud, rock and plant materials. The Salamanders were managing fine, and so was the Hydra, but the two big tanks were beginning to slip occasionally. Worse still, the track was beginning to disintegrate under their weight. Mkoll thought darkly about the weight of machines behind them, particularly the fifty-plus long-body troop trucks, which had nothing like the power or traction of the tracked vehicles.

Scintillating beetles sawed through the air between scout leader and major. Rawne kept one eye on the auspex. Both he and Mkoll knew considerable elements of Infardi had fled north into these woodlands after the battle, but no trace whatever had been found of them on the track. Somehow they'd got troops and fighting vehicles out of sight.

A cry came up from ahead and the spearhead stopped. Standing the scout troops and the armour to ready watch, Rawne and Mkoll went forward on foot. The lead Salamander had rounded a slow bend in the trail to find a massive cycad slumped across the track. The mass of rotting wood weighed many tonnes.

'Can you ram it aside?' Rawne asked the Salamander driver.

'Not enough purchase on this incline,' the driver replied. 'We'll need chains to pull it out.'

'Couldn't we cut it up or blast it?' asked Trooper Caober.

Mkoll had moved round to the uplifted rootball of the fallen trunk, which was sticky with peat-black soil and wormy loam. There were streaks of a dry, reddish oxide deposit on some of the root fingers. He sniffed it.

'Maybe we could get the Conqueror past. Lay in with its dozer blade,' Brostin was saying.

'Down! Down!' Mkoll yelled.

He'd barely uttered the words when las-fire stung out of the undergrowth alongside them. Rounds spanged off the vehicle hulls or tore overhanging leaves. The driver of the lead Salamander was hit in the neck and fell back into his machine's crewbay with a shriek.

Mkoll dived into cover behind the cycad trunk next to Rawne.

'How did you know?' Rawne asked.

'Fyceline traces on the tree roots. They used a charge to bring it over and block us.'

'Sitting fething target...' Rawne cursed.

The Ghosts were firing back now, but they could see nothing to aim at. Even Lillo, who happened to be in the crewbay of the lead Salamander and therefore had an auspex to refer to, could find no target. The auspex gave back nothing except a flat reading off the hot, dense mass of foliage.

'Cannons!' Rawne ordered, over his vox.

The coaxial and pintle mounts of the machines stuttered into life, raking the leaf canopy to shreds with heavy washes of fire. A moment later, Sergeant Horkan's Hydra drowned them all out as it commenced firing. The four, long barrelled autocannons of its anti-aircraft mount swivelled around and blasted simultaneous streams of illuminator rounds into the woodlands at head height, cropping trees, shredding bushes, pulverising ferns, liquidising foliage. A stinking mist of vaporised plant matter and aspirated sap filled the trackway, making the troops choke and retch.

After thirty seconds' auto-fire, the Hydra ceased. Apart from the drizzle of canopy moisture, the collapse of destroyed plants and the clicking of the Hydra's autoloader as it cycled, there was silence. The Hydra was designed to bring down combat aircraft at long range. Point-blank, against a soft target of vegetation, it had cut a clearing in the rainwood fifty metres deep and thirty across. A few denuded, broken trunks stood up amid the leaf-pulp.

Mkoll and Caober moved forward to check the area. The partially disintegrated remains of two Infardi lay amid the green destruction.

There was no sign of further attack.

Just a little ambush; just a little harrying, delaying tactic.

'Get chains round that tree!' Rawne ordered. At this rate, if the damn Infardi dropped a tree every few kilometres, it was going to take weeks to cross these rainwoods.

ABOUT A HUNDRED and twenty kilometres south of the rainwoods, a lone Chimera coughed its way down the dusty highway through an empty, abandoned village called Mukret. Since the dawn-stop that morning, it had borne the name 'the Wounded Wagon' on its flank, daubed in orange anti-rust lacquer by a hasty, imprecise hand.

The day was glaring hot, and Greer kept a close eye on the temp-gauges. The old heap's panting turbine was red-lining regularly, and twice now they'd had to stop, dump the boiling water-mix in the coolant system and replace it with water drawn from the river in jerry cans. Now they were out of coolant chemicals, and the mix in the flushed out system was so dilute it was essentially running on river water alone.

Greer pulled the vehicle to the roadside under the shade of a row of tree-ferns before the needles went past the point of no return.

'Fifteen minute break,' he called back into the cargo space. He needed to stretch his legs anyway, and maybe there would be time to show Daur a little more of the skills needed to drive the machine. An ability to swap drivers meant they would be able to keep going longer without rest stops.

Corbec's team dismounted into the sunlight and the dry air, seeking shelter at once under the ferns. The cabin fans and recirculators in the Chimera weren't working either, so it was like going on a long journey in an oven.

Corbec, Daur and Milo consulted the chart. 'We should get to Nusera Crossing by dark. That would be good. If they're in the rainwoods now, it means their rate of speed will have dropped, so we might just start catching them,' said Corbec. He turned aside, unpopped his water flask and knocked down a pill or two.

'The far side of the river bothers me,' Daur was saying. 'Seems likely that's where the mass of Infardi are concentrated. Things could get hotter for us too once we make the crossing.'

'Noted,' said Corbec. 'What are these here?'

Milo peered. The colonel was indicating a network of faint lines that followed the river north when it forked that way at Nusera. They radiated up into the Sacred Hills, echoing, though not precisely, the branches of the holy river's head waters. 'I don't know. It says "sooka" on the key. I'll ask Sanian.'

NEARBY, AT THE river's edge, Vamberfeld stood in the shallows skipping stones out over the flat water between the reed beds. A slight breeze stirred the feathery rushes on the far bank, which were starkly ash-white against the baked, blue sky.

He made one skip four times. Concentrating on simple actions like that helped him to control the shaking in his hand. The water was soothingly cool against his legs.

He skipped another. Just before it made its fifth bounce, a much larger stone flew out over his head and fell with a dull splash into the river. Vamberfeld looked round.

On the bank, Bragg grinned at him sheepishly.

'Never could do that.'

'So I see,' said Vamberfeld.

Bragg gingerly stepped out into the shallows, steering his clumsy bulk unsteadily over the loose stones of the bed.

'Maybe you could teach me?'

Vamberfeld thought for a moment. He took another couple of flat stones from his pants pocket and handed one to the big Tanith.

'Hold it like this.'

'Like this?' Bragg's meaty fingers dwarfed Vamberfeld's.

'No, like this. Flat to the water. Now, it's in the wrist. Make it spin as you release. Just so.'

Three neat splashes. Paff-paff-paff.

'Nice,' said Bragg, and tried. The stone hit the water and disappeared.

Vamberfeld fetched out two more stones. 'Try again, Bragg,' he said, and when the big man laughed he realised he had unwittingly made a joke.

Vamberfeld skipped a few more, and slowly, Bragg managed it too. One throw where Vamberfeld made four or five. The Verghastite suddenly, joyfully, realised that he was relaxed for the first time in recent memory. Just to be here, calm, in the sunlight, casually teaching a likeably gentle man to do something pointless like skip stones. It reminded him of his childhood, taking vacations up on the River Hass with his brothers. For a moment, the shaking almost stopped. Bragg's attention was fixed entirely on Vamberfeld's hands and demonstrations.

From the corner of his eye Vamberfeld saw the white rushes on the far side of the river sway in the breeze again. Except there was no breeze.

He didn't want to look.

'Hold it a little tighter, like that.'

'I think I'm getting it. Feth me! Two bounces!'

'You are getting it. Try another.'

Don't look. Don't look and it won't be there. Don't look. Don't look. Don't look.

'Yes! Three! Ha ha!'

Ignore the green shapes in amongst the rushes. Ignore them and they won't be there. And this moment won't end. And the terror won't come back. Ignore them. Don't look.

'Good shot! Five there! Can you do six?'

Don't look. Don't say anything. Ignore that urge to shout out: you know it will just start you shaking again. Bragg hasn't noticed. No one has to know. It'll go away. It'll go away because it isn't even there.

'Try again, Bragg.'

'Sure. Hey, Vambs... Why's your hand shaking?'

'What?'

It isn't. Don't look.

'Your hand's really starting to shake, pal. You okay? You look kinda sick. Vambs?'

'It's nothing. It's not shaking. Not. Try again. Try again.'

'Vambs?'

No. No. No no no no.

Shockingly loud, a lasrifle fired right behind them, the echo of the snap-roar rolling across the wide river. Bragg reeled round and saw Nessa crouched in a braced position on the bank, her long-las resting across a twist of roots. She fired again, out across the water.

'What the feth?' Bragg cried. His vox-link came alive.

'Who's shooting? Who's shooting?'

Bragg looked round. He saw the green shapes in the rushes over the river. There were silent flashes of light and suddenly las rounds were skipping like well-thrown stones in the water around him.

'Feth!' he cried again. Nessa fired a third, then a fourth shot. Derin appeared, scrambling down the bank behind her, lasgun in hand.

'Infardi! Infardi on the far shore!' Derin was yelling into his link.

Las-fire was punching up and churning the water right across the shallows. Bragg turned to Vamberfeld and saw to his horror the man was frozen, his eyes rolled back, his entire body spasming and vibrating. Blood and froth coated his chin. He'd bitten through his tongue.

'Vambs! Ah, feth it!'

Bragg grabbed the convulsing Verghastite and threw him over his shoulder. His wound screamed out in protest but he didn't care. He started struggling his way towards the shore. Derin was now firing on auto with his assault las in support of Nessa's hot-shots. Enemy rounds cut through the trunk and branches of the old trees above them with a peculiar, brittle sound.

Corbec, Daur and Milo appeared at the top of the bank, weapons raised. Dorden came bouncing and scrambling down the shady bank on his arse, and splashed out into the water, reaching for the lumbering Bragg.

'Pass him here! Pass him here, Bragg! Is he hit?'

'I don't think so, doc!'

A las-shot grazed Bragg's left buttock and he yowled. Another missed Dorden's head by a hand's breadth and a third hit the doctor's medikit and blew it open.

Dorden and Bragg manhandled Vamberfeld ashore and then dragged him up the bank into the cover of the roadwall. The five Ghosts behind them unleashed a steady salvo of fire at the far bank. Glancing back, Bragg saw at least one raft of green silk floating in the water.

Greer ran up from the Chimera, clutching Bragg's autocannon. Sanian followed him, a stricken look of fear on her face.

'What the hell's going on?' Greer asked, gazing in sick horror at the weirdly vibrating Vamberfeld. Vamberfeld's shaking hands were twisted into claw-shapes by the extreme muscular spasm. He'd wet himself too.

'Ah, feth. The nutter's lost it,' Greer said.

'Shut the feth up and help me!' Dorden snarled. 'Hold his head! Hold his head, Greer! Now! Make sure he doesn't smash it into anything!'

Bragg snatched the autocannon from Greer and ran back to the bank, locking in a drum-mag. The enemy fire was still heavy. Ten or twelve shooters, Bragg estimated. As he settled down to fire, he saw another Infardi tumble into the river, hit by Nessa. Clouds of downy white fibre were rising like wheat chaff from the rushes where the Imperial firepower was mashing it.

Bragg opened fire. His initial burst chopped into the river in a row of tall splashes. He adjusted his aim and began to reap through the rush stands, chopping them down, exposing and killing three or four green-clad figures.

'Cease fire! Cease fire!' Corbec yelled.

The gunfire from the opposite bank had stopped.

'Everyone okay?'

A muted chorus of answers.

'Back to the vehicle,' Corbec shouted. 'We have to get moving.'

* * *

THEY DROVE WEST out of Mukret for three kilometres and then pulled off the road, tucking the Chimera into the cover of a stand of acestus trees. Everyone was still breathing hard, faces shiny with sweat.

'Good pick up, girl,' Corbec said to Nessa. She nodded and smiled.

'Didn't you see them, Bragg?'

'I was talking to Vambs, chief. He started to go off weird on me and next thing they were shooting.'

'Doc?'

Dorden turned round from the supine Vamberfeld who was laid on a bed roll on the floor of the cargo bay.

'He's stopped fitting. He'll recover soon.'

'What was it, the trauma again?'

'I think so. An extreme physiological reaction. This poor man is very sick, sick in a way that's hard for us to understand.'

'He's a nut job,' said Greer.

Corbec turned his considerable bulk to face Greer. 'Any more talk like that and I'll break your face. He's one of us. He needs our help. We're going to give it to him. And we're not going to make him feel bad when he comes round either. Last thing he needs to feel is that we're somehow against him.'

'Spoken like a true medicae, Colm,' said Dorden.

'Right. Support. Can we all do that? Greer? Good.'

'What now?' asked Daur.

'We keep on for the crossing. Problem is, they likely know we're around now. We gotta play careful.'

IT TOOK THE rest of the afternoon to reach Nusera. They moved slowly and made frequent stops. Milo kept his ear to the old vox-caster, listening for the sound of enemy transmissions. There was nothing but white noise. He dearly wished they had an auspex.

They stopped about a kilometre short of the crossing, and Corbec, Milo and Nessa moved ahead on foot to scout. Sanian insisted on accompanying them. They crossed several irrigated fields, and a pasture gone to weed where the skeletal remains of two chelons lay, their vast shells calcifying in the sun. They passed through one wooded stretch where boxes of ornately carved wood were raised on stout, decorated posts. Corbec had seen many like them along the Tembarong Road.

'What are they?' he asked Sanian.

'Post tombs,' she replied. 'The last resting places of pilgrim-priests who die along the holy way. They are sacred things.'

The quartet edged through the glade, skirting the shadows of the silent post tombs. Sanian made a gesture of respect to each one.

Pilgrims who died along the way, Corbec thought. Miserably, he could identify with that all too well.

Passing through another dense stand of woods, Corbec thought he could smell the river. But his nose had been impaired by way too many years smoking cheap cheroots. Nessa had it spot on.

Promethium, she signed.

She was right. It was the stink of fuel. Another few hundred metres, and they began to hear the rumble of engines.

They crossed the mouth of an overgrown trail that joined the road from the north, and then bellied down in the final approach through the undergrowth to the crossing.

On the far side of the river, a column of lime green painted armour and transport elements was feeding onto the Tembarong Road from the arable land to the south. Corbec counted at least fifty vehicles, and those were only the ones in view. Infardi troopers milled about the slow moving procession, and over the growl of engines he could hear the chanting and the praise-singing. A refrain kept repeating, a refrain that featured the name Pater Sin over and over.

'Pater fething Sin,' Corbec murmured.

Milo watched the spectacle with a chill in his blood. After the Doctrinopolis, despite the catastrophe at the Citadel, the Infardi here were supposed to be broken, just fleeing remnants in the hinterlands. Here was a damn army, moving north with a purpose. And from the signs of battle the night before, Gaunt's force had encountered at least as many up in Bhavnager.

It seemed to Milo that the Infardi may have actually allowed the cities of Hagia to fall so that they might regroup ready for the approaching fleet-scale reinforcements. It was a wild idea, but one that smacked of truth. No one could ever predict the illogical tactics of Chaos. Faced with an imposing Imperial liberation force, had they simply given up the cities, left foul booby-traps like the Citadel behind them, and gone to ground ready for the next phase?

A phase they knew they would certainly win.

'No going through that way,' Corbec whispered, turning back to look at his companions. He sighed and looked down, apparently defeated.

'Feth... We might as well give up.'

'What if we follow the river north instead of the road?' Milo asked.

'There's no track, boy.'

'Yes, yes there is, chief. The... the whatcha call 'em. The sooka. Sanian, what are they?'

'We passed one just a while back. They are the herdsman trails, older even than the road of pilgrimage. The routes used by the drovers to take the chelon herds up into the high pastures, and bring them down again for market each year.'

'So they run up into the Sacred Hills?'

'Yes, but they are very old. Not made for machines.'

'We'll see,' said Corbec, his eyes bright again. He punched Milo on the arm playfully. 'Good head you got there, Brin. Smart thinking. We'll see.'

So it was that the *Wounded Wagon* began to thread its way up north along the sooka after dark that night, running east of the holy river. The track was very narrow for the most part, and its course worn into a deep trough by millennia of plodding feet. The Chimera slithered and bounced, jarring violently. Once in a while, members of the team had to dismount and clear overgrowth by the light of the hull searchlight.

They were now over a hundred and fifty kilometres behind the honour guard advance, travelling slower, and diverging steadily away to the north.

Vamberfeld slept. He dreamed of the herd-girl, her calf chelons and her piercing eyes.

TWELVE
THE HOLY DEPTHS

'One aching vista, everlasting.'

— Saint Sabbat, Biographica Hagia

GHOSTS. ICE-CLAD GHOSTS. Giants looming, impossibly tall, out of the dry, distant haze.

It had taken two full days for the honour guard column to crawl and squirm its way up through the dense, dark, smelly rainwoods. There had been sixteen random, inconsequential ambushes along the way. Gaunt's forces had skirmished with unseen harriers who left only a few dead behind. The progress lost Gaunt eighteen more men, one scout Salamander and a Chimera. But now, at dawn on the sixth day out from the Doctrinopolis, the honour guard began the laborious climb out of the rainwoods' humid mist and into the feet of the Sacred Hills. Above and around them, the mountain range rose up like silent monsters. They were already passing three thousand metres above sea-level. Some of the surrounding mountains topped out at over ten thousand metres.

The air was cool and dry, and the highland path ran through flat raised valleys where the soil was desiccated and golden.

Few plants grew, except a wind-twitching gorse, rock-crusting lichens and a ribbony kelp-like weed.

It was temperate, cool and clear. Visibility was up to fifty kilometres. The sky was blue, and the ridges of mountains stood clear of the lower rainwood fogs like jagged white teeth.

Six thousand years before, a child called Sabbat, daughter of a high pasture herdsman, had lived up in these inhospitable and awesomely beautiful highlands. The spirit of the Emperor had filled her, and caused her to abandon her herds and track her way down through the filthy swamps of the rainwoods on the start of a course that would lead her, in fire and steel and ceramite, to distant stars and fabulous victories.

One hundred and five years later, she had made the return journey, borne on a palanquin by eight Space Marines of the Adeptus Astartes White Scars chapter.

A saint, even from the moment of her martyrdom. An Imperial saint carried in full honour to her birthplace by the Emperor's finest warriors.

The local star group that now twinkled above her mountains in early evening was named after her. The planet was made sacred in her memory.

Saint Sabbat. The shepherd girl who came down from the mountains of Hagia to shepherd the Imperium into one of its most punishing and fast-moving crusades. One hundred inhabited systems along the edge of the Segmentum Pacificus. The Sabbat Worlds. A pan-planet civilisation.

Gaunt stood up in the crewbay of his lurching Salamander, gazing at the wide, high, clear scenery, the refreshing wind in his face. The sweat of two days in the rainwoods needed blowing away.

Gaunt remembered Slaydo reciting her history to him, back in the early days, as their crusade was being formed. It was shortly after Khulen. Everyone was talking excitedly about the new crusade. The High Lords of Terra were going to select Slaydo as Warmaster because of Khulen. The great honour would fall to him.

Gaunt remembered being called to the study office of the great lord militant commander. He had been just a commissar back then.

The study office, aboard the Citadel ship *Borealis*, was a circular wooden library of nine levels, lined with fifty-two million catalogued works. Gaunt was one of two thousand and forty officers attending the initial meeting.

Slaydo, a hunched but powerful man in his late one-forties, limped up to the lectern at the heart of the study office in his flame yellow plate armour.

'My sons,' he began, not needing a vox-boost in the perfect acoustics of the study office. 'It seems the High Lords of Terra approve of the work we've done together.'

A monumental cheer exploded out across the chamber.

Slaydo waited for it to die down.

'We have been given our crusade, my sons... the Sabbat Worlds!'

The answering shout deafened Gaunt. He remembered yelling until he was hoarse. No sound he'd ever experienced since, not the massed forces of Chaos, not the thunder of titans, matched the power of that cheer,

'My sons, my sons.' Slaydo held his augmetic hand up for peace. 'Let me tell you about the Sabbat Worlds. And first, let me tell you about the saint herself...'

Slaydo had spoken with passionate conviction about Saint Sabbat, the beati as he called her. It had seemed to Gaunt even then that Slaydo held her in a special regard. He was a dutiful man, who honoured all the Imperial worthies, but Sabbat was somehow dearest to him.

'The beati was a warrior,' Slaydo had explained to Gaunt months later, on the eve of the liberation of Formal Prime. 'She exemplifies the Imperial creed and the human spirit better than any figure in the annals. As a boy, she inspired me. I take this crusade as a personal matter, a duty greater than any I have yet undertaken for the Golden Throne. To repay her inspiration, to walk in her path and make free again the worlds she brought from darkness. I feel as if I am... a pilgrim, Ibram.'

The words had never left him.

THE WIDE, BARE plateau allowed them to make back time, but it lent them a sense of vulnerability too. In the lowlands, on the roads and tracks, the heavy column of armoured machines and carriers had seemed imposing and huge, dominating the environment. But out here, in the majestic uplands, they seemed lonely and small, exposed in the tree-less plains, dwarfed by the location.

Already, Lesp had reported the first few cases of altitude sickness. There was no question of stopping or slowing to assist acclimatisation. Surgeon Curth, ever the pragmatic thinker, had included decent quantities of acetazolamide in the drugs carried on the medical supply truck. This mild diuretic stimulated oxygen intake, and Lesp began prescribing it for the men worst affected by the thinner air.

Landmarks on the plateau itself were few, and their appearance became almost hypnotically fascinating to the troops. They stared as shapes spied distantly slowly resolved as they came closer. Usually they were nothing more than large boulders, erratics left by long departed glaciers. Sometimes they were single post tombs. Many of the Ghosts watched for hours as these lonely objects slowly receded from view in the distance behind them.

By mid-afternoon on the fifth day of travel, the temperature again dropped sharply. The air was still clear blue and the sun was bright, so bright in fact that several Ghosts had burned without realising it. But there was a biting wind now, moaning over the flatness, and the great shapes of the mountains no longer glowed translucent white in the brilliance. They had become a shade or two darker and duller, greying and misting.

'Snow,' announced ayatani Zweil, travelling with Gaunt. He stood up in the back of the Salamander, swaying at the motion, and sniffed the air. 'Snow definitely.'

'The air looks clear,' said Gaunt.

'But the mountains don't. Their faces are dark. Snow will be with us before the day's done.'

It was certainly colder. Gaunt had put on his storm coat and and his gloves.

'How bad? Can you tell?'

'It may flurry for a few hours. It may white out and murder us all. The mountains are capricious, colonel-commissar.'

'She calls them the Holy Depths,' Gaunt said idly, meaning the saint.

'She certainly does. Several times in her gospel, in fact. She came from up here and went down into the world. It's typical of her to think about them from the point of looking down. In her mind, the Sacred Hills rise up over everything. Even space and other planets.'

'I always thought it was a metaphor too. The great elevation from which the Emperor looks down on us all, his lowly servants toiling in the depths.'

Zweil grinned and toyed with his beard. 'What a profoundly bleak and inhospitable cosmos you inhabit, colonel-commissar. No wonder you fight so much.'

'So – it's not a metaphor.'

'Oh, I'm sure it is! I'm sure that stark image is precisely its meaning. Remember, Saint Sabbat was an awful lot more like you than like me.'

'I take that as a compliment.'

Zweil gestured at the ring of peaks. 'Actually, being at the top of a great mountain means only one thing.'

'Which is?'

'It means there's a long way to fall.'

As THE LIGHT began to fail, they made camp at the mouth of the next ascending pass. Mkoll estimated that the Shrinehold was still two days away. They raised tents and a strong perimeter. Heater units were put to work and chemical fires lit. No one had thought to bring kindling from the foothills and there was no wood to gather up here.

The snow began just before dark, billowing silently from the north. A few minutes before it began, a trooper on watch saw what he thought were contacts on the wide-band auspex. By the time he'd called up Gaunt and Kleopas, the snow had closed in and the sensor was blind.

But for the short time it lasted, it had looked like contacts. A mass of vehicles, moving north across the plateau behind them, twenty kilometres away.

'BACK! BACK NOW!' cried Milo, trying his best not to get caught in the sheets of liquid mud the Chimera's tracks were kicking up. Wheezing and puffing, the transport's turbines gunned again, and it slithered from side to side in the steep rut.

'Shut it down! Shut it down before it overheats!' shouted Dorden, exasperated. The engine whined and cut out. Quiet returned to the sooka trackway. Birds warbled in the gorse thickets and the gnarled vipiriums.

Greer jumped down from the back hatch and came around the side of the Wounded Wagon to survey the problem. A fast-moving stream, running directly alongside this stretch of sooka, had undercut the trail and the weight of the Chimera had collapsed it, leaving the machine raked over at a drunken angle.

They'd been on the sooka for over two days now, since Corbec's decision to avoid the Infardi at Nusera, and this was by no means the first time the transport had fallen foul of the track. But it was the first time they hadn't been able to right it again first time.

The chelon trails led up into the holy river headwaters and were for the most part steep. The narrow and sometimes winding trail had taken them up into wooded country where there was no other sign of human life. Using Sanian's knowledge, they had taken a route that avoided the worst of the lower spurs and gorges where the thick and unwholesome rainwoods flourished. Instead, they kept to more open ground where the shelving land was clad in breaks of trees, or small deciduous woods through which the trails rambled. The water was never far away: hectic rills and streams that sometimes shot out over lips in the crags and poured in little silver falls; or the mass of the main water itself, crashing down the sloping land and turning sudden drops into seething cataracts.

Each time they moved clear of treecover, it was possible to look back and see the vast green and yellow plain of the river basin below them.

'Maybe we could find a tree trunk and lever it,' suggested Bragg.

Greer looked at the big Tanith, then at the Chimera, and then back at the Tanith. 'Not even you,' he said.

'Does that work?' Corbec asked, pointing to the power-assisted cable drum mounted under the Chimera's nose.

'Of course not,' said Greer.

'Let's try and pack stuff under the tread there,' Corbec said, 'then Greer can try it again.'

They gathered rocks and logs from the trail and pieces of slate from the stream bed and Derin and Daur wedged them in under the track assembly.

The team stood clear and Greer revved the engines again. The tracks bit. There was a loud crack as a log fractured, and then the machine lurched forward and onto the trail. There was a half-hearted cheer.

'Mount up!' Corbec called.

'Where's Vamberfeld?' Dorden asked. The Verghastite had said little since the episode at Mukret and had kept to himself.

'He was here a second ago,' said Daur.

'I'll go look for him,' Milo volunteered.

'No, Brinny,' said Bragg. 'Let me.'

As the rest made ready, Bragg pushed off the side of the trail and lumbered into the glades. Birds called and piped in the leafy canopy at the tops of the tall, bare trunks. The place was full of sunlight and striated shadows.

'Vambs? Where'd you go, Vambs?' Bragg had taken a propriatorial interest in Vamberfeld's welfare since the stone skipping. The colonel had asked him to keep an eye on Vamberfeld, but to Bragg it wasn't an order he was following any more. He was a generous-hearted man, and he hated seeing a fellow Ghost in such a bad way.

'Vambs? They're all waiting!'

THROUGH THE GLADE, the land opened out into a wide, banking pasture dotted with wildflowers and heaps of stone. In one corner, against the line of the trees, Bragg saw the ruin of an old lean-to, a herdsman's shelter. He made his way towards it, calling Vamberfeld's name.

THERE WERE MANY chelon in the pasture, Vamberfeld noted. Not enough to be worth the drive to market, but the basis of a good herd. The cows were nosing together piles of leaf mulch ready to receive the eggs they would lay before the next new moons.

The girl sat cross-legged outside her lean-to, and sprang up warily the moment she saw Vamberfeld approaching.

'Wait, wait please...' he called. The words sounded funny. His tongue was still swollen from the bite he'd put through it in his fit, and he was self-conscious about the way it made his voice sound.

She disappeared into her hut. Cautiously, he followed.

The hut was empty except for old leaf-litter and a few sticks. For a moment, he thought she might be hiding, but there was nowhere to hide, and no loose boards at the rear through which she might have slipped. A couple of old jiddi-sticks lay on the floor inside the door, and on a hook on the wall hung the head-curl of a broken crook. It was very old, and the jagged end where it had snapped was dirty and worn. He took it down and turned it over in his hands.

'Vambs? Vambs?'

It took him a minute to realise the voice outside was calling his name. He went back out into the sunlight.

'Hey, there you are,' said Bragg. 'What were you doing?'

'Just... just looking,' he said. 'There was a girl and she...' He stopped. He realised that the pasture was empty now. There were no lowing chelons, no leaf-nests. The field was growing wild with weeds.

'A girl?'

'No, nothing. Don't worry about it.'

'Come on, we're ready to go now.'

They walked back to the sooka and rejoined the Chimera. Vamberfeld felt strangely dislocated and confused. The girl, the livestock. He'd definitely seen them, but...

It was only when they were underway again that he realised he was still holding the broken crook. He suddenly felt painfully guilty, but by then it was too late to go back and return it.

DESPITE CURTH'S BEST efforts, another of the casualties had died. Kolea nodded when she came to tell him and made an entry in the mission log. Night was falling over Bhavnager, the fourth since the honour guard had gone ahead. No vox contact had been made with them since then, though Kolea was confident that they might be well up into the Sacred Hills by now.

He'd just come back from an inspection tour of the stronghold. They'd made a good job of securing the town. The two Hydras Gaunt had left him guarded the approach highway where the Ghosts themselves had come in. The armour waited in the market place, ready to deploy as needed, except the Destroyer *Death Jester*, which was lurking on watch in the ruins of the temple precinct. Both south and north edges of the town were well defended by lines of Ghosts in slit trenches and strongpoints. Available munitions had been divided up so there was no single, vulnerable armoury point, and the emptied Chimera carriers retasked as troop support. The Conquerors had used their dozer blades to push rubble and debris into roadblocks and protective levees, drastically reducing the possible points of entry into the town. Chances were, if an attack came, they would be outnumbered. But they had the fabric of the town itself working for them and had made the best use of their weapons.

'When did you last sleep?' Kolea asked the surgeon, offering her a chair in the little ground floor room of the town hall that he'd taken as his command post. A long-gain vox-caster set burbled meaninglessly to itself in the corner next to the sideboard where his charts were laid out. Grey evening light poked in through the sandbags piled at the glass-less window.

'I can't remember,' she sighed, sitting down and kicking off her boots. She massaged her foot through a threadbare sock and then realised what she was doing.

'I'm sorry,' she said. 'That was very undignified.'

He grinned. 'Don't mind me.'

She sat back and stretched out her legs, gazing down over her chest at her toes as she wiggled them. The socks were worn through at the toes and heels.

'Gak! Look at me! I was respectable once!'

Kolea poured two generous glasses of sacra from a bottle Varl had given him and handed one to Curth.

'That's where you have me beat. I was never respectable.'

'Oh, come on!' she smiled, taking the glass. 'Thanks. You were a star worker back home, respectable mine worker, family man...'

'Well...'

'Gak!' she said suddenly, through a sip of the liquor. Her heart-shaped face was suddenly serious. 'I'm sorry, Gol, I really am.'

'What for?'

'The family man thing... That was really very crass of me...'

'Please relax. It's alright. It's been a while. I just think it's interesting, the way war is such a leveller. But for war, you and I would never have met. Never have spoken. Never have even been to each other's sectors of the city. Certainly never sat down with a drink together and wiggled our dirty toes at each other.'

'Are you saying I was a snob?' she asked, still smiling at his last remark.

'I'm saying I was an out-habber, a miner, lowest of the workforce. You were a distinguished surgeon running an inner hab collective medical hall. Good education, decent social circles.'

'You make me sound like some pampered rich kid.'

'I don't mean to. I just mean, look at what we were and now look at where we are. War does some strange things.'

'Admittedly.' She paused and sipped again. 'But I wasn't a snob.'

He laughed. 'Did you know any out-habbers well enough to call them by their first name?'

She thought hard. 'I do now,' she said, 'which is the real point. The point I have a feeling you were making anyway.'

He raised his glass to her and she toasted him back.

'To Vervunhive,' he said.

'To Vervunhive and all her hivers,' she said. 'Gak, what is this stuff?'

'Sacra. The poison of choice for the men of Tanith.'

'Ah.'

They sat a moment more in silence, hearing the occasional shouted order or chatter outside.

'I should be getting back to the infirmary,' she began.

'You need rest, Ana. Mtane can manage for a few hours.'

'Is that an order, Sergeant Kolea?'

'It is. I'm getting quite the taste for them.'

'Do you... think about them still?' she asked suddenly.

'Who?'

'Your wife. Your children. I'm sorry, I don't mean to pry.'

'It's alright. Of course I do. More than ever, just these last few days in fact.'

'Why?'

He sighed and stood up. 'The strangest thing has happened. I haven't told anyone. I haven't been sure what to say, or do for that matter.'

'I'm intrigued,' she said, leaning forward and cupping her glass.

'My dear Livy, and my two children... they all died in Vervunhive. I mourned them. I fought to avenge them for a long time. Just that vengeance took me through the resistance fighting, I think. But it turns out... my children aren't dead.'

'They're not? How? How do you know?'

'Here's where it gets strangest of all. They're here.'

She looked around.

'No, not in the room. Not on the planet now, I hope. But they're with the Ghosts. They've been with the Ghosts ever since Vervunhive. I just didn't know it.'

'How?'

'Tona Criid. You know her?'

'I know Tona.'

'She has two children.'

'I know. They're with the regimental entourage. I gave them their jabs myself during the medical screening. Healthy pair, full of... of... oh, Gol.'

'They're not hers. Not by birth. Bless Criid's soul, she found them in the warzone and took them into her protection. Guarded them throughout the war and brought them with her when she joined up. They regard her as their mother, unquestioningly now. Young, you see. So very young. And Caffran, he's as good as a father to them.'

She was stunned. 'How do you know this?'

'I found out by chance. She has holos of them. Then I asked around, very circumspectly, and got the story. Tina Criid rescued my kids from certain death. They now travel with our regiment in the support convoy. The price I pay for that blessing is... they're lost to me.'

'You've got to talk to her, tell her!'

'And say what? They've been through so much, wouldn't this just ruin what chances for a stable life they have left?'

Shaking her head, she held out her glass for a top-up. 'You have to... They're yours.'

He poured the bottle. 'They're content, and they're safe. The fact that they're even alive is such a big deal for me. It's like a... a touchstone. An escape from pain. It messed me up when I first found out, but now it... it seems to have released me.'

She sat back thoughtfully.

'This goes no further, of course.'

'Oh, of course. Doctor-patient confidentiality. I've been doing that my whole career.'

'Please, don't even tell Dorden. He's a wonderful man, but he's the kind of medic who'd... do something.'

'My lips are sealed,' she began to say, but a vox signal interrupted. Kolea ran out into the square, leaving Curth to pull her boots back on.

Mkvenner, his unit's chief scout, hurried up to him.

'Outer perimeter south has spotted movement on their auspex. Major movement. An armoured column of over a hundred vehicles moving this way.'

'Gak! How far?'

'Twenty kilometres.'

'And... I have to ask... Not ours, by any chance.'

Mkvenner smiled one of his lightless, chilling smiles. "Not a chance.'

'Make ready,' Kolea said, sending Mkvenner on his way. Kolea adjusted his vox-link microbead. "Nine to all unit chiefs. Respond.'

'Six, nine,' replied Varl.

'Eighteen, nine,' that was Haller.

'This is Woll, sergeant.'

'All stations to battle ready. Prime defenses. Arm weapons. Deploy armour to a southern line, plan alpha four. The Infardi are coming. Repeat, the Infardi are coming.'

THIRTEEN
ERSHUL IN THE SNOW

*'More snowflakes fall on the Holy Depths in a day than
there are stars left for me to conquer.'*

— Saint Sabbat, *Biographica Hagia*

THEY WERE HALFWAY up the pass when the enemy began firing on
them from the rear of the column.

It was ten o'clock on the morning of the seventh day, and the
honour guard had been slow getting started. Snow had blown
in all night and lay at least forty centimetres deep, drifting to a
metre in the open wind. Before dawn, with the Ghosts and
Pardus shivering in their tents, the snow had stopped, the sky
had cleared and the temperature had plummeted. Minus nine,
the air caking the rocks and metal with first frost and then hard
folds of ice.

The sun rose brightly, but took none of the edge off. It had
taken over an hour to get some of the trucks and the old
Chimeras started. The men were slow and hangdog, grumbling
at every move. Reluctantly, they tossed their packs up into the
troop transports and leapt up to take their places on ice-cold
metal benches.

A heated oat and water mix had been distributed, and Feygor brewed up a churn of bitter caffeine for the officers. Gaunt tipped a measure of amasec into each cup as it was handed round, and no one, not even Hark, protested.

Thermal kit and mittens had been brought as standard. The Munitorium had not underestimated the chill or the altitude, but the biggest boon to all the Ghosts was their trademark camo-cape which now served each man as a cold weather poncho. Zipped up to their throats in their fleece-lined crew-jackets and tank-leathers, the Pardus looked at the Ghosts enviously.

They had broken camp at eight forty, and extended their column up through the snow-thick pass. Occasional flurries whipped across them. The landscape was featureless and white, and the snow reflected the sunlight so fiercely that glare-shades came out before the issue-order was even given.

No trace of the phantoms from the night before could be found on the auspex. The convoy moved ahead at less than ten kph, churning and sliding as it groped for a track that was no longer identifiable.

The first few shells kicked up glittering plumes of snow. Near the head of the column, Gaunt heard the distinctive crack-thump, and ordered his machine to come around.

There was still no visual contact with the chasing enemy, and nothing on the auspex, though Rawne and Kleopas agreed that extreme cold made the sensor systems slow to function. It was also possible that the snow cover was bouncing signals wildly, cheating and disguising the auspex returns.

Gaunt's Salamander, bucking and riding over the snowfield and kicking up a wake of ice crystals, approached the back end of the file in time to see a salvo of high explosive shells thump across the rank. One of the heavy Trojans was hit and exploded, showering the white field with shrapnel and flaming scraps.

'One, four!'

'Four, one, go ahead.'

'Mkoll, keep your speed and pull the column ahead as fast as you can.'

Mkoll was riding a Salamander at the head of the line.

'Four, one. Acknowledged'

Gaunt exchanged voxes with the Pardus, and four tanks peeled back to support him: the *Heart of Destruction*, the *Lion of Pardua*, the *Say Your Prayers* and the Executioner *Strife*.

'Full stop!' Gaunt told his driver, the heat of his breath billowing in clouds through the freezing air. As the light tank slid to a halt, Gaunt turned to ayatani Zweil, who, with Commissar Hark and the Tanith scout Bonin, was riding with him.

'This is no place for you, father. Bonin, get him down and escort him to the rear trucks.'

'Don't fret, Colonel-Commissar Gaunt,' said the old man, smiling. 'I'd rather take my chances here.'

'I...'

'Honestly, I would.'

'Right. Fine.'

More shells whoomed into the snow cover. A munitions Chimera trundling slowly towards the rear of the van was hit a glancing blow but continued to struggle on.

'Auspex contact,' reported Hark from the lower level of the crewbay.

'Size? Numbers?'

'Nine marks, closing fast.'

'Roll!' Gaunt told the driver.

The command Salamander moved off, churning through the virgin snow. The three Conquerors and the old plasma tank were circling round from the convoy after them.

The enemy came into view through the mouth of the pass. Four fast-moving SteG 4s, the six-wheeled light tanks, fanning out ahead of three AT70s and a pair of Usurpers.

Their bright green paint jobs made them stand out starkly against the general white glare.

The SteGs, their big wheels wrapped in chains, were firing their light 40 mil weapons. Hypervelocity tank rounds whistled over the command Salamander.

Gaunt heard the deeper crump of the 105 mil Reavers and the even deeper, less frequent thunder of the big Usurpers.

Explosions dimpled the snow all around them.

'Tube!' Gaunt yelled to Bonin. Since Bhavnager, he'd kept a tread-fether in his machine. The scout brought it up loaded.

'Take us close,' Gaunt told the driver.

An AT70 made a hit on the *Say Your Prayers*, but the shot was stopped by the Conqueror's heavy armour.

The *Heart of Destruction* and the *Lion of Pardua* fired almost simultaneously. The *Heart* overshot but the *Lion* struck a SteG squarely and blew it over in the air.

With distance closing, Gaunt rose and aimed the tube at the nearest SteG. It was surging towards his bucking machine, turret weapon firing.

'Ease!'

Gaunt fired.

His rocket went wide.

'You're a worse fething shot than Bragg!' cursed Bonin.

Zweil started to laugh uproariously.

'Load me!' instructed Gaunt.

'Loaded!' Bonin yelled, slamming the armed rocket into the breach.

The sky, mountainside and ground suddenly exchanged places. Gaunt found himself tumbling over and over in the snow, winded.

A round from the SteG had hit the side of the Salamander jerking it over hard. It had righted itself, but not before Gaunt had been thrown clear. The wounded Salamander chugged to a halt, a sitting duck.

The SteG galloped up, swivelling its little turret to target the listing Salamander.

Spitting out snow, Gaunt got to his feet dazed. He looked about. The rear end of the missile launcher was jutting out of the snow ten metres away from him. He ran over and pulled it out, feverishly tapping the packed snow out of the tube mouth and the venturi.

Then he shouldered it and took aim, hoping to hell the fall hadn't dented the tube or misaligned the rocket. If it had, the tread-fether would explode in his hands.

The speeding SteG closed on the Salamander for the kill. Gaunt could see Hark standing up in the crewbay, firing his plasma pistol desperately at the attacking vehicle.

Gaunt braced and put the crosshairs on the SteG.

It exploded, kicking up an enormous gust of snow and debris.

Gaunt hadn't fired.

The *Heart of Destruction* roared past him in a spray of snow, smoke fuming from its muzzle break.

'You okay, sir?' Kleopas voxed.

'I'm fine!' Gaunt snapped, running towards the Salamander. Hark pulled him aboard.

'Are we alive still?' Gaunt snarled at Hark.

'Your scout's down,' said Hark. Bonin lay in the footwell, concussed from the impact.

Zweil smiled through his beard and held up his wizened hands. 'Me, I'm just dandy!' he declared.

'Could you see to Bonin?' Gaunt asked, and the ayatani jumped down, nursing Bonin into a braced, safe position.

'Move on!' cried Gaunt.

'S-sir?' the driver looked back out of the cave of the cockpit, terrified. Hark swept round and pointed his plasma pistol at the Pardus crewman.

'In the name of the Emperor, drive!' he yelled.

The Salamander roared away across the snow. Gaunt looked out and took stock of the situation.

The *Heart of Destruction* and the *Lion of Pardua* had knocked out the last two SteGs, and *Strife* had blown up a Reaver. The *Say Your Prayers* had been hit twice by Usurper shells and had come to a standstill. It looked intact, but ominous black smoke was pouring out of its engine louvres.

As Gaunt's Salamander slewed around, *Strife* fired on the nearest Usurper and detonated its munitions. Shrapnel whickered down over several hundred metres.

Gaunt braced himself and fired at the nearest AT70. The rocket hit its track guard. The battle tank reared up in the drifts and swung its turret around at the speeding Salamander. A heavy round blew into the snow behind them.

'Load me!' Gaunt demanded.

'Loaded!' Hark answered, and Gaunt felt the jolt of the rocket slamming home.

He took aim at the Infardi battle tank and fired.

Trailing smoke, the missile sped over the snow and hit the tank at the base of its turret. Internal explosions blew the hatches out and then burst the barrel off the tank-head.

Zweil whooped.

'Load me!' said Gaunt.

'Loaded!' said Hark.

But the battle was all done. The *Lion of Pardua* and the *Heart of Destruction* targetted and killed the remaining Usurper pretty much simultaneously and the *Say Your Prayers*, suddenly coughing back into life, crippled and then killed the last of the Reaver AT70s. Mechanical wrecks, sobbing out plumes of black smoke, marred the sugar-white perfection of the pass.

Kleopas's Conqueror turned hard around in a swirl of snow and bounced back alongside Gaunt's Salamander.

Kleopas appeared in the top hatch, holding his field cap in his hands and tugging at it. He pulled something off and tossed it to Gaunt.

Gaunt caught it neatly. It was the cap-badge of the Pardus regiment, worked in silver.

'Wear the mark proudly, tank killer!' Kleopas laughed as his machine sped away.

THROUGH HIS SCOPE, Kolea saw the musters of the enemy as they came down through the fruit glade onto Bhavnager. So many machines, so many troops. Despite his defences and his careful preparation, they would be overwhelmed. There was a horde of them. A gakking horde, with armour to match.

'Nine to all units, wait for my command. Wait.'

The Infardi legion advanced and spread out. They were almost on top of them. Kolea held fast. They would at least make a good account of themselves.

'Steady, steady...'

Without breaking stride, the enemy passed by.

They bypassed Bhavnager and continued up into the rain-woods. In under a half-hour, they were gone.

'Why so sad?' asked Curth. 'They left us alone.'

'They're going after Gaunt,' Kolea said.

She knew he was right.

IT WAS LIKE fething Nusera Crossing all over again. The way ahead was blocked. Through his scope, Corbec could see a long line of green-painted armour and transport units crawling northwards up the wide, dry pass below him. A legion strength force.

He shuffled back from the lip of the cliff and rose. Dizziness swirled through him for a moment. This cold, thin air was going to take quite some getting used to.

Corbec crunched down the slope of scree and down onto the sooka where the Wounded Wagon was drawn up. His team, pinch-faced and huddled in coats and cloaks, waited expectantly.

'We can forget it,' Corbec said. 'There's a fething great mass of enemy machines and troops heading north up the pass.'

'So what now?' whined Greer.

They'd been making good time up the sooka trails through the high pastures of the foot hills. The old Chimera seemed to respond better in the cooler climate. About an hour earlier they'd passed the edge of the tree-line, and now vegetation of any kind was getting thin and rare. The landscape had become a chilly, rock-strewn desert of pink basalt and pale orange halite, rising in great jagged verticals and sheer gorges that forced the ancient herding path to loop back and forth upon itself. The wind groaned and buffeted. Beyond, the awesome peaks of the Sacred Hills were dark and smudged with what Sanian said were snowstorms at the higher altitude levels.

They huddled around the chart-slates, discussing options. Corbec could feel the welling frustration in his team, especially in Daur and Dorden who, it seemed to him, were the only ones who felt the true urgency of the mission in their hearts.

'These here,' said Daur, pointing to the glowing screen of the chart with numb fingers. 'What about these? They turn east about six kilometres above us.'

They studied the radiating pattern of sooka branches that stretched out like thread veins.

'Maybe,' said Milo.

Sanian shook her head. 'This chart is not current. Those sooka are old and have been blocked for years. The herdsmen favour the western pastures.'

'Could we clear a way through?'

'I don't think so. This section here is entirely fallen away into the gorge.'

'Feth it all!' Daur murmured.

'There is perhaps a way, but it is not for our machine.'

'You said that about the sookas.'

'I mean it this time. Here. The Ladder of Heaven.'

FIVE THOUSAND METRES higher up and sixty kilometres to the north-west, the honour guard column climbed the ragged high passes in the driving snow. It was past dark on the night of the seventh day, but still they pressed on at a desperate crawl, head-lamps blazing into the dark. Blizzarding snow swirled through the beams of their lights.

According to the last reliable auspex reading, an enormous enemy force was half a day behind them.

The route they were following, known as Pilgrim's Pass, was becoming treacherous in the extreme. The track itself, climbing at an incline of one in six, was no more than twenty metres broad. To their left rose the sheer cliffs of the mountainside. To their right, invisible in the dark and the snow, it fell away in a scree-slope that tumbled almost vertically down to the floor of the gorge six hundred metres below.

It was hard enough to read the road in the day. Everyone was tense, expecting a wrong turn to send a vehicle tumbling off into the chasm. And there was also the chance of a rockslide, or a simple loss of grip in the snow. Every time the troop truck wheels slid, the Ghosts went rigid, expecting the worst... a long, inexorable slide to oblivion.

'We have to stop, colonel-commissar!' Kleopas urged over the link.

'Noted, but what happens if it continues like this all night? Come the dawn, we might be so buried in snow we can't move again.'

Another hour, perhaps two, Gaunt thought. They could risk that much. In terms of distance, the Shrinehold was close now. The duration of the journey was more determined by the conditions.

'Sabbat does love to test her pilgrims on the path,' chuckled Zweil, huddled up in a bed roll in the back of the Salamander's compartment.

'I'm sure,' said Gaunt. 'Feth take her Holy Depths.'

That made the old priest laugh so heartily he started coughing.

If anything, the snow seemed to be getting heavier.

Suddenly, there came a series of unintelligible bursts on the vox. Rearlamps ahead of them in the pelting flakes flashed and swung.

'Full stop!' Gaunt ordered and clambered out. He trudged forward into the wind and the driving snow, his boots sinking thirty or forty centimetres into the drifts.

Revealed only at the last minute by the groping auspex and by the driver's struggling eyesight, the track swung hard around a spur, almost at forty-five degrees. Even this close, Gaunt could barely see it himself. One of the pair of scout Salamanders fronting the column was dangling over the edge of the chasm, most of one entire track section hanging in space. Gaunt hurried up through the headlamp beams of the machines behind, joined by other Ghosts and vehicle crews. The four occupants of the stricken light tank: the Pardus driver, Vox-officer Raglon and Scout Troopers Mklane and Baen, were standing in the crewbay of the teetering machine, frozen in place, not daring to move.

'Steady! Steady, sir!' Raglon hissed as Gaunt approached. They could all hear rock and ice crumbling under the body of the scout machine.

'Get a line attached! Come on!' Gaunt yelled. A Pardus driver hurried forward with a tow-hook, playing out the plasteel-mesh cable. Gaunt took the hook and gently reached out, sliding it in place over one of the Salamander's hardpoint lugs.

'Tension! Tension!' he cried, and the electric drum of the vehicle behind them started to rotate, taking up the slack on the cable until the line was taut. The Salamander tilted back a little onto the track.

'Out! Now!' Gaunt ordered, and Raglon's crew scrambled out onto the snowy trail, dropping to their knees and gasping with relief.

The crews around them now began the job of hauling the empty machine back onto the path.

Gaunt helped Mklane up.

'I thought we were dead, sir. The road just wasn't there any more.'

'Where's scout one?' asked Gaunt.

They all stopped dead and turned to look out into the darkness. They'd been so busy saving one machine, no one had realised the other had vanished entirely.

He'd forced the pace, Gaunt reflected, and the scout crew had paid the price.

'Gaunt to convoy. Full stop now. We go no further tonight.'

'Maybe we do,' said ayatani Zweil, suddenly appearing at Gaunt's side. He pointed up into the darkness and the blizzarding snow. There was a light. Strong, yellow, bright, shining in the night above them.

'The Shrinehold,' said Zweil.

FOURTEEN
SHRINEHOLD

'In war, one must prepare for defeat. Defeat is the most insidious of our foes. It never comes the way we expect.'

— Warmaster Slaydo,
from *A Treatise on the Nature of Warfare*

THE HONOUR GUARD approached the Temple of the Shrinehold of Saint Sabbat Hagio at first light. The snows had stopped, and the mountain scenery was perfect, sculptural white under a golden sky.

The Shrinehold was a towering structure rising out of the basalt of a promontory spur that ran down from the ice-capped peak above. The road ran along the crest to a hefty gatehouse in the lower of two concentric walls. Within those walls stood the close-packed buildings of the Shrinus Basilica, the monastery of the tempelum ayatani shrinus, and a great square-sided tower topped by a golden gambrel roof with up-swept eaves. Prayer flags and votive kites fluttered from the tower. The buildings and walls of the Shrinehold were pink basalt. Shutters and doors were painted a bright gloss red and their frames edged in white. Beyond the walls and the tower, at

257

the very edge of the promontory, stood a massive stone pillar of black corundum on top of which the eternal light of the signal fire burned.

Gaunt halted the column on the causeway before the gate and approached on foot with Kleopas, Hark, Zweil, Rawne and an escort of six Ghosts. True to Sergeant Mkoll's estimate, it had taken eight days to make the journey. They needed to expedite the business here if they were going to make it back to the Doctrinopolis in the ten days remaining before complete evacuation. Gaunt didn't even want to start thinking about how hard that journey was going to be. The Infardi were closing on their heels in huge numbers and as far as he knew there was no other way down from the Sacred Hills.

The gigantic red doors under the grim carved aquila on the gatehouse swung open silently as they approached, and they strode in up the steps. Six blue robed ayatani brothers bowed to them but said nothing. They were taken up a wide flight of stone steps, which had been brushed clear of snow, to the gate in the inner wall, and then through into a lofty entrance hall.

The place was smoky brown and gloomy, with light entering through high windows, cold and pure. Gaunt could hear chanting, and the sporadic chiming of bells or gongs. The air was full of incense smoke.

He removed his cap and looked around. Colourful gleaming mosaics decorated the walls, showing the saint at various points in her hallowed life. Small holographic portraits set into lit alcoves along one wall depicted the great generals, commanders and Astartes who had served during her crusade. The great banner standard of Sabbat, an ancient and worn swathe of material, was suspended from the arched roof.

Ayatani of the tempelum ayatani shrinus entered the hall through the far doors, approached the Imperial retinue and bowed. There were twenty of them, all old, calm-faced men with tight, wrinkled skin worn by wind and cold and altitude.

Gaunt saluted. 'Colonel-Commissar Ibram Gaunt, commander of the Tanith First, Imperial Crusade Liberation Army. These are my chief officers, Major Rawne, Major Kleopas and Commissar Hark. I am here under orders from Lord Militant General Lugo.'

'You are welcome to the Shrinehold, sir,' said the leader of the brothers, his blue robes a deeper shade of violet. His face was as weatherbeaten as his colleagues', and his eyes had been replaced by an augmetic visor that made his stare milky and blank, like chronic cataracts. 'My name is Cortona. I am ayatani-ayt of this temple and monastery. We welcome you all to the shrine, and praise your diligence in making the arduous trek here at this time of year. Perhaps you will take refreshment with us? You are also free to make devotion at the shrine, of course.'

'Thank you, ayatani-ayt. Refreshment would be welcome, but I should make clear that the urgency of my mission means I have little time to spare, even for pious observances.'

The Imperials were taken through into an anteroom where soda farls, dried fruit and pots of a warm, sweet infusion were laid out on low, painted tables. They sat: Gaunt and his men on squat stools; the ayatani, including Zweil, on floor mats. Refreshment was passed round by junior esholi in white robes.

'I am touched that your lord general has seen fit to be concerned for our welfare,' Cortona continued, 'but I fear your mission here has been a waste of effort. We are fully aware of the enemy forces that seek to overrun this world, but we have no need of defence. If the enemy comes, the enemy comes and that will be the way of things. Our holy saint believed very much in natural fate. If it is decreed by destiny that this Shrinehold should fall to the enemy, and that our lives are to be forfeit, then it is decreed. No amount of tanks and soldiers can change that.'

'You'd let the Chaos breed just walk in?' Rawne asked, incredulously.

'Watch your mouth, major!' Hark hissed.

'It is an understandable question,' said Cortona. 'Our belief system may be hard to comprehend for minds versed and schooled in war.'

'Saint Sabbat was a warrior, ayatani-ayt,' Gaunt pointed out smoothly.

'She was. Perhaps the finest in the galaxy. But she is at rest now.'

'Your concerns are moot anyway, with respect, father,' Gaunt went on. 'You have misjudged our purpose here. We have not been sent to defend you. Lord General Lugo has ordered me to recover the relics of the saint and escort them with full honour to the Doctrinopolis, prior to the evacuation of Hagia.'

The calm smile never left Cortona's face. 'I fear, colonel-commissar, that I can never allow that to happen.'

'YOU QUITE TOOK my breath away,' murmured Zweil. 'I never imagined that was why you were coming to the Shrinehold! Beati's blood, colonel-commissar! What were you thinking?'

'I was obeying orders,' said Gaunt. They stood together on the terrace of the Shrinehold's inner wall, looking out across the bright snows towards the gorge.

'I thought you'd been sent to protect this place! I knew the tempelum ayatani would be none too pleased with a military intervention, but I left that to you.'

'And if I'd told you my full purpose, would you have advised me to turn back?'

'I would have told you what ayatani-ayt just told you. The saint's relics can never be taken from Hagia. It's one of the oldest doctrines, her deathbed prophecy. Even the likes of this General Lugo, or your esteemed Warmaster Macaroth, would be fools to break it!'

'I've read it. You know I've read the gospels closely. I just assumed it was... a whim. A minor detail.'

Zweil shook his head. 'I think that's where you keep going wrong, my boy. Half the time you read the scriptures hunting for absolute literal sense, the other half you try too hard to decipher hidden meanings! Textual interpretation indeed! You need balance. You need to understand the fundamental equilibrium of faith as it matters to us. If you expect the ayatani to devoutly and strictly keep the customs and relics and traditions of the beati alive, then you must equally expect us to treat the instruction of her scriptures with absolute conviction.'

'It is written,' Gaunt began thoughtfully, 'that if the remains of Saint Sabbat are ever taken from Hagia, if they are ever removed by accident or design, the entire Sabbat Worlds will fall to Chaos forever.'

'What's not clear about that?'

'It's an open prophecy! A colourful myth designed to intensify devotion and worship! It couldn't actually happen!'

'No?' Zweil gazed out across the Sacred Hills. 'Why not? You believe in the saint, in her works, in her incorruptible sanctity. Your belief in her and all she represents shines from you. It brought you here. So why wouldn't you believe in her deathbed prophecy?'

Gaunt shrugged. 'Because it's too... insane! Too big, too far-fetched! Too unlikely...'

'Maybe it is. Tell me, do you want to test it by taking her from this world?'

Gaunt didn't reply.

'Well, my boy? Do you know better than the sector's most venerated martyr? Does Lugo or the Warmaster? Will you risk losing everything, a thousand inhabited systems, forever, just to find out? Never mind your orders or their seniority, have they the right to take that risk either, or order you to do it?'

'I don't believe they do. I don't believe I do,' replied Gaunt quietly after a long pause.

'I don't believe you even have to consider the question,' said Hark, approaching them from behind. 'You have utterly unambiguous orders, sir. They leave no room for interpretation. Lugo made your duty plain.'

'Lugo made a mistake,' Gaunt said, fixing Hark with a clear, hard stare. 'It's not one I care to take any further.'

'Are you breaking orders, sir?' asked Hark.

'Yes, I am. It hardly matters. My career's over, my regiment's finished, and there's every chance we won't get out of here alive anyway. I'm breaking orders with a clear conscience, because it's about fething time I showed a bit of backbone and stopped blindly obeying men who are clearly and demonstrably wrong!'

Zweil's gaze darted back and forth between the two Imperial officers in total fascination, hanging on every word. Hark slowly put on his silver-braided cap, sighed heavily, and moved his hand to open the button-down cover of his holster.

'Oh, don't even bother, Hark,' Gaunt snarled contemptuously and walked away.

THEY WERE HIGH enough now for the snow that Sanian had warned them about to become a reality. It was light but persistent, and settled on their clothes and eyelashes. Further up the pass, snow clouds choked visibility so badly the great mountains themselves were temporarily invisible, masked out by the storm.

They had finally said goodbye to the Wounded Wagon two hours earlier, abandoning it at a point on the sooka where an old rockslide had long since carried the last of the negotiable track away. Loading up with everything they could carry, they had continued on foot.

The track was as thin and desolate as the air. To their right towered the sheer south faces of the innermost and highest Sacred Hills. To their left, a great slope of scree and bare rock arced downwards into the mysterious shadows of gorges and low passes far below. Every few steps, one of them caught a loose stone with their toe, and it would skitter and slither away down the decline.

The Ladder of Heaven had been cut by early pilgrims soon after the foundation of the Shrinehold six millennia before. They had engineered the work with zealous enthusiasm, seeing it as a sacred task and an act of devotion. A fifty kilometre staircase rising four thousand metres up into the peaks, right to the Shrinehold. Few used it now, Sanian had explained, because the climb was arduous, and even hardy pilgrims preferred the march up the passes. But that softer option wasn't open to them now.

Sanian led them to the foot of the Ladder as the first snows began.

It didn't look like much. A narrow, worn series of steps carved into the mountainside itself, eroded by weather and age. Lichens clung like rust to the surfaces. Each step was about sixteen centimetres high, a comfortable enough pace, and the steps were uniformly two metres deep from front to back, except where they sectioned and turned. The Ladder wove up through the rocks and disappeared above them.

'This looks easy enough,' said Greer, stepping lightly up the first few.

'It isn't, I assure you. Especially with the weather closing like this. Pilgrims used to choose this approach as an act of chastening,' said Sanian.

They started up, Greer eagerly hurrying ahead, followed by Daur, Corbec and Dorden, then Milo and Sanian, Nessa, Derin and finally Vamberfeld and Bragg.

'He'll kill himself if he doesn't pace his climb,' Sanian told Milo, pointing to Greer far ahead of them.

The main group fell into a rhythm. After about twenty minutes, Corbec began to feel oppressed by the sheer monotony of the task. He started to roam with his mind, trying to occupy his thoughts. He considered the distance and altitude, the depth and width of the steps. He did a little sum or two in his head.

'How many steps do they say there are?' he called back to Sanian.

'They say twenty-five thousand.'

Dorden groaned.

'That's just what I made it,' Corbec beamed, genuinely pleased with himself.

Fifty kilometres. Troops could cover that in a day, easy. But fifty kilometres of steps...

This could take days. Hard, painful, bone-numbing days.

'I maybe should have asked you this about five hundred metres ago, Sanian, but how long does this climb usually take?'

'It depends on the pilgrim. For the dedicated... and the fit... five or six days.'

'Oh sacred feth!' Dorden groaned aloud.

Corbec concentrated on the steps again. Snow was beginning to settle on them. In five or six days, when they reached the Shrinehold, Gaunt should be virtually all the way back to the Doctrinopolis if he was going to make the evac. They were wasting their time.

Then again, there was no way in creation Gaunt's honour guard was going to get down the mountain past that Infardi host. Chances were he'd use the Shrinehold as his base and fight it out from there.

They'd have to wait and see. There was no point in going back now. There was nothing to go back for.

ALONE, IBRAM GAUNT pulled back the great old bolt and pushed open the door of the Shrinehold's sepulchre. The voices of male esholi filtered out, singing a solemn, harmonius, eight-part chant. Cold wind moaned down the monastery's deep airshafts.

He didn't know what to expect. He realised he had never imagined coming here. Slaydo, the Emperor rest him, would have been envious.

The room was surprisingly small, and very dark. The walls were lined with black corundum that reflected none of the light from the many rows of burning candles. The air smelled of smoke, and musty dryness, the dust of centuries.

He stepped in, closing the door after him. The floor was made of strange, lustrous tiles that shimmered in the candlelight and made an odd, plastic sound as he walked on them. He realised they were cut and polished sections of chelon shell, pearlescent, with a brown stain of time.

To either side of where he stood were alcove bays in the corundum. In each glowed a life-size hologram of a White Scars Space Marine, power blades raised in salutes of mournful triumph.

Gaunt walked forward. Directly ahead of him was the reliquary altar. Plated with more polished chelon shell, it shone with ethereal luminescence. Inlaid on its raised front was a beautiful mosaic of coloured shell pieces depicting the Sabbat Worlds. Gaunt had no doubt it was cartographically precise. Behind the altar rose a huge, domed cover that overhung the altar block like a cowl. It was fashioned from a single chelon shell, a shell that had come from an incredibly massive animal, far larger than anything Gaunt had seen on Hagia. Beneath it, behind the altar, lay the reliquary itself, a candlelit cavern under the shell. At the front were two hardwood stands with open lids in which, behind glass, lay original manuscripts of the gospels.

Gaunt realised his heart was beating fast. The place was having an extraordinary effect on him.

He moved past the gospel stands. To his left stood a casket on which lay various relics half-wrapped in satin. There was a drinking bowl, a quill pen, a jiddi-stick worn black with age, and several other fragments he couldn't identify.

To his right, on top of another, matching casket, lay the saint's Imperator armour, painted blue and white. It showed the marks of ancient damage, blackened holes and grooves, jagged dents where the paint had been scraped off. The marks of the nine martyring wounds. There was something odd about it. Gaunt realised it was... small. It had been purpose-built for a body smaller than the average male Space Marine.

Ahead of him, at the very rear of the shell dome, lay the holy reliquary, a bier covered in a glass casket.

Saint Sabbat lay within.

She had wanted no stasis field or power suspension, but still she was intact after six thousand years. Her features had sunk, her flesh had desiccated, and her skin was dark and polished. Around her skull there were traces of fine hair. Gaunt could see the rings on her mummified fingers, the medallion of the

Imperial eagle clasped in her hands across her bosom. The blue of her gown had almost entirely faded, and the dry husks of ancient flowers lay around her on the velvet padding of the bier.

Gaunt didn't know what to do. He lingered, unable to take his eyes off the taut, withered but incorruptible form of the beati.

'Sabbat. Martyr,' he breathed.

'She's under no obligation to answer you, you know.'

He looked around. Ayatani Zweil stood beyond the altar, watching him.

Gaunt made a dignified, short bow to the saint and walked back out past the altar to Zweil.

'I didn't come for answers,' he whispered.

'You did. You told me so, as we were coming from Mukret.'

'That was then. Now I've made my choice.'

'Choices and answers aren't the same thing. But yes, you have. A fine choice, may I add. A brave one. The right one.'

'I know. If I doubted that before, I don't now I've seen this. We have no business moving her. She stays here. She stays here as long as we can protect her.'

Zweil nodded and patted Gaunt on the arm. 'It's not going to be a popular choice. Poor Hark, I thought he was going to shit out a kidney when you told him.' Zweil paused, and looked back at the reliquary. 'Forgive my coarse language, beati. I am but a poor imhava ayatani who ought to know better in this holy place.'

They left the sepulchre together, and walked down the drafty hall outside.

'When will you make your decision known?'

'Soon, if Hark hasn't told everyone already.'

'He may remove you from command.'

'He may try. If he does, you'll see me breaking more than orders.'

NIGHT WAS FALLING, and another storm of snow was racing down from the north-west. Ayatani-ayt Cortona had allowed the Imperial forces to pitch their camp inside the outer wall of the Shrinehold, and the space was now full of tents and chemical braziers. The convoy vehicles had been drawn up in the lea of the wall outside, except for the fighting machines, which had ranged out and dug in, hull down, to guard the approach up the gorge to the promontory. Troop positions had also been dug in the snow banks outside, and the heavy weapons fortified. Anything coming up the pass was going to meet heavy resistance.

Making use of an anteroom in the monastery, Gaunt assembled the officers and section chiefs of the honour guard. The Shrinehold esholi brought food and sweet tea, and none of the priesthood complained about the amasec and sacra being portioned around. Ayatani-ayt Cortona and some of his senior priests had joined them. The lamps twitched and snowstorm winds banged at the shutters. Hark stood at the back of the room, alone, brooding.

Before he went in to join them, Gaunt took Rawne to one side, out in the chilly hall.

'I want you to know this first,' Gaunt told him. 'I intend to disobey Lugo's orders. We are not moving the saint.'

Rawne arched his eyebrows. 'Because of this fething stupid old prophecy?'

'Exactly because of this fething stupid old prophesy, major.'

'Not because it's all over for you?' asked Rawne.

'Explain.'

Rawne shrugged. 'We've known from the start that Lugo's got you cold. When you return to the Doctrinopolis, be it empty-handed or with this old girl's bones, that's the end. End of command, end of you, end of story. So as I see it, you really haven't got anything to lose, have you? Not to speak of. Telling Lugo to feth off and shove his orders up his own very special Eye of Terror isn't going to make things any worse for you. In fact, it might leave you feeling better when they come to drag you away.'

'You think I'm doing this because I don't care any more?' asked Gaunt.

'Well, do you? This last week, you've not been the man I started serving under. The drinking. The rages. The foul, foul fething moods. You failed. You failed badly. At the Doctrinopolis, you fethed up good and proper. You've been a wreck ever since. Oh...'

'What?' growled Gaunt.

'Permission to speak candidly, sir. With effect retroactive.'

'Don't you always, Rawne?'

'I fething hope so. Are you still drinking?'

'Well, I...'

'You want me to believe you're right, that you're doing this for real reasons and not just because you couldn't give a good feth about anything any more, then smarten up. Clean up. Work it out. I've never liked you, Gaunt.'

'I know.'

'But I've always respected you. Solid. Professional. A warrior who works to a code. Sure, because of that code Tanith burned, but you stuck by it no matter what anyone else thought. A man of honour.'

'That's the closest you've ever come to complimenting me, major,' said Gaunt.

'Sorry sir, it won't happen again. What I need to know is this... Is it that code now? Is it honour? This fething mission is an honour guard... Do you mean it to deserve that title?'

'Yes.'

'Show me then. Show us all. Show us this isn't just spite and bile and frustration coming out of you because you fethed up and they caught you for it. Show us you're not just a drunken wreck going down fast and bitterly trying to take everything and everyone with you. It's over for you, any way you cut it, but it isn't for us. If we go along with you, the lord general will have us all court martialled and shot. We've got something left to lose.'

'I know,' said Gaunt. He paused for a moment, and watched the driving snowflakes build and pile up against the glass of the hall windows.

'Well?'

'Would you like to know why this matters to me, Rawne? Why I took the disaster at the Doctrinopolis so badly?'

'I'd be fascinated.'

'I've given the better part of the last two decades to this crusade. I've fought hard every step of the way. And here on Hagia, the blind stupidity of one man... our dear lord general... forced my hand and ruined all that work. But it's not just that. The crusade that I've devoted these years to is in honour of Saint Sabbat, intended to liberate the planets she first made Imperial worlds six thousand years ago. I hold her in special regard, therefore, and am dedicated to her honour, and that bastard Lugo made me fail on the very world sacred to her. I didn't just feth up during a crusade action, major. I fethed up during a crusade action on the saint's own holy shrineworld. But it's not just that either.'

He paused and cleared his throat. Rawne stared at him in the gloom.

'I was one of Slaydo's chosen, hand-picked to wage this war. He was the greatest commander I've ever known. He took on this crusade as a personal endeavour because he was absolutely and utterly devoted to the saint. She was his totem, his inspiration, the role model on which he had built his military career. He told me himself that he saw this crusade as a chance to pay back that debt of inspiration. I will not dishonour his memory by failing him here. Here, of all places.'

'Let me guess,' said Rawne. 'It's not just that either, is it?'

Gaunt shook his head. 'On Formal Prime, in the first few months of the crusade, I fought alongside Slaydo in a fierce action to take the hive towers. It was one of the first big successes of the crusade.

'At the victory feast, he brought his officers together. Forty-eight of us, the chosen men. We caroused and celebrated. We all got a little drunk, Slaydo included. Then he... he became solemn, that bitter sadness that afflicts some men when they are at their worse for drink. We asked him what was wrong, and he said he was afraid. We laughed! Great Warmaster Slaydo, afraid? He got to his feet, unsteady. He was one hundred and fifty years old by then, and those years had not been kind. He told us he was afraid of dying before finishing his work. Afraid of not living long enough to oversee the full and final liberation of the beati's worlds. It was his one, consuming ambition, and he was afraid he would not achieve it.

'We all protested... he'd outlive us all! He shook his head and insisted that the only way he could ensure the success of his sacred task, the only way he could achieve immortality and finish his duty to the saint, was through us. He called for an oath. A blood oath. We used bayonets and fething table knives to cut our palms and draw blood. One by one we clasped his bleeding hand and swore. On our lives, Rawne, on our very lives. We would finish his work. We would pursue this crusade to its end. And we would damn well protect the saint against any who would harm her!'

Gaunt held out his right hand, palm open. In the blue half-light, Rawne could still make out the old, pale scar.

'Slaydo fell at Balhaut, that battle of battles, just as he feared he would. But his oath lives on, and in it, Slaydo too.'

'Lugo's making you break your pact.'

'Lugo made me ride rough-shod through the saint's Doctrinopolis and set ablaze her ancient temples. Now Lugo wants me to defy the beati and disturb her final rest. I apologise if I seemed to take any of that badly, but now perhaps you can see why.'

Rawne nodded slowly.

'You had better tell the others,' he said.

GAUNT WALKED INTO the centre of the crowded anteroom, declined a drink offered to him by an esholi, and cleared his throat. All eyes were on him and silence fell.

'In the light of developments in the field and... other considerations, I hereby inform you I am making an executive alteration to our orders.'

There was a murmur.

'We will not be proceeding as per Lord General Lugo's instruction. We will not remove the Shrinehold relics. As of now, my orders are that the honour guard digs in here and remains in defence of the Shrinehold until such time as our situation is relieved.'

A general outburst filled the room. Hark was silent.

'But the lord general's orders, Gaunt–' Kleopas began, rising.

'Are no longer viable or appropriate. As field commander, judging things as they stand here on the ground, it is within my purview.'

Intendant Elthan rose, quivering with rage. 'But we'll be killed! We have to return to the Doctrinopolis landing fields by the timetable or we will not be evacuated! You know what's coming, colonel-commissar! How dare you suggest this!'

'Sit down, Elthan. If it helps, I'm sorry that non-combatants such as yourself and your driver crews have been caught in this. But you are servants of the Emperor. Sometimes your duty is as hard as ours. You will obey. The Emperor protects.'

A few officers and all the ayatani echoed the refrain.

'Sir, you can't just break orders.' Lieutenant Pauk's voice was full of alarm. Kleopas nodded urgently at his junior officer's words. 'We'll all face the strictest discipline. Lord General Lugo's orders were simple and precise. We can't just disobey them!'

'Have you seen what's coming up the pass behind us, Pauk?'
Everyone turned. Captain LeGuin was standing at the back of
the room, leaning against the wall. 'In terms of necessity alone,
I'd say the colonel-commissar was making a sound decision.
We can't get back to the Doctrinopolis now even if we wanted
to.'

'Thank you, captain,' nodded Gaunt.

'Stuff your opinions, LeGuin!' cried Captain Marchese, commander of the Conqueror P48J. 'We can always try! That's what
the lord general and the Warmaster would expect! If we stay
here and fight it out, we might resist for the next week or so.
But once that fleet arrives, we're dead anyway!'

Several officers, Ghosts among them, applauded Marchese's
words.

'We follow orders! We take up the relics and we break out
now! Let's take our chances in a stand-up fight against the
Infardi! If we fail, we fail! Better to die like that, in glory, than
to wait it out for certain death!'

Much more support now.

'Captain Marchese, you should have been a commissar. You
turn a good, rousing phrase.' Gaunt smiled. 'But I am commissar. And I am commander here. We stay, as I have instructed.
We stay and fight.'

'Please reconsider, Gaunt!' cried Kleopas.

'But we'll die, sir,' said Sergeant Meryn.

'And die badly, come to that,' growled Feygor.

'Don't we deserve a chance, sir?' asked Sergeant Soric, pulling
his stout frame upright, his cap clasped in his hands.

'Every chance in the cosmos, Soric,' said Gaunt. 'I've considered all our options carefully. This is the right way.'

'You're insane!' squealed Elthan. He turned and gazed
imploringly at Hark. 'Commissar! For the Emperor's sake, do
something!'

Hark stepped forward. The room went quiet. 'Gaunt. I know
you've considered me an enemy all along. I can see why, but
God-Emperor knows I'm not. I've admired you for years. I've
studied how you've made command choices that would have
been beyond lesser men. You've never been afraid of questioning the demands of high command.'

Hark looked round at the silent room and then his gaze
returned to Gaunt.

'I got you this mission, Gaunt. I've been with the lord general's staff for a year now, and I know what kind of man he is. He wants you to shoulder the blame for the Doctrinopolis to cover his own lack of command finesse.

'After the disaster at the Citadel, he would have had you drummed out on the spot. But I knew damn well you were worth more than that. I suggested a final mission, this honour guard. I thought it might give you a chance to redeem yourself, or at least finish your career on a note of respectability. I even thought it might give Lugo time to reconsider and change his mind. A successful salvation of the shrineworld relics from under the nose of an overwhelming enemy force could even be turned into a famous victory with the right spin. Lugo might come out a hero, and you, consequently, might come out with your command intact.'

Hark sighed and straightened the front of his waistcoat. 'You break orders now, there's no coming back. You'll put yourself right where Lugo wants you. You'll turn yourself into the scapegoat he needs. Furthermore, as an officer of his personal commissariate, I cannot allow it. I cannot allow you to continue in command. I'm sorry, Gaunt. All the way along, I've been on your side. You've just forced my hand. I hereby assume control of the honour guard, as per general order 145.f. The mission will continue to the letter of our orders. I wish it could have been different, Gaunt. Major Rawne, relieve Colonel-Commissar Gaunt of his weapons.'

Rawne rose slowly. He walked across the packed room to Gaunt and then stood at his side, facing Hark. 'I don't think that's going to happen, Hark,' he said.

'That's insubordination, major,' murmured Hark. 'Follow my instructions and relieve Gaunt of his weapons now or I'll have you up on charges.'

'I can't have been clear,' said Rawne. 'Go feth yourself.'

Hark closed his eyes, paused, opened them again and drew his plasma pistol.

He raised it slowly and aimed it at Rawne. 'Last chance, major.'

'Who for, Hark? Look around.'

Hark looked around. A dozen sidearms were pointing at him, aimed by Ghost officers and a few Pardus, including LeGuin and Kleopas.

Hark holstered his weapon. 'I see you give me no choice. If we survive, this incident will be brought to the attention of the Crusade commissariate, in full and frank detail.'

'If we survive, I'll look forward to that,' said Gaunt. 'Now let's make ready.'

OUT IN THE blizzarding night, at waymark 00.02 at the head of the pass, Scout-trooper Bonin and Troopers Larkin and Lillo were dug into an ice bunker. They had a chemical heater puffing away in the base of the dug-out, but it was still bitterly cold. Bonin was watching the portable auspex unit while Larkin hunted the flurrying darkness with the night scope of his long-las. Lillo chaffed his hands, waiting by the tripod-mounted autocannon.

'Movement,' Larkin said quietly.

'Nothing on the screen,' replied Bonin, checking the glowing glass plate of the auspex.

'See for yourself,' said Larkin, moving aside so that Bonin could slide in to view through the scope of the positioned sniper weapon.

'Where?'

'Left a touch.'

'Oh feth,' murmured Bonin. Illuminated in ghostly green, he could see blurs of light on the pass below. Hundreds of lights were moving up the precipitous track towards them. Headlamps glaring in the falling snow.

'There's lots of them,' said Bonin, moving back.

'You haven't seen the half of it,' mumbled Lillo, staring at the auspex screen. Bright yellow sigils wobbled around the contour lines of the holo-map. The tactical counter had identified at least three hundred contacts, but the number was rising as they watched.

'Get on the vox,' said Larkin. 'Tell Gaunt all fething hell is coming up the pass.'

FIFTEEN
THE WAITING

*'Actual combat is a fleeting part of war.
The bulk of soldiering is waiting.'*

— Warmaster Slaydo,
from *A Treatise on the Nature of Warfare*

WHEN THE SNOWING stopped just before dawn, the Infardi advance guard began their first assault up the top of the pass. A bombardment was launched by their reserve tanks and self-propelled guns, but most of it fell short of the Shrinehold walls. Six SteGs and eight Reavers churned through the snow towards the promontory, and a hurrying line of four hundred troops followed them.

They were met by the Pardus armour and the dug-in sections of the Tanith First-and-Only. Hull-down, *Grey Venger* picked off the first four armour units before they were even clear of the spur. Their burning carcasses dirtied the snowfield with blackened debris and fire.

Heavy weapon emplacements opened up to meet the infantry. In a quarter of an hour, the white slopes were scattered with green-robed dead.

A SteG and an AT70 pushed in past the outer defence, behind *Grey Venger's* field of fire. They were met and destroyed by Kleopas's *Heart of Destruction* and Marchese's P48J.

The Infardi fell back.

GAUNT STRODE INTO the tent where Ghost troopers were guarding the Infardi officer taken prisoner at Bhavnager. The wretch was shivering and broken.

Gaunt ordered him to be released and handed him a small data-slate.

'Take this back to your brethren,' he said firmly.

The Infardi rose, facing Gaunt, and spat in his face.

Gaunt's punch broke his nose and sent him tumbling onto the snowy ground.

'Take this back to your brethren,' he repeated, holding out the slate.

'What is it?'

'A demand for them to surrender.'

The Infardi laughed.

'Last chance... Go.'

The Infardi got up, blood from his nose spattering the snow, and took the slate. He went out through the gate and disappeared down the slope.

The next time the Imperials saw him, he was strung spread-eagled across the front of an AT70 that was ploughing up the approach to the outer line. The tank waited, stationary, as if daring the Imperials to shoot or at least daring them to notice.

Then it fired its main gun. The screaming Infardi officer had been tied with his torso over the muzzle of the tank cannon.

A conical spray of red gore covered the snow. The AT70 turned and trundled back to its lines.

'An answer of sorts, I suppose,' Gaunt said to Rawne.

ON THE LADDER, barely a quarter of the way up, Corbec's team woke in the chill of dawn to find themselves half buried in the overnight snow. Each of them had lain down on a step in their bedroll. Shaking and slow, they got up, cold to the marrow. Corbec looked up the winding stairs. This was going to be murder.

* * *

FOR FIVE STRAIGHT days, the Infardi made no attempt to attack again. Gaunt was beginning to believe they were stalling until the fleet's arrival. For the Imperials dug in behind the Shrinehold defences, the waiting was becoming intolerable.

Then, at noon on the fourteenth day of the mission, the enemy tried again.

Armour ploughed up out of the gorge, and shells wailed at the Shrinehold. Caught in the initial rush, the Conqueror *Say Your Prayers* and two Chimera were lost. Smoke from the wreck of the dead Conqueror trailed up into the blue.

The rest of the Pardus armour met the assault and slugged it out. Ghosts under Soric and Mkoll ran forward from their ice trenches and countered the enemy push on foot up the pass.

From their dug-outs, the Tanith snipers began to compete. Larkin could outscore Luhan easily enough, but Banda was something else. Seeing a competition, Cuu put money on it. His wager, Larkin was furious to discover, was on the Verghastite loom-girl.

It took two straight hours for the Imperials to repulse the attack. They were exhausted by the end of it.

ON THE SIXTEENTH day, the Infardi tried yet again, in major force. Shells hit the Shrinehold's walls and tower. A blizzard of las-fire streaked the air, raining on the Imperial lines. Once they could see they were hurting their enemy, the Infardi charged, five or maybe six thousand cultist-warriors, pouring in through the advancing files of their war machines. From the wall, Gaunt saw them coming.

It was going to be bloody.

HIGH UP ON the punishing Ladder of Heaven which seemed to go on forever, Corbec stopped to get his breath back. He'd never known exhaustion like this, or pain, or breathlessness. He knelt down on the snow-covered step.

'Don't... don't you dare go... go quitting on me now!' Dorden exclaimed, vapour gusting from his lips, as he tried to pull Corbec to his feet. The chief medic was thin and haggard, his skin drawn and pale, and he was struggling for breath.

'But doc... we should never... never have even tried...'

'Don't you dare, Corbec! Don't you dare!'

'Listen! Listen!' Daur called back to them. He and Derin were about forty steps above them, silhouetted against the bright white sky.

They heard a rolling roar that wasn't the constant wind. A buffeting, thunderous drone, mixed over what they slowly realised were the voices of thousands of howling, chanting men.

Corbec got up. He wanted to just lie down and die. He couldn't feel his feet any more. But he got up and leaned against Dorden.

'I think, my old friend, we might be there at last. And I think we've arrived at a particularly busy time.'

A few steps behind them, the others had caught up, all except Greer who was now lagging a long, long way behind. Bragg and Nessa sat down in the snow to catch their breaths. Vamberfeld stood panting with his eyes closed. Milo looked at Sanian, whose weary face was clouded by what he supposed to be grief.

It wasn't. It was anger.

'That's the sound of war,' she wheezed, fighting her desperate fatigue. 'I know it. Not enough that war comes to my world, that it tears through my home town. Now it comes here, to the most sacred place of all, where only peace should be!'

She looked up at Dorden. 'I was right, you see, doctor? War consumes everything and everyone. There is only war. Nothing else even matters.'

THEY CLAMBERED ON, up the last few hundred metres of curling staircase, soul-weary and delirious with cold and hunger. But to know the end was at hand lifted them up for that last effort.

The sounds of the combat grew louder, magnified by the echoes that came off the mountain faces and the gorge.

They readied their weapons with trembling, clumsy hands, and advanced, Corbec and Bragg covered the way ahead, taking one step at a time.

The steps ended in a wide snow-covered platform of rock, the cliff edge of which showed the ancient traces of a retaining wall. They were climbing up onto a great promontory of rock, a flat-topped buttress of mountain that stuck out from the mountainside above a vast gorge. A walled, keep-like structure that could only be the Shrinehold itself lay to their left, dominating the promontory. Between it and the place where the wide promontory extended out from the top of the pass, full-scale battle raged. They were bystanders, hidden from view half a kilometre from the edge of the fighting. Banks of sooty smoke and ash rolled through the freezing mountain air.

A tide of Infardi war machines and troops, inexorable as a glacier, was moving forward from the head of the pass and up the promontory past them. In the sloping snowfield in front of the Shrinehold, the Chaos forces were being met head-on by the Imperial defenders. Shell holes had been torn in the Shrinehold's outer wall, and vehicles were on fire. The fighting was so thick they could barely make sense of it.

'Come on,' said Corbec.

'We're going into that?' moaned Greer. 'We can barely walk any more, you crazy bastard!'

'That's Colonel Crazy Bastard to you, pal. No, we're not going into that. Not directly. We'll follow the edge of this promontory around. But that's where we're going, and we've got to get in there sooner or later. Dead on my damned feet I may be, but I've come a fething long way to be part of this.'

GAUNT WAS IN the thick of the fighting at the foot of the outer wall. He hadn't been in a stand-up fight this fierce since Balhaut. It was so concentrated, so direct. The noise was bewildering.

Nearby, Lieutenant Pauk's Executioner was firing beam after beam of superheated plasma into the charging ranks, leaving lines of mangled corpses in the half-melted snow. Both the *Heart of Destruction* and the *Lucky Bastard* had run out of main gun shells, and were reduced to bringing in their bulk and coaxial weapons in support of the Ghosts. Brostin, Neskon and the other flame troopers were out on the right flank, spitting gouts of yellow flame down the field that turned the hard-packed snow to slush and sent Infardi troops screaming back, their clothes and flesh on fire.

The Imperials were holding, but in this hellish confusion, there was a chance that command coherency could be lost as wave after wave of the Chaos-breed stormed forward.

Gaunt saw the first couple of enemy officers. Just energised blurs moving amongst their troops, each one protected in the shimmering orb of a refractor shield. Nothing short of a point-blank tank round could touch them. He counted five of them amid the thick echelons of advancing enemy. Any one of them might be the notorious Pater Sin, come all this way to snatch his final triumph.

'Support me!' Gaunt cried to the fireteam at his heels, and they pushed out in assault, tackling the Infardi, sometimes hand to hand. Gaunt's bolt pistol fired shot after shot, and the power sword of Heironymo Sondar whispered in his fist.

Two Ghosts beside him were cut down. Another stumbled and fell, his left arm gone at the elbow.

'For Tanith! For Verghast! For Sabbat!' Gaunt yelled, his breath steaming the air. 'First-and-Only! First-and-Only!'

There was good support to his immediate left. Caffran, Criid, Beltayn, Adare, Memmo and Mkillian. Flanking them, Sergeant Bray's section, and the remains of a fireteam led by Corporal Maroy.

Scything with his sword, Gaunt worried about the right flank. He was pretty sure Corporal Mkteeg was dead, and there was no sign of Obel's section, or of Soric who, with Mkoll, had operational command of that quarter.

One of the Infardi officers was close now, cackling aloud, invisible in his ball of shield energy against which the Imperial las-fire twinkled harmlessly. Using him as mobile cover, the Ershul foot troops were pounding at the Ghosts. Memmo tumbled, headshot, gone, and Mkillian dropped a second later, hit in the thigh and hip.

'Caffran! Tube him!' Gaunt yelled.

'It won't breach the shield, sir!'

'Put it at his feet, then! Knock the fether over!'

Caffran hurled a tube-charge, spinning it end over end. It bounced in the thick snowpack right at the Infardi officer's feet and went off brightly.

The blasts didn't hurt the Ershul officer, but it effectively blew the ground out from under him and he fell, his refractor shield hissing in the snow.

Gaunt was immediately on him, yelling out, stabbing down two-handed with his power blade. Criid, Beltayn and Adare were right at his heels, gunning down the Ershul-lord's body-guard.

Power sword met refractor shield. The shield was a model manufactured by Chaos-polluted Mechanicus factories on the occupied forgeworld Ermune. It was powerful and effective. The power sword was so old, no one knew its original place of manufacture. It popped the shield like a needle lancing a blister.

The fizzling cloak of energy vanished and Gaunt's sword blade plunged on, impaling the screaming Infardi revealed inside.

Gaunt wrenched the sword out and got up. The Infardi nearby, those who hadn't yet been dropped by his Ghosts, backed off and ran in fear. By killing the officer in front of their eyes, he'd put a chink in their insane confidence.

But it was a tiny detail of triumph in a much greater battlestorm. Major Rawne, commanding units nearer to the main gate, could see no respite in the onslaught. The Infardi were throwing themselves at his position as fast as his troops in the snow-trenches and on the wall parapet could fire on them. A row of self-propelled guns was working up behind the enemy infantry, and their munitions now came whistling down, throwing up great bursts of ice and fire. Two shells dropped inside the wall and one hit the wall itself, blowing out a ten metre chunk.

Rawne saw the *Grey Venger* advancing over the snow, streaking titanic stripes of laser fire at the Usurper guns. One was hit and sent up a fiery mushroom cloud. Rocket grenades slapped and banged off the *Venger's* hull. The *Lion of Pardua* smashed directly through a faltering pack of Infardi troopers, dozer blade lowered, fighting to get a shot at the heavy gun units too. A tank round, coming from Emperor alone knew where, destroyed its starboard tracks and it lurched to a stop. The shrieking Infardi were all over it, mobbing the hull, their green figures swarming across the crippled tank. Rawne tried to direct some of his troop fire to assist the Conqueror, but the range was bad and they were too boxed in. Tank hatches were shot or blasted open, and the mob of Infardi dragged the *Lion's* crew out screaming.

'Feth, no!' Rawne gasped, his warm exhalation becoming vapour.

Without warning, another tank round hit the *Lion*, and blew it apart, exploding several dozen Infardi with it. Killing the Imperial armour seemed to be all the enemy cared about.

In a snow-trench ten metres left of the major, Larkin cursed and yelled out 'Cover me!' as he rolled back from his firing position. Troopers Cuu and Tokar moved up beside the prone Banda and resumed firing.

The barrel of Larkin's long-las had failed. He unscrewed the flash suppressor and then twisted and pulled out the long, ruined barrel. Larkin was so practiced at this task he could swap the XC 52/3 strengthened barrels in less than a minute. But his bag of spares was empty.

'Feth!' He crawled over to Banda, shots passing close over his head. 'Verghast! Where're your spare rods?'

Banda snapped off another shot, and then reached round and pulled the clasp of her pack open. 'In there! Down the side!'

Larkin reached in and pulled out a roll of vizzy-cloth. There were three XC 52/3s wrapped in it.

'This all you got?'

'It's all Twenish was carrying!'

Larkin locked one into place, checked the line, and rescrewed his suppressor. 'They're not going to last any fething time at this pace!' he grunted.

'Should be more in the munition supplies, Tanith,' said Cuu, clipping a new power cell into his weapon.

'Yeah, but who's going back into the Shrinehold to get them?'

'Point,' murmured Cuu.

Larkin blew on his mittened hands and began firing again.

'What's the tally?' he hissed at Banda.

'Twenty-three,' she said without looking round.

Only two less than him. Feth, she was good.

Then again, who wouldn't score when they had this many damned targets to fire at?

RAWNE GOT A fireteam forward as far as the cover provided by one of their own burning Chimeras. Lillo, Gutes, Cocoer and Baen dropped into the filthy snow beside him, firing through the raging smoke that boiled out of the machine. A moment later, Luhan, Filain, Caill and Mazzedo moved up close and provided decent crossfire under Feygor's command.

Rawne waved a third team – Orul, Sangul, Dorro, Raess and Muril – round to the far side of the Chimera. They were reaching position when an Infardi counter-push hit. Two rounds from an AT70 erupted like small volcanoes in their midst. Filain and Mazzedo were obliterated instantly. Cocoer was gashed by flying metal and fell screaming. Steam rose from his hot blood in the chill air. Gutes and Baen ran forward to drag the bawling, bloody Tanith into cover, but Gutes was immediately hit in the leg by a las-round. Baen turned in surprise and took two hits in the lower back. His arms lurched up and he fell on his face.

Infardi troops rushed in from the left, weapons blazing. In the savage short-range firefight that followed, first Orul and then Sangul were killed by massive torso injuries. Dorro managed to get Baen and Cocoer into cover and then he was hit in the jaw with such destructive force his head was virtually twisted off.

Rawne found himself pinned with Luhan, Lillo, Feygor and Caill, firing in support of Raess and Muril who were closer to the trio of wounded Ghosts.

'Three! This is three! We're pinned!'

The blackened wreckage of a Munitorium troop truck fifty metres ahead splintered and rolled as something big pushed it aside. For a moment, Rawne felt relief, sure it was one of the Pardus Conquerors.

But it wasn't. It was a SteG 4, squirming through the heavy snowcover on tyres that were encrusted with slush, oil and blood.

'Feth! Back! Back!'

'Where the gak to, sir?' Lillo wailed.

The SteG fired and the whooping shell slammed through the dead Chimera.

There was a chilling wail from behind Rawne's position. Part animal shriek, part pneumatic hiss, a sound that swooped from high pitch to low. The output of a powerful beam weapon ripped into the front of the SteG and a rush of pressurised flame blew out the side panels. It bounced to a halt, streaming smoke.

'Fall back! Get clear!' Commissar Hark yelled to Rawne and his soldiers as he fired again into the midst of a charging Infardi platoon. They half-carried and half-dragged Gutes, Cocoer and Baen back the twenty metres to the nearest snow-work cover.

'I'm surprised to see you,' Rawne told Hark flatly.

'I'm sure you are, major. But I wasn't just going to sit in the Shrinehold and wait for the end.'

'You won't have to wait long, commissar,' said Rawne, changing clips. 'I'm sure you'll be pleased to note that this is it. The last stand of Gaunt and his Ghosts.'

'I...' Hark began and then fell silent. As a commissar, even an unpopular, unwelcome one, it was his foremost duty to rally, to inspire the men and to quell just that kind of talk. But he couldn't. Looking out at the forces that swept in to overrun and slaughter them, there was no denying it.

The cold-blooded major was right.

In the very heaviest part of the battle, Gaunt knew it too. Troopers fell all around him. He saw Caffran, wounded in the leg, being dragged to cover by Criid. He saw Adare hit twice, convulse and drop. He saw two Verghastite Ghosts thrown into the air by a shell burst. He almost fell over the stiffening corpse of Trooper Brehl, the blood spats from his wounds frozen like gemstones.

A las-round hit Gaunt in the left arm and spun him a little. Another passed through the skirt of his storm coat.

'First-and-Only!' he yelled, his breath smoking in the cold. 'First-and-Only!'

Something happened to the sky. It changed abruptly from frozen chalk-white to fulminous yellow, swirling with cloud patterns. A sudden, almost hot wind surged up the gorge.

'What the gak is that?' Banda murmured.

'Oh no,' mumbled Larkin. 'Chaos madness. Fething Chaos madness.'

Silent auroras of purple and scarlet rippled across the sky. Crimson blooms swirled out and stained the sky like ink spots in water. Lightning strikes, searing violet-white, sizzled and cracked down, accompanied by thunderclaps so loud they shook the mountain.

The savage fighting foundered and ceased. Beneath the alien deluge, the Infardi fled back down to the pass, leaving their wounded and their crippled machines behind them. The mass exodus was so sudden, they had cleared the approach fields of the Shrinehold in less than ten minutes.

The Imperials cowered in terror beneath the twisting light-show. Vehicle engines stalled. Vox signals went berserk in whoops of interference and swarms of static. Many troopers wrenched their microbead ear-plugs out, wincing. Vox-officer Raglon's ears were bleeding by the time he'd managed to pull off his headset. Wild static charge filled the air, crackling off weapons, making hair stand on end. Greenish corposant and ball lightning wriggled and flared around the eaves and roofs of the Shrinehold.

In the face of final defeat, something had saved Gaunt's honour guard, or at least allowed it a temporary reprieve.

Ironically, that something was Chaos.

'I HAVE CONSULTED the monastery's sensitives and psyker-adepts,' said ayatani-ayt Cortona. 'It is a warp storm, a flux of the empyrean. It is affecting all space near Hagia.'

Gaunt sat on a stool in the Shrinehold's main hallway, stripped to the waist as Medic Lesp sutured and bound up his arm. 'The cause?'

'The arch-enemy's fleet.' replied Cortona.

Gaunt raised an eyebrow. 'But that's not due to reach us for another five days.'

'I don't believe it has. But a fleet of that size, moving through the aether, would create a massive disturbance, like the bow wave of a great ship, pushing the eddies and swirls of the warp ahead of it.'

'And that bow wave has just broken over Hagia? I see.' Gaunt stood up and flexed his bandaged arm. 'Thanks, Lesp. Immaculate needlework as ever.'

'Sir. I don't suppose there's any point advising you to rest it?'

'None whatsoever. We get out of this, I'll rest it all you like.'

'Sir.'

'Now get to the triage station and do some proper work. There are many more needy than me.'

Lesp saluted, collected up his medicae kit and hurried out. Pulling on his shirt, Gaunt walked with Cortona to one of the open shutters and gazed out at the seething, malign fury of the sky above the Sacred Hills.

'No getting off planet now.'

'Colonel-commissar?'

Gaunt looked round at the elderly high priest. 'There's nothing good about that storm, ayatani-ayt, but there's some satisfaction to be derived from it at least. If I had followed my orders and returned to the Doctrinopolis, I wouldn't have reached it until tomorrow, even under the best conditions. So even if I'd got in before the evacuation deadline, I'd have been trapped.'

'Like Lugo and the last few hundred ships undoubtedly are,' said Hark, suddenly there and in the conversation. A typical Hark-esque no-warning appearance.

'You sound almost pleased, Hark.'

'Hagia is about to be wiped from space, sir. Pleased is not the right word. But, like you, I wager, there is some cruel delight to be drawn from the idea of Lord General Lugo suffering along with us.'

Gaunt began to button up the braid froggings of his tunic. 'Major Rawne, another bête noir of yours, told me you did us proud in the fight today. Saved him and a good many others.'

'It wasn't service to you. It was service to the Golden Throne of Terra. I am a soldier of the Imperium and will make a good account of myself until death, the Emperor protects.'

'The Emperor protects,' nodded Gaunt. 'Look, commissar... for whatever it's worth, I have no doubts as to your courage, loyalty or ability. You've fought well all the way along. You've tried to do your duty, even if I haven't liked it. It took, I have to admit, a feth of a lot of guts to stand up in that room and try and take command off me.'

'Guts had nothing to do with it.'

'Guts had *everything* to do with it. I want you to know that you'll receive no negative report from me... if and when I ever get to make one. No matter what kind of report you choose to make. I bear you no ill will. I've always taken my duty to the Emperor fething seriously. Completely fething seriously. How could I possibly resent another man doing the same?'

'I... thank you for your civility and frankness. I wish things could have been... and could yet be... different between us. It would have been a pleasure to serve with you and the First-and-Only without this cloud of resentment hanging over me.'

Gaunt held out his hand and Hark shook it.

'I think so too.'

The doors to the hall swung open and cold air billowed in, bringing with it Major Kleopas, Captain LeGuin, Captain Marchese and the Ghost officers Soric, Mkoll, Bray, Meryn, Theiss and Obel. They stomped their boots and brushed flakes from their sleeves.

'Join me,' Gaunt told Hark. They joined the officers.

'Gentlemen. Where's Rawne?'

'There was some perimeter alert, sir. He went to check it out,' said Meryn.

Gaunt nodded. 'Any word on Corporal Mkteeg?'

'He was found alive, but badly shot up. They slaughtered his squad but for two other men,' said Soric.

'What is this, sir?' asked Corporal Obel. 'What drove the Infardi back? I thought they had us there, I really did.'

'They did, corporal. They honestly did. But for the damndest luck.' Gaunt quickly explained the nature of the storm effects as best as he understood it. 'I think this sudden warp storm shocked the Ershul. I think they thought it was some apocalyptic sign from their Dark Gods and simply... lost it. It is an apocalyptic sign from their Dark Gods, of course. That's the down side. Once they've regrouped, they'll be back, and stronger too, would be my wager. They'll know almighty hell is coming to help them.'

'So they'll assault again?' asked Marchese.

'Before nightfall would be my guess, captain. We must restructure our force disposition in time to meet the Ershul's next attack.'

'Is that what we're calling them now, sir?' asked Soric.

'Call them whatever you like, Soric.'

'Bastards?' suggested Kleopas.

'Scum-sucking warp-whores?' said Theiss.

'Targets?' said Mkoll quietly.

The men laughed.

'Whatever works for you,' said Gaunt. Good, there was some damn morale left yet.

'Bray? Obel? Drag over that table there. Captain LeGuin, I see you've brought charts. Let's get to work.'

They'd just spread out the tank hunter's maps when Gaunt's vox beeped.

'One, go.'

It was Vox-officer Beltayn. 'Major Rawne says to get out front, sir. Something's awry.'

Awry! Always with that nervous, understated awry! 'What's actually awry this time, Beltayn?'

'Sir... it's the colonel, sir!'

* * *

GAUNT RAN OUT down the steps, through the snow lying between the inner and outer walls, towards the gate.

Rawne and a section of men were just coming in, bringing with them ten haggard, stumbling figures, caked in dirt and rime, half-starved and weary.

Gaunt's eyes widened. He came to a halt.

Trooper Derin. Try Again Bragg. The Verghastite Ghosts Vamberfeld and Nessa. Captain Daur, supporting a half-dead Pardus officer Gaunt didn't know. Dorden... Great God-Emperor! Dorden! And Milo, Emperor protect him, carrying a Hagian girl in his arms.

And there, at the head of them, Colonel Colm Corbec.

'Colm? Colm, what the feth are you doing here?' Gaunt asked.

'Did... did we miss all the fun, sir?' Corbec whispered, and pitched over into the snow.

SIXTEEN
INFARDI

'It was always her greatest weapon. Surprise, you would call it,
I suppose. The scope of her ability to produce the unexpected.
To turn the course of an engagement on its head, even the worst of
defeats. I saw it happen many times. Something from nothing.
Triumph from disaster. Until the very end, when at the last,
she could no longer work her miracles.
And she fell.'

— Warmaster Kiodrus, from *The Path to the Nine Wounds:*
A History of Service with the Saint

THE NIGHT OF the sixteenth day fell, but it was not proper night.
The surging maelstrom of the warp storm lit the sky above the
Shrinehold with pulses and cyclones of kaleidoscopic light and
electromagnetic spectres. The snows had ceased, and under the
silent, flickering glare, the embattled Imperials stood watch at
battle-readiness, gazing at the reflections of the rapidly fluctu-
ating colour patterns on the snowfield and the ice of the Sacred
Hills.

It was the stillest time, almost tranquil. Vivid colour roiled
and swelled, broke and ebbed, all across the heavens. Barely a

breeze stirred. Perhaps as a result of the warp-eddies, the temperature had risen to just above zero.

In an anteroom in the monastery, ayatani carefully lit the oil lamps and then left without a word.

Gaunt put his cap and gloves on a side table. 'I... I'm very pleased you're here, but the commissar in me wants to know why. Feth, Colm! You were wounded and you had orders to evacuate!'

Corbec sat back on a daybed under the bolted, gloss-red shutters, his camo-cloak pulled around him like a shawl, and a cup of hot broth in his hands.

'Both facts true, sir. I'm afraid I can't really explain it.'

'You can't explain it?'

'No, sir. Not without sounding so mad you'll have me clapped in irons and locked in a padded cell immediately.'

'Let's risk that,' said Gaunt. He'd poured himself a glass of sacra, but realised he didn't really want it. He offered it to Rawne, who shook his head, and then to Dorden, who took it and sipped it. The Tanith chief medic sat near the central fire pit. Gaunt had never seen him look so old or so tired.

'Tell him, Colm,' Dorden said. 'Tell him, damn it. I didn't believe you at first either, remember?'

'No, you didn't.' Colm sipped his broth, put it down, and pulled a box of cigars from his hip pouch. He offered them around.

'If I may,' said ayatani Zweil, rising up from his floor mat to take one. With a surprised grin, Corbec lit it for him.

'Haven't had one for years,' smiled Zweil, enjoying the first few puffs. 'What's the worst it could do? Kill me?'

'Least of your worries now, father,' said Rawne.

'Too true.'

'I'm waiting, Colm,' said Gaunt.

'I... ah... let me see... how best to put it... I... well, the thing of it was... at first...'

'The saint spoke to him,' said Dorden abruptly.

Zweil exploded in a coughing fit. Corbec leaned forward to thump the old priest on the back.

'Corbec?' growled Gaunt.

'Well, she did, didn't she?' said Dorden. He turned to Gaunt and Rawne. 'Don't look at me like that, either of you. I know how mad it sounds. That's how I felt when Colm told it to me.

But answer me this... What in the name of the good God-Emperor would make an old man like me come all this way too? Eh? It almost killed me. The fething Ladder of Heaven! It nearly killed all of us. But none of us are mad. None of us. Not even Colm.'

'Oh, thanks for that,' said Corbec.

'I need more,' began Gaunt.

'A whole fething lot more,' agreed Rawne, helping himself to a stiff drink after all.

'I had these dreams. About my old dad. Back on Tanith, Pryze County,' said Corbec.

'Aha. Here we go...' said Rawne.

'Get out if you don't want to listen!' spat Dorden. Rawne shrugged and sat. The mild old medic had never spoken to him like that before.

'He was trying to tell me something,' Corbec went on. 'This was right after I'd been through the clutches of that Pater Sin.'

'Trauma, then?' suggested Gaunt.

'Oh, very probably. If it makes it easier for you, we can pretend I slogged three hundred fething kilometres just because I wanted to be with you at the last stand of the Ghosts. And these people were fool enough to follow me.'

'That is easier to pretend,' said Rawne.

'Agreed, major,' said Gaunt. 'But humour us, Corbec, and tell us the rest.'

'Through my father, in my dreams, the saint called me. I can't prove it, but it's a fact. She called me. I didn't know what to do. I thought I was cracking up. Then I discovered Daur felt the same way. From the moment he was injured, he'd been taken by this niggle, this itch that wouldn't go away, no matter how hard he tried to scratch it.'

'Captain?' asked Gaunt. Daur sat over in the corner and so far he'd said nothing. The cold and fatigue of his hard journey had played hell with his wound-weakened state.

'It's as the colonel describes. I had a... a feeling.'

'Right,' said Gaunt. He turned back to Corbec. 'And then what? This feeling was so strong you and Daur broke orders, deserted, and took the others with you?'

'About that,' admitted Corbec.

'Breaking orders... Where have I heard that recently?' murmured Zweil, relighting his cigar.

'Shut up, father,' said Gaunt.

'Corbec told me what was going on,' said Dorden quietly. 'He told me what was in his head and what he planned to do. I knew he was trying to rope in able-bodied troopers to go with him. I tried to argue him out of it. But...'

'But?'

'But by then the saint had spoken to me too.'

'Feth me!' Rawne exclaimed.

'She'd spoken to you too, Tolin?' asked Gaunt steadily.

Dorden nodded. 'I know how it sounds. But I'd been having these dreams. About my son, Mikal.'

'That's understandable, doctor. That was a terrible loss for the Ghosts and for you.'

'Thank you, sir. But the more Corbec talked to me about his own dreams, the more I realised they were like mine. His dead father. My dead son. Coming to each of us with a message. Captain Daur was the same, but in a different way. Someone... something... was trying to communicate with us.'

'And so the three of you deserted?'

'Yes sir,' said Daur.

'I'm sorry about that, sir,' said Corbec.

Gaunt breathed deeply in contemplation. 'And the others? Were they spoken to?'

'Not as far as I know,' said Corbec. 'We just recruited them. Milo had come back with the wounded and desperately wanted to rejoin the company, so he was easy to convince. He brought in the girl, Sanian, her name is. She's esholi. We knew we needed local knowledge. But for her guidance we'd have been dead many times over by now. Shot, or frozen on the mountainside.'

'She found our way for us,' joked Dorden darkly. 'I pray to the Golden Throne she finds her own now.'

'Bragg, well, you know Try Again. He'd do any damn thing I tell him,' said Corbec. 'He was so eager to help. Derin, too. Vamberfeld, Nessa. When you've got a colonel, a captain and a chief medic asking you to break the rules and help them out, life or death, I think you go for it. None of them are to blame. None should be punished. They gave their all. For you, really.'

'For me?' asked Gaunt.

'That's why they were doing it. We'd convinced them it was a life or death mission above and beyond orders. That you'd have approved. That you'd have wanted it. That it was for the good of the Ghosts and for the Imperium.'

'You say you had to convince them, Corbec,' said Rawne. 'That implies you had to lie.'

'None of us lied, major,' said Dorden bluntly. 'We knew what we had to do and we told them about it. They followed, because they're loyal Ghosts.'

'What about the Pardus... Sergeant Greer is it?'

'We needed a driver, sir,' Daur said. 'I'd met Greer a little while before. He didn't need much convincing.'

'You told him about the saint and her messages?'

'Yes, sir. He didn't believe them, obviously.'

'Obviously,' echoed Rawne.

'So I...' Daur faltered, ashamed. 'I told him we were deserting to go and liberate a trove of ayatani gold from the Sacred Hills. Then he went along willingly, just like that.' Daur clicked his fingers.

'At last!' said Rawne, refilling his shot glass. 'A motivation I can believe.'

'Is there a trove of ayatani gold in the Sacred Hills?' Zweil asked, blowing casual but perfect smoke rings.'

'I don't believe so, father,' said Daur miserably.

'Oh good. I'd hate to be the last to know.'

Gaunt sat down on a stool by the door, ruminated, and stood up again almost at once. Corbec could tell he was nervous, edgy.

'I'm sorry, Ibram...' he began.

Gaunt held up a commanding hand. 'Save it, Colm. Tell me this... If I believe this miraculous story one millimetre... What happens now? What are you all here for?'

Corbec looked at Dorden, who shrugged. Daur put his head in his hands.

'That's where we all kind of run out of credibility, sir,' said Corbec.

'That's where it happens?' Rawne chuckled. 'Excuse me, Gaunt, but I thought that moment had passed long ago!'

'Perhaps, major. So.... none of you have any idea what you're supposed to do now you're here?'

'No, sir,' said Daur.

'Not a clue,' said Corbec.

'I'm sorry,' said Dorden.

'Very well,' said Gaunt. 'You should return to the billets arranged for you and get some sleep.'

The three members of the Wounded Wagon party nodded and began to get up.

'Oh no, no, no!' said Zweil suddenly. 'That's not an end to it! Not at all!'

'Father,' Gaunt began. 'It's late and we're all going to die in the morning. Let it go.'

'I won't,' said Zweil. He stubbed out his cigar butt in a saucer. 'A good smoke, colonel. Thank you. Now sit down and tell me more.'

'This isn't the time, father,' said Gaunt.

'It is the time. If this isn't the time, I don't bloody know what is! The saint spoke to these men, and sent them out after us on a holy cause!'

'Please,' said Rawne sourly.

'A holy cause! Like it or not, believe it or not, these men are Infardi!'

'They're what?' cried Rawne, reaching for his laspistol as he leapt up.

'Infardi! Infardi! What's your word for it...? Pilgrims! They're bloody pilgrims! They have come all this way in the name of the hallowed beati! Don't spurn them now!'

'Sit down, Rawne, and put the sidearm away. What do you suggest we do, Father Zweil?'

'Ask them the obvious question, colonel-commissar.'

'Which is?'

'What did the saint say to them?'

Gaunt ran his splayed hands back though his cropped blond hair. His left arm throbbed. 'Fine. For the record... What did the saint say to you?'

'Sabbat Martyr,' Dorden, Corbec and Daur replied in unison.

Gaunt sat down sharply.

'Oh sacred feth,' he murmured.

'Sir?' queried Rawne, getting up. 'What does that mean?'

'That means she's probably been speaking to me too.'

'SANIAN?' MILO CALLED her name as he edged down the dim corridors of the Shrinehold.

The wind outside wailed down the flues of the airshafts. Bizarre reflections of light from the warp storm outside spilled across the tiled floor from the casements. He saw a figure sitting on one of the hallway benches.

'Sanian?'

'Hello, Milo.'

'What are you doing?'

He could see what she was doing. Clumsily and inexpertly, she was field-stripping and loading an Imperial lasrifle.

She looked around at him as he approached, put down the chamber block and the dirty vizzy-cloth, and kissed him impetuously on the cheek. Her fingers left a smudge of oil on his chin.

'What was that for?'

'For helping me.'

'Helping you to do what?'

She didn't reply immediately. She was trying to screw in the rifle's barrel the wrong way.

'Let me,' said Milo, reaching around her to grip the weapon. 'So what have I helped you to do?'

She watched as his expert hands locked the rifle system together.

'Praise you to the saint, Brin. Praise you.'

'Why? What have I done?' he asked as she took the weapon from his hands.

'You,' she smiled. 'You and your Ghosts. From them, I have found my way. I am esholi no longer. I see the future. I see my way at last.'

'Your way? So... what is it?'

Outside, the warp storm blistered across the night sky.

'It's the only way there is,' she said.

'I'M SORRY, BUT this is crazy!' Rawne cried, hurrying to catch up with Gaunt, Dorden, Corbec, Zweil and Daur as they strode down the long cloisters of the Shrinehold heading for the holy sepulchre.

'What is this commotion?' asked an ayatani, coming out of a pair of inner doors.

'Go back to bed,' Zweil told him as they rushed past.

Gaunt stopped dead and they slammed into him from behind.

He turned around. 'Rawne's right! This is fething stupid! There's nothing in it!'

'You said yourself some voice has murmured "Sabbat Martyr" to you several times,' reminded Dorden.

'It did! I thought it did! Feth! This is madness!'

'How long have we been thinking that?' Dorden looked aside at Corbec.

'It doesn't matter how stupid it feels,' Zweil said. 'Get in there. Into the sepulchre! Test it!'

'I've already been there! You know that!' said Gaunt.

'On your own, maybe. Not with these other Infardi.'

'I wish you'd stop using that word,' said Rawne.

'And I wish you'd bugger off,' Zweil told him.

'Stop it! All of you!' cried Gaunt. 'Let's just go and see what happens...'

'VAMBS?' WHISPERED BRAGG, pushing open the heavy, red door of the sepulchre. He wasn't sure where he was, but it looked a feth of a lot like a place he shouldn't be.

The chamber was dark, the air was smoky and the floor was squeaky. Bragg edged across the shiny tiles carefully. They looked valuable. Too valuable for his big boots. 'Vambs? Mate?'

Scary holos of Space Marines loomed out of alcoves in the black walls.

'For feth's sake! Vambs?'

Behind the polished altar and under a big hood of what looked to Bragg like bone, he saw Vamberfeld, bending over a small hardwood casket in the shadows.

'Vambs?' Bragg approached the altar. 'What are you doing in here?'

'Look, Bragg!' Vamberfeld held up an object he had taken from the casket. 'It's her jiddi-stick! The cane used by Sabbat herself to drive her chelon to market.'

'Great. Uhm... I reckon you oughta put that back...' Bragg said.

'Should I? Maybe. Anyway, look at this, Bragg! Remember that broken crook I found? See? It matches exactly the broken haft they have here! Can you believe it? Exactly! I think I found a piece of the saint's actual crook!'

'I think I should get you to the doc, mate,' Bragg said carefully. 'We shouldn't be in here.'

'I think we should. I think I should.'

The sepulchre door creaked open behind them.

'Feth! Someone's coming in,' said Bragg, worried. 'Stay here. Don't touch anything else, okay? Not a thing.' He walked back into the main area of the sepulchre.

'What the feth are you doing here?' Vamberfeld heard Bragg ask a few seconds later.

He turned and stared out of the gloomy reliquary. His friend Bragg was talking to someone.

'Same as you, Tanith. I've come for the gold.'

'The gold? What fething gold?' Vamberfeld heard Bragg reply.

'Don't screw with me, big guy!' the other voice said.

'I have no intention of screwing with you. Put that auto down, Greer. It's not funny any more.'

Don't. Not in here, Vamberfeld thought. Please not in here. His hand was starting to shake.

He got up and came out of the reliquary. Greer was standing inside the big red door, which he'd closed behind him. He looked sick and desperate and twitchy. His skin was haggard and blotchy from the ordeal they'd all been through. He was pointing a guard-issue autopistol at Bragg.

The moment Vamberfeld appeared, Greer flicked the muzzle to cover him as well.

'Two of you, huh? I expected as much, that's why I came down here. Trying to cheat me out of my cut, huh? Did Daur put you up to this or are you stabbing him in the back too?'

'What the good feth are you talking about?' asked Bragg.

'The gold! The damn gold! Stop playing innocent!'

'There is no gold,' said Vamberfeld, trying to stop his hand shaking. 'I told you that.'

'Shut up! You're not right in the head, you psycho! You've got nothing I wanna hear!'

'Why don't you put the gun down, Greer?' asked Bragg, taking a step forward. The gun switched back to cover him.

'Don't move. Don't try that crap. Show me the gold! Now! You got here before me, you must've found it!'

'There is no gold,' Vamberfeld repeated.

'Shut the hell up!' spat Greer, swinging the gun back to cover the Verghastite.

'This is getting out of hand,' said Bragg. 'We gotta calm down...'

'Okay, okay,' Greer seemed to agree. 'Look, we'll split it three ways. Gold's heavy. I can't carry it all, and there's no way I'm staying here tonight. Chaos is going to be all over this shithole any time. Three way split. As much as we can take. You help me carry it back down the Ladder to the Chimera. What do you say?'

'I'd say... One, you know we'd never make it back all that way, especially laden down... Two, the whole planet's falling to Chaos, so there's nowhere to run to... And three, there is no fething gold.'

'Screw you, then! I'll take what I can myself! As much gold as I can carry!'

'There is no gold,' said Vamberfeld.

'Shut up, you head-job!' screamed Greer, aiming the gun at Vamberfeld. 'Make him shut up, Tanith! Make him stop saying that!'

'But it's true,' said Vamberfeld. His hand was shaking so much. So hard. Trying to make it stop, he pushed it into his pocket.

'What the hell? Are you going for a weapon?' Greer aimed the gun straight-armed at Vamberfeld, his finger squeezing.

'No!' Bragg lunged at Greer, grappling frantically at his weapon.

The pistol discharged. The round hit Vamberfeld in the chest and threw him over onto his back.

'Vambs!' Bragg raged in horror. 'God-Emperor feth you, you bastard!' His massive left fist crashed into Greer's face, hurling the Pardus back across the sepulchre with blood spurting from his broken nose and teeth. The gun fired again twice, sending one bullet through Bragg's right thigh and the other explosively through the front of the chelon-shell altar in a spray of lustrous shards.

Bragg lunged at Greer again, big hands clawing.

The Pardus sergeant's first shot didn't even slow Bragg down, even though it went right through his torso. Neither did the second. The third finally brought Bragg down, hard on his face, at Greer's feet.

'You stupid pair of bastards!' Greer snarled contemptuously at the fallen men, trying to staunch the blood pouring out of his smashed face.

The Verghastite lay on the floor beside Bragg, face up, staring at the roof shadows high above through sightless eyes. Bragg was face down. A wide and spreading lake of blood seeped out across the ancient, precious tiles from each of them. The Pardus sergeant strode in towards the sepulchre.

'WHAT THE FETH! Did you hear that?' Corbec cried.

'Shooting! From the sepulchre,' said Gaunt. He pulled his bolt pistol out and started to run. The others raced after him, Dorden lagging, his weary legs too leaden.

They burst into the sepulchre, Gaunt's boot slamming the massive door wide.

'Oh, feth me, no! Doc!' bellowed Corbec, gazing at the bodies and the blood.

'Who would do this?' Zweil gasped.

'There! Down there!' cried Rawne, his laspistol already drawn.

In the reliquary itself, Greer dived for cover behind the altar. He'd overturned the hardwood relic casket in his frantic search, spilling the ancient pieces across the floor. The glass covers over the gospel stands were smashed. The venerated Imperator armour was half-slumped off its palanquin.

'Where is it? Where's the gold, you bastards?' he screamed, ripping off several shots. Rawne cried out in pain as he was twisted round off his feet. Gaunt grabbed Zweil and threw himself down on top of the old priest as a shield. Corbec and Daur ducked hard. Dorden, just reaching the door, sought cover behind the frame.

'Greer! Greer! What the feth are you doing?' bawled Corbec.

'Back off! Back the hell off or I'll kill you all!' yelled Greer, firing three more shots that punched into the shrine's door or chipped the black corundum of the walls.

'Greer!' cried Daur. 'It's me! Daur! What are you doing?'

Several more shots whined over his head.

Daur had his laspistol out. He glanced at Corbec, hunched on the polished tiles next to him.

A meaningful look.

'Greer! You'll blow everything! You'll ruin it for us!'

'Where is it, Daur?' shouted Greer, slamming a new clip into his sidearm's grip. 'It isn't here!'

'It is! Gak it, Greer! You're screwing up all the plans!'

'Plans?' murmured Rawne through gritted teeth. Dorden was hastily dragging him back into the cover of the doorway. The bullet had punched through Rawne's forearm.

'You weren't going to do anything until I gave you the word!'

Daur yelled, trying to edge forward. Greer fired again, crazing several six thousand year old shell-tiles.

'Plans change! You Ghosts were gonna ditch me!'

'No! We can still do this! You hear me? You want to? I can show you the gold! Go with me on this!'

'I dunno...'

'Come on!' cried Daur, and leapt upright, turning to point his laspistol at Corbec, Gaunt and the others.

'Drop the guns! Drop them!'

'What?' stammered Gaunt.

'I guess you got us, Daur,' said Corbec, tossing aside his laspistol and staring at Gaunt as hard as he could.

'I got them covered, Greer! Come on! We can run for it! Come on! I'll take you to the gold and we can leave these bastards to die! Greer!'

Greer rose from behind the altar, his gun in his hand. 'You know where the gold is?'

Daur turned, his aimed weapon swinging from the sheltering Ghosts to point at Greer.

'There is no gold, you stupid bastard,' he said, and shot Greer between the eyes.

Dorden ran into the room and knelt by the bodies of Bragg and Vamberfeld. 'They're a mess, but I've got pulses on both. Thank the Emperor the maniac wasn't packing a las. We need medic teams here right now.'

Standing in the doorway, clutching his bloody arm, Rawne spoke into his microbead. 'Three, in the sepulchre. I require medical teams here right now!'

Gaunt got back to his feet, and helped the winded Zweil up.

'Captain Daur, perhaps you'd give me a warning next time you plan to play a bluff that wild. I almost shot you.'

Daur turned to the colonel-commissar and held out his laspistol, butt-first. 'I doubt there'll be a next time. This is my fault. I led Greer on. I knew he was dangerous, I just didn't realise how gakking far he'd go.'

'What are you doing, Daur?' asked Gaunt, looking at the gun.

'It's a court martial offence, sir,' said Daur.

'Oh, at least,' said Corbec, with a wide grin. 'Saving the lives of your commanding officers like that.'

'Nice,' Rawne nodded at Daur. 'I never realised you were such a devious bastard, captain.'

'We'll talk about this later, Daur,' said Gaunt, and walked past the altar and Greer's spread-eagled corpse. He stared in dismay at Greer's wanton desecration.

'Just so I'm absolutely sure,' Zweil whispered to Daur. 'There really isn't a trove of ayatani gold here, is there?'

Daur shook his head. 'Just, you know, checking.'

Gaunt righted the relic casket and began putting the scattered fragments back reverently.

'What's keeping Lesp?' growled Dorden. He was trying to keep compression on Bragg's most serious injury. 'I need a medicae kit. Both of them are bleeding out! Colm! Get some pressure there on Vamberfeld's chest. No, higher. Keep it tight!'

The sound of running footsteps came from outside. Milo and Sanian burst in through the doorway and stopped dead.

'I heard shooting,' said Milo, out of breath. 'Oh, great God-Emperor! What's happened? Bragg!'

'Everything's under control, lad,' said Corbec, his hands drenched in Vamberfeld's blood. He wasn't convinced. In the reliquary, Gaunt seemed almost beside himself with agony as he tried to set things right.

'What was that?' asked Rawne sharply, looking around.

'What was what?' said Corbec.

'That noise. That hum.'

'I didn't... Oh, yeah. That's kind of scary.'

'A vibration!' said Rawne. 'The whole place is shaking!'

'It must be the Infardi attacking!' said Milo.

'No,' said Zweil with remarkable calm. 'I think it must be the Infardi reaching the sepulchre.'

The candles flickered and went out all at once. Pale, undersea light washed through the ancient tomb, green and cold. The holograms of the Adeptus Astartes dissolved and vanished, and in their place columns of bright white hololithic light extended from floor to ceiling. The black stone walls sweated and a pattern of previously invisible geometric blue bars glowed into life out of the stone, all the way around the chamber. Everything shook with the deep, ultrasonic growl.

'What the feth is happening?' stammered Rawne.

'I can hear...' Daur began.

'So can I,' said Dorden, looking up in wonder. Silent, phantom lights like ball lightning shimmered and circled above their heads.

'I can hear singing,' said Corbec. 'I can hear my old dad singing.' There were tears in his eyes.

In the reliquary, Gaunt slowly rose to his feet and gazed at the bier on which Saint Sabbat lay.

He could smell the sweet, incorruptible fragrance of spices, acestus and islumbine. The body of the saint began to shine, brighter and brighter, until the white radiance was too bright to stare at.

'Beati...' Gaunt murmured.

The light streaming out from the bier was so fierce, all the humans within had to close their eyes. The last thing Corbec saw was the faint silhouette of Ibram Gaunt, kneeling before the saint's bier, framed by the white ferocity of a star's heart.

THE LIGHT DIED away, and the sepulchre returned to the way it had been before. Blinking, speechless, they gazed silently at each other.

For the time it had lasted, no more than a few seconds, a calm but inexorable psychic force of monumental power had penetrated their minds.

'A miracle,' murmured Zweil, sitting down on the floor. 'A proper miracle. A transcendant miracle. You all felt that, didn't you?'

'Yes,' sobbed Sanian, her face streaming with tears.

Dorden nodded.

'Of course we did,' said Corbec quietly.

'I don't know what that was, but I've never been so scared in my life,' said Rawne.

'I'm telling you, Major Rawne. It was a miracle,' said Zweil.

'No,' said Gaunt, emerging from the reliquary. 'It wasn't.'

SEVENTEEN
SABBAT'S MARTYR

'There are no miracles. There are only men.'

— Saint Sabbat, epistles

THE ERSHUL'S FINAL assault began at two o'clock on the morning of the seventeenth day. In the silence of a snow-less, clear night, under the spasming auroras of the warp storm, they committed their entire strength to the attack on the Shrinehold. Support columns of reinforcements had been pushing up the pass all day and into the night. The Ershul were legion-strength. Nine thousand devotee-warriors. Five hundred and seventy armoured machines.

Just under two thousand able-bodied Imperial troops defended the Shrinehold, supported by the last four Conquerors, one Executioner, one Destroyer, and a handful of Chimeras, Salamanders and Hydra batteries. All they had on their side was the strategic strength of their walled position and the comparative narrowness of the approach across the promontory.

The staggering power of the Ershul bombardment hammered down onto the Imperial lines. The honour guard did not fire back. They were so low on ammunition and shells they had to wait to pick their targets. The Ershul host advanced towards them.

Standing on the inner wall, Gaunt surveyed their approaching doom through his scope. Even by his best estimate, they would be able to hold out for no more than twenty or thirty minutes.

He turned and looked at Rawne and Hark. Rawne's arm was thickly bandaged.

'I don't really think it matters how we fight this now, but I want you both to head down and rally the men for as long as you can. Do anything you can to buy time.'

The men nodded.

'The Emperor protects,' Gaunt said, shaking them both by the hand.

'We're not done yet, sir,' said Hark.

'I know, commissar. But remember... sometimes the carniv gets you.'

The officers strode away down the wall steps together.

Walking towards their deaths, Gaunt thought, taking one last look at the major and the commissar. And I should be there with them.

He turned and hurried back to the sepulchre where the others were waiting.

'A MIRACLE!' AYATANI-AYT Cortona was declaring yet again, his principal clerics gathered around him.

'I keep telling you it's not,' growled Zweil, 'and I have it on good authority.'

'You are just imhava! What do you know?' snapped Cortona.

'A feth of a lot more than you, tempelum,' said Zweil.

'You've been hanging out with the wrong crowd, picking up filthy language like that,' Corbec said to Zweil.

'Story of my woebegotten life, colonel,' said Zweil.

Gaunt entered the sepulchre and everyone turned to him.

'There is so little time, I have to be brief. This was not a miracle.'

'But we all felt it! Throughout the Shrinehold! The blessed power, singing in our minds!' cried Cortona.

'It was a psychic test pattern. The activation signature of an ancient device that I believe is buried under the shrine.'

'A what?' asked one of the ayatani.

'The Adeptus Mechanicus constructed this place to house the saint. I believe they laced the entire rock underneath us with dormant psyker technology the power – and purpose – of which we can only guess at. Was I the only one who got that from the psychic wave? It seemed quite clear.'

'Technology to do what?' sneered Cortona.

'To protect the beati. In the event of a true catastrophe, like this influx of the warp. To safeguard her final prophesy.'

'Preposterous! Why did we not know of it then?' asked another Shrinehold priest. 'We are her chosen, her sons.'

'Six thousand years is a long time,' said Corbec. 'Time enough to forget. Time enough to turn facts into myths.'

'But why now? Why does it manifest now?' asked Cortona.

'Because we came. Her Infardi. Gathered together in her sepulchre, we triggered the mechanism.'

'How?'

'Because our minds responded to the call. Because we came. Because through us, the mechanism recognised the time for awakening had come.'

'That's nonsense! Blasphemy, even!' cried the ayatani-ayt. 'It presumes you soldiers are more holy than the sacred brotherhood! Why would it wake for you when it has never woken for us?'

'Because you're not enlightened. Not that way,' said Zweil, drawing a gasp from the priests. 'You tend, and keep vigil, and reread the texts. But you do so out of inherited duty, not belief. These men really believe.' He gestured to Corbec, Daur and Gaunt.

There was a lot of angry shouting.

'There's no time to debate this! You hear that? The forces of Chaos are at the gates! We have a chance to use the technology the saint has left for us. We have barely any time to figure out how.'

'Sanian and I have been studying the holograms, sir,' said Milo. He gestured to the glowing bars of light in the shrine's corundum walls, lights that had not yet faded.

'There are depictions of her holy crusade,' said Sanian, tracing certain runes. 'The triumphs of Frenghold, Aeskaria and Harkalon. A mention of her trusted commanders. Here, for instance, the name of Lord Militant Kiodrus...'

'You're going to have to cut to the chase,' Gaunt interjected. 'We've only got a few minutes left.'

Sanian nodded. 'The activation mechanism for the technology appears to be here.' She pointed to a small runic chart glowing on the wall. 'The pillar of the eternal flame, at the very tip of the promontory.'

'How are we to use it?'

'Something must be put in place,' said Sanian, frowning. 'Some trigger-icon. I'm not sure what this pictogram represents.'

'I am,' said Daur. He rose from his stool and took the silver trinket from his pocket. 'I think this is what we need.'

'You seem remarkably sure, Ban' said Gaunt.

'I've never been so sure about anything, sir.'

'Right. No more time for talk. Pass me that and I'll–'

'Sir,' said Daur. 'It was given to me. I think I'm supposed to do this.'

Gaunt nodded. 'Very well, Ban. But I'm coming with you.'

'RALLY! RALLY, MY brave boys and girls!' Soric yelled above the roar of explosions. Infardi shells had torn the gate and the front part of the inner wall away. 'This is what we were born for! Deny the arch-enemy of mankind! Deny him now!'

GAUNT, CORBEC, MILO, Sanian and Daur approached the back gate of the outer Shrinehold wall. The din of battle behind them was deafening.

They readied their weapons. Sanian hefted up her lasrifle.

'We're going to get killed out there,' Milo told her. 'Are you sure you want to do this?'

'My way, remember? War. War is the only true way and I have found it.'

'For Sabbat!' cried Gaunt and threw open the gate.

'POWER BATTERIES HAVE failed!' Pauk's gunner told him.

'Restart them! Restart them!' the lieutenant shouted.

'The couplings have burnt out! We've put too much stress on them!'

'Hell, there's got to be a way to–' Pauk began.

He never finished his sentence. Usurper shells atomised the old Executioner tank *Strife*.

* * *

'PULL THE LINE back! Feygor, pull the line back!' Rawne yelled. The Ershul or whatever their fething name was were all over their positions now.

THE PILLAR SEEMED a hundred kilometres away across the snow, gleaming at the very end of the jagged promontory. Gaunt and his party ran forward in the snow, las-fire from the circling enemy flank zapping over and between them.

'Come on!' Gaunt yelled, firing his bolt pistol at the green-clad Ershul storming forward to cut them off.

'No! No!' Corbec yelped as a las-round hit his leg and brought him down.

Sanian turned and fired her gun on full auto, ripping into the enemy. She wasn't used to the recoil and it threw her over into the snow.

'Sanian! Sanian!' Milo stopped to pull her up as Gaunt and Daur ran on. 'Come on! I'll get you back to the–'

The butt of her gun hit Milo in the side of the head and he fell over unconscious.

'Bless you, Milo, but you won't rob me of this,' she muttered. 'This is my way. I'm going to take it, in the name of the saint. Don't try to stop me. Forgive me.'

She ran after the others, leaving Milo curled in the snow.

Twenty metres ahead of her, Daur was hit. He fell sideways into the snow, screaming in anger.

Gaunt stopped and ran back to him. The wound was in his side. He was yelling. There was no way he was going to be able to carry on.

'Ban! Give me the trigger-icon! Ban!'

Daur held the silver trinket out, clasped in his bloody fingers. 'Whoever does this will die,' he said.

'I know.'

'The psychic burst told me that. It needs a sacrifice. A martyr.'

'I know.'

'Sabbat's martyr.'

'I know, Ban.'

'The Emperor protects, Ibram.'

'The Emperor protects.' Gaunt took the silver figurine and began to run towards the pillar. Ban Daur tried to rise. To see. The las-fire of the enemy was too bright.

* * *

THE THUNDER OF war, of armageddon, shook the walls. Hands bloody, Dorden fought to save Bragg's life in the Shrinehold antechamber Lesp had turned into a makeshift infirmary.

'Clamp! Here!'

Lesp obeyed.

It was futile, Dorden knew. Even if he saved Bragg's life, they were all dead.

'Foskin!' Dorden yelled over as he worked. 'How's Vamberfeld doing?'

'I thought you had him,' said Foskin, jumping up from his work on another of the injured.

'He isn't here,' said Chayker.'

'Where the feth has he gone?' Dorden cried.

THROUGH THE PRISMATIC scope of his sight, LeGuin saw Captain Marchese's P48J blow out in a swirl of sparks.

Barely a second later, the same AT70 that had killed Marchese and his crew put a shell through the side of the *Grey Venger*. LeGuin's layer and loader were both disintegrated. The Destroyer lurched and stopped dead, its turbines failing for the very last time. Fire swirled through the compartment, up under LeGuin's feet. His hair was singed.

He tried the hatch above him. It was jammed shut.

Resignedly, Captain LeGuin sat back in his command chair and waited for the end.

Freezing cold air gusted in around him as the hatch opened.

'Come on! Come on!' Scout Sergeant Mkoll yelled down at him, his arms outstretched. LeGuin looked around himself for a moment at the ruined interior of his beloved tank. 'Goodbye,' he said, and then reached up and allowed Mkoll to pull him out.

Mkoll and LeGuin had got twenty metres from the *Grey Venger* when it exploded and flattened them both.

'TOO MANY! TOO many! cried Larkin, firing through his last remaining barrel.

Beside him, a las-shot struck Trooper Cuu in the shoulder and threw him back into the bloody snow.

'Oh, feth! Too many!' Larkin murmured.

'No, Tanith,' smiled Banda beside him as she fired again and again. 'Not nearly enough.'

'Think I win my wager,' croaked Cuu, staring up at the warp storm that blistered overhead. 'Sure as sure.'

GAUNT WAS JUST thirty metres from the pillar, running through the blitz of shots. Infardi were closing all around him.

He didn't feel the las-round hit his shin, but his leg went dead and he fell, tumbling over and over in the drifts.

'No,' he cried out. 'No, please...'

A figure bent over him. It was Sanian, her lasrifle trained on the advancing enemy. She sprayed off a burst and then turned to Gaunt.

'I'll take it. Let me.'

Gaunt knew he couldn't move unaided. 'Just help me up, girl. I can make it.'

'Give it to me! I can move faster alone! It's what she wants!'

Hesitating, Gaunt reached out his hand, the trigger-icon in it. 'Do it right, girl,' he said through pain-gritted teeth.

She took the silver icon.

'Don't worry, I–'

Fierce las-fire exploded in the snow around them.

Three Ershul troopers were just a few metres away.

Sanian turned to fire, the unfamiliar lasrifle awkward in her hands.

The closest Ershul aimed his weapon to kill her. She threw herself down in desperation.

Pin-point las-fire toppled her would-be killer and the two Ershul behind him.

Spraying las-shots into the face of the enemy, Milo ran to them both, blood streaming from his head.

'Good work, Milo,' said Gaunt, struggling for breath and rising on his elbow to fire his bolt pistol.

'The icon! Where is it?' Milo called, looking around. 'I can make it! It's not far! Where the feth is it?'

'It was here! I had it in my hand!' Sanian replied, groping about in the snow as blisteringly intense shots fell around them. 'Where is it? Oh, God-Emperor! Where the hell is it?'

MAJOR KLEOPAS WAS smiling. He didn't need his augmetic implant to see it. The view through the scope was clear. The last round fired from the *Heart of Destruction* had destroyed a Reaver in a bloom of fire.

But it was the last round. The last round ever.

His valiant crew was dead. Flames filled his turret basket, igniting his clothes. He couldn't move to escape. Shrapnel had destroyed his legs and severed his spine.

'Damn. You. All. To. Hell,' he gasped out, word by word, as the inferno surged up around him and consumed him.

THE GHOSTS AROUND him were falling back in panic in the face of the overwhelming host.

'There's nowhere to run to,' mumbled Commissar Hark, firing at the foe. Blood from a head wound was running down his cheek and he'd lost his cap.

An Ershul officer, another swirling ball of shield energy, loomed ahead of him. He'd killed three of its kind so far. Hark hoped this was Pater Sin.

'For the saint! For the Ghosts! For Gaunt!' he bellowed at the top of his voice.

He fired his plasma pistol and the shield exploded.

HALF-BURIED IN the snow under the enemy onslaught, Sanian cried out, 'Oh my lord! Look! Look!'

Returning fire, Gaunt and Milo both looked around.

'Good feth,' Gaunt stammered.

IT WAS COLD out there, on the edge of the promontory. From below the lip, howling gorge winds cut like knives. Overhead, the warp storm blistered the heavens.

The pillar stood just ahead, a massive finger of corundum, fire flaming from the top of it.

Close now.

It was hard going. He'd been hurt badly. Including the chest wound Greer had dealt him, he had seven wounds. Las-fire from the Ershul had stabbed at him ferociously these last ten metres.

Daur's silver trinket was clamped tightly in his hands. It had just been lying there, in the snow, as if it was waiting for him.

A las blast clipped his calf. Eight.

Almost there.

He could see her piercing eyes. The little girl, the herder. He could smell the wet stink of the chelons' nests and the cold wind of the high pastures.

He could smell the fragrances of acestus and wild islumbine.

Vamberfeld slumped against the cold, hard side of the watch flame pillar. He uncurled his fingers from the silver trinket and placed it in the recess, just like he had been shown during the miracle.

His hand wasn't shaking any more.

That was good.

An Ershul bolter round blew out the back of his head.

Vamberfeld fell back into the snow, a sad smile on his face.

Nine.

EIGHTEEN
HONOUR GUARD

*'Taken at face value, we were clearly mad.
Actually, I believe we're clearly mad most of the rest of the time,
so go fething figure.'*

— Colm Corbec, at Hagia

FROM DEEP INSIDE its planetary core, obeying ancient instructions, the mechanisms of the saint came alive. Vast psychic amplifiers woke and broadcast their signal.

For just an instant.

An instant enough to send abject fear into the souls of the Chaos spawn infesting the planet.

An instant enough to cremate the minds of Ershul hosts choking up across the promontory.

An instant enough to blow back the warp storm with such force that the advancing fleet was tumbled aside.

An instant enough to show Tolin Dorden his smiling son again, to show Colm Corbec one last glimpse of his father, to show Ban Daur a final vision of the old woman with the shockingly white hair in the refugee crowd.

To show Trooper Niceg Vamberfeld the hard, penetrating eyes of the chelon herdsgirl in the last moment of his life.

OUTSIDE THE SHRINEHOLD, under a cold, blue sky, Ibram Gaunt limped out, and down a churned up mass of snow and stone that used to be steps. He was clad in full dress uniform.

The remnants of the convoy waited below.

Beyond them, littered across the snows of the promontory, lay the fused and charred skeletons of nine thousand Chaos-touched humans and the blackened wrecks of over five hundred war machines.

'Hark?'

Hark stepped up and saluted the colonel-commissar.

'Units present and numbers correct, sir.'

'Very good.' Gaunt paused and looked back along the promontory at the lonely post tomb the tempelum ayatani had erected in the snow and rock beside the corundum pillar of the eternal watch fire.

Gaunt climbed up into his waiting Salamander.

'Honour guard, mount up!'

'As the commander orders, mount up and make ready!' Hark relayed down the line. Cries came back.

'Column ready to move out, sir,' Hark reported.

Gaunt thought of Slaydo for a moment and the old blood pact. He touched the scar on his palm. Then he took one last look back at Vamberfeld's lonely post tomb.

'Honour guard, advance!' he cried, making a sweeping gesture with his hand.

The units began to rumble forward, under a spotless sky of frozen blue, down towards the head of the pass.

ABOUT THE AUTHOR

Dan Abnett lives and works in Maidstone, Kent, in
England. Best known for his comic work, he has
written everything from Rupert the Bear to Batman in
the last ten years, and is currently scripting Legion of
Superheroes and Superman for DC Comics, and
Sinister Dexter and Durham Red for 2000 AD.
His work for the Black Library includes the popular
strips Darkblade and Titan, a clutch of novels featuring
the celebrated Imperial Guard unit known as Gaunt's
Ghosts (with more on the way), Inquisitor Eisenhorn,
and two fantasy titles *Gilead's Blood* and
Hammers of Ulric. There is, it seems,
no stopping him.

More Gaunt's Ghosts from the Black Library

FIRST & ONLY
A Gaunt's Ghosts novel
by Dan Abnett

'THE TANITH ARE strong fighters, general, so I have heard.' The
scar tissue of his cheek pinched and twitched slightly, as it
often did when he was tense. 'Gaunt is said to be a resourceful
leader.'

'You know him?' The general looked up, questioningly.

'I know *of* him, sir. In the main by reputation.'

GAUNT GOT TO his feet, wet with blood and Chaos pus. His
Ghosts were moving up the ramp to secure the position. Above
them, at the top of the elevator shaft, were over a million
Shriven, secure in their bunker batteries. Gaunt's expeditionary
force was inside, right at the heart of the enemy stronghold.
Commissar Ibram Gaunt smiled.

*IT IS THE nightmare future of Warhammer 40,000, and mankind
teeters on the brink of extinction. The galaxy-spanning Imperium is
riven with dangers, and in the Chaos-infested Sabbat system,
Imperial Commissar Gaunt must lead his men through as much in-
fighting amongst rival regiments as against the forces of Chaos.
FIRST AND ONLY is an epic saga of planetary conquest, grand
ambition, treachery and honour.*

More Gaunt's Ghosts from the Black Library

GHOSTMAKER
A Gaunt's Ghosts novel
by Dan Abnett

THEY WERE A good two hours into the dark, black-trunked forests, tracks churning the filthy ooze and the roar of their engines resonating from the sickly canopy of leaves above, when Colonel Ortiz saw death.

It wore red, and stood in the trees to the right of the track, in plain sight, unmoving, watching his column of Basilisks as they passed along the trackway. It was the lack of movement that chilled Ortiz.

Almost twice a man's height, frighteningly broad, armour the colour of rusty blood, crested by recurve brass antlers. The face was a graven death's head. Daemon. Chaos Warrior. *World Eater!*

IN THE NIGHTMARE future of Warhammer 40,000, mankind teeters on the brink of extinction. The Imperial Guard are humanity's first line of defence against the remorseless assaults of the enemy. For the men of the Tanith First-and-Only and their fearless commander, Commissar Ibram Gaunt, it is a war in which they must be prepared to lay down, not just their bodies, but their very souls.

More Gaunt's Ghosts from the Black Library

NECROPOLIS
A Gaunt's Ghosts novel
by Dan Abnett

GAUNT WAS SHAKING, and breathing hard. He'd lost his cap somewhere, his jacket was torn and he was splattered with blood. Something flickered behind him and he wheeled, his blade flashing as it made contact. A tall, black figure lurched backwards. It was thin but powerful, and much taller than him, dressed in glossy black armour and a hooded cape. The visage under the hood was feral and non-human, like the snarling skull of a great wolfhound with the skin scraped off. It clutched a sabre bladed power sword in its gloved hands. The cold blue energies of his own powersword clashed against the sparking, blood red fires of the Deathwatcher's weapon.

ON THE SHATTERED world of Verghast, Gaunt and his Ghosts find themselves embroiled within an ancient and deadly civil war as a mighty hive-city is besieged by an unrelenting foe. When treachery from within brings the city's defences crashing down, rivalry and corruption threaten to bring the Tanith Ghosts to the brink of defeat. Imperial Commissar Ibram Gaunt must find new allies and new Ghosts if he is to save Vervunhive from the deadliest threat of all – the dread legions of Chaos.

More Warhammer 40,000 from the Black Library

XENOS
Book 1 of the Eisenhorn trilogy
by Dan Abnett

THE THUNDERING SOUND rolled through the thawing vaults of Processional Two-Twelve. Fists and palms, beating at coffin hoods. The sleepers were waking, their frigid bodies trapped in their caskets. I could hear footsteps above the screams. Eyclone was running. I ran after, passing gallery after gallery of frenzied, flailing forms. The screaming, the pounding... God-Emperor help me, I will never forget that. Thousands of souls waking up to death, frantic, agonised. Damn Eyclone. Damn him to hell and back.

THE INQUISITION MOVES amongst mankind like an avenging shadow, striking down the enemies of humanity with uncompromising ruthlessness. Inquisitor Eisenhorn faces a vast interstellar cabal and the dark power of daemons, all racing to recover an arcane text of abominable power – an ancient tome known as the Necroteuch.

More Warhammer 40,000 from the Black Library

SPACE WOLF
A Warhammer 40,000 novel
by William King

RAGNAR LEAPT UP from his hiding place, bolt pistol spitting death. The nightgangers could not help but notice where he was, and with a mighty roar of frenzied rage they raced towards him. Ragnar answered their war cry with a wolfish howl of his own, and was reassured to hear it echoed back from the throats of the surrounding Blood Claws. He pulled the trigger again and again as the frenzied mass of mutants approached, sending bolter shell after bolter shell rocketing into his targets. Ragnar laughed aloud, feeling the full battle rage come upon him. The beast roared within his soul, demanding to be unleashed.

IN THE GRIM *future of Warhammer 40,000, the Space Marines of the Adeptus Astartes are humanity's last hope. On the planet Fenris, young Ragnar is chosen to be inducted into the noble yet savage Space Wolves chapter. But with his ancient primal instincts unleashed by the implanting of the sacred Canis Helix, Ragnar must learn to control the beast within and fight for the greater good of the wolf pack.*

More Warhammer 40,000 from the Black Library

RAGNAR'S CLAW
A Warhammer 40,000 novel
by William King

ONE OF THE enemy officers, wearing the peaked cap and greatcoat of a lieutenant, dared to stick his head above the parapet. Without breaking stride, Ragnar raised his bolt pistol and put a shell through the man's head. It exploded like a melon hit with a sledgehammer. Shouts of confusion echoed from behind the wall of sandbags, then a few heretics, braver and more experienced than the rest, stuck their heads up in order to take a shot at their attackers. Another mistake: a wave of withering fire from the Space Marines behind Ragnar scythed through them, sending their corpses tumbling back amongst their comrades.

FROM THE DEATH-WORLD of Fenris come the Space Wolves, the most savage of the Emperor's Space Marines. Ragnar's Claw explores the bloody beginnings of Space Wolf Ragnar's first mission as a young Blood Claw warrior. From the jungle hell of Galt to the polluted cities of Hive World Venam, Ragnar's mission takes him on an epic trek across the galaxy to face the very heart of evil itself.

IN THE GRIM DARKNESS OF THE FAR FUTURE, THERE IS ONLY WAR...

You can recreate the ferocious battles of the Imperial Guard and the Space Marines with WARHAMMER 40,000, Games Workshop's world famous game of a dark and gothic war-torn future. The galaxy-spanning Imperium of Man is riven with dangers: aliens such as the ravaging orks and the enigmatic eldar gather their forces to crush humanity – and in the warp, malevolent powers arm for war!

To find out more about Warhammer 40,000, as well as Games Workshop's whole range of exciting fantasy and science fiction games and miniatures, just call our specialist Trolls on the following numbers:

In the UK: 0115-91 40 000

In the US: 1-800-394-GAME

or look us up online at:

www.games-workshop.com